About the Authors

Karin Baine lives in Northern Ireland with her husband, two sons, and her out-of-control notebook collection. Her mother and her grandmother's vast collection of books inspired her love of reading and her dream of becoming a Mills & Boon author. Now she can tell people she has a *proper* job! You can follow Karin on Twitter, @karinbaine1 or visit her website for the latest news—karinbaine.com

Annie O'Neil spent most of her childhood with her leg draped over the family rocking chair and a book in her hand. Novels, baking and writing too much teenage angst poetry ate up most of her youth. Now Annie splits her time between corralling her husband into helping her with their cows, baking, reading, barrel racing (not really!) and spending some very happy hours at her computer, writing.

Alison Roberts is a New Zealander, currently lucky enough to be living in the south of France. She is also lucky enough to write for the Mills & Boon Medical Romance line. A primary school teacher in a former life, she is also a qualified paramedic. She loves to travel and dance, drink champagne, and spend time with her daughter and her friends.

The Hot Docs on Call

COLLECTION

July 2019

August 2019

September 2019

October 2019

November 2019

December 2019

Hot Docs on Call: Healing His Heart

KARIN BAINE

ANNIE O'NEIL

ALISON ROBERTS

MILLS & BOON

First Published in Great Britain 2019
By Mills & Boon, an imprint of HarperCollins *Publishers*
1 London Bridge Street, London, SE1 9GF

HOT DOCS ON CALL: HEALING HIS HEART
© 2019 Harlequin Books S.A.

Falling for the Foster Mum © Harlequin Books S.A. 2017
Healing the Sheikh's Heart © Harlequin Books S.A. 2017
A Life-Saving Reunion © Harlequin Books S.A. 2017

Special thanks and acknowledgement are given to Karin Baine, Annie O'Neil and Alison Roberts for their contribution to the *Paddington Children's Hospital* series

ISBN: 978-0-263-27674-9

1219

MIX
Paper from
responsible sources
FSC C007454

FSC
www.fsc.org

This book is produced from independently certified FSC™ paper to ensure responsible forest management.

For more information visit: www.harpercollins.co.uk/green

Printed and bound in Spain
by CPI, Barcelona

FALLING FOR THE
FOSTER MUM

KARIN BAINE

This one's for Jennie, Stephen and Samantha, my London travelling companions/supervisors because we all know I can't be trusted out on my own! Along with John, you've always been so supportive of my writing and it's much appreciated xx. Thanks to Catherine, Abbi and Chellie who've helped me so much with my research.

PROLOGUE

QUINN GRADY WAS officially the worst mother in the world. Barely a week into the job and her charge was already lying in the hospital.

Simon mightn't be her *real* son but that made her role as his foster mum even more important. As someone who'd been passed from pillar to post in the care system herself, it meant everything to her to provide a safe home for him. Yet here she was, sitting on her own in the bright corridors of the Paddington Children's Hospital, nerves shredded, waiting for news on his condition.

She'd done everything by the parenting handbook, even when life had thrown her that 'I'm not ready to be a dad' curveball from Darryl right before Simon had come into her life. Her focus had remained on his welfare regardless of her own heartbreak that her partner had gone back on his word that he was going into this with her. The sleepless nights she'd spent with her mind running through every possible scenario she might encounter as someone's guardian hadn't prepared her for this.

A fire at the school.

As she'd waved a tearful goodbye this morning and watched Simon walk away in his smart, new uniform she'd half expected a phone call. He'd looked so small, so lost, she'd almost been waiting for the school to call and ask her to pick him up, to come and hug him and tell him everything was going to be all right.

Not this. A fire was totally beyond her control. She couldn't have prevented it and she couldn't fix it. Apparently all she could do was fill in endless forms and she hadn't even been able to do that until she'd contacted the local fostering authority to notify them about what had happened. Watching the frantic staff deal with the influx of injured schoolchildren, she'd never felt so helpless.

She knew Simon was badly hurt but she hadn't been able to see him yet until they stabilised him. He could have life-changing injuries. Or worse. What if he didn't make it? Her stomach lurched, terror gripping her insides at the thought of his suffering. This was supposed to have been a new start for both of them, to wipe out the past and build a better future. Now all she wanted was to see him and know he was okay.

She fidgeted in the hard plastic chair doing her best not to accost any of the nurses running from department to department. Perhaps if she was a *proper* mum she'd feel more entitled to demand constant information on his condition.

'Are you Simon's mother?'

A vision in green scrubs appeared beside her. His lovely Irish lilt was the comfort blanket she needed at this moment in time.

'No. Yes.' She didn't know the appropriate response for this kind of situation.

As a pair of intense, sea-green eyes stared at her, waiting for an answer, she realised her temporary status didn't matter. 'I'm his foster mother.'

It was enough to soften the doctor's features and he hunched down beside her chair.

'I'm Matthew McGrory, a burns specialist. I've been brought over to assess Simon's condition.'

Quinn held her breath. *Good news or bad?*

She searched his face for a sign but apart from noting how handsome he was up close she discovered nothing.

'How is he?'

Good?

Bad?

'Would you like to come through and see for yourself?' The doctor's mouth tilted into a smile.

That had to be positive, right?

'Yes. Thank you.' She got to her feet though her legs weren't as steady as she needed them to be. Nonetheless she hurried down the corridor, powering hard to keep up with the great strides of a man who had to be at least six foot.

He stopped just outside the door of the Paediatric Intensive Care Unit, the last barrier between her and Simon, but an ominous one. Only the most poorly children would be on the other side and he was one of them. Not for the first time she wished she had someone to go through this with her.

'Before we go in, I want you to be prepared. Simon has suffered severe burns along with some smoke inhalation. It's not a pretty sight but everything we're doing is to minimise long-term damage. Okay? Ready?'

She nodded, feigning bravery and nowhere near ready. Whatever the injuries, they would affect her and Simon for a long time but they were in this together.

'He needs me,' she said, her voice a mere whisper as she tried to pull herself together. She wondered if clinging to the hunky doctor's arm for support was an option but he was already opening the door and stepping into the ward before she could make a grab for him.

They passed several cubicles but she couldn't make out any of the faces as the small bodies were dwarfed by monster machinery aiding their recovery.

'Oh, Simon!' Her hand flew to her mouth to cover the gasp as she was led to the last bed on the row. She wouldn't have recognised him if not for the glimpse of curly hair against the pillow.

The face of the little boy she'd left at the school gates only hours ago was now virtually obscured by the tubes and wires going in and out of his tiny form keeping him alive. His pale torso was a contrast to the mottled black and red angry skin of his right arm stretched out at his side. Lying there, helpless, he looked even younger than his meagre five years.

Quinn's knees began to buckle at the enormity of the situation and the tears she'd been desperately trying to keep at bay finally burst through the dam.

Strong hands seemed to come from nowhere to catch her before she fell to the floor in a crumpled heap of guilt and manoeuvred her into a chair.

'I know it's a lot to take in but he's honestly in the best place. Simon has severe burns to the face and arm and we have him intubated to help him breathe after the smoke inhalation. Once the swelling has gone down and we're happy there's no damage to his eyes, we'll move him to the burns unit for further treatment.'

She blinked through her tears to focus on the man kneeling before her.

'Is he going to be okay?' That was all she needed to know.

'The next forty-eight hours will be crucial in assessing the full extent of his burns. He'll need surgery to keep the wounds clean and prevent any infection and there's a good chance he'll need skin grafts in the future. I won't deny it'll be a long process, but that's why I'm here. I'm a reconstructive surgeon too and I will do my very best to limit and repair any permanent scarring. The road to recovery is going to be tough but we're in this together.' This virtual stranger reached out and gave her hand a squeeze to reassure her but the electric touch jolted her back into reality.

She was a mum now and following in the footsteps of her own amazing adoptive mum, who'd moved heaven and earth to do what was best for her. It was time for her to step up to the plate now too.

'I'll do whatever it takes. Simon deserves the best.' And something told her that the best was surgeon Matthew McGrory.

CHAPTER ONE

Two months later

QUINN WISHED THEY did an easy-to-read, step-by-step guide for anxious foster mums going through these operations too. It was difficult to know what to do for the best when Simon resisted all attempts to comfort him pre-op.

He turned his face away when she produced the well-worn kids' book the hospital had provided to explain the surgical process.

She sighed and closed the book.

'I suppose you know this off by heart now.' Not that it made this any easier. After the countless hours he'd spent on the operating table they both knew what they were in for—pain, tears and a huge dollop of guilt on her part.

She hadn't caused the fire or his injuries but neither had she been able to save him from this suffering. Given the choice she'd have swapped places with the mite and offered herself up for this seemingly endless torture rather than watch him go through it.

'Can I get you anything?' she asked the back of his head, wishing there was something she could do other than stand here feeling inadequate.

The pillow rustled as he shook his head and she had

to suppress the urge to try and swamp him into a big hug the way her mother always had when she'd been having a hard time. Simon didn't like to be hugged. In fact, he resisted any attempt to comfort him. That should've been his *real* mother's job but then apparently she'd never shown affection for anything other than her next fix. His too-young, too-addicted parents were out of the picture, their neglect so severe the courts had stripped them of any rights.

Quinn and Simon had barely got to know each other before the fire had happened so she couldn't tell if his withdrawal was a symptom of his recent trauma or the usual reaction of a foster child afraid to get attached to his latest care giver. She wasn't his parent, nor one of the efficient medical staff, confident in what they were doing. For all she knew he'd already figured out she was out of her depth and simply didn't want to endure her feeble overtures. Maybe he just didn't like her. Whatever was causing the chasm between them it was vital she closed it, and fast.

As if on cue, their favourite surgeon stepped into the room. 'Back again? I'm sure you two are sick of the sight of me.'

That velvety Irish accent immediately caught her attention. She frowned as goose bumps popped up across her skin. At the age of thirty-two she should really have better self-control over an ill-conceived crush on her foster son's doctor.

'Hi, Matt.' An also enchanted Simon sat upright in bed.

It was amazing how much they both seemed to look forward to these appointments and hate them at the same time. Although the skin grafts were a vital part of recovery, they were traumatic and led to more night terrors once they returned home as Simon relived the events of the fire in his sleep. He'd been one of the most seriously burned children, having been trapped in his classroom by falling debris. Although the emergency services had thankfully rescued him, no one had been able to save him from the memories or the residual pain.

Matt, as he'd insisted they call him, was the one constant during this whole nightmare. The one person Simon seemed to believe when he said things would work out. Probably because he had more confidence in himself and his abilities than she did in herself, when every dressing change made her feel like a failure.

The poor child's face was still scarred, even after the so-called revolutionary treatment, and his arm was a patchwork quilt of pieced together skin. Technically his injuries had occurred in school but that didn't stop her beating herself up that it had happened on her watch. Especially when the fragile bond they'd had in those early days had disintegrated in the aftermath of the fire. Unlike the one he'd forged with the handsome surgeon.

Matt moved to the opposite side of the bed from Quinn and pulled out some sort of plastic slide from his pocket. 'I've got a new one for you, Simon. The disappearing coin trick!' he said with flare, plucking a ten pence piece from the air.

'Cool!'

Of course it was. Magic was a long way away from the realities of life with second- and third-degree burns. Fun time with Matt before surgery offered an escape whilst she was always going to be the authority figure telling him not to scratch and slathering cream over him when he just wanted to be left alone.

Somehow Simon was able to separate his friend who performed magic tricks from the surgeon who performed these painful procedures, whereas she was the one he associated with his pain. It was frustrating, especially seeing him so engaged when she'd spent all day trying to coax a few words from him.

'I need you to place the coin in here.' He gave Simon the coin and pulled out a tray with a hole cut out of the centre from the plastic slide.

Concentration was etched on his face as he followed instructions and once Quinn set aside her petty jealousy she appreciated the distraction from the impending surgery. After all, that's what she wanted for him—to be the same as any other inquisitive five-year-old, fascinated by the world around him. Not hiding away, fearful of the unknown, the way he was at home.

'Okay, so we push it back in here—' he slid the tray back inside the case '—and this is the important bit. We need a magic word.'

'Smelly pants!' Simon had the mischievous twinkle of a child who knew he could get away with being naughty on this occasion.

'I was thinking along the more traditional abracadabra line but I guess that works too.' Matt exchanged a grin across the bed with her. It was a brief moment which made her forget the whole parent/doctor divide and react as any other woman who'd had a good-looking man smile at her.

That jittery, girlish excitement took her by surprise as he made eye contact with her and sent her heart rate sky high. Since Darryl left her she hadn't given any thought to the opposite sex. At least not in any 'You're hot and I want you' way. More of a 'You're a man and I can't trust you' association. She wasn't prepared to give away any more of herself—of her time or her heart—to anyone who wouldn't appreciate the gift. All of her time and energy these days was directed into the fostering process, trying to make up for the lack of two parents in Simon's life. Harbouring any form of romantic ideas was self-indulgent and, most likely, self-destructive.

She put this sudden attraction down to the lack of adult interaction. Since leaving her teaching post to tutor from home and raise Simon, apart from the drive-by parents of her students, and her elderly neighbour, Mrs Johns, the medical staff were the only grown-ups she got to talk to. Very few of them were men, and even fewer had cheekbones hand-carved by the gods. It was no wonder she'd overreacted to a little male attention. The attraction had been there since day one and she'd fought it with good reason when her last romantic interlude had crashed her world around her. Everything she'd believed in her partner had turned out to be a lie, making it difficult for her to trust a word anyone told her any more. She kept everyone at a distance now, but Matt was such a key figure in their days that he was nigh on impossible to ignore. As the weeks had gone on she found herself getting into more arguments with him, forcing him to take the brunt of her fears for Simon and the annoyance she should have directed at herself.

Matt waved his hand over the simple piece of plastic which had transformed Simon's body language in mere seconds.

'Smelly pants!' he shouted, echoed by his tiny assistant.

The magician-cum-surgeon frowned at her. Which apparently was equally as stimulating as a smile.

'It'll only work if we all say the magic words together. Let's try this again.'

Quinn rolled her eyes but she'd go along with anything to take Simon's mind off what was coming next.

'Smelly pants!' they all chorused as Matt pulled out the now empty tray.

'Wow! How did you do that?' Simon inspected the magic chamber, suitably impressed by the trick.

'Magic.' Matt gave her a secret wink and started her tachycardia again.

Didn't he have theatre prep or intensive hand-scrubbing to do rather than showing off here and disturbing people's already delicate equilibrium?

'I wish I could make my scars disappear like that.' Simon's sudden sad eyes and lapse back into melancholy made Quinn's heart ache for him.

'I'm working on it, kiddo. That's why all of these operations are necessary even though they suck big-time. It might take a few waves of my magic wand but I'll do my very best to make them disappear.'

Quinn folded her arms, binding her temper inside her chest. He might mean well but he shouldn't be giving the child false hope. Simon's body was a chequered, vivid mess of dead and new flesh. He was never going to have blemish-free skin again, regardless of the super-confident surgeon's skills, and she was the one who'd have to pick up the pieces when the promises came to nothing. Again.

'You said that the last time.' Not even Simon was convinced, lying back on the bed, distraction over.

'I also said it would take time. Good things come to those who wait, right?' It was a mantra he'd used since day one but he clearly wasn't *au fait* with the limited patience of five-year-olds. Unlike Quinn, who'd had a crash course in tantrums and tears while waiting for the miraculous recovery to happen before her very eyes. Her patience had been stretched to the limit too.

'Right,' Simon echoed without any conviction.

'I'll tell you what, once you're back from theatre and wide awake, I'll come back and show you how to do a few tricks of your own. Deal?'

Quinn couldn't tell if it was bravado or ego preventing the doctor from admitting defeat as he stood with his hand held out to make the bargain. Either way, she didn't think it was healthy for him to get close to Simon only to let him down. He'd had enough of that from his birth parents, who'd given up any rights to him in favour of drugs, foster parents, who'd started the adoption process then abandoned him when they'd fallen pregnant themselves, and her, who'd sent him to get burned up in school. It might have failed her once but that protective streak was back with a vengeance.

'We couldn't ask you to do that. I'm sure you have other patients to see and we've already taken up so much of your time.' She knew these extra little visits weren't necessary. They had highly skilled nurses and play specialists to make these transitions easier for the children. These informal chats and games made her feel singled out. As if he was trying to suss out her capability to look after Simon outside of the hospital. The nurses had noticed too, remarking how much extra time he'd devoted to Simon's recovery and she didn't appreciate it as much as they probably thought she should. He wasn't going to sneak his way into her affections the way Darryl had, then use her fostering against her; she'd learned that lesson the hard way. She could do this. Alone.

'Not at all. I'm always willing to pass on my secrets

to a budding apprentice.' He held out his hand again and Simon shook it with his good arm, bypassing her concerns.

'I just mean perhaps you should be concentrating on the surgery rather than performing for us.' The barb was enough to furrow that brow again but he had a knack for getting her back up. Handsome or not, she wouldn't let him cause Simon any more pain than necessary.

The wounded look in his usually sparkling green eyes instantly made her regret being such a cow to him when he'd been nothing but kind to Simon since the accident. His smile was quickly back in place but it no longer reached anywhere past his mouth.

'It's no problem. I can do both. I'll see you soon, kiddo.' He ruffled Simon's hair and turned to leave. 'Can I have a word outside, Ms Grady?'

As he brushed past her, close enough to whisper into her ear, Quinn's whole body shivered with awareness. A combination of nerves and physical attraction. Neither of which she had control over any longer.

'Sure,' she said although she suspected he wasn't giving her a choice; she felt as though she was being called into the headmaster's office for misbehaving. A very hot headmaster who wasn't particularly happy with her. Unsurprising, really, when she'd basically just insulted him on a professional level.

She promised Simon she'd be back soon and took a deep breath before she followed Matt out the door.

'I know you're having a tough time at the moment but I'd really appreciate it if you stopped questioning my dedication to my job in front of my patient.'

It was the first time Quinn had seen him riled in all of these weeks. He was always so calm in the face of her occasional hysteria, so unflappable through every hurdle of Simon's treatment. Although it was unsettling to see the change in him, that intense passion, albeit for his work, sent tingles winding through her body until her toes curled, knowing she was the one who'd brought it to the fore. She found herself wondering how deep his passions lay and how else they might manifest…

He cleared his throat and reminded her she was supposed to speak, to argue back. She questioned what he was doing, he pulled her up on it and claimed rank when it came to Simon's health care—that was the way this went. It kept her from going completely round the bend imagining the worst that could happen when she'd be the one left dealing with the consequences on her own. She was supposed to be the overprotective mother voicing her concerns that everything being done was in her son's best interests, just as he was the one to insist he knew what he was doing. Fantasising about Matt in any other capacity, or his emotions getting the better of him, definitely wasn't in their well-rehearsed script.

'Yeah…well… I'd appreciate it if you didn't give Simon false hope that everything will go back to normal. We've both had enough of people letting us down.' Not that she knew what normal was, but although he deserved a break, they had to be realistic too.

'I'm not in the habit of lying to my patients…'

'No? What about this miracle spray-on skin which was supposed to fast-track his recovery? It's been two months and his burns are still very much visible. I should've known it was too good to be true when you would only use it to treat his facial burns and not the ones on his arm. I mean, if it was such a wonder cure it would make sense to use it everywhere and not make him go through these skin grafts anyway.' She was aware her voice had gone up a few decibels and yet she couldn't seem to stop herself when something good she'd believed was going to happen hadn't. This time it wasn't only *her* hopes that were being dashed.

Matt simply sighed when Quinn would've understood if he'd thrown his hands up and walked away. Deep down she knew he'd done his best, and yet, they were still here going through the same painful process.

'I can only reiterate what I told you at the start. It will take time. Perhaps the progress we have made isn't as noticeable to you because you see him every day, but the scars *are* beginning to fade. It's as much as we can hope for at this stage. As I explained, this is a new treatment, not readily available everywhere in the UK, and funding is hard to come by. The burns on Simon's arm are full thickness, not suitable for the trial, otherwise I'd have fought tooth and nail to make it happen. But he's young—his skin will heal quicker than yours or mine. Besides, I'm good at what I do.' There wasn't any obvious arrogance in his words or stance. It was simply a statement of fact. Which did nothing to pull her mind out of the gutter.

'So you keep telling me,' she muttered under her breath. However, despite his conscientious efforts, Simon no longer resembled the child she'd been charged with minding, either physically or mentally.

'I meant what I said. I'm not in the habit of lying to sick kids, or their beautiful mothers.' His forehead smoothed out as he stopped being cross with her.

The renewed smile combined with the reassuring touch of his hands on her shoulders sent those shivers back Irish dancing over her skin. She was too busy squealing inside at the compliment to correct him again about being Simon's *foster* mother.

Unfortunately, in her experience she couldn't always take people's word as truth. It wasn't that long ago Darryl had sworn he was in this thing with her.

'I hope not,' she said, the cold chill moving to flatten the first fizz of ardour she'd felt since her ex abandoned her and the future they'd planned together.

Simon's fate was entirely in this man's hands. Matt's skills on the operating table would determine his long-term appearance and probably his self-esteem along with it. It was too much to expect her to put her faith entirely in the word of a virtual stranger. Especially when the men closest to her had littered her life with broken promises and dreams.

Quinn Grady was a grade-A pain in the backside. In the most understandable way. Matt had seen his fair share of anxious parents over the years. His line of work brought people to him in their most fragile, vulnerable state and it was only natural that emotions ran high, but she'd spent most of the last couple of months questioning his every decision, seemingly doubting his ability to get Simon through the other side of his injuries. It was exhausting for all of those concerned. Normally he outlined his treatment plan and got on with it but somehow this case had drifted off course.

The spray-on skin was a relatively new treatment. Instead of these painful skin grafts, a small sample of healthy skin was removed from the patient and placed in a processing unit where it reproduced in a special suspension solution which was then sprayed over the damaged area where it continued to grow and multiply. There was no risk of the patient's body rejecting it because it was from the patient's own cells. The regenerative nature of this process meant the wounds healed rapidly in comparison to traditional techniques, such as the one he was performing now. If it wasn't for the extensive burns on Simon's arm, where he'd defended himself from the flames, he wouldn't have to go through the skin grafts or worry about scarring because the spray-on skin would stretch with him as he grew.

He'd expected Quinn to be wary; he'd had to convince her as well as the board that this was worth trialling, but the constant clashing had tested him. Naturally, she wanted instant results, for the burns to fade and heal overnight, but that wasn't how it worked. Almost every day she demanded to know 'Why?' and he couldn't always give her the answer she wanted. *He* knew the results were favourable compared to some he'd seen, and indeed, Simon's facial burns were exceptionally better healed than those on his arm but he was still disfigured. For now. Until the boy resembled his pre-fire self, Matt was going to take the flak, and so far he'd been happy to do so.

He knew he'd probably become too involved with Simon's case, more so than the other children he'd seen at Paddington's as a result of the fire at Westbourne Grove Primary School. Perhaps it was because his burns had been so extensive, or perhaps the reason was closer to home. The single foster mum reminded him a lot of himself and the hand he'd been dealt once upon a time.

Although he assumed she'd voluntarily agreed to take on the responsibility for other people's children. His role as a stand-in father had been thrust upon him when his dad had died and left him in charge of his younger siblings.

Matt recognised the fear in Quinn's brilliant blue eyes, even when she was giving him grief. He'd spent over a decade fretting about getting his sisters through their childhood in one piece with much the same haunted expression staring back at him in the mirror.

It was only now that Bridget, the youngest of the brood, had gone off to university he was able to relax a little. Of course, that didn't mean he wasn't still handling relationship woes or doling out crisis loans, but at least he could do most of his parenting over the phone these days, unless they came to visit him in London.

It meant he had his life back, that he'd been able to leave Dublin and take this temporary contract. When his time was up here he would have no reason to feel guilty about moving on to somewhere shiny and new and far from Ireland.

Quinn wouldn't have that luxury for a long time with Simon being so young. As his foster mother, she was probably under even more pressure to get him through his injuries, and naturally, that had extended to his surgeon. If fostering authorities were anything like social services to deal with, she'd have to jump through hoops to prove her suitability as a parent.

Life was tough enough as a substitute parent without the added trauma of the fire for her and Simon. Especially when she appeared to be doing this on her own. He hadn't spotted a wedding ring, and to his knowledge there hadn't been any other visitors during Simon's hospitalisation. When the cancer had claimed his father, Matt had been in much the same boat and being a sounding board for Quinn's frustrations was the least he could do to help. Unless her comments were in danger of unnecessarily upsetting Simon.

A boy needed a strong mother as much as a father. Matt's had been absent since shortly after Bridget's birth, when she'd suddenly decided family life wasn't for her. With his father passing away only a few years later, there had been no one left for them to turn to. For him to turn to. He'd had to manage the budget, the bills, the parent/teacher meetings and the numerous trips to A&E which were part and parcel of life with a brood of rambunctious kids, all on his own. Most of the time it had felt as though the world was against him having a life of his own.

He knew the struggle, the loneliness and the all-encompassing fear of screwing up and he would've gone out of his way to help anyone in a similar situation. At least, that's how he justified his interest. It wasn't entirely down to the fact he enjoyed seeing her, or the sparks created every time they had one of their 'discussions.' Attraction to single mothers wasn't something he intended to act upon and certainly not with the parent of one of his patients.

He'd only just gained his freedom from one young family and he wasn't ready, willing or able to do it again. As it was, he would be in young Simon's life for a long time to come. Perhaps even longer than Quinn. There were always going to be more surgeries as the child grew and his skin stretched. Treatments for scar tissue often took months to be effective and new scar contractures, where the skin tightened and restricted movement, could appear a long way down the line in young patients who were still growing.

'He's out.' The anaesthetist gave the go-ahead for the team to begin.

Time was of the essence. Generally they didn't keep children under the anaesthetic for more than a few hours at a time in case it proved too much for their small bodies to cope with. Hence why the skin grafts were still ongoing months later. Before they could even attempt the graft they had to clean the wound and harvest new skin from a separate donor site.

And Quinn wondered why recovery was taking so long.

'Saline, please. Let's get this done as quickly and accurately as we can.' Despite all the support in the operating theatre from the assisting staff, Matt had never borne so much responsibility for a patient as he did now.

Simon was completely at his mercy lying here, lost among the medical equipment surrounding the operating table. The slightest slip and Matt would have to face the wrath of the Mighty Quinn.

He smiled beneath his surgical mask at the thought of her squaring up to him again, her slight frame vibrating with rage as the mama bear emerged to protect her cub. She was a firebrand when she needed to be, not afraid of voicing her opinion if she thought something wasn't right. Matt didn't take offence; he was confident in the decisions he made on his patient's behalf and understood Quinn's interference came from a place of love. That didn't mean he wanted to give her further reason to berate him or challenge his authority.

He was as focused as he could be as they debrided Simon's wounds, cleaning and removing the dead tissue to clear the way for the new graft so it would take. As always, he was grateful for his perfect eyesight and steady hands as he shaved the thin slices of tissue needed for the graft. His precision as he prepared this skin before placing it on the wound could impact on Simon for the rest of his life.

No pressure.

Just two vulnerable and emotional souls relying on him to work his magic.

CHAPTER TWO

IF WAITING WAS an Olympic event, Quinn would never make it through the qualifying rounds.

Although she'd had enough experience to know to come prepared, she hadn't been able to sit still long enough to read her book or make any lesson plans for her tutored students. She'd even added an extra body to the picket line outside to save this hospital from closure in the hope it would take her mind off Simon going under the knife again. It was hard to believe anybody thought it was a good idea to merge this place with another outside the city when so many walked through the doors every day, and she was happy to wave a placard if it meant Simon's treatment continued here without any disruption.

The kids called it the Castle because of the beautiful architecture, and the story-like turrets and spires certainly gave it more character than any modern glass building could hope to replicate. Quinn had actually found it quite an imposing place at first but that could have been because of what she'd had to face inside the walls. These days it had almost become their second home and the people within were now all so familiar she didn't want anything to change.

'How's Simon?'

'You poor thing…'

'And you're out here? With us?'

'Have you heard how Ryan Walker is?'

'He's still an inpatient. I don't think there's been any real improvement. Even if he gets to go home I think the family are going to need a lot of help.'

'And they have a toddler to look after too. It's such a burden for them. For you too, Quinn, with Simon.'

The other Westbourne Grove Primary parents on the picket line had been well-meaning but the chit-chat hadn't helped her paranoia. Ryan, who'd suffered a serious head injury during the fire, was still critical and he and Simon were among the last of the children still receiving treatment. The raised eyebrows and exchanged glances at her presence anywhere other than Simon's bedside made her wonder if she had done the right thing in participating in the event and she'd abandoned her post in a hurry. Perhaps a *real* mother would've acted differently when her son was in surgery and she worried people would think she wasn't compassionate when that couldn't have been further from the truth.

That little boy meant everything to her. He might only be with her for a short time but she was as invested in him as if he was her own flesh and blood. All she wanted was for him to feel safe and loved and she'd failed on both accounts, if his continued apathy towards her was anything to go by. Perhaps when these operations became less frequent, and without the constant disruption of hospital appointments, they might actually find the time and space to bond.

She tossed her uneaten, soggy ham sandwich back into the crumpled aluminium foil. Not even the chocolate biscuit nestled in her pre-packed lunchbox could tempt her into eating. She had no appetite for anything other than news on Simon's condition. It might be a standard procedure for the staff but she knew there were risks for any surgery under general anaesthetic—breathing difficulties, adverse reaction to medication, bleeding—she'd done her Internet research on them all. Of course, none of these had occurred thus far but that didn't mean they *couldn't* happen.

In a world so full of danger she wondered how any parent ever let their offspring over the doorstep alone. It was taking all of her courage just to let Simon get the treatment recommended by the experts. At the end of the day, parental responsibility had been handed over to her and it was her job to keep him safe until adoption took place with another family.

That permanent knot in her stomach didn't untangle even when she saw him safely wheeled back onto the ward.

'How did it go?' she asked the first person who walked through the doors towards her. Of course that person had to be Matt.

Deep down she was grateful; the surgeon was the best person to keep her informed. It was just…he was always here, disturbing her peace of mind, reminding her he was doing a better job of taking care of Simon than she was.

Matt saw no reason to prolong Quinn's misery any longer. 'It all went well. No complications or unforeseen problems. Now we just have to wait for this young man to come around again.'

It had been a long day for him with surgery and his outpatient clinic but Quinn had every right to be kept in the loop and he'd wanted to end the day on a high for all of them by coming to speak to her. He wanted to be the one to smooth out the worry lines on her brow. Besides, he'd rather she torture him for information than take out her frustrations on the rest of the staff. He could handle it better because he understood it better. After being thrown in at the deep end and having to learn on the job, he hadn't exactly been a model parent either when he'd fought his siblings' battles.

'Thank goodness.'

The fleeting relief across her face and the glimpse of the pretty, young woman beneath the mask of combative parent was Matt's reward for a job well done.

She followed the bed into the private cubicle with him, never letting go of Simon's hand although he was still drowsy from the anaesthetic.

'Once he comes around and he's ready for home, we'll make sure you have painkillers to take with you. If there's any further problem with itching or infection let us know.'

'I think I've got the number on speed dial,' she said with the first sign of humour of the day.

Matt knew they'd been through this routine countless times but it was part of his duty to make sure the correct treatment was followed up at home. Quinn's co-operation was just as important as his in the recovery.

'As usual, we'll need you to try and keep the dressings dry until you come back to have them changed. You've got an appointment with the child psychologist too, right? It's important that Simon has help to process everything he's going through.' Never mind the fire itself, the surgery alone could be traumatic enough for someone so young to get past. He already seemed so withdrawn and Matt wanted to make sure they were doing all they could as a team to make him better.

'The psychologist, the physiotherapist, the dietitian—

we've got a full house in appointment bingo.' Her voice was taking on that shrill quality which was always an indication of an impending showdown.

'I know it's a lot to take on but it won't be for ever. It's all to ensure Simon recovers as quickly and effectively as possible so you can both go back to your normal routine outside of these hospital walls.' He didn't know what that included since she seemed to spend every waking moment here. Almost as if she was afraid to go home.

These days he had an entirely different outlook on his personal time. There was nothing he loved more than reclaiming the peace and quiet of his apartment and the freedom of doing whatever he felt like without having to fit around other people's schedules.

'Don't.' Her small plea reached in and squeezed his insides, making him wonder how on earth he'd managed to upset her in such a short space of time.

'Don't what?' He didn't understand the sudden change in her body language as she let go of Simon's hand to wrap her arms around her waist in self-comfort.

'Don't make any more promises you have no way of keeping.'

Matt frowned. He was supposed to be the harbinger of good news, not enemy number one. 'Ms Grady, Quinn, I've assured you on many, many occasions we are doing everything in our control—'

'I've heard it all before but there always seems to be one thing after another—infections, fevers, night terrors, haemo-wotsit scars—'

'Hemotrophic.'

'Whatever. Life is never going to be *normal* when every surgery creates further problems.' Her voice, now reaching levels only dogs and small unconscious children could hear, brought a murmur from Simon before he drifted off to sleep again.

This wasn't the time or the place for one of her dressing-downs about how nothing he did was good enough. Venting or not, Simon didn't need to hear this.

He placed a firm hand under Quinn's elbow and, for the umpteenth time since they'd met, he guided her out of the room. Whatever was going on he couldn't continually let her undermine him in front of his patient. If Simon didn't believe he could help him he might lose hope altogether.

Quinn dug her heels in but it only took a pointed glance back at the bed and an extra push to get her moving again.

'I'm not a child,' she insisted, shaking him off.

'Then stop acting like one. This is a conversation that needs to be held away from impressionable young ears.' His own temper was starting to bubble now. Why couldn't she see he would do anything to help them? She seemed determined to make this situation more difficult than it already was. Perhaps it was time he did back off if his presence here was partly to blame for getting her riled. Once he'd said his piece today he'd go back to his official role of reconstructive surgeon and nothing more.

She huffed into the corridor for another round of their battle of wills. He waited until the door was firmly closed behind them and there was no audience to overhear what he was about to say.

'The graft was a success. That's what you should be focusing on here.'

'That's easy for you to say. You're not the one he runs away from crying when it's time to bathe him, or the one who has to rock him back to sleep when he wakes from the nightmares, screaming.' Quinn's eyes were shimmering with tears, the emotions of the day clearly coming to a head.

He kept an eye out for a female member of staff who'd be in a better position to comfort her. For him to hug her was stretching the boundaries of his professionalism a tad too far. Whilst he sympathised, at the end of the day, she wasn't one of his siblings and not his direct responsibility.

'Perhaps it would help to talk to one of the other parents? I know they're bound to be going through the same struggles right now.' He didn't doubt she was having a tough time of it personally but he really wasn't the one to guide her through it.

This was why he should treat all patients exactly the same and not let sentiment, or physical attraction to a parent, cloud his judgement.

'They probably are but I'm not part of the *clique*. I'm the new kid on the block as much as Simon. Most of them have known each other for years through the Parent Teacher Association and I haven't even been around long enough to organise a playdate for Simon, much less myself. Even if I did, I'd probably have to make sure they all had background checks done first. Not the way to start any budding friendship, I'm sure you'll agree. No, we've managed this far on our own without inviting strangers in to witness our misfortune. I think we can persevere a little longer.'

She was insisting she could go it alone but those big blue eyes said otherwise and prevented Matt from walking away when he knew that was the best thing he could do to save himself.

'The staff here will always be available for you and Simon but I do think perhaps our personality clash isn't helping your stress levels. Unless there are any complications I'm sure the nurses can take care of you until the next scheduled surgery. I'll make sure I keep my promise to him today though. I will come back when he's awake and show him that magic trick.'

This time he did manage to move his feet, but as he took a step away, Quinn took one closer.

'Oh, yeah. It's so easy for you to gain his trust. A few stupid magic tricks and he thinks you're the best thing since sliced bread, but me? He hates me. I've given up my job, lost my partner and abandoned any hope of a social life so I could focus on fostering, and for what? I've failed at that too.'

The thing he'd been dreading most finally happened. The dam had burst and Quinn was weeping onto his scrubs. There was no possibility of him leaving her now. She needed a shoulder to cry on and it was simply rotten luck for both of them—he'd been the wrong person at the wrong time.

'He doesn't hate you. You're in a…transition period. That's all. After all of the trauma it's going to take a while for him to settle down.' He heard the chatter of passersby and took it upon himself to reposition Quinn so she was against the wall and his body was shielding her from view. She was so slight in his arms, so fragile, it was a natural instinct to want to protect her.

As if he didn't have enough responsibilities in his life.

She shook against him, her sobs wracking so hard through her petite frame he was afraid she might break.

'I. Wish. I. Was. More. Like. You,' she hiccuped against his chest.

'I've never performed a sex change and I think it might be weird if I started making clones of myself.' He wanted to add that it would be a shame to tamper with the beautiful body she'd been given but it sounded inappropriate even in a joke. He wasn't supposed to be thinking about her soft curves pressed against him right now in anything other than a sympathetic and completely professional manner.

The sobbing stopped and she lifted her head from his chest, either because she'd rediscovered her sense of humour or he'd completely creeped her out. He held his breath until he read her face and exhaled when he saw the wobbly smile start to emerge.

'I mean, you're a natural with Simon, with all the kids. I'm starting to think I'm not cut out for parenthood.' Her bottom lip began to quiver again in earnest and Matt made it his personal mission to retrieve that smile.

He tilted her chin up with his thumb so she stopped staring at the floor to look at him instead. She needed to believe what he was telling her. Believe in herself.

'I've picked up a few child-wrangling tips along the way. Parenting isn't easy and that parent/child bond simply needs a little nurturing. I have a few short cuts I can share with you if you promise never to breathe a word of my secrets. I would hate to dent my reputation as the resident child-whisperer.'

'Heaven forbid. I'm sure that would break the hearts of many around here who worship the ground you walk on.' She blinked away the tears and for a split second it would be easy for Matt to forget where he was and do something stupid.

If they weren't standing in a hospital corridor he

might've imagined they were having 'a moment.' She'd made it clear she wasn't one of his devoted followers and yet her body language at present said entirely the opposite.

Matt's stomach growled, a reminder he hadn't eaten anything substantial since mid-morning, and distracted him from her dilated pupils and those swollen pink lips begging him to offer some comfort. He couldn't go back on his word to help but he did need a timeout to regain his composure and remember who he was. That definitely wasn't supposed to be a man prepared to cancel a hot date in order to spend some unpaid overtime counselling families.

'Listen, there's a pub across the road—the Frog and Peach. Why don't I meet you over there in ten minutes to talk things over? We can grab a drink or a bite to eat and come straight back here the minute Simon wakes up.' There was nearly always a contingent from the hospital propping up the bar at the end of their shift and he was counting on someone else to jump in and come to Quinn's aid before he committed to something else he'd come to regret. The phone call he was going to have to make would end his most recent love interest before it even began.

She gave a wistful glance at the room behind her before she answered. The sign of a true mother thinking of her son before herself, even though she didn't realise it.

'I'll leave word to contact us the second he opens his eyes.' He wasn't going to beg but he did want to fulfil his obligations ASAP so he could finish his working day and head home. Alone.

'Only if you're sure...' Her hesitation was as obvious in her doe-like eyes as it was in her voice.

Matt wasn't any more certain this was a good idea than Quinn but a chat in a pub had to be infinitely safer than another five minutes with her in his arms.

CHAPTER THREE

QUINN SCROLLED THROUGH her phone, paying little attention to the social media updates on the screen. She wasn't in contact with any of these people; they weren't part of her *actual* life. Recent events had proved that to her. Virtual acquaintances could be chock-full of sympathy and crying emoticons on the Internet but a distinct lack of physical support from anyone other than Mrs Johns next door had made her see an online presence was a waste of her valuable time. This sudden interest in what people were having for dinner, or who had the cutest kitten meme, was simply to occupy her hands and give the impression she was at ease on her own.

Matt had directed her towards the pub across the road and assured her he'd be with her as soon as he could get away. The Frog and Peach, as nice as it was, was a busy hub in Paddington and she was self-conscious sitting outside, occupying one of the much sought after tables.

She envied the carefree patrons meeting their friends to toast the end of their working day. It reminded her of the camaraderie she'd once had with her fellow teachers inside and outside of the school. A friend was the one thing she was desperately missing right now—someone she could share a laugh with, or pour her heart out to without judgement. Mrs Johns was the closest thing to that, volunteering to babysit if she ever needed a hand, but it wasn't the kind of relationship where she could really confide everything that was getting her down at the minute. She only really had her mum to talk to on the end of the phone for that, but even then she was almost ashamed to be totally honest about her situation and admit she wasn't coping when her mother had been her fostering inspiration. When she did return home to her Yorkshire roots, she wanted it to be a journey of triumph with Simon as happy as she'd been as a child who'd finally settled.

Quinn drained the water from her glass. After the day she'd had fretting over the surgery and making a fool of herself crying on Matt's shoulder, she could probably do with something stronger but she wouldn't touch alcohol while Simon was under her care. She took her responsibilities seriously and she couldn't sit here getting pie-eyed when she still had to get them both home across the city.

'Are you finished?' A male member of staff was at her side before she managed to set the empty glass down.

She nodded but felt the need to explain her continued occupation of valuable drinking space. 'I'm just waiting for someone.'

There was a brief flicker of something replacing the irritability in the young man's eyes and Quinn's cheeks burned as she realised it was sympathy. He thought she'd been stood up. It was the natural assumption, she supposed, as opposed to her waiting for her foster son's surgeon, who she'd emotionally tortured until he'd agreed to meet her here.

'I'm sure he'll be here any minute.' She began to defend her party-of-one residency but the busy waiter had already moved on to clean the next table, uncaring about her social life, or lack of one.

Unfortunately, the jitterbugs under her skin weren't entirely down to her anticipation of an evening in a hot doctor's company. The excitement of a singleton let loose in the city didn't last for ever and these days the skippety-hop of her heart tended to come from fear of what was going to happen to Simon next.

Still, as Matt finally came into view across the street there was a surge of girlish glee she'd imagined had vanished out the door with her ex. There was something about seeing him in his casual clothes that felt forbidden, naughty even. She was so used to him in his formal shirt and trousers combo, or his scrubs, that a pair of jeans and tight T-shirt seemed more…intimate.

There was something voyeuristic watching him negotiate the traffic, oblivious to her ogling. It was amazing how one scrap of plain material became so interesting when stretched across the right body, marking out the planes of a solid chest and rounding over impressive biceps. As he jogged across the road, with his jacket slung over his arm, Matt had no clue how good he looked.

Long-dormant butterflies woke from their slumber, mistaking the handsome man coming towards Quinn as a potential date, and fluttered in her stomach as she followed his progress. They quickly settled when she turned to check her reflection in the window and was reminded this was more of a pity party than a hook-up.

She knew the second he spotted her in the crowd on the pavement as a smile spread across his lips and he lifted a hand to wave. He'd been incredibly understanding considering her sometimes erratic behaviour and this was above and beyond the call of duty. It also did nothing to diminish her crush.

'Hey,' he said as he pushed his way through to reach her table, the last of the evening sun shining behind him and lighting his short blond hair into a halo. It made him almost angelic, if it wasn't for that glint in his ever shifting blue-green eyes which said there was potential for mischief there. It made her curious to find out if there was a wicked side to Saint Matt when he was off duty.

'Hi, Matt.' She pulled out a chair for him and couldn't resist a smug grin as the surly waiter passed by and did a double take.

'Do you want to go inside to order? The smokers tend to congregate out here…unless you'd prefer that?'

'It's okay, I'm not a smoker.' It earned him more Brownie points too—as if he needed them—he obviously didn't approve of the habit.

She popped her phone back in her bag and got up to follow him. It was easy to see him when he was head and shoulders above most of the crowd, but soon the mass of bodies was too thick for her to fight through to reach him.

'Excuse me…sorry…can I just get past?'

On the verge of giving up and heading back out for some fresh air, she felt a large hand clamp around her wrist and pull her through the people forest. Somehow she ended up taking the lead with Matt creating a force field around her with his body alone. She revelled in that brief moment of nurturing where someone put her welfare first. It had been a long time since anyone had been protective of her feelings and she missed that kind of support.

Since moving away from home it had been in rare supply at all. Even Darryl, who she'd thought she'd spend the rest of her days with raising children, had put his selfish needs before her or any potential foster kids.

'There's a table over here.' Matt cleared away the dirty dishes left behind by the previous occupants so they could take the comfy leather sofas by the fire. He obviously wasn't the sort of man who only thought of himself. It showed in his every action. Even if her jealousy had prevented her from appreciating the extra care he'd given to Simon, Matt's generous nature would make some lucky woman very happy indeed. A woman who wouldn't second-guess his every gesture, waiting to find out what ulterior motive lay behind it.

'I'm sorry I've been such a nuisance.' She leaned forward in the chair, taking a sudden interest in the patina of the wooden table, unable to meet Matt's eyes. It would be fair to say she'd been an absolute horror to him these past weeks. Now the hysteria had subsided and the voice of reason had restored calm, her bad behaviour became very apparent. Based on her past experience with men, her paranoia had led her to question his judgement, his professionalism and his methods when the man had simply been trying to do his job. It was a wonder he hadn't called security to remove her from the premises at any point. His patience clearly stretched further than hers.

'Don't worry. You're an anxious mum. I get it.' He reached across the table and squeezed her hand, pumping the blood in her veins that bit faster.

She flashed her eyes up at him, surprised at the soft warmth of his touch and the very public display of support. Matt met her gaze and there was a connection of solidarity and something…forbidden, which both comforted and confused the hell out of her.

'Are you ready to order?'

At the sound of an intruder, they sprang apart, the moment over, but the adrenaline continued surging through Quinn's body as though they'd been caught doing something they shouldn't. She began to wonder if the gum-chewing waiter was stalking her, or was more interested in her date.

Doctor. Friend. Not date.

'I…er… I'll have the burger and fries.' Matt snatched up the menu and barely glanced at it before ordering. She could read into that by saying he was as thrown by his actions as she was, or he simply ate here a lot.

'The chicken salad wrap, please.' Her appetite had yet to fully re-emerge since the fire but it would be nice to sit and enjoy a meal in company. In Matt's company. Except he was on his feet and following the waiter back towards the bar.

'I should've ordered drinks. I'll go and get some. Wine? Beer? Soft drink?' He called from an increasing distance away from her, walking backwards, bumping into furniture and generally acting as though he couldn't wait to get away from her.

Second-thoughts syndrome. He'd probably only suggested doing this to prevent another scene at his place of work.

'Just water, please.' She sighed, and slouched back in her chair, whatever spark she'd imagined well and truly extinguished.

A romantic interest from any quarter was nothing more than a fantasy these days anyway. She was going through enough emotional turmoil without leaving herself open to any more heartache. No, she should be grateful for what this was—a meal in adult company and a short respite from her responsibilities. Simon would be awake soon enough and the next round of anxious parenting would begin.

As she took in her new surroundings from her place of safety in the corner, she supposed it was a nice enough place. It had old-fashioned charm—Victorian, she guessed from the dark wood interior—and not the sort of establishment which immediately sprang to mind for a well-heeled surgeon. Matt was young, fashionable and, from what she could see, totally unencumbered by the ties she was bound by. Not that she regretted any of her choices, but if their roles were reversed she'd probably be living it up in some trendy wine bar hoping for a Matt clone to walk through the door and make her night. By weeping her way to a dinner invitation she'd no doubt spoiled the night for many single ladies across the city waiting for him to show.

'The food shouldn't be too long.' Matt took a seat opposite and placed a jug of iced water and two glasses on the table between them.

At least his agitation seemed to have passed as he poured the water with a steady hand. He was probably saving the heavy drinking for whenever he got rid of her and he could cut loose without having to babysit her.

'So…you were going to give me a tutorial in basic child-rearing…'

They may as well get this over with when they knew they both had other places to be. Ten minutes of him telling her where she was going wrong and they could all get back to their real lives, which, for her, generally didn't include pub dinners with handsome men. It was the highlight of an otherwise fraught day, it had to be said.

'Hey, I never claimed to be an expert. All I can do

is pass on the benefit of my experience in dealing with young children in very trying circumstances.'

'All suggestions for helping gain a five-year-old's trust will be gratefully received.' As was the arrival of her dinner. Although she hadn't been hungry up until now, it was infinitely more appetising than the sandwich she'd binned earlier, and it was a nice change from potato smiley faces and alphabet spaghetti which were the only things Simon would eat at present.

'A cheap magic set,' Matt managed to get out before he took a huge bite out of his loaded burger. He attacked it with such a hunger it gave Quinn chills. There was more than a hint of a wild thing lurking beneath that gentlemanly exterior and a glimpse of it was enough to increase her appetite for more than the bland safe option she'd chosen.

'Pardon?'

She had to wait until he'd swallowed for an answer.

'I use bribery as a way in. I keep a box of child-friendly toys in my office for emergencies. Toy cars, colouring books, bubbles… I've even got a couple of hand puppets I break out when they're too shy to speak directly to me. I find being a friend makes the whole experience less traumatic for them.' He snagged a couple of fries from the plate and tossed them into his mouth, making short work of them too before she'd even taken her first bite.

'Tried that. He's got a room full of new toys at my place but apparently you can't buy your way into a child's heart. I think you've just got a knack with kids that apparently I don't.' It was something she'd assumed would happen naturally since she'd been in the system herself and could relate to the circumstances which would bring foster children to her.

Unfortunately, she was finding it took more than enthusiasm and a will for things to work out to make an impression on Simon. Not every child would fit seamlessly into family life the way she had. Not that it had been easy for her either when her adoptive father had decided he couldn't hack it, but she'd had a special bond with her mother from the first time they'd met and they'd faced all the unexpected obstacles together. At least until she became an adult and decided she should venture out into the big wide world on her own. She wanted that same show of strength they'd had for her to enable her and Simon to work through the aftermath of the school fire but it wasn't going to happen when he kept shutting her out.

Matt shrugged. 'I don't know about that but I've had a lot of practice.'

Quinn nearly choked on her tortilla wrap. 'You have kids of your own?'

It would certainly explain how comfortable he was in that parenting role if there were a load of mini-Matts running around. The lack of wedding ring had blinded her to that possibility. Then again, marriage wasn't always a precursor to fatherhood. He could also be an absentee father but he didn't seem the type to have abandoned little Irish babies around the countryside either.

He spluttered into his glass. 'Hell, no!'

The emphatic denial should've pleased her to know he wasn't a feckless father but it was a stark reminder that the life she'd chosen wasn't for everyone. At least he was upfront about it, unlike Darryl, who'd pretended to be on board with family life and bailed at the last minute.

'You're not going to tell me you actually hate kids or

something, are you?' Her heart sank in anticipation of more disappointment. She couldn't bear to find out this affable surgeon had been nothing more than an act. If so, he deserved an Oscar for well and truly duping everyone who knew him from the Castle.

The sound of his deep chuckle buoyed her spirits back up again.

'Not at all. They're grand. As long as I'm not in charge of them outside work.'

'Ah, you're not the settling down type, then?' It was blatant nosiness but he seemed such perfect husband and father material she couldn't let it pass without comment. Not that she was actively looking for either when it hadn't worked out so well the first time around. She'd clearly been out of the dating scene too long since she was sitting here thinking about playing happy families with the first man to show her any attention.

'I've only just been released into the wild again. My dad died a while back, when I was in medical school. Cancer. I was left to raise my three sisters on my own. Bridget, the youngest, enrolled in college last year and moved away so I feel as though I'm finally starting my adult life. Child free.' He took a short break from devouring his dinner, the subject interfering with his appetite too.

Both she and Matt's siblings had been lucky they'd had someone special who'd been willing to sacrifice everything to provide for them. She wanted to do the same for Simon if he'd only let her.

'That must've been tough.' She was barely coping with one small boy and a part-time job. It was almost incomprehensible to imagine a young Matt raising and supporting a family while studying at the same time. Just when she thought this man couldn't be any more perfect his halo shone that bit brighter.

It was a shame that no-kids rule put him firmly off-limits. Along with the whole medical ethics thing and the fact she'd chosen celibacy over trusting a man in her life again. As if she'd ever stand a chance anyway after he'd witnessed her puffy panda eyes and been drenched in her tears of self-pity. He'd probably endured a lot more as a single parent and cried a lot less.

'Do you want some of my chips? Help yourself.' He shoved his plate towards her and it took a second to figure out why he was trying to feed her.

'Er...thanks.' She helped herself to a couple to detract from the fact she'd probably been staring at him longingly.

Better for him to think she was greedy than love struck. She wasn't too happy about the nature her thoughts had taken recently either.

'It wasn't easy but we survived and you will too. You figure this stuff out as you go along.'

It was good of him to share some of his personal details with her—he didn't have to and she knew he'd only done it to make her feel better. It did. He was no longer an anonymous authority figure; he was human and he was opening up to her. A little knowledge of his private life made it easier to trust another kindred spirit. She supposed it was only fair she gave something of herself too, although he'd probably already heard more than enough about her for one day.

'I thought with my background this would all be familiar territory. I was a foster kid myself. My birth parents were too young to handle parenthood and I bumped around the system until I was finally adopted. My mum never seemed to struggle the way I have, even when her husband walked out. I'm afraid history repeated itself. My ex left me too when I decided I wanted to foster.' It was difficult not to take it personally that any important male figures in her life had abandoned her. From the emotional outbursts and irrational behaviour Matt had probably already figured out why no man wanted to face a future with her.

'We're all full of good intentions, but it's not long before a cold dose of reality soon hits home, eh?' He was smiling at her but Quinn was convinced there was a barbed comment in there. Perhaps he'd meant well by asking her to meet here but he'd found it tougher going than he'd imagined listening to her whining.

'I'm sorry. I shouldn't be lumbering you with all my problems. It's not part of your job description and I'm putting you off your food.'

'Not at all.' He wedged the last bit of his burger into his mouth to prove her wrong.

'I tutor from home so it's been a while since I've had any adult company to vent with. Lucky you, you get to hear me offload first.'

'It's a hazard of the job. I'm a surgeon-cum-counsellor.' His grin said he didn't mind at all.

It was a relief to get off her chest how much these past two months had impacted on her and not be judged on it. She was doing enough of that herself by constantly comparing herself to her mother when the circumstances were so different. She'd been a young girl in the country, desperate for a family, and Simon, well, he wasn't more than a baby and had already been through so much. He'd been passed around like an unwanted guest and now he was burned and traumatised by the fire, with no real idea of what was going to come of him.

Her mother had had an advantage simply by living in her rural surroundings. Fresh air and wide open spaces were more conducive to recovery and peace of mind than the smog and noise of the city. However, this was the best place for him to be for his treatment and there was no choice but to soldier on, regardless of location.

'Do you have a couch in your office we can share?' It wasn't until he raised his eyebrow in response she realised how inappropriate that sounded. Today, it was becoming a habit.

An image of more inappropriateness on the furniture behind closed doors with Matt filled her head and made her hot under her black tank top and slouchy grey cardigan. If she'd had any intention of flirting she definitely would've picked something more attractive than her slummy mummy attire. Comfy leggings and baggy tops were her security blanket inside the hospital and hadn't been meant for public display.

'I mean… I feel as though I should be lying on your couch…you taking notes. As a counsellor, obviously. Not some sort of sofa fetishist who gets off on that sort of thing. I'll shut up now before you do actually use your authority to call the men in white coats to lock me up.' Quinn clapped her hands over her face as if they provided some sort of invisibility shield for her mortification. Unfortunately, they weren't a sound barrier either as she heard Matt cough away his embarrassment.

Very smooth. Not.

Far from building the beginnings of a support system with Matt as a friend, she'd created an even bigger chasm between them with her weirdness. She'd made it crystal clear to herself, and Matt, through her awkward small talk and vivid imagination that she fancied the pants off him. Why else would she be stumbling over her words and blushing like a schoolgirl trying to make conversation with him.

Great. On top of everything else she was actually picturing him with his pants fancied all the way off! The poor man had no clue about the monster he'd created by being so nice to her.

A sweaty, red-faced monster who'd apparently woken up from hibernation looking for a mate.

CHAPTER FOUR

FOR A SECOND Matt thought he was going to need someone to perform the Heimlich manoeuvre on him to dislodge the French fry in his throat. The shock of Quinn's imagery had made him swallow it whole.

He gulped down a mouthful of water, relief flooding through him as it cleared his blocked airway.

She hadn't tried to choke him to death on purpose. There'd been absolutely no malice or deliberate attempt on his life as far as he could tell, when Quinn emanated nothing but innocence and the scarlet tint of embarrassment. Neither, he suspected, had she meant to flirt with him but his body had responded all the same to the idea of them rolling around in his office. Around this woman he lost all control of himself, body and mind. Not to mention his common sense.

His first mistake had been to come here outside of work, only to be compounded by swapping details of their personal lives. Then there was the touching. Offering a reassuring hand, or shoulder to cry on, was part and parcel of his job, but probably not when they were lost in each other's eyes in a crowded pub.

She drew that protective nature of his to the fore when he'd spent this past year trying to keep it at bay. He'd only intended to show her she wasn't alone because he knew how it was not to have anyone to turn to when you were weighed down with family stresses. She didn't have to apologise for the feisty spirit she'd shown as they clashed over Simon's treatment; she'd need it to get her through. He simply hadn't expected that spark of attraction to flare to life between them as if someone had flicked a switch.

It had thrown him, sent him scurrying to the bar to wait until it passed. Quinn was the mother of one of his patients.

A mother. His patient.

Two very good reasons to bypass that particular circuit, but no, he kept on supplying power.

Telling her about his family was an eejit move. That was personal and this wasn't supposed to be about him. He listened, he diagnosed and he operated but he never, ever got personally involved. Not only had he given something of himself by revealing his family circumstances, now he knew her background too. The fact she'd been through the foster system only made her strength all the more remarkable to him.

She was a true survivor and yet she was still willing to give so much of herself to others. He needed to direct her somewhere those qualities weren't a personal threat to his equilibrium.

'You know, if you're at a loss for company, I can introduce you to members of the hospital committee. I'm sure you've heard the board is trying to close the place down and we'd be only too glad to have someone else fighting in our corner.' It would give her something to focus on other than Simon's treatment and, in turn, might create a bit of distance between them too. She might make a few more friends into the bargain. Friends who weren't afraid to get too close to her in case it compromised their position or freedom.

'I did do a spot of picketing today. It would be such a shame to see the place close. Especially after everything you've done for Simon there. What happens to you if they do close? What happens to us?'

He could see the absolute terror in her eyes, that brilliant blue darkening to the colour of storm-filled skies, at the thought of more disruption in their lives. It was also an indication that she was relying on him being present in her life for the foreseeable future and that wasn't an expectation he could live up to.

'I'd hate to see the place get phased out. Hopefully the campaigning and fundraising will make a difference. As for me, I'm on a temporary contract. I'll move on soon enough anyway. Like I said, I prefer to be footloose and fancy free these days.'

'Simon will miss you terribly.' She broke eye contact and diligently tidied the empty plates into a pile for the server to collect.

A dagger jabbed Matt in the heart at the idea that he'd be the one to cause either of them any further distress.

'Don't worry, I'll be around for a while yet and if I stay local there's always a chance he'd get referred to me anyway.' At least by then he would've had a cooling off period from this particular case.

Quinn nodded, although the lip-chewing continued.

This was the first time his casual new lifestyle had given him cause to rethink his idea of moving from one place to another whenever the mood took him. Whilst the notion of experiencing new people and places was more attractive than remaining stagnant in Dublin, he hadn't given any thought to patients who might get too attached, or vice versa.

It would be tough to leave his patients here when the time came, but better for him. He'd spent a huge chunk of his life on hold, waiting until others were ready to let go of him. This was supposed to be *his* time to spread his wings and not get dragged back into any more family dramas.

Despite the hustle and bustle of the pub around them, he and Quinn fell into an uneasy silence. His attraction to her was in direct competition with his longing for a quiet, uncomplicated life. The two weren't compatible, and whichever won through, it would undoubtedly leave the bitter taste of loss behind.

The vibration in his pocket shocked him back into the present, his pager becoming a cattle prod to make sure he was back on the right path. Although the message informing him Simon was awake had come too late to save him from himself or from straying onto forbidden territory.

'Simon's awake. We should head back.' And put a stop to whatever this is right now.

Quinn's face lit up at the news, which really wasn't helping with the whole neutral, platonic, not-thinking-of-her-as-anything-other-than-a-parent stance he was going to have to take.

'Oh, good! What are we waiting for?'

There was genuine joy moving in to chase the clouds of despair away in those eyes again. Whether Quinn knew it, or wanted it, Matt could see Simon was the most important thing in her life. He knew fostering was only supposed to be a temporary arrangement until a permanent home for the child was secured and if she wasn't careful with her heart she'd end up getting hurt. If he'd had to, Matt would've fought to the death with the authorities to gain custody over his siblings and he knew he'd have been heartbroken to see them shipped out to strangers after everything he'd done for them.

He didn't know what Quinn's long-term plans were, but it was important she didn't lose sight of her own needs or identity in the midst of it all. At least he'd had his career to focus on when his family had flown the nest and stripped him of his parent role.

Quinn was the sort of woman who needed to be cared for as well as being the nurturer of others.

He didn't know why he felt the need to be part of that.

The good news that Simon was awake was a welcome interruption for Quinn. She wasn't proud of the display she'd put on today and it would be best if she and Simon could just disappear back to the house and take her shame with her. At least she could unleash her emotions there without sucking innocent bystanders into the eye of the storm along with her.

Poor Matt, whose only job was to operate on Simon and send them on their way, had run the gauntlet with her today. Irrational jealousy, fear, rage, self-pity and physical attraction—she'd failed to hide any of them in his presence. That last one in particular gave her the shame shudders. He'd been antsy with her ever since that sofa comment.

That sudden urge to crumple into a melting puddle of embarrassment hit again and she wrapped her cardigan around her body, wishing it had a hood to hide her altogether.

She wasn't stupid. That suggestion she should join the hospital committee was his subtle way of getting her to back off and go bother someone else. He'd made his position very clear—he was done with other people's kids unless it was in the operating theatre.

'Are you cold?' Matt broke through her woolly invisibility shield with another blast of concern. He was such a nice guy, it was easy to misinterpret his good manners for romantic interest and that's exactly what she'd done.

If she asked around she'd probably find a long line of lonely, frightened women who were holding a candle for him because of his bedside manner. One thing was sure, when he did move on he'd leave a trail of broken hearts behind him.

'Yeah.' She shivered more at the thought of Matt leaving than the sudden dip in temperature as they ventured outside. He'd become a very big part of their lives here and she couldn't imagine going through all of this without him.

Warmth returned to her chilled bones in a flash as perfect gentleman Matt draped his jacket around her shoulders. In another world this would have been a romantic end to their evening and not a doctor's instinct to prevent her from adding hypothermia to her list of problems. She should have declined the gesture, insisted it wasn't necessary when they'd soon be back indoors, to prevent her from appearing any more pathetic than she already did. Except the enveloping cocoon of his sports coat was a comfort she needed right now. It held that spicy scent she associated with his usually calming presence in its very fabric.

She supposed it would be weird if she accidentally on purpose forgot to return it and started wearing it as a second skin, like some sort of obsessed fan.

When they reached the hospital lobby she had no option but to extricate herself from the pseudo-Matt-hug. If she didn't make the break now there was every likelihood she'd end up curled up in bed tonight using it as a security blanket.

'Thanks. That'll teach me for leaving home without a coat. Mum would not be happy after all those years of lecturing me about catching my death without one.' Although she'd be tempted to do it again for a quick Matt fix if she thought she could achieve it without the cringeworthy crying it had taken to get one.

He helped her out of his jacket and shrugged it on over his broad shoulders.

Yeah, it looked better on him anyway.

Given their difference in height and build she'd probably looked even more of a waif trailing along behind him. So not the image any woman wanted to give a man she was attracted to. If she was to imagine Matt's idea of a perfect partner it would be one of those oh-so-glamorous female managers who seemed to run the departments here, with their perfect hair and make-up looking terribly efficient. Nothing akin to a messy ponytail, and a quick swipe of lipgloss on a bag lady who didn't know if she was coming or going most of the time. Any romantic notion she held about Matt needed to be left outside the doors of this elevator.

'You don't have to go up with me. I know this place like the back of my hand. Thanks for your help today but I can take it from here. We'll see you again at our next appointment.' She jabbed the button to take her back to Simon, trying not to think about who, or what, Matt had planned for the rest of the night without her.

'I'm sure you can but I promised Simon I'd come and

see him. Remember? I wouldn't want to renege on our deal.' Matt stepped into the lift behind her.

It wasn't unexpected given his inherent chivalry but as the steel doors closed, trapping them in the small space together, Quinn almost wished he had gone back on his word so she could breathe again. In here there were no other distractions, no escape from the gravitational pull of Matt McGrory.

She tried not to make eye contact, and instead hummed tunelessly rather than attempt small talk, meaning that the crackling tension remained until another couple joined them on the next floor. Extra bodies should've diffused her urge to throw herself at him and give in to the temptation of one tiny kiss to test her theory about his hidden passion, but the influx only pushed them closer together until they were touching. There was no actual skin-to-skin contact through the layers of their clothes but the static hairs on the back of her neck said they might as well be naked.

Another heavyset man shoulder-barged his way in, knocking Matt off balance next to her.

'Sorry,' he said, his hand sliding around her waist as he steadied himself.

Quinn hoped her cardi wasn't flammable because she was about to go up like a bonfire.

His solid frame surrounded her, shielding her from any bumps or knocks from the growing crowd. He had a firm grip on her, protecting her, claiming her. She thought it was wishful thinking on her part until they arrived at their floor and he escorted her out, refusing to relinquish his hold until they were far from the crowd. His lingering touch even now in the empty corridor was blowing her he's-only-being-polite theory out of the water. Surely his patience would've run out by now if all of this had simply been him humouring her?

It was a shame he hadn't come into her life before it had become so complicated, or later, when things were a bit more stable. Pre-Darryl, when she hadn't been afraid to let someone get close, or post-Simon, when she might have some more control over what happened in her life.

He'd made it clear he wasn't interested in a long-term relationship with anyone but she didn't want to close the door on the idea altogether. Men like Matt didn't come around very often and someday she knew she'd come to regret not acting on this moment. Perhaps if one of them actually acknowledged there was more going on between them other than Simon's welfare she might stand a chance of something happening.

'Matt, I think we should talk—'

Before she could plant the seed for a future romantic interlude, Matt sprang away from her *à la* scalded cat. She barely had time to mourn the loss of his warmth around her when she spotted the reason for the abrupt separation.

'Hey, Rebecca.'

Another member of staff headed towards them. A woman whose curves were apparent even in her shapeless scrubs. The rising colour in Matt's cheeks would've been endearing if it wasn't for the fact Quinn was clearly the source of his sudden embarrassment.

'Hi, Matt. What on earth are you still doing here? Weren't you supposed to be going somewhere tonight?' A pair of curious brown eyes lit on Quinn and she immediately realised how selfish she'd been for monopolising his time. It hadn't entered her head that he would've given up a glamorous night out to sit listening to her tales of woe in a dingy pub.

Matt slid his green-eyed gaze at her too, and Quinn hovered between the couple, very much an outsider in the conversation. There was clearly something unsaid flying across the top of her head. Metaphorically speaking, of course. She had the advantage of a couple of inches in height on the raven-haired doctor. But it was the only one she had here, as she didn't know what they were talking about, or indeed, what relationship they might have beyond being work colleagues. It wasn't any of her business, yet she had to refrain from rugby-tackling the pretty doctor to the ground and demanding to know what interest she had in Matt.

Okay, so she was a little more invested in Matt than she'd intended.

'I…er…changed my mind. I wanted to check in on one of my patients, Simon, one of the kids from the school fire. This is his mum, Quinn. Quinn, this is Rebecca Scott, a transplant surgeon here at the Castle.'

Finally, she was introduced into the conversation before she started a catfight over a man who wasn't even hers.

'I'm so sorry you were caught up in that. I know it's been horrendous for all involved but I hear Simon's treatment's going well?' Rebecca reached out in sympathy and dampened down any wicked thoughts Quinn might've harboured towards her.

'It is. In fact, I'm just going to see him now after his surgery.'

'Well, he's definitely in the best hands.' There was admiration there but Quinn didn't detect anything other than professional courtesy.

'Yes, he is. Listen, Matt, I'm going to go and see how he is. I'll catch up with you later. Nice to meet you, Rebecca.' She didn't hang around for Matt's inevitable insistence he accompany her, nor did she look back to overanalyse the couple's body language once she'd left. They had separate lives, different roles in Simon's future, which didn't necessarily equate to a relationship or a debt to each other. She was confusing her needs with his and a clear head was vital in facing the months ahead. It was down to her to prepare Simon for his future family and she couldn't do that whilst pining for one of her own. Until then, she'd do well to remember it was just the two of them.

'What are you doing?' Rebecca moved in front of Matt, blocking his view of Quinn walking away.

'Hmm?' He was itching to follow her so they could see Simon together but the manner in which she'd left said she didn't want an audience for the reunion. She could be emotional at the best of times and seeing her five-year-old post-surgery would certainly give her cause for more tears. He'd give her a few minutes' privacy before he joined them, and as soon as he'd fulfilled his promise to the boy, he'd do what he should've done in the first place and go home.

Quinn rounded the corner and vanished from sight. It had been a long day for all of them and he didn't want to abandon her when she was so fragile. Instead, he turned his attention back to Rebecca to find her with her arms folded, eyebrows raised and her lips tilted into a half-smile.

'I told Simon I'd show him how to do a few magic tricks before he went home. I thought cheering him up was more important than a few drinks with someone I hardly know.'

'I believe you,' she said, her voice dripping with enough sarcasm to force Matt to defend his presence here post-shift.

'What? You think there's something going on with me and Quinn? She's having a nightmare of a time with Simon and he seems to respond better when I'm around. That's all.' He shut down any gossip fodder without the utterance of a lie. Anything remotely salacious resided entirely in his head. For now.

'Uh-huh? It's not like you to turn down a hot date for a charity case.' Rebecca wasn't about to let this drop and he knew why when he'd been enthusing about the date he'd lined up all week, only to have blown it off at the last minute. It was no wonder he'd developed something of a reputation due to his reluctance to settle down with one woman.

It was true; there'd been a few female interests over the course of his time in London but that didn't mean he jumped into bed with a different partner every week. Sometimes he simply enjoyed a little company. However, the slight against his character was nothing to the umbrage he took to Quinn being denigrated to a pity date. After two months of sparring and making up, he'd go as far as to say that they'd bonded as friends.

He pursed his lips together so he wouldn't defend her honour and give Rebecca any more ammunition to tease, or admonish, him.

'You know me, I'm never short of female company.' Generally he wasn't big-headed about such matters but it was better to shrug it off as a non-event than turn it into a big deal. The girl he was supposed to be seeing tonight, Kelly—or was it Kerry?—was just someone he'd met the other day. It was nothing special and neither of them had been particularly put out when he'd phoned to call it off so he could meet with Quinn instead. He wasn't a player and it wasn't as if he was trying to keep his options open. There was a good chance he'd never see or speak to Kelly/Kerry again.

'No, but it is quite uncharacteristic of you to be so... hands on, at work.'

So she'd seen him with his arm around Quinn. He couldn't even defend his actions there. There'd been no excuse for him to maintain that close contact after they'd exited the packed lift except for his own pleasure. He'd enjoyed the warmth of her pressed into him, her petite frame so delicate against his bulk and the scent of her freshly washed hair filling his nostrils until he didn't want anything else to fill his lungs.

'Simon's a special boy. He's in foster care and I guess I do have a soft spot for him. He's one of the first patients I've been able to treat with spray-on skin, so I'm particularly interested in his progress for use in other cases.' He didn't delve into any other personal aspects of his affinity for the pair. Rebecca knew he had younger sisters, but as this was his new start, he hadn't seen the need to divulge his personal struggles to reach this point. As far as anyone needed to know, he was simply escorting an anxious mother back to her son post-surgery.

'It's easy to get attached. I guess I was hoping for some juicy gossip to take my mind off things.'

'Well, I'm not the one everyone's talking about around here. The rumour mill's gone into overdrive now Thomas is back.'

Rebecca's sigh echoed along the corridor at the mention of her ex-husband. It might have come across as a dirty trick to shift focus from one taboo subject to another but he was genuinely concerned for his friend too. By all accounts the end of her marriage had been traumatic. The car crash which had claimed the life of her young daughter had also proved too much for the marriage to survive. Now her ex, a cardiologist, was here on loan, it was bound to be awkward for both of them.

Matt had seen grief rip apart many families in his line of work and in that respect he was lucky to have kept his own together. The alternative didn't bear thinking about.

'Me and Thomas? There's no story to tell, I assure you. In fact, we haven't exchanged a word since he got here. You'd never believe we knew each other, never mind that we were married once upon a time.' Her smile faltered as she was forced to confront what were obviously unresolved issues with her ex.

'How long has it been since you saw him last?'

'Five years, but in some ways it feels like only yesterday.' The hiccup in her voice exposed the raw grief still lingering beneath the surface.

'I'm sure it's not easy. For either of you.' They'd both lost a child and it was important to remember they'd both been affected. He didn't know Thomas but he knew Rebecca and she wouldn't have given her heart away to someone who wasn't worthy of her.

'It's brought a lot of memories back, good and bad. At some point I think we do need to have an honest conversation about what happened to clear the air, something we never managed when we were still together. Perhaps then we might both get some closure.'

Given that they were going to be working together, they'd need it. According to the staff who'd seen them together, the tension was palpable, and it wasn't like Rebecca not to speak her mind. As she'd just proved with this ambush. Thank goodness she hadn't spotted them getting cosy in the pub or he'd really have had a job trying to explain himself.

'I hope you sort things out. Life's too short to stay mad.'

'We'll see. When all is said and done this isn't about us. We're only here to do our jobs.' On cue, her pager went off and put an end to their impromptu heart-to-heart. She shrugged an apology as she pushed the call button for the elevator.

'I'm sure it'll all work out in the end.'

Rebecca was a professional, the best in her field, and there was no way she'd let personal matters interfere with her patients' welfare. That was one of the golden rules here and one he'd do well to remember himself.

'We've all got to face our demons at some time, I guess. Right, duty calls. Stay out of trouble.'

If he was going to do that, he wouldn't be heading to Simon's room, straight towards it.

CHAPTER FIVE

ALTHOUGH SEEING SIMON had come through the surgery successfully was always a relief, his aftercare never got any easier. Each stage of the treatment was often punctuated with a decline in his behaviour once they left the hospital grounds. From the moment he opened his eyes it was as if they'd taken two steps backwards instead of forward.

She'd stroked his hair, told him what a brave boy he was, promised him treats—all without the normal enthusiastic response of a child his age in return. Of course, they'd see the psychologists, who would do their best to get him to open up and help him work through the trauma, but the onus was still on her to get him past this. With a degree in child psychology herself, she really thought she'd make more progress with him. At least get him to look at her. She'd aced her written exams but the practical was killing her. Most kids would only be too glad to get out of here and go home—she knew she would be—but no amount of coaxing could get him to even acknowledge her.

When Matt strolled into the room and instantly commanded his attention she had to move away from any items which could suddenly become airborne. Although, after their dinner chat, she was able to watch their interaction through new eyes.

He'd had more experience in parenthood than her, his ease very apparent as he engaged Simon in his magic know-how. Perhaps that's what made the difference. He was comfortable around children, whereas she'd had virtually no experience other than once being a child herself. Even then, she hadn't socialised a great deal. Her mother had worked hard to keep a roof over their heads and often that meant missing out on playdates and birthday parties to help her at her cleaning jobs.

It could be that Simon's unease was in direct correlation to hers and he was picking up on the what-the-hell-am-I-doing? vibes. In which case his lack of confidence in her was understandable. Unfortunately, the fostering classes she'd attended hadn't fully equipped her to do the job. Unlike star pupil Matt, who was deep in conversation sitting on the end of Simon's bed.

'What's with all of the whispering going on over there?' She dared break up the cosy scene in an attempt to wedge herself in the middle of it.

There was more whispering, followed by a childish giggle. A sound she thought she'd never hear coming from Simon and one which threatened to start her blubbing again. She was tempted to throw a blanket over Matt's head and snatch him home with her to keep Simon entertained.

'Can't tell you. It's a secret.' Simon giggled again, his eyes bright in the midst of the dressings covering his face.

'Magician's code, I'm afraid. We can't divulge our secrets to civilians outside our secret circle.' Matt tapped the side of his nose and Simon slapped his hand over his mouth, clearly enjoying the game.

Quinn didn't care as long as he was talking again and having fun.

'Hmm. As long as we're not suddenly overrun with rabbits pulled out of hats, then I'll just have to put up with it. Tell me, what do you have to do to be part of this prestigious group anyway?' She perched on the bed beside Matt, getting a boost from sitting so close to him as much as from the easy-going atmosphere which had been lacking between her and Simon.

'We're a pretty new club so we'll have to look into the rules and regulations. What do you say, Simon? What would it cost Quinn to join?' Matt's teasing was light relief now her green-eyed, monstrous alter ego had left the building. This wasn't about one-upmanship; he was gaining Simon's confidence and trust and gradually easing her in with him.

'Chocolate ice cream!' he shouted without hesitation.

'We can do that.' She was partial to it herself and something they could easily pick up on the way home. A small price to pay for a quiet night.

'That should cover her joining fee…anything else?' Matt wasn't going to let her off so easily.

'Umm…' Simon took his time, milking her sympathy for all it was worth with Matt's encouragement.

He eventually came back with 'The zoo!' knowing he had her over a barrel.

There was no way she could say no when they were making solid progress. Not that she was against the idea; it simply hadn't crossed her mind that he would want to go.

'Nice one.' Matt high-fived his mini-conspirator and Quinn got the impression she'd walked straight into a trap.

'A day at the zoo? I've never been myself, but if that's the price I have to pay to join your club I'm in.' It was worth it. He hadn't expressed a desire to leave the house since the fire, unwilling to leave the shadows and venture out into the public domain, so this was a major breakthrough.

It could also turn out to be an unmitigated disaster, depending on how he interacted with other visitors. He'd already endured much staring and pointing from the general public who didn't understand how lucky he was just to survive the injuries, but it was a risk worth taking. If things went well it could bring them closer as well as give him a confidence boost.

'You've never been to the zoo?' Matt was still staring at her over that particular revelation.

'We never got around to it. Mum was always working weekends and holidays to pay the bills and I tagged along with her.' It wasn't anyone's fault; spending time together had simply been more important than expensive days out.

'You don't know what you're missing. Lions, penguins, gorillas...they're all amazing up close.'

She couldn't tell who was more excited, both big kids bouncing at the idea. Although she was loath to admit it, there was a fizz in her veins about sharing the experience with Simon for the first time too. As if somehow she could recapture her childhood and help him reconnect with his at the same time.

'Matt has to come too!' Simon tried to wedge it into the terms and conditions of the deal but he was pushing his luck now.

'I've been before. This is something for you and your mum to do together.' Matt turned and mouthed an apology to her and the penny dropped that he'd been trying to broker this deal for her benefit alone.

'Matt has lots of other patients to treat and he'd never get any work done if he had to keep taking them all to the zoo whenever they demanded it. We'll go, just the two of us, and make a day of it.' Quinn could already sense him shrinking back into his shell. Negotiating with an infant was a bit like trying to juggle jelly—impossible and very messy.

'You can take loads of photos and show me the next time you're here.'

Bless him, Matt was doing his best to keep his spirits up but the spark in Simon had definitely gone out now he knew his favourite surgeon wasn't involved. She knew the feeling.

'Right, mister, it's getting late. We need to get you dressed and take you home.' Any further arguments or tantrums could continue there, out of Matt's earshot. She wouldn't be surprised to find out he'd taken extended leave the next time they were due back to see him.

'I don't have a home!' Simon yelled, and single-handedly pulled the sheet up over his head, his body shaking under the covers as he sobbed.

Quinn genuinely didn't know what to do; her own heart shattered into a million pieces at his outburst. He didn't count her as his mum, didn't even think of her house as a place of safety, despite everything she'd tried to do for him.

She was too numb to cry and stood open-mouthed, staring at Matt, willing him to tell her what to do next. It wasn't as if she could leave him here until he calmed down; he was her foster child, her responsibility, and it was down to her to provide a home he'd rather be in-stead of here.

The foster authorities would certainly form that opin-ion and it was soul-crushing to learn he'd take a hospital bed on a noisy ward over the boy-friendly bedroom she'd painstakingly decorated in anticipation of his arrival.

She'd been happy to have one parent—why couldn't he?

'You're being daft now. I know for a fact you and Quinn live in the same house. I bet you've even got a football-themed room.' As usual Matt was the one to coax him back out of his cotton cocoon.

'I've got space stuff.' Simon sniffed.

'Wow! You're one lucky wee man. I had to share a room with my sisters so it was all flowers and pink mushy stuff when I was growing up.'

'Yuck!'

'Yuck indeed.' Matt gave an exaggerated shudder at the memory but it gave Quinn a snapshot of his early life, outnumbered by girls.

'Do you wanna come see?' He peeked his head above the cover to witness the fallout of his latest demand.

This time Matt turned to her for answers.

They were stuffed.

If she said no, she hadn't a hope of getting Simon home without a struggle and she was too exhausted to face it. A 'yes' meant inviting Matt further into their personal lives and they couldn't keep relying on him to solve their problems. He'd made it clear he didn't want to be part of any family apart from the one he'd already raised. In her head she knew it was asking for trouble but her heart said, 'Yes, yes, yes!' So far, he'd been the one blazing ember of hope in the dark ashes of the fire.

She gave a noncommittal shrug, leaving the final decision with him. It was a cop out on her behalf, but if he wanted out, now was the time to do it. She was putting her faith in him but his hesitation was more comforting than it should've been. At least she wasn't the only one being put on the spot and it proved some things were beyond even his control. His mind wasn't made up one way or the other about getting further entangled in this mess and that had to be more promising than a firm no.

'My apartment isn't too far away... I suppose I could get my car, drop you two home and take a quick peek at your room...' The confidence had definitely left his voice.

A five-year-old had got the better of both of them.

'I really couldn't ask you to—'

'Cool!' Simon cut off the polite refusal she was trying to make so Matt didn't feel obligated, even though she didn't mean it. Inside, she was happy-dancing with her foster son.

'Well, it would save us a taxi fare.' She folded easily. A ride home would be so much less stressful than the Tube or a black cab. As efficient as the London transport system was, it wasn't traumatised-child-friendly. The fewer strangers Simon had to encounter straight after his surgery, the better.

'I'll go get the car and meet you out front in about thirty minutes. That should give you plenty of time to get ready.' He bolted from the room as soon as she gave the green light. It was impossible to tell whether he wanted to put some distance between them as soon as possible, or whether he intended to get the job done before he changed his mind. Whatever his motives, she was eternally grateful.

For the first night in weeks, she wasn't dreading going home.

* * *

Matt stopped swearing at himself the moment he clocked the two figures huddled at the hospital entrance waiting for him. He'd been beating himself up about getting roped into this, but seeing them clutching each other's hands like two lost bodies in the fog, he knew he'd done the right thing. He wouldn't have slept if he'd gone home and left Quinn wrestling a clearly agitated child into the back of a taxi. For some reason his presence was enough to diffuse the tension between the two and, as Simon's healthcare provider, it was his duty to ease him back to normality after his surgery. Besides, it was only a lift, something he would do for any of his friends in need.

The only reason he'd hesitated was because he didn't want people like Rebecca, or Quinn, reading too much into it. He really hadn't been able to refuse when he'd had two sets of puppy dog eyes pleading with him to help.

'Nice car.' Quinn eyed his silver convertible with a smile as he pulled up.

'A treat to myself. Although I don't get out in it as often as I'd hoped. Much easier to walk around central London.' It had been his one great extravagance and what might appear to some as a cliché; to him it had been a symbol of his long-awaited independence.

Yet here he was, strapping a small child into the back seat...

'Yeah. This is made for long drives in the country with the top down.' She ran her hand over the car's smooth curves, more impressed than a lot of his friends who thought it was tragic attention-seeking on his part.

'That's the idea.' Except now he had the image of Quinn in the passenger seat, her ash brown hair blowing in the wind, without a care in the world, he wondered if it was time he traded it in for something more practical, more sedate.

Quinn's modest house was far enough from the hospital to make travel awkward but it had the bonus of peace and quiet. It was the perfect suburban semi for a happy family and the complete opposite of his modern bachelor pad in the heart of the city. He at least had the option of walking to PCH and did most days. Since moving to London he'd fully immersed himself in the chaos around him. Probably because he'd spent most of his years at the beck and call of his siblings, his surroundings dictated by the needs of his dependents. This kind of white picket fence existence represented a prison of sorts to him and he couldn't wait to get back to his alternative, watch-TV-in-my-pants-if-I-want-to lifestyle.

'You can't get much better than a taxi straight to your door.' He pulled the handbrake on with the confidence of a man who knew he'd be leaving again soon. This was the final destination for any feelings or responsibility he felt for Quinn and Simon today. Tomorrow was another day and brought another list of vulnerable patients who would need him.

'I really can't thank you enough, Matt. I wasn't up to another burst of tantrum before we left.' Quinn's slow, deliberate movements as she unbuckled her seat belt showed her weariness and reluctance to go inside.

The stress she was under was relentless—juggling Simon's injuries with the fostering process and her job. All on her own. The two of them could probably do with a break away from it all.

He glanced back at Simon. 'Someone's out for the count now. He shouldn't give you any more trouble.'

'If I can get him up to bed without disturbing him I might actually get a few hours to get some work done. Then I'll be on standby for the rest of the night with pain relief when he needs it.' She was yawning already at the mere mention of the night ahead.

'Make sure you get a couple of hours' sleep too.'

'That's about as much as we're both getting at the moment.' She gave a hollow laugh. The lack of sleep would definitely account for the short tempers and general crankiness, not to mention the emotional outbursts.

'Why don't you open the door and I'll carry Sleeping Beauty inside for you?'

She was strong and stubborn enough to manage on her own, he was sure—after all, she'd been coping this far on her own—but it didn't seem very gentlemanly to leave her to carry the dead weight of a sleeping child upstairs. If he delivered Simon directly to his bed there was more chance of him getting out of here within the next few minutes. That was his excuse and he was sticking to it.

Quinn opened her mouth as if to argue the point, then thought better of it, going to open the door for them and leaving him to scoop Simon out of the back seat. It was an indication of how weary she was when she gave in so easily.

As Matt carried Simon up the steep staircase to bed, careful not to jar his arm in the process, he knew he'd made the right call. Leaving a tired, petite Quinn to manage this on her own would have been an accident waiting to happen. He'd had enough experience of doing this with baby sisters who'd sat up long past their bedtimes to negotiate the obstacle with ease.

'Which way?' he mouthed to Quinn, who was waiting for them on the landing.

'In here.' She opened one of the doors and switched on the rocket-shaped night light at the side of the small bed.

Matt eased him down onto the covers and let Quinn tuck him in. She was so tenderly brushing his hair from his face and making sure he was comfortable that in that moment an outsider wouldn't have known they were anything other than biological mother and son.

They tried to tiptoe out of the room together but Simon unfurled his foetal position and rolled over.

'Do you like my room, Matt?' he mumbled, half asleep and hardly able to keep his eyes open.

'Yeah, mate. You're one lucky boy.' He could see how much effort Quinn had gone to in order to create the perfect little boy's room. From the glow-in-the-dark stars on the ceiling, to the planet-themed wallpaper, it had been co-ordinated down to the very last detail. The sort of bedroom a young boy sharing a council flat with three sisters could only have dreamed about.

'Now Matt's seen your room he has to go and you need to get some sleep.' Quinn tucked the loosened covers back around him.

'What-about-the-zoo?' he said in one breath as his eyes fluttered shut again.

'We'll do that another day,' she assured him, and tried to back out of the room again.

'Can-Matt-come-too?' He wasn't giving in without a fight.

Quinn's features flickered with renewed panic. This wasn't in the plan but they knew all hell would break loose again if he left and denied this request. Their silence forced Simon's eyes open and Matt had to act fast or get stuck here all night trying to pacify him.

'Sure.' He glanced back at her and shrugged. What choice did he have? With any luck Simon would forget the entire conversation altogether. Especially since the required answer sent him back to sleep with a smile on his face.

This time they made it out of the room undetected and Quinn released a whoosh of breath from her lungs as she eased the door behind them.

'I thought we'd never get out of there alive.' She rested her head against the back of the door, all signs of tension leaving her body as her frown lines finally disappeared and a smile played upon her lips. It was a good look on her and one Matt wished he saw more often.

'We're not off the hook yet but hopefully we've stalled the drama for another day.' Preferably when he was far from the crime scene.

'I appreciate you only agreed to the zoo thing to get him to go to sleep. Don't worry, I won't hold you to it.' She was granting him immunity but he remembered something she'd said about people letting her down and he didn't want to be another one to add to her list.

'It's no problem at all. I told you, I love the zoo.' It just wasn't somewhere he'd visited since his sisters had entered their teenage years. An afternoon escorting the pair around the sights wasn't a big deal; he'd been the chaperone on a few organised hospital trips in his time and this wouldn't be too dissimilar. It would be worth a couple of hours of his free time to see them happy again.

'Thanks for the idea, by the way. I kind of fell apart when he said he didn't have a home to go to.' The crack in her voice was evidence of how much the comment had hurt.

'He's frightened and it's been another tough day for both of you. It's easy to hit out at the ones closest to us. I've lost count of the amount of times my sisters told me they hated me and they couldn't wait to move out. They didn't mean it, and nor does Simon. It's all part of the extras package that comes with parenthood, I'm afraid.'

There'd been plenty of rows over the years as teenagers rebelled and he'd been the authority figure who'd had to rein them in. However, they were still a close family and he was the first person they'd call if they needed help.

'I'd hate to think I was making things worse for him. He seems so unhappy.' The head was down as the burden of guilt took up residence again on her shoulders.

He crouched down before her so she had to look at him. 'Hey, I don't know Simon's background but I do know he's a lucky boy to have you as a foster mother. You're a wonderful woman, Quinn, and don't you forget that.'

She fluttered her eyelashes as she tried to bat away the compliment but he meant every word. The burden she'd taken on with Simon's injuries and her determination to make a loving home for the duration of his time with her took tremendous courage. A strong, fiery soul wrapped up in one pretty package was difficult not to admire.

Now free from the responsibilities of work and away from the stares of co-workers and impressionable youngsters, Matt no longer had anyone to stop him from doing what he'd wanted to do for a long time.

He leaned in and pressed his mouth to hers, stealing the kiss they'd been dodging since their time in the pub. It wasn't his ego make-believing she wanted this too when her lips were parted and waiting for him.

Away from the hospital they were more than an over-attentive doctor and an anxious parent. In another time, in different circumstances, he wouldn't have waited a full day before taking her in his arms the way he did now.

He bunched her silky hair in his hands and thought only of driving away the shadows of doubt already trying to creep in and rob him of this moment. The instant passion which flared between them was a culmination of weeks of building tension, fighting the attraction and each other. Every fibre of his being, with the exception of several erogenous zones, said this was a bad idea. She was a single mother and this went against all of his self-imposed rules. This new carefree lifestyle was supposed to mean he went with the flow, free to do whatever he wanted. And in the here and now, Quinn was exactly what he wanted, so he ignored the voice that told him to leave and never look back, and carried on kissing her.

Either Quinn had died and gone to heaven or her exhaustion had conjured up this mega-erotic fantasy because it couldn't possibly be happening. It was beyond comprehension that she was actually making out with her foster son's surgeon in her own house.

The tug at her scalp reminded her it was very real.

Matt took her gasp as an invitation to plunge his tongue deeper into her mouth, stealing what was left of her breath. He was so thorough in his exploration, yet so tender, he confused her senses until she couldn't think beyond his next touch.

His fingers wrapped around her hair, his mouth locked onto hers, his hard body pressed tightly against her—it was too much for her long-neglected libido to process at once. It was as though every one of her forgotten desires had come to life at once, erasing the loneliness of these past man-free months.

Her ex's betrayal had devastated her so much she'd convinced herself romance in her life didn't matter but Matt McGrory had obliterated that theory with one kiss. It most certainly *did* matter when it reminded her she was a hot-blooded woman beneath the layers of foster mum guilt. She'd forgotten how it was to have someone kiss the sensitive skin at her neck and send shock waves of pleasure spiralling through her belly and beyond. In fact, she didn't remember ever swooning the way she was right now.

Today, Matt had successfully operated on Simon, talked sense into her when she'd been virtually hysterical, held her when she'd cried, supported her when she'd fallen apart and carried a sleeping child to his bed. He was perfect. It was a crying shame the timing was abominable.

He slid a hand under her shirt and her nipples immediately tightened in anticipation of his touch. If he ventured any further than her back she doubted she'd be able to think clearly enough to put a stop to this. As enjoyable as the feel of his lips on her fevered skin was, this wasn't about her getting her groove back on. Simon was her priority and she wouldn't do anything to jeopardise that.

Matt was his surgeon and this could lead to all sorts of complications regarding his treatment and the fostering authorities. That wasn't a risk she was willing to take. She wanted to break the cycle of selfish behaviour which had plagued her and Simon to date, and if it kept her heart protected a while longer, all the better.

'I think we should probably call it a day.' She dug deep to find the strength to end the best night she'd had for a long time.

With her hands creating a barrier between their warm bodies, she gave him a feeble push. Her heart wasn't in the rejection but it did stop him in his tracks before he kissed his way to her earlobe and discovered her kill switch. His acquiescence did nothing to ease her conscience or the throbbing need pulsating in her veins.

'You're probably right.' He took a step back, giving them some space to think about the disaster they'd narrowly averted. Then he was gone.

One nod of the head, a meek half-smile and it was Goodnight, Josephine.

Quinn exhaled a shaky breath as the front door clicked shut.

It had been a close call and, now she knew the number, it was going to be a test of endurance not to put him on speed dial.

CHAPTER SIX

IT HAD BEEN several days since the infamous kiss but Quinn hadn't laid eyes on Matt at all. Quite a feat when she'd spent every waking moment back at the hospital. She thought he'd be there when Simon had his dressings changed, an ordeal in itself. Although it was the nurses who routinely did that job, he usually called in to see how they were. He was definitely avoiding her.

Whilst his noticeable absence had prevented any awkwardness between them after locking lips together, a sense of loss seemed to have engulfed her and Simon as a result. They'd become much too invested in his company and now she had very fond, intimate memories to make her pine for him too.

It had been her decision to stop things before they'd gone any further. Hot kisses and steamy intervals didn't bring any comfort when there was no commitment behind them. Passion didn't mean much to her these days when she'd found out the hard way men used it to hide their true intentions. She'd thought Darryl had loved her because he was so attentive in that department but when it came down to putting a child's needs before his he'd shown how shallow he really was. She wouldn't be duped for a second time into believing a man's interest in her body was anything more than just that. Darryl had nearly broken her spirit altogether with his betrayal, to the point she'd questioned her own judgement about foster care. What was the point if the whole ideal of a happy family was a sham concocted so the male species could satisfy their own selfish needs?

It was meeting Simon which had convinced her she'd taken the right path and she wouldn't be so easily diverted from it again. A handsome face and a kissable mouth weren't enough for her to risk her or Simon's future if she was dumped again and sent spiralling back down into despair. Things were difficult at the moment but she was still soldiering on, wasn't ready to give up the fight. One more knock to her confidence might well change that. No, she'd made the right call and she'd just have to learn to live with it. Regardless of how much she wanted Matt to be the man she'd always thought would be the head of her perfect little family.

Today, to distract herself from the events of that evening, she'd joined the committee fighting to save the Castle. Whilst Simon was busy with his physiotherapist, who was working with him to make sure he maintained the movement in his right arm, she had some time to herself. She chose to spend it putting the world to rights with other committee members over a latte in the canteen. Her position also allowed her to keep watch on the door in case of a glimpse of the elusive Mr McGrory.

'I'm so glad you've joined us, Quinn. It'll really help our cause to have parents of our patients on board, as well as the staff. This is about the children, and showing the board the Castle is an important part of the community, and is more than just a lucrative piece of land.' Victoria Christie sat forward in her chair, fixing Quinn with her intense hazel eyes. She was a paramedic, the head of the committee and apparently very passionate about the cause.

With her buoyant enthusiasm she was the perfect choice for a front woman and Quinn got the impression she would attach herself to the wrecking ball should the dreaded demolition come to fruition.

'I'm only too happy to help. I'll sign a petition, wave a placard, write a personal impact statement…whatever it takes to make a difference. Matt…er… Mr McGrory suggested I join since I spend most of my days here anyway.' Mostly, she suspected, to get her out of his lovely blond hair, but at least it was a more productive way of filling her time than fretting and crying on shoulders of very busy surgeons.

'Matt's very passionate about his work and his patients. He's one of the good guys.' The tall blonde she'd been introduced to at the start of this meeting was Robyn Kelly, head of surgery at the hospital and the committee's PR person.

Quinn shifted her gaze towards the pile of papers on the table outlining their press coverage so far in case her blush gave away her thoughts about that very personal, private moment she'd spent with her colleague at her house.

'He's been very patient with Simon, and me, but we're well on the way to recovery. I hope future patients are as lucky to have him on their side.' She smiled as brightly as her pained cheeks would allow. In truth, she didn't want anyone to get as close as she had been to him but that didn't mean she'd deny another family his expertise.

'That's a really good idea!' Victoria slammed her

cup back down on the table, sloshing the contents into the saucer.

'What is?' With one hand Robyn quickly moved the newspaper cuttings out of the path of the tea puddle slowly spreading across the table, and used the other to soak up the mess with a napkin.

She exuded a self-confidence Quinn had once had, before a runaway boyfriend and being catapulted into life as a single foster parent had robbed her of it. With a little time and more experience she hoped she'd soon be able to clear up her own messes as swiftly and efficiently.

Although she'd never regret her decision to leave her full-time teaching position to raise Simon, she did envy both women to a certain degree. They were still career women, free to gossip over coffee without feeling guilty about taking some 'me' time. It was just as well they'd been so welcoming, arranging this meet as soon as she'd expressed an interest in the committee. Otherwise her jealousy might have got the better of her again.

'Personal impact stories, of course. Perhaps we could collate short statements from patients and their families, past and present. They could give an account of what the hospital has done for them and what it would mean to lose its support.

'That could add a really heartfelt element to the cause...'

'I could make a start with the families of the other children who were treated after the school fire.' Quinn knew most of them by sight now, if not personally, and they were certainly aware of Simon. Their kids had been discharged from the hospital long ago whilst he and Ryan, who'd suffered the most serious injuries, were still receiving treatment.

This new mission would give her an introduction into a conversation which didn't have to solely revolve around Simon's trauma. She wasn't the one who bore the physical scars but even she was sick of the sympathetic murmuring every time they walked past.

'Fantastic. That would be better coming from you, a concerned parent, rather than a soon-to-be-out-of-work member of staff.' Victoria's smile softened her features and her praise endeared her to Quinn even more.

'We might even get the papers to run a series of them to really hammer home how much a part of the children's recovery the Castle has become. Honest raw emotion versus cold hard cash... I think my contacts at the paper would be only too glad to wage war on some corporate fat cats.' Robyn was furiously scribbling in a reporter's notebook she'd plucked from her handbag.

'Quinn, I'll pass your name on to a few of the patients who want to help. You could be the co-ordinator for this leg of the campaign, if that's not too much trouble?' After draining her cup, Victoria got to her feet and effectively ended the meeting.

'Not at all. I could even make up some questionnaires to hand out if it would make things easier?' Admin she could do, and while paperwork had been the bane of her teaching career it was something positive here. It gave her an identity which wasn't merely that of Quinn, the single mother. She still had one useful function.

'I'll leave the details to you and try to organise a collection point for the completed papers. I'm really glad you've joined us, Quinn.' Another smile of acceptance and a firm handshake to solidify her role on the team.

Robyn, too, was packing up to leave. 'All excellent suggestions. I'll be sure to put your name forward for a medal or something at the next board meeting if we pull this off. In the meantime, I'm going to go make some more phone calls.'

She gave a sharp nod of her head as though to assure Quinn she'd just passed some sort of initiation test before she vanished out the door after Victoria. It seemed she was the only one not in a hurry to get anywhere.

She took her time finishing her latte and the caffeine seemed to have kicked in as she went to collect Simon with a renewed bounce to her step. Her well-received ideas today gave her hope that somewhere down the line she might come up with another brainwave to aid Simon as well as the hospital.

She rounded the corner and stopped dead, the rubber soles of her shoes squealing in protest on the tiled floor as she pulled on the emergency handbrake.

Unless her eyes were deceiving her, Simon and Matt were walking towards her. Panic slammed into her chest that something was wrong; there was also a fluttering in her pulse, followed by irrational fear again…then relief because they were both smiling. And finally, a surge of gratefulness she'd chosen a dress today instead of her jeans and cardi.

So, her wardrobe choices had become decidedly more feminine this week. It was an ego boost; she felt better inside when she knew she looked good on the outside. It held no significance where Matt was concerned. She definitely hadn't been paying more attention to her make-up and clothes in case she ran into him again so she looked her best. That would mean she regretted telling him to leave the other night which wasn't possible. Her primary focus would always be Simon and any other future foster children over men with wanderlust in their bewitching green eyes.

'Hey. Is everything all right?' She managed to keep her voice steady and un-chipmunk-like regardless of her heart pounding a dizzying beat.

All of the thoughts she'd had about him since that night hit her at once as the sight of him reminded her she hadn't exaggerated the effect he had on her. Her lips tingled with the memory of him there, her skin rippled with goose bumps as though his hand still rested upon her and the hairs stood on the back of her neck where he'd kissed her so tenderly.

She supposed it would be really out of order to grab the fire extinguisher off the wall and hose herself down before she forgot where she was and tried to jump Matt's bones.

'I thought I'd call in and see how things were going.' He ruffled Simon's hair, not meeting her eyes.

Did he mean that in a purely professional capacity? Was he checking in to see how she was after their moment of madness, or just Simon? Why was she overanalysing his every word like a neurotic teenager when she was the one who'd called it a night? She'd forfeited her right to be on his watch-list when she'd directed him towards her front door rather than her bedroom door.

And now her imagination was really going into overdrive, along with her heart rate. Any minute now her tachycardia was going to require a hospital stay of her own if she couldn't stop thinking about Matt without his scrubs.

She cleared her throat and refocused. He was wearing clothes. They were in public. He had Simon by the hand. Anything remotely erotic beyond that was in her disturbed mind.

'We're chugging along as usual.' The only disruption to their carefully organised schedule were the distractions she was seeking to stop her obsessing over a certain medic. 'Oh, and I've volunteered my services to the hospital committee.'

'Good. Good. We can use all the help we can get.' Matt rocked forward and back on his toes, displaying the same unease about seeing each other after their last meet.

Yet, he'd come to seek her out. Albeit using Simon as some sort of barrier between them.

'How did you get on today, sweetheart?' It was never fun waiting on the sidelines no matter what the purpose of the visit because there was no telling how his mood would be at the end of these appointments. No child enjoyed sitting still for too long or being poked and prodded by doctors and nurses. Although there was no dragging of heels when he was with Matt. She should really capitalise on that and get him home while there were some happy endorphins going on.

'Okay.' It was probably as good an answer as she could hope for.

'I took the liberty of checking on Simon while I was here. Everything seems to be healing nicely.'

'Yes. Thanks to you and the rest of the staff.' Praise where it was due, Matt was very skilled at what he did and everyone here was working to ensure Simon's scarring would be as minimal as possible.

'And you. Aftercare at home is equally as important.'

Quinn didn't know how to respond to his kind acknowledgement that she'd contributed to his recovery in some small way. So far, she'd only seen the areas in which she'd failed him.

As they ran out of things to say to each other, memories of that kiss hovered unattended between them, the air crackling with unresolved sexual tension.

'Matt says we can go to the zoo tomorrow.' Leave it to Simon to throw her even more off guard with extra last-minute drama.

'I don't think so.' They'd had this conversation so she could prepare him for the disappointment when they ended up going alone, impressing upon him the importance of Matt's job and how he couldn't take time off when small boys demanded it.

She wouldn't expect Matt to keep his word given the circumstances, when he'd either be nursing a bruised ego or breathing a sigh of relief after she'd rebuffed him. Although, strictly speaking, she hadn't rejected his advances; she'd simply declined a further sample of his wares before she became addicted.

Simon's bottom lip dropped, indicating the moment of calm was about to come to an abrupt end.

'If you have other plans I totally understand. I really should have got in touch sooner.' Matt raked his hand over his scalp, mussing his usually neat locks.

Quinn found it oddly comforting to find she wasn't the only one trying to keep her cool.

'No plans.' Certainly none which included spending another day in adult male company because she apparently had trouble containing herself when left alone with one.

'Good. It's a date, then.' Matt's very words, no matter how innocently intended, shattered her fragile composure.

Whatever deal these two had struck this time, there

was no going back on it; otherwise Simon would never forgive her for it. She couldn't afford to be the bad guy here.

'Great,' she said, smiling sweetly while glaring daggers at Matt. She didn't understand why he'd insisted on making this happen when it had been made very clear socialising between them wasn't a good idea at all.

Matt strolled towards the designated meeting point for his day out with Quinn and Simon. He never imagined he'd be back playing the stand-in father figure so soon but he couldn't go back on his word to Simon.

Okay, he wasn't being *totally* altruistic; he hadn't been able to stop thinking about Quinn, or that kiss they'd shared, no matter how hard he'd tried to avoid her. In the end he'd resigned himself to see this through, spurred on in part by the glimpses he'd caught of her flitting in and out of the department like a ghost until he hadn't been entirely sure if she was anything but a figment of his overactive imagination.

It was difficult to convince yourself you weren't interested in someone when they were at your place of work every day and driving you to distraction when you knew how it was to hold them, taste them, be with them.

In the cold light of day he should've been relieved when she'd sent him home for a cold shower. After all, he'd had more than enough family duty stuff to last him a lifetime. Instead, he and his dented male pride had brooded, mourned the loss of something which could've been special.

It was seeing Quinn carry on taking care of Simon regardless of her own wants and feelings which had made him see sense in the end. Forget the playboy car and bachelor pad in the city; he was a thirty-five-year-old man, an adult, and Simon was the child who had to come first.

Now he was committed to this he was going to make it a day to remember. One which wouldn't be dictated by hospitals and authorities for Quinn and Simon. If Matt had learned anything about raising younger sisters, it was how to have fun and keep their young minds occupied away from the harsh realities of life.

Quinn had declined his offer of a lift but he hadn't minded since it reduced his responsibilities for the afternoon. It gave the impression he was more of a tour guide today rather than a date, or part of the family, and that suited him fine. As soon as they were back on the train home he was off the clock with a clear conscience and his promise kept.

Little Venice, with its pretty barges and canals, was only a short distance from his apartment and the Tube station. The perfect place to pick up a couple of tourists already waiting on the bridge for him. They were watching the boats below, oblivious to his arrival, and Matt took a moment to drink in the sight.

Quinn, dressed in a daisy-covered strappy yellow sundress and showing off her toned, tanned limbs, was the embodiment of the beautiful sunny morning. Simply stunning. Simon, too, was in his summer wear, every bit as colourful in his red shirt and green shorts. Quinn knelt to slather on sun cream to Simon's exposed skin and plonked a legionnaire-style cap on his head. As per instructions, she wasn't taking any chances of the sun aggravating his already tender skin.

'Look, Quinn. It's Matt!' Simon spotted him over the top of his foster mother's head and was suddenly running at him full pelt.

'Oof!' A five-year-old hug missile knocked out what was left of his breath after seeing Quinn.

'Hi,' she said, brushing her hair from her eyes as he walked towards her.

Matt held out his hand to help her back to her feet, with Simon still attached one-handed to his waist. 'It's nice to see you too.'

'Sorry, he's very excited.' With a warning to calm down before Matt changed his mind, Quinn untangled the little person from him. The threat wasn't the least bit likely but it did the job.

'Me too.' Matt's grin reflected that of his co-chaperone for the day and sealed a non-verbal agreement that they'd put their indiscretion behind them and start over.

'Where are the animals?' Simon piped up, understandably anxious when he'd been promised monkeys, giraffes and all kinds of exotic new friends, only to find water and barges as far as the eye could see.

It was all part of Matt's plan to build the excitement a while longer and capture Simon's attention for the main event.

'They're at the zoo, which we're going to, but a tourist trip around London isn't complete without taking in a show.' He could see Quinn frowning at him out of the corner of his eye but the surprise was just as much for her.

Simon skipped between the two adults as they walked down towards the red-and-yellow barge covered with a huge stripy canvas top. They must've looked like any other young family from a distance and he was surprisingly comfortable with that thought…as long as it was short-lived. Today all Matt wanted was for Simon to feel comfortable and the beaming faces beside him said the lie was worth telling.

'A puppet show?' Quinn's eyes were wider than those of the other children trooping past them on the gangplank into the quirky theatre barge.

'I've heard the kids love it and it'll get Simon used to being on board before we take a water taxi on up to the zoo.' Apart from being the perfect excuse for him to see it for himself, the dimly lit area would also serve as a gentle icebreaker into the general public. He didn't want Simon to become too overwhelmed by the hordes of people who'd undoubtedly be at the zoo on a day such as this.

'You really do think of everything.'

It was a compliment, not a criticism, but it was truer than Quinn would ever know. He hadn't left anything to chance, having planned every tiny detail of this trip in those moments he'd lain awake since agreeing to it.

Matt escorted them to their tiered seats looking down on the small stage, away from prying eyes. The one concern he'd had was that Simon might find the small space too claustrophobic. On his initial admission his notes had mentioned he'd been trapped in one of the classrooms and Quinn had mentioned his nightmares regarding his entrapment and not being able to find his way out. He needn't have worried. Simon was as enthralled with the old-fashioned marionettes adorning the walls as any of the other children. Matt was the only one experiencing difficulties with the low ceiling and small walkways and that was purely down to his height.

'I've never seen a real puppet show before.' Quinn leaned in to whisper in the darkness, her thighs touching his on the small bench where they sat, her excitement inadvertently increasing his.

'Well, they say it's recommended for small kids from five to ninety-five and I think we fall right in the middle of that age bracket.' He reached across to whisper back, the soft waves of her hair brushing his cheek, and it was all he could do not to nuzzle closer and breathe in her sweet scent. This was supposed to be a PG-rated show and he didn't want to run the risk of being asked to walk the gangplank of shame because he couldn't control himself around her.

'In that case, we're the perfect audience.' Her eyes glittered in the darkness as she hugged Simon close.

'Perfect.' Matt ignored the rising curtain, mesmerised by Quinn's childlike wonder instead.

Quinn was in her very own fairy tale. So far she and Simon had been enchanted by their favourite childhood tales brought to life by puppets and had a good old singalong to some very familiar nursery rhymes. Simon had really thrown himself into the audience participation, as had Matt.

Perhaps it was the relative safety of dimmed lighting which brought her boy out of his shell, or maybe he was simply following the exuberance of Matt's tuneless singing, but in that hour no one could tell he was different from any other boisterous child.

Matt had whisked them straight onto another barge when the show ended and they'd trundled along the tranquil waterways towards the zoo. It was the best route they could've taken, so peaceful, and a world away from the crowded streets beyond the green banks.

She'd been on boats before but never the barges. The hand-painted green-and-red beauty they were travelling on transported them to another era, a parallel universe where everything was well in her world.

How was it Matt could take such a simple idea and turn it into something special?

That was the talent which charmed adults as much as the children.

He was sitting with Simon now, spending the journey time pointing out the sights through the tiny side windows. He had a love and knowledge of the world around him that he was keen to share. Then there was that fun side to him as he encouraged his sidekick to wave at passers-by and make silly noises every time they went under a bridge. A distraction, she guessed, from the odd curious stare and a fear of the dark.

It was probably the first time in his young life he had two adults working together to put his needs above their own. She hoped one day he would have this for real even if she wouldn't. There would be a family for Simon someday but she doubted she'd ever find another Matt who'd take her and her planned foster brood on for anything other than an afternoon. She wasn't lucky that way.

Their gentle journey came to an end in a leafy area which still seemed miles from civilisation. As if sensing her confusion, Matt reached his arm across the seat and rested his hand on her shoulder.

'The waterbus tours have their own entrance into the zoo so there's no need for us to join the queues at the main entrance.'

A warmth started in the pit of Quinn's stomach and gradually spread its way through her system and it wasn't purely because they couldn't seem to help themselves from making body contact when and where they could. On this occasion it was Matt's thoughtfulness which had really captured her heart. Something which had been sadly lacking from the people in her and Simon's lives to date. Without making a big deal about it, he'd carefully constructed a tailor-made route into the busy zoo to suit all of a traumatised child's needs.

From the magical puppet theatre, to the tranquil method of transport, and now this, the trouble he'd gone to just so they could arrive at their destination relaxed brought a lump to her throat.

If only she and Simon had had male role models who took such care of others, they mightn't have had the past heartaches they were both still trying to overcome.

They waited until all the other passengers had disembarked before they left their seats, with Quinn hesitant to leave the sweet memories of their journey here to rejoin the masses on the other side of the hill.

'Your sisters are very lucky to have you,' she said as Matt helped her ashore. If he treated his siblings as well as he did his patients and families they would never have been in doubt about being loved, and that was the most important aspect of growing up in any family.

His brow knitted together trying to fathom what to make of her compliment. She had no doubt he'd experienced the same general struggles as she'd had as a single parent, yet the very fact he didn't expect thanks for getting through them spoke volumes. A person didn't become a parent for awards and accolades but to create the best possible start in life for their children. Be it younger siblings or foster children. Simply by doing her best for Simon, Quinn was beginning to see she was already the best mother he'd ever had.

Simon squeezed her hand as they moved through to the main part of the zoo with people as far as the eye could see. She squeezed back, reassuring him she was here whenever he needed her. That was all she could do for as long as he was with her—love him and protect him as well as she could. Someday that might be enough for him.

As more children, and adults who should've known better, turned to stare at the little boy with the scars and burned skin, she held him closer. Matt took up residence on the other side so they created a protective barrier around him. Somehow they'd get through this together.

CHAPTER SEVEN

'Is it still the done thing to go to the zoo? Should I feel guilty about walking freely around here peering in at caged animals?' As excited as she was to be here, she did have a social conscience and the child-versus-adult argument about it in her head was in danger of tainting the experience.

'There are two very different schools of thought but the zoo today is much more than the sideshow attraction it used to be. It's educational and provides a natural environment for the animals. Then there are the conservation projects which are funded through the admission fees...'

'Okay. Okay. I'm sold. I can enjoy the view safe in the knowledge I'm not contributing to any ill treatment.' She trusted Matt's judgement. He'd done his homework and he wasn't the sort of man to throw his weight behind a cause unless it was for the greater good. He was principled and not the type to bend the facts to suit his own agenda. Unlike her ex, who'd pretended he wanted a family so he could move in with her.

Quinn shooed away the negative thoughts from her past to replace them with the positive. Such as Matt, positively yummy in his casual clothes again this morning. As he turned to study the map, she was free to ogle his backside encased in black denim and the perfect V of his torso wrapped in dark grey cotton.

'What are you smiling at, Quinn?' Simon quizzed, drawing Matt's attention back from the map.

Caught in the act of perving at Matt's physical attributes, lies didn't come easy to her. 'I, er… I was just thinking nice thoughts.'

She spun on her heel and started walking again, ignoring the smirk on Matt's face and the heat of her own.

'What ones?' Simon tugged her hand with the unfiltered curiosity only a child could get away with.

The puppets. The boat. Matt's butt.

She could've said any of those things and they would've been true.

In the end she went with, 'About how much fun I'm having with you both today.'

Curiosity satisfied, Simon moved on to his new topic of interest, staring at the pictures of ice creams depicted on an advertising board.

'Can I have one?'

'It's a bit early for ice cream but we can get one later. All good boys and girls deserve a treat now and then, don't you think, Quinn?' Matt was so close his breath tickled the inside of her ear and did something to her that made her a very bad girl.

She so wanted him to be talking about more than a child or an ice cream.

Up until now she'd been the very model of restraint but she was wondering if she deserved a treat too? They did say a little of what you fancy was good for you and there was no denying what it was she fancied more than anything.

'Absolutely. Life can get very dull if you don't give in to temptation once in a while.' She locked eyes with

Matt so that all pretence they were still talking about dairy products vanished without trace.

Eye contact definitely constituted flirting when the heat flaring between them was hotter than the morning sun. They'd proved they could be adults, and whatever did or didn't happen between them personally wouldn't become an issue where Simon was concerned. There was no fostering law against her seeing someone either, except the one she'd created herself. By trying to protect her heart she might actually be denying herself the best thing that had walked into her life since Simon.

Despite the unexpected trials and tribulations which had made their journey more difficult than it should've been, she couldn't imagine her existence without Simon in it. Or Matt, for that matter, and therein lay the danger. The damage had already been done, because she knew when the time came for these two to leave, all she'd have left would be a broken heart and some wonderful memories.

Today was all about making those memorable moments and as long as they avoided any empty promises they might actually get to make a few. Matt was a boost to her confidence when he did his best to convince her she could handle whatever fate threw at her. That was every bit as enticing as the soft lips which had caressed hers and the warm hands she could still imagine on her skin. He was right. She did deserve a treat.

Away from impressionable young eyes who might read more into an adult relationship than was true, she wanted one more taste of her dishy doc.

They made their way around the exhibits, each animal becoming Simon's new favourite as he was introduced to their habitats, and eventually circled back to the area where they'd started. Their route had been dictated according to which animals Simon wanted to see rather than the logical, more traditional route everyone else was following. It had probably added a few extra miles to their journey but that could be to their advantage later when exhaustion caught up with him.

Quinn had to admit a pang of self-pity for her inner child when she was only getting to experience this herself at the age of thirty-two. Watching Simon's face light up every time a penguin swam close or a monkey swung by, she ached for the little girl who'd been denied this joy with her own parents.

Every child should experience the fun and wonder to be had in the world beyond school and the foster system and she vowed to do it for whoever entered her care. It didn't have to be the zoo, or with Matt, but she wanted her future foster children to have at least one day of simply being a kid.

'You wish you could get in there, don't you?'

'Sorry?' Quinn panicked that Matt had caught her ogling his backside again.

'The meerkat tunnels. I can see you're busting to get in those with him.' He nodded over towards Simon, who'd popped his head up in the plastic capsule overlooking the enclosure.

'Yeah. This place is great, so interactive for the kids, but us adults might want to find out what it's like to be a meerkat for the afternoon too.' She covered herself quickly, happy to acknowledge her play envy before her relationship daydreams. After all, she didn't know if Matt saw her as anything other than an acquaintance now.

He'd certainly been in control of any more urges to kiss her. More's the pity.

Despite the flirting and the unnecessary touching, which she could have misconstrued entirely, he hadn't made another move on her.

'Poor Quinn. I hear they do some adult-only tours of the zoo at night. Perhaps we should sign up for one?' He was teasing her but he painted an enticing picture of an intimate party of two having some fun together at night.

'It seems to me that we both missed out on the whole childhood fun thing. It mightn't be a bad idea for us to have some quality time in the dark.' Her temperature rose with the bold proposal, as did Matt's eyebrows.

'Hold that thought,' he growled into her ear as Simon came running back to greet them.

'When are we getting something to eat?'

'Soon.' She was glad he was getting his appetite back and she would simply have to set aside her hunger for anything other than lunch until she and Matt were alone again.

Matt thought he'd imagined the heat shimmering between them, a manifestation of his own frustration that he and Quinn hadn't progressed to anything beyond that one sizzling kiss. He'd wanted more but when she'd given him his marching orders he'd done his best to ignore the temptation. That was until he'd seen the darkening of her eyes, the sapphire fire matching the one burning inside him.

He wasn't a man to disappoint anyone if he could help it but there was a time and place for everything and at this very moment they had a hungry boy to feed.

He'd arranged a special child-sized lunch for them. Although the restaurant was crowded with most tables and chairs occupied, they were able to slip into a quiet side room where they served a more civilised afternoon tea.

'This is amazing! You're really spoiling us today.' Quinn clapped her hands together as the arrangement of mini-rolls, sandwiches and bite-sized cakes and scones arrived, presented on a small picnic bench.

'You're worth it,' he said, hoping he sounded more complimentary than cheesy.

He meant it. She should have someone treating her every day and making her feel special. The delight on her face and her grateful smile puffed Matt's chest out that he'd been the one to put it there and he didn't want anyone else to have the privilege.

When he'd planned this day he'd convinced himself he'd be glad when it was over, his responsibility to the pair outside the hospital over for good. Now that they were coming to the last stages, he was beginning to have second thoughts. He could honestly say this was one of the best days he'd had since moving to London and that was entirely down to the company. It would be stupid to end things here and now simply because there was a child involved. There'd always been children in his life. Children who weren't his. If Quinn was willing to be brave about it, then so was he. A relationship didn't have to mean a family and he was sure he could keep the two separate. Especially when the arrangements were all so fluid.

When they'd eaten their fill they headed to the indoor exhibits they'd bypassed in favour of some of the more exotic creatures.

'We are now entering the Rainforest Life,' he said in the style of a nature documentary voiceover artist.

Simon ran ahead into the tropical wilderness, hopped up on mini-desserts and fruit juice.

'He's going to have one hell of a crash when that sugar rush wears off.' Quinn attempted to scold him but he knew she'd savoured every mouthful of that lunch. Each heavenly groan and lick of her lips attested to her pleasure as well as increasing his discomfort. He'd heard those sounds before and intended for her to make them again soon, somewhere more private.

'Look at him!' Simon was off again, following the path of a bright blue bird flitting through the plants and vines.

'He's pretty.' Quinn was observing the exotic display from the balcony beside him, unaware she was adding to the beauty of it all.

Never mind the rare birds flying overhead or the small monkeys swinging freely through the vines, this was all about Quinn for him. The pure delight she took in her surroundings was refreshing and contagious. He'd been so caught up in material possessions and showing he could cut it as a single man in the city, he'd forgotten what it was to just enjoy life. The barrier he'd erected to protect himself had become as much of a prison as that council flat in Dublin.

Given the chance he'd swap his fancy car to travel on a barge anywhere if she was part of the deal. It was as if he was recapturing that lost childhood of his too, by being with her.

He'd been forced to grow up too quickly. From his mother walking out on her family, through his father's illness, and ultimately his death, Matt had never had time for the mischief and fun other kids had experienced. With Quinn he didn't have to be embarrassed in his joy at a puppet show when she was here spinning around, letting the mist fall on her face and telling the sloth how sleepy he looked. Matt had had enough of being the adult and there was plenty of room for his inner child, not to mention the randy teenager.

They stepped out of the light and moved into the nocturnal area. Faced with the creatures of the night, including giant rats and flitting bats, it wasn't long before he found Quinn cuddled up next to him.

'I don't know how Simon is enjoying this.'

'He's a boy. We like gross stuff.'

'I don't want to stay in here,' she whispered, fear pitching her voice until only the bats could probably hear.

Matt felt her hand graze by his knuckles as she fumbled for his reassurance in the dark. He took hold of her and turned so she could make him out in the dimmed light.

'I'll keep you safe.'

In that moment they were locked into their own world, staring into each other's eyes and holding hands like lovers who'd just sworn their lives to one another. The rest of the group had moved on, leaving them alone so the only sounds he could hear now were scurrying animals and the frantic beat of his heart for Quinn.

He cupped her face in his hands and found her mouth easily with his, honing in as if she was a beacon of light guiding him home. This time, instead of pushing him away, she wound her arm around his neck and pulled him closer. He dropped his hands to her waist as she sought him with her tongue and leaned her soft curves against him.

'Have you seen this? He's got really big eyes.' The sound of Simon's voice from across the room somewhere broke through the darkness, alerting them to his presence and throwing a bucket of cold water over them.

'I think that's a bush baby.' Matt's breath was ragged as he fought to regain control so Simon wouldn't think anything was amiss.

'We should probably follow the rest on to the next exhibit.' Quinn was already backing away from him.

'We'll talk about this later,' he whispered, low enough so only she would hear.

'I'm a mum. I have mum things to do.' That uncertainty was back in her wavering voice and Matt fumbled for her hand again in the blackness. He didn't want the guilt to start eating away at her for enjoying a moment of her own.

'Don't forget, the adult fun starts after the *real* dark.' This wasn't over and although she couldn't see him wink, he was sure he sensed her smile.

Somehow they'd find a way to be together without compromising their roles in Simon's life.

His peace of mind depended on it.

Quinn stumbled back out towards Simon and the rest of the visitors tripping out of the exhibit. Her unsteadiness on her feet was more to do with Matt's epic bone-melting prowess than the unfamiliar territory. He had a way of completely knocking her off balance when she was least expecting it.

Yes, she'd encouraged him with a few flirtatious gestures, but phew, that had taken hot to a whole new level. Wrapped in his embrace she'd forgotten who she was, where she was or what day of the week it was, and let the chemistry consume her.

Dangerous. Irresponsible. Intoxicating.

It only made her crave more.

If Simon hadn't reminded them that they weren't here alone, they could've created quite a scene. They were lucky he hadn't seen anything of their passionate embrace or they would've had some explaining to do. Unfortunately, now as she made her way back into the light, the interruption had left her throbbing with unfulfilled need which only Matt could help relieve.

As he'd pointed out, they had things to say, things to do, but they'd have to wait until Simon was safely tucked up in bed and her parental duties were over for the day. The anticipation of where and when they might get to explore this exciting new development uninterrupted was an aphrodisiac in itself. As if she needed it! Quinn was finally starting to believe there could be room in her life for more than foster children. If she dared risk her heart again.

Simon's pace began to slow up and it struck her for the first time about how much energy this day had taken out of him. Not that his enthusiasm had waned once.

'Can we go to the shop now?' His eyes were wide and it was no wonder. A building stuffed to the rafters with soft toys and souvenirs was probably one of the highlights for most of the children. For her, there'd been many others. With one in particular still lingering on her lips, and she wasn't talking about the cakes.

'Sure. What do you say about taking in the rest of the way from a giraffe's point of view?' Matt, obviously picking up on his sudden weariness too, stooped down and gently hoisted Simon up onto his shoulders. It was a balancing act to avoid jarring Simon's right side but he managed it, holding on to make sure his passenger was comfortable and secure.

Rather than make a fuss, he'd found a way to turn

a potential meltdown into something fun. A tired and cranky tot was just as difficult to reason with as a frightened, injured one.

Crisis averted, Simon perched happily on Matt's broad shoulders for the remainder of their walk around the grounds with a hand resting on his head. If either of them were in any discomfort they made no mention of it. The smiling twosome blended into the crowd of other fathers and sons and Quinn had to remind herself it was an illusion. It wasn't real. Matt wasn't always going to be around, but for now, it was good for Simon to have someone other than her who actually wanted the best for him.

'I wanna get down.' He only became restless once they reached the shop entrance, so Quinn helped Matt lift him off his shoulders so they could let him loose.

Matt cricked his neck from side to side and massaged his neck. 'I'm getting too old for that.'

'Never.' She got the impression he'd done this sort of thing a lot for his kid sisters. It seemed a shame he was so set on making sure he never committed to fatherhood again. He'd have made a great dad for some lucky child.

'My thirty-five-year-old aching muscles beg to differ. You, on the other hand, strike me as someone who's young at heart and never too old to appreciate these.' He lifted a cuddly bush baby, its big eyes begging Quinn to take him home.

'It's so cute.' She hugged it close, unable to resist the aww factor.

'And a souvenir from our time in the night life exhibit.' His devilish arched eyebrow and wicked smirk immediately flicked her swoon switch.

She'd never been a bad girl, always on her best behaviour, trying to please people so they wouldn't have cause to reject her. Matt drew out that reckless side she'd suppressed for so long and she kind of liked it.

She knew the score. Unlike Darryl, Matt had never said he'd stick around and raise foster kids with her. He was going to leave no matter what. She didn't have to be a good girl where he was concerned, and based on previous experience he had a hell of a naughty side she wouldn't mind getting to know better. Arousal rushed through her like a warm summer breeze, bringing promises of hot sweaty nights to follow.

It would've been futile to try and stop him from taking the poignant reminder of their day together over to the cash register when he hadn't let her pay for anything so far. She went to look for Simon, who'd disappeared behind the shelving at the front of the shop, probably lining up a selection of animal friends he'd talk Matt into buying for him.

When she walked around the corner she was horrified to find him in tears, surrounded by a group of older boys.

'What's going on?' She went straight into mama bear mode, defending her young and putting a barrier between Simon and whatever was upsetting him.

The three backed off, still laughing, and tossed a plastic monkey face mask at her feet. 'The freak might look better with one of those.'

At that point Matt came striding over, a formidable figure with a thunderous look on his face which sent Simon's tormentors scurrying out of the shop. 'Are you two okay?'

Quinn was winded from the cruelty she'd witnessed directed at Simon but she hugged him close, letting his tears soak through her dress.

'He's only a baby,' she gasped to Matt, her own tears bubbling to the surface.

They'd had a lovely day and now the actions of some stupid kids had set them back at square one, undoing all the progress they'd made by bringing him here.

Matt crouched down so he was level with Simon's bowed head. 'Hey, wee man. Don't you listen to them.'

Every jerky sob broke her heart a little bit more as Simon clung to her with his one good arm. If she had her way she'd wrap him up in cotton wool so this kind of thing would never happen again. A child this young shouldn't have had to go through so much in his short life.

'No one's ever going to want to be my mummy and daddy because of my stupid face.'

The emotional punch of Simon's words knocked them both into silence.

That belief was at the very heart of the child's fears and why he wouldn't let anyone get too close. He genuinely thought his injuries made him unlovable and that few minutes of taunting had given credence to his worries.

This time Quinn was forced to swipe away a rogue tear but she steeled herself against any more. For her to become an emotional wreck now wasn't going to do Simon any favours.

'Well, I know people who think the world of you. Why else would they have bought you your very own spider monkey?' Matt opened the long arms of the cuddly primate and attached them around Simon's neck. 'I've got some zoo mugs for us too. Why don't we go back to my house to test them out?'

Simon glanced up at her with puffy, red, irresistible eyes. 'Can we?'

'Sure,' she said as brightly as she could muster, thankful that the master of distraction had found a quick and simple way to ease his immediate pain. It was going to have to be down to her to find the long-term solution and show him how loved he was.

Matt stood up and spoke quietly for her ears only. 'I know this wasn't in the plan but my place is closer. We can get a taxi there, get him calmed down again before we get you home.'

She nodded, afraid to verbalise her thanks in case she burst into grateful tears.

Just as he'd reassured Simon, he took her hand and squeezed it. 'Everything's going to be grand.'

She didn't know why but even in the most trying circumstances she believed him.

'Take us home, Matt.' She sighed, content to let the pretence go on a while longer.

CHAPTER EIGHT

THE BACK OF a taxi was a luxury compared to the packed trains or buses at rush hour. The busy streets somehow seemed further away from the sanctity of their private black carriage. It was a shame Quinn's mind couldn't defend against the outside stresses as well as the thick glass windows.

The tears had dried on Simon's face now as he played with the stuffed animals on his lap. Finally sharing what had been troubling him seemed to have taken a weight off his mind, but it hadn't eased hers any. She'd been digging for so long to find out the cause of his inner turmoil she'd imagined it would bring relief. That they would deal with it and move on, naively thinking it would make her better equipped to help him. Far from it. She knew all too well that fear of never belonging, never being loved, and how it never really left, not completely. Despite the efforts of those who'd eventually taken her in. She was always waiting for that moment of final rejection which repeated itself over and over. It had to be the same for Simon, even before his injuries were added to fears which weren't completely unfounded.

Adoption was a long and complicated process and the odds of finding a family for him could well have been worsened with his serious medical, and probable future psychological, problems which not everyone would be willing to take on. Her heart ached for him, and between her and Matt, they had to work together to help him transition into the next phase of the process and find his for ever family.

Matt's home was everything she'd expected it to be on arrival—modern, expensive and in the busy hub of the city—everything hers wasn't. His apartment spoke volumes about their contrasting lifestyles and future plans. He was very much enjoying his freedom as a man about town, whilst her Victorian terraced house had been built with family predominantly in mind.

The floor-to-ceiling windows were impressive, as was the view of the river, but for her it lacked the personal touch, the evidence of family, to make it a home.

However, Matt did his best to make them comfortable for the short time they'd be here. She was certain he'd never intended for them to cross his threshold and this had been nothing more than an emergency stop to prevent her going home with the company of a distressed child to look forward to. Yet, here he was washing up after home-made omelettes and freshly squeezed orange juice as though he'd expected them for dinner all along.

'Were you a Boy Scout? You're always prepared, no matter what catastrophe I bring to your door.' Literally, in this case.

Matt laughed as he stacked the dishwasher. 'I'm no Boy Scout. I still do a big weekly shop, a leftover habit from having a houseful of ravenous teenagers, I suppose.'

'Well, I appreciate it and apparently Simon does too.' She passed him an empty plate. At least Simon's appetite was improving despite the new drama.

'It's not a problem. Actually, it's been a while since I cooked for anyone. I forgot how much I enjoy doing it.' He leaned against the kitchen worktops and for the first time looked almost unhappy about living on his own.

'Are you seriously telling me you haven't brought women back to show all of this off? Most men would have photos of this as their profile picture all over social media.' Not that he would need to use his money to draw interest. A man who could cook and clean, on top of everything else, was designed for seducing women, her included. No matter how much he tried to hide it, domesticity was very much a part of him.

'I didn't say that. I've just never cooked for any of them. That's what expensive restaurants are for.' The wink he gave her made her sick to the stomach thinking of the women who'd been here before her under entirely different circumstances.

'I guess I'm more one for home-cooked meals than whatever's fashionable.' She sniffed, despising those who'd put more store in the material things Matt could give them instead of appreciating the qualities which made him who he was—a kind-hearted, generous man, with the patience of a saint. A man she was falling much too hard for and yet she was powerless to stop herself. She was unable to resist when there was still so much to discover about him, and herself.

He'd been generous with his time where Simon was concerned but his support had also boosted her confidence that she wasn't the only stand-in parent in history who'd struggled. As everything in her life had been, this was a rough patch she simply had to fight her way through and that was something she was well practiced in.

'Hey, I only break out the chef's apron for very special guests.' Matt held her chin between his thumb and forefinger and parted her lips.

Her eyelids were already fluttering shut before he settled his mouth on hers, much too briefly. She peered over his shoulder to see how much of this little moment Simon had witnessed. It wouldn't do to have two of them confused about what was happening between her and Matt.

'I think the excitement's all got too much for him.' Matt followed her gaze to the small figure hunched up on the end of the leather sofa.

'How on earth am I going to get him home now?' Although it was a blessed relief to see him so soundly asleep, she didn't relish the thought of having to wake him to get him home and run the risk of him not getting back to sleep again.

'You know what they say, let sleeping five-year-olds lie.' Matt didn't appear to be in a hurry for her to leave, unmoving from his position in the open-plan living room between her and her sleeping babe.

'I think you'll find that's dogs,' she said, gently nudging him aside so she could go and check on Simon.

'It won't do him any harm to sleep there for a while. I swear I'll take you both home as soon as he's awake.' He crossed his heart. 'Scout's promise.'

She narrowed her eyes at him but he did make her laugh. 'He can't be comfortable in that position though.'

He was curled into the foetal position, his head bent awkwardly over the arm of the chair. It was cramp waiting to happen. Worse, it could aggravate his injuries if he lay like that too long.

'I can move him into the spare bedroom. There's plenty of space for him to stretch out there and sleep undisturbed.'

'You'll have to be careful not to wake him.' She hovered as Matt scooped him up into his big strong arms as though he weighed nothing.

'Don't worry, he's sound asleep.'

Simon didn't so much as flinch as they transferred him down the hall, his arms and legs hanging limply from Matt's hold. The fresh air had obviously done him the world of good.

Matt elbowed the door open and Quinn couldn't have been more surprised about what lay behind it if she'd found an S&M dungeon rigged up. The room was decorated in pretty pinks and purples, flowers and fairies, and everything he'd said he'd despised in home décor growing up. At the far side of the room next to a mountain of children's toys and teddy bears was a child-sized bed and a white wooden cot. The perfect little girl's room and nursery.

'Is there something you want to tell me?' He'd made such a big production about not wanting family responsibilities, she hoped she wasn't about to discover he was, in fact, a divorced dad of two little girls. She didn't think she could handle it if he'd lied to her about who he was when that was the very man she'd fallen for.

He carefully laid Simon on top of the bed covers and pulled a comforter over him before he attempted to explain himself.

'I told you I have sisters. Anne, the eldest, is married with two daughters, Jaime and Lucy. Sometimes they come visit.' He fussed around, closing the curtains and making sure the floor was clear of any debris Simon could trip over.

It was a far cry from the self-centred bachelor he'd portrayed and she wondered why he'd withheld this snippet of information. Perhaps his family situation would have put off a different type of woman, one who'd have been horrified at the thought of being required to babysit or change dirty nappies someday. Not her.

She backed out of the room with a snigger. 'So, basically, you're a granddad?'

Matt rolled his eyes and closed the door softly behind him. 'See? This is why I don't generally share the details of my personal life. It changes the way people see me. I have two sides. To the outside world I'm a young, single, successful surgeon. To my family, I'm an agony aunt and a doting uncle. I don't tend to let the two worlds collide.'

'And which side am I seeing?' They were standing toe to toe in the hallway and Quinn was sure he could hear her heart thumping against her ribcage. The more she got to know the *real* Matt, the more she wanted to believe they stood a chance of making this work.

'Well, Quinn, you are an anomaly.' He reached out and tucked a strand of her hair behind her ear. 'Somehow you've managed to set a foot in both camps and I'm not sure how I feel about that.'

It was the kind of honesty she appreciated. He wasn't promising her the world to get what he wanted, only telling her that she'd made him think about what they were getting into and that was enough for now.

'Me either.' She didn't know what each step further into his life meant for her down the line except more heartache but for now the one thing she was sure of was that she wanted him.

She leaned closer but Matt was already there to meet her, meshing his lips with hers as though they'd always meant to fit together.

Her conscience drifted between taking him by the hand and leading him to the bedroom, or setting up camp outside Simon's door in case he needed her. 'What about Simon? What if he wakes up and doesn't know where he is?'

She couldn't blame Matt for wanting to avoid ready-made families when they were such a passion killer at the most inopportune moments. Every time their make-out sessions got steamy it seemed to trigger the baby alarm.

No hanky-panky! You have a child to think about!

Not what any hot-blooded man wanted interrupting his love life and Matt wouldn't have any trouble finding a willing partner elsewhere if he kept getting sex-blocked by a five-year-old and his panicky mum.

She was already preparing herself for the 'This isn't going to work' speech as Matt took off towards the living room. She trudged behind him and wondered how they were going to put the time in during Simon's unexpected nap now. A game of chess perhaps? Or maybe he had a photo album of all of his glamorous, readily available exes she could flick through while they waited. If she'd had a coat she would've fetched it.

'I have one of these.' Instead of his sex life in pictures, he produced a baby monitor and set it on the coffee table with a proud flourish as if he'd solved the world's hardest equation. For her, he had.

No matter what obstacles crept up he always found a way over them. He didn't quit at the first sign of trouble and that was new to her as far as men were concerned. It was difficult not to get too attached to someone who, so far, had done everything possible to show her she could trust him. Rely on him.

'Of course you do,' she said with a great big grin.

All the signs were pointing to a brother and uncle who took his family duties very seriously even if he didn't want people to know. He was a loving family man whether he liked it or not. It was the idea of taking on someone else's which was the sticking point for him, and prevented any notion of a relationship between them.

'I'll just nip in and turn on the one in the bedroom so we can hear if he gets up. I'll be two seconds.'

Quinn took a seat on the sofa to wait for him coming back, fidgeting with the hem of her dress and unable to sit still, thinking about what was going to happen next as if she was waiting for her first kiss.

Things with Matt had gone far beyond that. This would be the only quality time they'd spent together alone and she was afraid it mightn't live up to the hype of that fevered embrace in the dark corner of the zoo.

He wanted her to stick around. He'd told her there was more to come. Surely the next step they were about to take wasn't all in her head?

'Would you like a drink?' Matt was back, padding into the kitchen.

'A glass of water would be nice, thanks.' Suddenly, her tongue was sticking to the roof of her mouth and her hands were clammy. Just what every guy was looking for in a hot date. Not.

She thought of all those other women he'd had here who'd never seen the kitchen. They were probably too busy ripping his clothes off in a frenzy to get to the bedroom to care. She must seem so dull in comparison but she no longer saw herself as sexy, spending her days watching cartoons and washing dirty clothes, lucky if she'd had a chance to brush her hair that morning, so why should she expect a man to?

At least with advance warning she'd be spending the day with Matt, she'd been able to put an effort into her clothes and make-up today. It couldn't hurt to try and reconnect with her inner sex siren, who'd disappeared under a mountain of paperwork and rejection.

The sofa dipped as Matt sat down next to her and handed her a glass of water. She took a sip and flicked her tongue out to wet her parched lips, fully aware he was watching her every move. He reached up to rub the back of his neck and Quinn seized the opportunity to get physical.

'Turn around and I'll give you a quick massage. You've earned one after all the carrying you've done today.' She set her glass on the floor and kicked off her shoes so she could kneel on the couch beside him.

'I probably should have stretched before I started bench pressing dead weights.' He turned around so she was faced with the solid wall of his back. She bit back the comment about bench pressing her anytime in case that bordered more on the side of desperate and crass rather than sexy and irresistible. This too-long abstinence had really brought out the worst in her.

With trembling hands she kneaded his shoulders, the thick muscle resisting her attempts to manipulate the tissue.

'Perhaps you should…er…take your shirt off. You're really knotted up in there.' Not very subtle and as bold as she dared but he complied nonetheless, shrugging the shirt off over his head.

'Wow,' she mouthed as she got to see the impressive

physique beneath for the first time in the flesh, albeit from the back. If only she could find the excuse to start massaging the pecs she knew would be on the other side of that muscular frame.

She worked her fingers over his warm skin, smoothing her hand down the length of his spine until she reached the waistband of his jeans. With a sudden burst of bravado, or lust, she slid her hand beneath and reached around until she felt that smooth V of taut skin leading down to...

Matt sucked in a sharp breath and clapped his hand over hers, stopping her pathetic seduction attempt dead in its tracks.

'I'm sorry... I...' What? How the hell was she going to pass this off as anything other than a blatant grope?

She rocked back on her heels, contemplating a commando-style roll onto the floor so she could crawl away without having to look him in the eye again, but he had too firm a grip on her wrist.

He spun around so she had no option but to face him. Okay, it wasn't all bad; she'd got a sneak peek at the goods, but she would need something good to remember anytime she replayed this humiliation in her head. For the record, she was pretty sure they'd used a mould of his chest and abs for those superhero costumes with the fake muscles.

'You don't have to try so hard, Quinn.' He was smiling, not recoiling in disgust, which she took as a good omen.

'Wh-what do you mean?' She tossed her hair back, aiming for the nonchalance of a woman who stuck her hand down a man's pants whenever she felt like it.

'You don't have to force this. Let it happen naturally.'

In slow motion he moved closer until his breath whispered on her lips, turning her to a rag doll liable to slip off the furniture in a cascade of molten limbs. She closed her eyes and let nature take its course.

He captured her in a soft kiss, leaned her back against the cushions as he took possession of her. It was true—there was no need for planning or acting out a part she thought she needed to play when chemistry did all the work.

Quinn was lying flat out beneath him, clinging to him, although there was no chance of going anywhere with his weight pinning her down. They were both where they needed to be.

She'd surprised him by taking the lead when, to date, she'd been the one reluctant to let this go further than snatched kisses. It wasn't unwelcome, parts of him were throbbing with delight, but he'd needed to take back some control. Not of her, or the situation, but of himself.

He was getting too caught up in her and Simon. Although bringing them back here had been more of an intervention than an invitation into his personal life, the result had been the same. They were invading his personal space, and his heart.

He'd raged inside today after Simon had been bullied by those kids, ached for him, and Quinn, who'd had to deal with the fallout. All he'd wanted to do was take some of that pain away, regardless that it meant compromising himself in the process.

If he took his own advice and simply let this thing take its natural course he could find himself saddled with more parental duties he hadn't asked for. That's why he needed a clear head, to focus on something other than his own pleasure—Quinn's.

These big blue eyes peered up at him with such trust and longing it was a test of strength not to take the easy route to instant gratification and sod the consequences. Even though it was killing him, this self-punishment would serve as a reminder to him not to start something he couldn't finish. Like getting involved with a single mother.

Quinn didn't have any such reservations as she pulled him ever closer until his chest was crushing hers, her soft mounds rubbing against him and undoing his restraint bit by bit. Eager to feast his eyes on her naked flesh, he slipped the shoestring straps of her dress down her arms and peeled away her strapless bra. Her cherry-peaked breast fit easily into the palm of his hand, so ripe and ready he couldn't resist a taste. He took her in his mouth and suckled her sweetness.

He shifted his position slightly so the evidence of his arousal wasn't so uncomfortable for either of them but Quinn tilted her hips so it nestled between her thighs instead. He released her sensitive nub with a groan as his resolve eroded by the second, clearly underestimating the effect she'd have on him even with his trousers firmly buttoned up. A fact which hadn't gone unnoticed by a partner who was doing her best to address that problem, popping his buttons open one by one.

This woman was driving him crazy and if he wasn't careful his good intentions would soon give way to lust, a short-term solution to his current predicament but undoubtedly with long-term consequences. He needed to bring this to some sort of conclusion which made her feel good without giving too much of himself in the process.

He inched his hand up her thigh and, with a quick tug, divested her of her undies. Her giggle as he tossed them onto the floor only spurred him on in his devilment. With a trail of kisses, over her clothes this time, he made his way down the centre of her body and ducked his head under the skirt of her dress.

'Matt—' she gasped, her hands immediately lighting atop his head, but she didn't ask him to stop.

He took his time savouring that first taste of her, teasing his tongue along her folds before parting her to thrust inside her core. She bucked against him, drawing him deeper between her thighs. He cupped her buttocks, holding her in place so he could direct his attention straight to that sweet spot.

He circled that little nub of flesh, sucking and licking his way to heaven until her breathy pants almost brought him to climax too. She tightened around him and he could sense that impending release. Her fingers were digging into his shoulders, her body rising and falling with the clench and release of her inner muscles.

She was slick with arousal, inviting him to join with her on the climb to that final peak but he couldn't take the chance he'd never want to come back down to earth. He withdrew, only to plunge back inside her again, and again, until she came apart beneath him. It was a shame he couldn't hear her cries of ecstasy as she slapped a hand over her mouth to muffle the sound. There was nothing he wanted more than to hear and see her completely undone, not holding anything back and without a trace of self-consciousness, but he understood why she couldn't turn off that mothering instinct. When he was long gone, she still had Simon to think about.

He sat back, giving Quinn space to recover as she fought to catch her breath, and a chance to regain his own composure. Not an easy task when her face was flushed, her pupils dilated and she was still half naked.

The lights on the baby monitor flashed, accompanied by the sound of rustling sheets, saving Matt from himself. Simon was stirring and he'd made a vow to get them home the minute that happened. It was his get-out clause before he did something even more stupid than falling for this beautiful woman he'd just ravished on his sofa.

'I'll go check on him,' he told her, keen to get a minute alone to gather his thoughts now both of their worlds had been rocked.

'Thanks.' Quinn sat up and adjusted her clothes to cover her nakedness, suddenly bashful. She'd no need to be embarrassed. He was the one who'd screwed up.

Whether he'd given in to temptation or not he'd still fallen for the one woman he couldn't have. Quinn came as part of a package deal, and although he was fond of Simon, there was every chance her foster brood could expand later on and he wasn't signing up for that. He hadn't left his family to move out to London only to have his longed-for independence curtailed by someone else's children.

He and Quinn were on completely different paths but they couldn't seem to stop intersecting and complicating things. Something had to give and it sure as hell wasn't going to be his freedom. Whilst he was treating Simon, cutting off all contact was out of the question, even if he thought he could.

The whole day had been an eye-opener for him but his resistance had been stretched to breaking point for now. If he didn't get his house guests back to their own home soon, he'd find this slipping into a long-term arrangement and this was supposed to be his time, a new start. He wasn't going to fall into the same old trap.

Matt McGrory was young, free and single, and that was the way it would stay. He just had to keep chanting that mantra to himself so he'd start believing it, or find someone else to take his place in Quinn and Simon's affections.

CHAPTER NINE

THE LAST FEW days had passed Quinn by in an out-of-body, did-that-actually-happen? daze.

There had to be a catch somewhere in a man who'd spent the day piggybacking a five-year-old around the zoo, and at night had made her pleasure his sole purpose. At this moment in time she didn't care what that flaw might be when her body was still glowing from the after-effects of his attentions.

Even now, another delicious shudder rippled through her at the memory of his lips on her. The only problem was, she hadn't seen the man of the moment since. She'd convinced herself it was because he was so busy at work, too invested to believe what they'd shared could be ignored so easily.

She turned her face away from the patients and staff walking towards her in the hospital corridor in case they read her X-rated thoughts. Her infatuation with the surgeon was probably there on her smiling face for the world to see and she could do without lectures from do-gooders who might take it upon themselves to warn her off a man committed to bachelorhood. They couldn't tell her anything she hadn't already told herself.

You're going to get hurt. He won't commit.

She didn't want to hear it when it was all too late anyway. She was in love with Matt and for once she didn't want to think about the consequences. That day had shown her how important it was for her to take some time for herself and that didn't always have to include getting naked with Matt, as enjoyable as that had been. The smallest thing such as a chat, a meal or a walk without stressing about Simon's issues had made her feel lighter than she had in months. A state of mind which would benefit them both.

Simon had been much more content the next morning than usual. The day's exertions had meant he'd slept through the night, even after Matt had driven them home, and the rarity of his uninterrupted sleep had improved the atmosphere between them.

To date, she hadn't availed of any outside help to care for her boy. She'd wanted to prove she could manage on her own and turned down any offers of respite care in case it disrupted Simon any further. There was also the fear that it would highlight her inadequacies even more. Now she was beginning to rethink those ideas of extra support.

That was how she'd come to be at the hospital now without her little bundle of curls in tow. He'd been excited when she'd suggested he could spend some time with Mrs Johns, as had her widowed neighbour when she'd broached the subject of babysitting. She was on the list of approved contacts with the authorities as she'd volunteered to help from day one when she found out there'd be a little one in the street. Quinn had only given her name in case she needed someone at a moment's notice in an emergency but perhaps she and Simon needed to venture beyond the bubble they'd created for themselves since the fire.

No doubt he'd be spoiled and filled to the brim with home-baked goods by the time she returned, but a young boy should have doting elders, playdates and adventures. A grown woman should have coffee mornings, gossip and a love life where possible. It was time to bring some normality back into their lives.

Of course, she'd seen to her other responsibilities before she'd gone in search of the man who'd convinced her she didn't need to remain celibate in order to be a good mother.

She'd added her voice to the ongoing protest out front for the first shift of the day and she'd had a ball this time with the knowledge that Simon was safe and happy. There was a rush of feel-good endorphins from volunteering her services to a good cause and they didn't come any greater than trying to save this iconic building from decimation. Perhaps she could make this a regular thing and when Simon went back to school permanently she might think about volunteering somewhere else that might need her help. They were already in the process of rebuilding the school and she would need something to distract her when it was time for him to go back there.

For now, she was collecting personal statements from some of the parents she'd seen coming and going on a regular basis.

'That's fantastic. I really appreciate your help,' she said, adding another paper bullet to the committee's arsenal of weapons against the board's decision.

'Anything I can do to help. We'd be lost without this place and we've made so many friends here I can't imagine starting over somewhere new.' Mrs Craig's daughter,

Penny, was a regular feature around the Castle's corridors, an outpatient but still dependent on oxygen at all times. Quinn had heard on the grapevine she was waiting for a life-saving heart transplant.

'Neither can I.' She'd spent those first days after the fire praying Simon would pull through, not eating or sleeping until she knew for sure he was going to survive. What Mrs Craig and Penny had been through, still had to go through, didn't bear thinking about. For her treatment to be transferred elsewhere away from the staff, who'd probably become like family, would be a wrench. Quinn knew how it was to rely on these people, get closer than she should, and how devastating it would be when they were no longer part of her life.

This was exactly the kind of emotional impact the money men didn't stop to consider when they were cost-cutting and paper shuffling.

'Are you Simon's mum?' The little girl in question wheeled her way in between the two adults, demanding attention, though she was difficult to ignore dressed in her pink tutu anyway.

'Yes. I'm his foster mum, Quinn. Pleased to meet you.' She held out her hand to shake on their introduction.

'I'm Penny and I know everyone here,' she said matter-of-factly.

'And quite the celebrity, I believe.' Quinn gave the mother a knowing smile. All of the kids had their own way of coping with life on the wards but Penny's integration into the hospital community and her self-confidence was something she envied on Simon's behalf.

'Nosy, more like,' Mrs Craig muttered under her breath.

'You're seeing Matt, aren't you?' Penny tilted her head to one side to study her.

Quinn's cheeks were on fire. She hadn't been able to keep her feelings hidden for long. Goodness knew how he'd react when he saw her again if it was plain enough for a child to see she was mad about him. He probably wouldn't be renewing any local contracts again soon, that was for sure.

'Er—'

'He's not here today. I wanted to show him my new tiara but Rebecca says he's off today.' She patted the pretty plastic band perched on her head as if it was a perfectly good reason for Matt to make time to see her—though knowing him, he probably would.

'Penny, I'm sure you're supposed to be doing something other than gossiping in the corridor. Come on and let Quinn get on with her job.'

'Okay, okay.' She spun her chair around towards the elevator.

Quinn gave her thanks again and waved goodbye. The news about Matt's sudden absence had unsettled her all over again.

He hadn't said anything that night about taking time off. In hindsight, he hadn't said much after Simon had woken up. She'd been too caught up in her own orgasmic euphoria and subsequent worry about getting Simon home without disturbing him too much to contemplate Matt's state of mind. He'd given so much without taking anything for himself. Whilst she'd taken so much pleasure in his unselfishness in the moment, now she was scrutinising his motives. Very few men would've been happy to be left unattended to and it wasn't because he'd been immune to the heat of the moment. She'd seen and felt the hard evidence of his arousal against her.

They could've found a way to be together. If Matt had

suggested she and Simon stayed the night she would've jumped at the chance. His readiness to get rid of all traces of them from his apartment didn't marry with her idea of carrying on where they'd left off.

Okay, he was never going to declare his undying love and set up house with them but it didn't bode well if he needed time off to recover after only a few hours in their company.

It wasn't as if he lived a million miles away. Her brain flashed through all the possibilities his actions could mean. She wanted to make it clear she wasn't expecting anything from him other than what they already had together.

All she wanted was a little more time together to explore what was happening between them and the effect it was having on her. Emotional significance aside, if they focused on the physical progression of their relationship they could have a good time together before his contract ended and he disappeared for good. If nothing else, she needed to return the favour he'd done her. She didn't like to be in anyone's debt.

She started off at a brisk pace towards the shiny, modern apartment block with her sights set on ripping Matt's clothes off and seducing him. Unfortunately, the doubt crows soon caught up with her, flapping their wings in her face to slow her down.

Did she really have the right to turn up, unannounced, on his doorstep? He could be sick, or perhaps this wasn't about her at all. There were a multitude of reasons he might not want to see her right now.

She could stand outside staring through the glass of the lobby like a child at a toy shop window on Christmas Eve, or she could stop wasting her precious time and find out the answer.

With her finger poised to buzz him, she braced herself to start overanalysing the tone of his voice over the intercom. The door suddenly swung open and one of the residents held it open for her. Clearly she wasn't a threat to anyone's security—except, perhaps, her own.

'Thanks,' she said as Mr Suit rushed on to whatever meeting he was going to, paying no mind to who he'd let into his building.

Every crisp step along the marble hallway towards Matt's apartment made her stomach roll more violently. If anyone from the hospital was aware she was here they'd probably advise him to get a restraining order. He was Simon's surgeon. Then again, what they'd shared that night broke whatever rules and boundaries long before she'd walked in off the street.

She took a deep breath before she knocked on the door, not knowing what to expect from this encounter. He mightn't even be home. After all, he had family and doctor commitments she wasn't party to. It wasn't likely he'd take time off at short notice to sit at home in the shadows to avoid running into a one-night stand, or whatever she was to him. If he wasn't in she could pretend this had never happened and let him make the next move.

Suddenly, the door whooshed open and her breath was sucked into a vacuum.

'Quinn! The very person I need to speak to.'

Not the welcome she'd expected, particularly as he was slamming his front door shut behind him and jangling his car keys.

'I...er...you haven't been around much—'

'I know. I know. Wait, where's Simon?'

'He's staying with a neighbour. I thought we could both do with a playdate this morning.' With one obviously going better than the other.

'Good idea,' he said, but he was still walking away from his apartment rather than dragging her back inside.

'I can see you're busy. Maybe we'll catch up another time.' She could salvage some dignity if she walked away now without forcing a conversation about what significance she held in his life. She had her answer right here with a closed door in her face.

Matt slowed his brisk pace as if it had only occurred to him how odd her visit was. 'You didn't make the journey all the way here just to see me, did you?'

It sounded such a desperate act when he put it that way that she immediately had to deny it. 'No. I was at the hospital anyway helping the committee. Young Penny said she'd heard you'd taken some leave. I thought I'd call in and see if you were sick or something.' If she'd stopped to buy grapes on the way here she might've made that more plausible.

He laughed. 'Ah, yes. Penny. There are no secrets where she's concerned.'

'I was collecting statements from the parents.' That was right up there with 'I carried a watermelon' in lame excuses but she didn't want him to think she'd been stalking the corridors seeking him out.

'They're definitely one of the most familiar families at Paddington's and Penny is such a live wire despite her condition.' He was clearly fond of the little girl even though she wasn't one of his own patients. Another indication that his devotion went far beyond the parameters of his job description.

'She is and I can report back and tell her you're fine

and there's no need for her to worry.' Quinn scooted outside into the sunlight first, taking the path back to the hospital so she didn't trip on her lies. It was her who'd wanted to know why he wasn't at work and her who'd stumble back home with her tail tucked between her legs for thinking she could simply turn up here and take what she wanted from Matt, ignoring his wishes, which clearly included being left alone.

That heavy weight was back on her shoulders, almost doubling her over with the effort of having to carry it again.

'Aren't you coming with me?'

It took a strong hand wrapped around her waist for the words to register.

'Do you want me to? I mean, you were on your way out before I got here.' *Without me.*

'It will make this easier. I would've had to contact you anyway to make the final decision.' He practically bounced into the front seat of his car, pumped up by whatever he had planned.

'That sounds ominous. Where are we going?'

'It's a surprise. Relax. It's nothing bad. Just sit back and enjoy the ride.'

The car purred to life at his touch, much the way she had.

They stopped and started their way out of the city until eventually they made their way onto the quieter roads. She had no clue how long they were going to be in the car or how far they'd be driving but she didn't care. For now, she was content to sit back and relax in his company as he'd suggested. It wasn't what she'd planned but it was preferable to the scenario where he told her he didn't want to see her again.

She trusted him to give her a good time. He hadn't let her down yet.

Matt was in the dark about what had brought Quinn to his door but her visit was providential. He'd been contemplating a major commitment for her and Simon so it was only polite he should seek her opinion on the matter.

Since that day he'd spent with them, and most of the evening, he'd been trying to concoct a plan to keep them in his life without stepping into the role of surrogate dad again. It would be easy to get carried away, especially when a different part of his body other than his brain was trying to make decisions for him.

If he'd given in to what it was he'd really wanted he'd be in an ever bigger mess where Quinn was concerned. That first-hand experience of bringing up a family was the only thing which had prevented him from taking her to his bed, letting Simon sleep the night in his spare room and waking up to a new domesticity he hadn't asked for. His fear of that had somehow won out over his libido. He couldn't promise that would always be the case so he'd hit on the idea of a third wheel in their relationship, or a fourth if he included Simon.

'A dog pound?' Quinn's raised eyebrows drew into a frown as they pulled up outside the animal rescue centre in a blend of undisguised curiosity and disappointment. Exactly what he'd been trying to avoid.

He'd delayed getting back in touch when he knew nothing he said or did could possibly match up to any expectations she might have had after that night. Now, he was counting on the tried and tested distraction technique of canine cuteness.

'It's an idea I've been toying with. Pet companions are known to be very therapeutic, loving unconditionally without judging people's appearances or background. You saw what a great time Simon had at the zoo. He loves animals and this could really help build his confidence.' It would also give them the sort of close companionship that they were both craving on a long-term basis.

Quinn was silent as they entered the reception and he hoped it was because she was mulling over the idea of adopting a dog, not that she was filled with quiet rage at him.

'It's a nice idea, in theory, but it's not very practical. I have enough to deal with without adding house-training a puppy to the list.'

'This one's a year old, fully trained. No extra work.' A puppy would've secured the deal because who wouldn't fall in love with a bundle of fur but she wouldn't have thanked him for the puddles around the house or using her furniture for oversized chew sticks. He'd been there when Siobhan, his middle sister, had suckered him into housing one of a litter of unwanted pups. Thankfully, she'd taken the little poop machine with her when she'd moved out soon after.

'This one?' She raised an eyebrow, seemingly unimpressed as he showed her the computer printout of his research subject.

'Frankie. She's a collie cross. I saw her online and made this appointment to come and see her before I spoke to you. You know, to make sure she's suitable for you and Simon.' He gave his details to the receptionist and waited for them to bring out the dog he thought could be the answer to everyone's prayers.

'How very thoughtful of you.' The sarcasm wasn't lost on him. It had been very presumptuous of him to make these arrangements, supposedly on her behalf, without giving her the heads-up. He preferred to think of it as being proactive.

'She's supposed to be a lovely wee thing.' He'd made sure this was a dog they could be satisfied was comfortable around children, and from everyone he'd spoken to, she was very good-natured.

'Wee?' Quinn was nearly knocked off her feet by the black-and-tan slobber monster which accosted her.

'Well, those handbag dogs aren't for boys. She's a good sturdy size for cuddling.'

It was his turn to pet the reason they were here and he was rewarded with a rough doggie tongue licking his face.

'What's wrong with her neck?' Quinn hunkered down to inspect the patch of shaved fur and jagged scars zigzagging around her throat.

'They found her wandering the streets. Someone had let the skin grow over her puppy collar and the vet had to operate to remove it. Hence the name "Frankie," after Frankenstein's monster.' He'd seen the pictures and read the case file so she'd already claimed a place in his affections. Quinn's too, by all accounts, as she stroked and cuddled the pooch.

'Poor girl. You deserve a pretty name. If you were mine I'd call you Maisie.'

'Maisie?' He tried to suppress a grin and failed. The scarred, scrawny mutt looked as girlie as he did.

'Every girl should be treated like a princess. Calling her after a monster will do nothing for her self-esteem. If I'd ever had a daughter, Maisie's the name I would've chosen.' For such a young woman, she sounded as though she'd given up on the idea of ever having kids of her own. Fostering probably seemed enough of a challenge without bringing up her own children minus a partner. Still, if Maisie filled that particular void too, then Matt's job here was done.

'We'll have to bring Simon up for a visit but I can register our interest now in case someone else wants her in the meantime.'

'I'm sure he'll love her, Matt, but would it really be fair to give him a dog only to take it off him when he moves on? I couldn't break his heart again.' She was already distancing herself from the mongrel, who just wanted to be loved too.

Matt hadn't considered the long-term consequences. It was so unlike him to go for the temporary solution, but she was right—he couldn't use the dog as a sticking plaster. The moment Simon had to leave her behind would devastate him all over again and who was to say Quinn would want to be tied down to a pet once Simon had gone.

There was no other option but for him to take her on if he wanted this adoption to go ahead. It was a commitment he'd never anticipated making but a dog had to be less trouble than raising kids, surely?

'What if I adopt her? You and Simon could help with her when I'm at work. He can still bond with her but technically she'll be my dog.' A single man was still a single man with a pet. It would be company for him instead of coming home to that empty apartment at the end of every shift. He'd hate to let this opportunity pass for Simon and Maisie to find some comfort in each other.

'You mean joint custody?' Naturally, Quinn wanted clarification. She was a woman who didn't like to leave room for misunderstandings.

It was surprising, then, that she'd yet to quiz him on his intentions as far as she was concerned. It was the main reason he'd maintained a little distance because he genuinely didn't know what either of them wanted to come from this relationship. If Quinn in her usual forthright manner told him she expected some sort of commitment to her and Simon, he'd be forced to walk away and he wasn't ready for that yet.

'I guess...' Adopting a stray dog was more than he'd committed to in a long time, stretching the boundaries of his comfort zone and the best promise he could give in regards of a future together.

For the duration of Simon's stay with her, he and Maisie would be a part of their lives and that was the most he could give of himself without compromising his own plans. He'd still be moving on to pastures new someday, except now he'd have a slobbery hound in tow.

'Simon's going to be so excited.' Quinn dropped down to hug the new family friend and Matt didn't know if she or the dog had the biggest smile on their face.

He had to admit he felt good to have been the one to have orchestrated this. Quinn's happiness was his weakness and most likely guaranteed to be his greatest downfall but he reminded himself he was a live-in-the-moment guy and bundled in on the fun. As he joined the group hug, the excitement proved too much for Maisie, who slipped out of their hold for a mad dash around the room.

'Thank you for this.' Quinn dropped a kiss on his mouth as they tumbled to the ground. He wanted to freeze time, keep her there for ever so they didn't have to worry about anything except keeping that simple contact between them.

When she was with him, touching him, happy to be with him, he wanted to give her the world. He'd already broken all the singleton rules and was about to adopt a stray dog just so this feeling would last. He was afraid of what he would do next in the name of love.

There was no doubt about it. Given the lengths he'd gone to and his wish to lie here with her for ever, he was totally head over heels for Quinn Grady. It should've made him want to bolt from the room, pack his bags and catch the first flight back to Dublin but that wouldn't solve the problem. Wherever he went he knew he'd be thinking of her. The only way to get this out of his system was to let it run its course until they reached some sort of crisis point where having him in her life was no longer tenable. She was going to have to be the one to make that decision because, for once, Matt wasn't the one in charge. His heart was.

CHAPTER TEN

'WE HAVE A small communal garden she can use, and of course there's the nearby park.' Matt's application for Maisie-homing hadn't been as easy as simply signing a form, and rightly so. The animal shelter had insisted on doing a home visit to see for themselves that the ground-floor apartment was a suitable environment for her, and Quinn had agreed to be here for it.

She was still in shock he'd come up with the idea in the first place, never mind taken on primary responsibility of a dog to aid Simon's recovery. An act which certainly wouldn't have been part of his Hippocratic oath. This level of kindness couldn't be taught; it was pure Matt.

She didn't want to get her hopes up, much like she didn't want Simon to get too attached to him, or Maisie. At least by getting Matt to adopt the dog she'd managed to put some sort of safety prevention in place. When their dalliance inevitably came to its unsatisfactory conclusion they could go their separate ways without any ill will or duty to the other. The dog would be his responsibility, and Simon was hers.

'And where will doggie sleep?' The lady with the clip-board peered in the various rooms sussing out what prep-arations Matt had made for his new house companion.

'This is her bed here and Quinn's going to let her in and out while I'm at work.' Matt proudly showed off the comfy new dog bed full of new toys and treats he and Simon had picked out at the pet store.

It was all Simon could talk about since Matt had told him the news. He'd been clear to point out Maisie would be his but Simon could help out.

'Yes, we'll take her for walks and make sure she gets plenty of exercise when Matt's not here.' It was something she was looking forward to too. It would get them both outdoors more and be a step towards his recovery if the dog had his attention rather than the people around him. All thanks to Matt.

'I'll take a quick look at the garden to make sure it's safe and secure for Maisie but I don't think we'll have any problems giving the adoption the green light.' The lady who held Maisie's future in the palm of her hand gave a thumbs up before she ventured outside.

Quinn breathed a sigh of relief and left Matt to deal with any last-minute details with the inspector. If the process for adopting children was as straightforward it would have made life a lot easier for Simon. He might have found a family and settled down a long time ago if he hadn't been caught up in the bureaucracy for so long. Although that would've meant she'd never have got to meet him, and no matter what hardships they'd endured so far, she couldn't imagine being without him. Evidently she wasn't able to keep her emotions out of any relationship.

For someone who'd only ever meant to provide a safe and loving home for children until they'd found their adoptive families, she'd managed to fall for Simon and Matt along the way. They'd saved her at a time when she'd been at her loneliest. Now she knew how it was to be part of a family, however accidental, however dysfunctional, her life was never going to be the same without either of them. Regardless of what the future held, this was the most content she'd ever been and she'd learned never to take that for granted.

Happiness had come late in her childhood, infrequently in her adulthood, and was something she intended to make the most of for however long she was able to give and receive it.

'I don't think that could've gone any better. It won't be long before we hear that pitter-patter of little feet around here.' Matt was every inch the proud new adoptive dad when he returned.

Quinn would be lying if she said she didn't experience a pang of longing for a man who'd feel that way about children. In an ideal world Matt would be as joyful about the prospect of adding foster children to his family as he was about the dog. Maybe if she had a partner like that to support her she might've found the strength to adopt Simon herself, confident she could give him a more stable life than the one his neglectful parents had provided.

'I should go back. It's not fair on Simon, or Mrs Johns, to make a habit of this.'

'Twice isn't a habit. It's simply making the most of a good thing.' He advanced towards her with a hunger in his eyes that made her pulse quicken as fever took hold of her body.

This was the first time they'd been truly alone with no outside distraction from the simmering sexual attraction and no reason to stop it bubbling over.

'So, it's okay to do something naughty twice without having to worry it's the wrong thing?' She took a step forward to meet him, resting her hands on his chest, desperate to make body contact again.

'Definitely. Especially if you didn't technically *do it* first time around.' He teased her lips with the breath of innuendo, leaving her trembling with anticipation.

'If you say so—' She plucked the top button of his shirt open, ready to get the party started once and for all. They mightn't ever get the chance to do this again and then she really would have regrets. She'd had a sample of how good they could be together and not following it up seemed more idiotic than taking the risk.

If Simon wasn't in the picture she wouldn't hesitate to give herself to Matt and when this was over the only consolation she'd have was that she'd been true to herself.

'I do.' His mouth was suddenly crushing hers, the force of his passion hard and fast enough to make her head spin.

She trembled from the sheer intensity of the embrace as he pulled her close. Her knees went completely from under her as Matt swept her up into his arms, her squeal of surprise quietened by his primitive growl. She clung tightly to him, her hands around his neck, her mouth still meshed to his, afraid to break contact in case she started overthinking this again. When he was touching her it was all that mattered.

He strode down the hallway and she heard the heavy thud as he kicked the bedroom door open to carry her inside. She'd never gone for macho displays but, somehow, knowing the usually unflappable Matt was so impatient to get her to bed was the greatest turn-on ever.

He booted the door shut behind them again, ensuring they were completely cut off from the rest of the world. There was just her, Matt and a bed built for two.

They fell onto the mattress together, each pulling at the other's clothes until they were naked with no barriers left between them. They'd had weeks of foreplay, months if she counted all of those arguments at the hospital, and she didn't want to wait any longer.

She was slick with desire as they rolled across the bed in a tangle of limbs and kisses. Once Matt had sheathed himself in a condom he grabbed from his night stand, he thrust inside her. His hardness found her centre so confidently and securely she knew she'd found her peace.

Matt had finally lost his control, yet joining with Quinn brought him more relief than fear. He'd been strong for too long, trying to do the right thing by everyone when his body had been crying out for this. For Quinn.

He moved slowly inside her at first, testing what little there was left of his restraint, luxuriating in her tight, wet heat. She was a prize he knew he didn't deserve and one he'd only have possession of for a very short time. Quinn was her own woman who wouldn't be so easily swayed by great sex. It would soon become clear he didn't have anything else to bring to the party. If she expected anything more he'd only leave her with extra scars to deal with.

Quinn tightened her grip around his shaft to remind him this wasn't a time for inner reflection and stole the remnants of his control. As much as he wanted to pour inside her he also wanted this to be something she wouldn't regret. This should be a positive experience they could both look back on fondly, not a lapse of judgement they'd come to resent.

They'd gone into this fully aware this wasn't the beginning of some epic love story. No matter how he felt about her this couldn't be about anything more than sex.

He could never say he loved her out loud; that would place too much pressure on him to act on it when it wasn't a possibility. He wasn't about to turn his life upside down again for the sake of three little words.

She ground her hips against him, demanding he show her instead. Carnal instinct soon took over from logical thinking as he sought some resolution for them both.

His strokes became quicker with Quinn's mews of pleasure soon matching the new tempo. He captured her moans with a kiss, driving his tongue into her mouth so he had her completely anchored to him. She didn't shy away from his lustful invasion but welcomed it, wrapping her legs around his back to hold him in place.

Matt's breath became increasingly unsteady as he fought off the wave of final ecstasy threatening to break. Only when Quinn found her release would he submit to his own.

He gripped her hips and slammed deep inside her. Once, twice, three times—he withdrew and repeated the rhythm. The white noise was building in his head, his muscles beginning to tremble as his climax drew ever nearer.

Quinn lifted her head from the pillows, her panting breath giving way to her cries of ultimate pleasure and he answered her call with one of his own. His body shook with all-encompassing relief as he gave himself completely to her. For that brief moment he experienced pure joy and imagined how it would be to have this feeling last. Making love to someone he was actually in love with was a game changer. He couldn't picture sharing his bed with anyone else again and that scared him half to death. The other half was willing to repeat the same mistake all over again.

He disposed of the condom and rolled onto the bed beside her, face first into the mattress, content to die here of exhaustion instead of having to get up again and face reality.

'What do we do now?' Quinn turned onto her side so he had a very nice view of her pert breasts.

'Try and breathe,' he said, unable to resist reaching out to cup her in his hand even through his exhaustion.

'I mean after that.'

He knew exactly what she meant but he didn't have the answer. At least, probably not the one she wanted to hear. She wanted to know what happened now they'd finally succumbed to the chemistry, to their feelings, but for him he couldn't let it change anything.

To enter into a full-blown relationship with Quinn entailed having one with Simon too. One which went beyond professional or friendship. He couldn't do that in good conscience when he could never be the father Simon needed. He wouldn't give him any more false hope.

He was done with the school runs, the birthday parties and the angsty teenage rebellion stage. Whilst he didn't regret being the sole provider for his sisters, he was too jaded and tired to go through it all again.

Yet, he was advancing ever further towards the vacancy.

'You're fostering Simon, right? Someday he'll be adopted and you'll start the process over with someone new?'

'Well…yes. The children are only placed temporarily in my care until a family can be found for them.' Quinn frowned at him and he could tell the idea of not having the boy around was already becoming a touchy subject. They'd both got in over their heads but Matt was determined he, at least, was going to keep swimming against the tide.

'What if we apply the same restriction to our relationship?' It was the only logical way this could continue without any one of them coming to serious harm.

'You want me to foster you too?' Quinn danced the flat of her hand down his back, over the curve of his backside and across his thigh until he was back to full fighting strength and falling for her blatant attempt to leave this discussion for another time.

'More of a co-dependency until you've found your for ever family too.' In his heart he couldn't let it go on once Simon left her. There could never be a future for them as a couple because there would always be a child in need and Quinn's heart was too open to deny anyone the love they craved.

It wouldn't be fair to stop her simply because his heart was closed for business.

She sighed next to him, the heavy resignation of the situation coming from deep within a soul still searching for its mate. It was too bad it couldn't be him, then his own wouldn't be howling at the injustice he was doing to it.

'I'm beginning to think that's an impossible dream.'

'You're a great foster mother, a beautiful woman and an incredible lover.' He traced his thumb across her lips, hating they were talking about the next man who'd get to kiss them.

'Yeah?' She coquettishly accepted his compliment and he was in danger of digging a hole in the mattress as his libido decided they should make the most of their time together in bed.

'Yeah, and I think we should make a few more memories so I never forget.' Not that it was likely.

Quinn was the one woman, other than his sisters, who'd ever truly touched his heart and gave his life more meaning simply by being in it. The same probably couldn't be said about him when he'd only be able to give her fun and sex at a time when she needed stability. When she looked back she'd see they'd muddled personal feelings with the intensity of Simon's treatment. What he didn't want was for her to end up hating him for taking advantage of her. If they kept it light, kept it fun, kept it physical, there'd be no need to get into the heavy emotional stuff he had no room for any more.

He threw an arm across Quinn and rolled onto his back, bringing her with him so she straddled his thighs. With her sex pressed against his, the logical side of his brain finally shut up.

Quinn wasn't stupid. Sex was Matt's way of avoiding deep and meaningful conversation. She didn't blame him. Nothing good was going to come of them in their case. When Simon left, so would he, if not sooner. At some point in the near future they'd both be gone, leaving nothing but memories and a void in her heart. It was much easier to take pleasure where she could find it in the here and now than face the prospect of that pain. She'd rather have this kind of procrastination than ugly crying over bridal magazines for a relationship that would never happen.

For every fake idyll that popped into her head of her and Matt and their foster brood, she ground her hips against him to block it out. The rush of arousal instantly channelled her thoughts to those of self-pleasure instead of an impossible dream.

With her hands braced on Matt's sturdy chest, she rocked back and forth. His arousal strengthened as she slid along his length so she took him in hand and guided him into her slick entrance, giving them both what they craved for now. They fit perfectly, snug, as if they'd both found their other halves.

Matt was watching her, his eyes hooded with desire, but this time he was letting her make all the moves. Only thinking of herself for once, taking what she wanted, was kind of liberating. With a firm hand she teased the tip of his shaft along her folds until she was aching to have him inside her again. She anchored herself to him and that blessed relief soon gave way to a new need. Every circular motion of her hips brought another gasp of self-pleasure and a step closer to blinding bliss.

She doubled over, riding out the first shudders of impending climax. Matt sat up to capture one of her nipples with his mouth and sucked hard until it blurred the pleasure and pain barriers. Her orgasm came quickly and consumed her from the inside out, leaving her body weak from the strength of it.

Matt held her in place as he thrust upwards, finally taking his own satisfaction. Each time his hungry mouth found her breast or his deft fingers sought to please her again, another aftershock rippled through her. Only when she felt him tense beneath her, his grip on her tighten and the roar of his triumph ring in her ears did she finally let exhaustion claim her.

'That was…unexpected. Great, just…unexpected.'

As much for her as it was for him. She didn't recall ever being that confident in the bedroom before.

'I'm full of surprises, me.' She gave him a sly smile and hoped now he saw her as much more than a fragile foster mum he didn't want to be lumbered with for the rest of his days. There was still a sexy, independent-thinking, fun-loving woman inside her. She just hoped he assumed it was *her* husky voice he was hearing and not the raw-throated mutterings of a girl brought to the edge of tears by great sex.

He slung his arm around her shoulders and pulled her close. She didn't know how long they'd been locked away in this room, in their own world of fire and passion where time didn't matter. There was that residual parental guilt that perhaps she'd spent too long indulging her own needs while neglecting her son's but the warmth of Matt's skin against hers and the steady rhythm of his heart beating beneath her ear soon convinced her to stay here for a while longer. Simon was safe, and in Matt's arms, so was she.

'We'll pick Simon up once we've had a rest,' he mumbled into her hair.

Without prompting, Matt had raised the matter, something she'd been hesitant to do in case she ruined the moment. Her last thought as she drifted off to sleep was a happy one.

CHAPTER ELEVEN

'CAN I WALK HER? Please?' Simon hovered between Quinn and Matt, eyeing the dog's lead as if it was the hottest toy of the year.

Quinn glanced at Maisie's *official* owner for confirmation it was okay even though she and Simon walked her in the park practically every day.

'Sure.' Matt handed over control without a second thought. It was that kind of trust between him and Simon which was helping to build up the boy's confidence. That, and a hyperactive dog which kept them all too busy to dwell on any unpleasantness.

They'd fallen into a new routine, one which included exercising the dog and therefore getting Simon out and about in between hospital visits. Dare she say it, things had begun to settle down and they had so much going on now Simon's scars no longer seemed to be their main focus. Especially when those on his face were slowly beginning to fade.

As well as their dog-sitting duties, Quinn had the hospital committee meetings to attend and Simon was working towards his return to school. There'd been a phased return to classes held in the nearby hall, and although he'd been nervous, it had helped that some of his classmates were still being treated for minor injuries, including some burns. They understood what had happened to alter his appearance better than most but it didn't stop Quinn worrying.

'Hold on tight to Maisie's lead and don't go too far ahead,' she shouted after the enthusiastic duo haring through the park, although the sound of happy barking and childish laughter was music to her ears.

'They'll be grand. With any luck they'll tire each other out.' Matt cemented his place as the laid-back half of the partnership content to hang back and let the duo explore the wide open space, whist she remained the resident worrywart.

'Getting that dog was the best decision we could have made.' She knew pets were sometimes used as therapy for patients but she hadn't expected such impressive results so quickly. Simon was finally coming out of the shadows back into the light.

'Not *the* best decision.'

Quinn gave a yelp as he yanked her by the arm behind a nearby tree. He quietened her protest with his mouth. The kiss, full of want and demanding at first, soon softened, making her a slave to his touch. Okay, taking that long-awaited step into the bedroom had been one of the highlights of her year, perhaps even her lifetime. That in itself caused her more problems, as once would never be enough.

'We should really make sure those two aren't getting up to any mischief.'

'Like us?' He arched that devil eyebrow again, daring her to do something more wicked than snatching a few kisses out of sight.

She swallowed hard and tried to centre herself so she didn't get carried off into the clouds too easily.

'I hope not,' she muttered under her breath. If Simon was in a fraction of the trouble she was in right now she'd completely lose the plot.

'I want you.' Matt's growl in her ear spoke directly to her hormones, sending them into a frenzy and making her thankful she had a two-hundred-year-old oak tree to keep her upright.

These illicit encounters were all very exciting, but for someone as sexually charged as Matt, her inability to follow it through to the bedroom again would get old real quick.

Now that she'd discovered how fiercely hot their passion could burn, left unchecked there was nothing she'd enjoy more than falling into bed with him, but it was difficult to find enough Simon-free time to revel in each other the way they wanted to.

It was wrong to keep asking Mrs Johns to babysit and she was afraid if she started sleeping over at Matt's she would have to inform the foster authorities of his involvement in her life. That meant forcing him into a commitment he'd been very clear he didn't want and could signal the end of the good thing they had going. No matter how frustrated she was waiting for some more alone time it had to be better than never seeing him again.

Matt grazed his teeth along her neck, gave her a playful nip, and she began to float away from common sense all over again.

A snuffling sound at her feet and a wet tongue across her bare toes soon grounded her. She should have known open-toed sandals were a bad move for a dog walk.

'Maisie?'

The dog apparently had a shoe fetish, having already chewed one of Matt's expensive work shoes and buried the other. It was just as well she was cute or she might have found herself back in doggie prison. Thankfully, Matt's soft spot for waifs and strays was greater than his affinity for Italian leather. Although it must have been a close call.

'Yay! She found you.' Simon came into view still attached to the other end of the lead and Quinn was quick to push Matt aside.

'She's a good tracker.' She bent down to rub Maisie's ears. It wasn't their canine companion's fault she didn't understand the necessity for discretion.

'Whatcha doin' here?' Simon tilted his head to one side as he assessed the scene.

'We...er—' She struggled for a cover story.

'Were playing hide and seek. You won.' Matt stepped in with a little white lie to save her skin. He could very well have told Simon the truth that they were together and stopped all of this pretence but that would entail following up with an *actual* relationship which involved sleepovers and paperwork. Perhaps Matt's eyes were open to all the baggage that she'd bring and he'd decided it wasn't worth the effort after all.

She had a horrible feeling their fragile relationship was already on the countdown to self-destruction.

'Is it our turn to hide?' Simon's eyes were wide with excitement, the biggest smile on his face at the prospect of the game. It was going to be tough when it went back to being just the two of them.

She forced down the lump in her throat. 'Yup. We'll count to twenty and come and find you.'

Surely none of them could get into too much trouble in that short space of time?

She was rewarded with another beaming smile and a lick. Neither of which came from Matt.

'I'm as fond of a quickie as the next guy but twenty seconds? You wound me.' He clutched his chest in mock horror at the slight against his stamina.

That pleasure might seem like an age ago now but she could attest that it definitely wasn't a problem. She evaded eye contact and ignored the renewed rush of arousal as her body recalled the memory in graphic detail or they'd be in danger of losing Simon in the woods altogether.

'One…two…three…'

'You're killing me, you know.' He shook his head and from the corner of her eye Quinn saw him adjust the crotch of his trousers. A sight which was becoming more common with the increased rate of these passionate clinches. It wasn't fair on either of them.

'I don't mean to be a tease.' She gestured towards his groin area.

'I know but we really need to find a way to make this work.'

'Your penis?' She wanted to make him laugh, to steer the conversation away from that area of conflict they'd never be able to resolve satisfactorily.

It almost worked. He laughed at least.

'No, I'm fine in that department as you very well know. I mean us. We can't go on indefinitely hiding as though we're doing something wrong.'

'It's not as simple as clearing a space in my bathroom cabinet for your hair care products.' Her levity was waning as he made her face the reality of their situation.

'Of course. I'll require considerable wardrobe space too.'

'For an overnighter?'

'I do like a selection so I can dress according to my mood.'

Why couldn't life be as easy as their banter? Then perhaps her stomach wouldn't be tied up in knots waiting for the asteroid to hit and annihilate her world.

'All joking aside, we both know having you stay at my place, or us at yours, will only confuse Simon more than we already have. If we become an official couple I'll have to let the foster people know. I probably should've done that already but I didn't want to jinx this by putting it down on paper.'

The warmth of Matt's hands took the chill from her shoulders as he reassured her. 'As long as we're not signing a contract of intent I don't see why that should change things between us. It's understandable they'll want to protect Simon with background checks on anyone in his life but it's none of their business what our arrangement is. We can remain discreet where he's concerned. I'm the last person who wants him thinking I'm his replacement father. I can come over when he's asleep, leave before he's awake and make that time in between ours.'

She shivered, although there was no breeze in the air. It was a tempting offer, better than she expected in the circumstances. Yet there was something cold about the proposition. It snuffed out the last embers of hope that he'd ever want more than a physical relationship with her. Somewhere in her romantic heart she'd still imagined he could've been nudged further towards a more permanent role in their family. This was exactly the reason she'd wanted to keep Simon protected, because it was too late for her.

'That could work,' she said, not convinced it was the answer but the best one available for the moment.

At some point she was either going to have to push for more or sever all ties. Neither of which she was brave enough to do without prompting. The one consolation was that he was willing to stick around in some capacity and hadn't used this as an excuse to walk away. These days she took all the positives where she could find them and that new attitude had propelled her and Simon further forward than she could have hoped for.

Not that she was ready to admit it to anyone until she was one hundred percent sure it was the right thing to do, but she was thinking of making her and Simon's relationship more permanent. He was finally settling into her home, relaxing in her company and opening up to her. It wouldn't be fair to ask him to start all over again in a new town, with a new family and go to a school where they knew nothing of what he'd been through. Above everything else, she loved him as though he was her own son. He mightn't be of her flesh and blood, but she hurt when he hurt, cried when he cried, and seeing him happy again made her happy. They needed each other.

Adoption wasn't going to be straightforward, not even for a foster parent. She needed a bit more time to be certain it was right for both of them before she committed to the decision. There was no way she'd promise Simon a future if she thought she couldn't deliver. It would also be the end game for her and Matt.

His whole take on their relationship was based on the temporary nature of hers with Simon too. There was no way he'd stay involved once he found out she had ideas of becoming a permanent mum and all of the baggage that entailed. She wasn't ready to say goodbye to Matt either. For the meantime, it was better if the status quo remained the same.

'We'll talk it over later. When Simon's in bed.'

She would've mistaken his words for another wicked hint of what he wanted to do to her except he was taking her hand and leading her back towards Simon and the dog. It was his way of telling her he understood her concerns and was happy to comply. She swore her heart gave a happy sigh.

'Nineteen…twenty. Here we come, ready or not.'

Simon wasn't difficult to spot, his red jacket flashing in the trees and Maisie rolling in the grass beside him.

Quinn motioned for Matt to flank him from the far side whilst she approached from the other.

'Gotcha!' she said as she tagged him. It was only then she noticed his poor face streaked with tears.

'What's wrong, wee man?' Matt crouched down to comfort him too, as Quinn fought the urge to panic or beat herself up. She'd only left him for a few minutes.

'Are you hurt? Did you fall?' She rolled up his trousers searching for signs he'd cut himself or had some sort of accident.

He sniffed and shook his head. 'I thought you weren't coming for me.'

She was numb for the few seconds it took for the enormity of his fears to hit home. Simon longed for stability, had to be confident there'd be at least one person constant in his life taking care of his interests, or he'd never feel truly safe. Ready or not, it was her time to commit.

She hugged Simon tight and kissed the top of his head. 'I'm always going to be here for you. I love you very, very much and don't you ever forget it.'

Another sniff and a big pair of watery green eyes stared up at her.

'Thanks… Mum,' he said softly, as if testing the name on his lips. It almost had her sobbing along with him.

There was zero chance of her letting him go back into the system again without a fight. Whatever happened now, Simon was going to be the biggest part of her future and his happiness was her greatest reward.

She pulled him close again, channelling her love and hope for him in the embrace, and caught a glimpse of Matt's face over the top of his head as he joined in on the group hug. He was including himself in this moment of family unity when he could easily have stepped back and played no part in it. It was impossible not to let that flutter of hope take flight again when everything finally seemed to be coming together. She'd been brave enough to make that leap for Simon's sake and now it was Matt's turn to decide who, and what, he wanted.

It was a three-letter word—not the three little words Matt couldn't bring himself to say—which spelled the beginning of the end.

Mum.

He was happy for Quinn. It had been a beautiful moment watching them create a bond that nothing in this world could break. Including him. Not that he intended to come between them but he simply wasn't compatible with the new set-up. It was early days so it wasn't clear what role they expected him to play as the dynamics changed, but he was already becoming antsy about it.

Now they were back at Quinn's. She was putting Simon to bed, the dog was snoring by his feet and the scene would've been enough to content any family man.

Except he wasn't a family man. Not with Quinn and Simon at least.

He enjoyed the lifestyle he had now. The one before they'd gatecrashed his apartment. He'd worked hard to gain his freedom and he wasn't about to trade it in for another unplanned, unwanted fatherhood. Some part of him had hoped that might change, that he might step forward and be the man they all needed him to be. Yet the overriding emotion he'd felt as they'd hugged wasn't happiness. That generally didn't bring on heart palpitations and an urge to run.

He was as fond of Simon as he was his own sisters and nieces and he was in love with Quinn, but it wasn't enough to persuade him to stay for ever. What if it didn't last anyway? He knew from experience his conscience wouldn't let him walk away from a child who counted on him for support and he didn't want to become emotionally tied to two families. It would be a step back and he wasn't afraid to admit he wasn't up to the job this time around if it meant saving everyone unnecessary pain later on.

Quinn tiptoed back downstairs from Simon's bedroom and curled up beside him on the settee. She rested her head on his chest the way she did most nights when they had five minutes together and yet tonight it seemed to hold more significance than he was comfortable with.

This wasn't about sex; it was about unwinding with each other at the end of the day, sharing the details of their struggles and triumphs. The companionship was becoming as important as the physical stuff, as were the emotions. Stay or go, it was going to hurt the same.

Her contented sigh as she cuddled into him reached in and twisted his gut. If only he was as settled there wouldn't be an issue but he was dancing over hot coals, afraid to linger too long and get burned.

'That was some day,' he said as he stroked the soft curtain of her hair fanned across his chest.

'Uh-huh. I never saw it coming. I mean, I was having a hard time thinking about him moving on but to hear him call me Mum—' Her voice cracked at the sentiment and Matt's insides constricted a little tighter.

'It's a big deal.'

'We'll have to get the ball rolling and make our intent known regarding the adoption. The sooner he knows this is his real home, the better.' She was full of plans, more invigorated by the breakthrough than Matt was prepared for.

'We?' Matt's fingers tangled in her hair, his whole body tense. This was exactly how he hadn't wanted this to play out.

'It's a figure of speech.' She sat bolt upright, eyes wide and watching his reaction. He wasn't that good an actor and neither was she. Slip of the tongue or not, Quinn didn't say things she didn't mean. She was already including him in the plans for Simon's future.

He leaned back, creating a healthy space between them so he could think clearly without the distraction of her softness pressed against him.

'Quinn—'

'Would it really be so bad though? I know we've danced around the subject but we *are* in a relationship, Matt. I need to know if you're behind me in this before we go any further.'

Nausea clawed its way through his system, his breathing shallow as the walls of his world moved in around him. He may as well be back living in that tiny council flat in Dublin where he'd barely enough room to breathe.

'Of course I'm behind you. I think adopting Simon will be good for you both.'

Quinn took a deep breath. 'I need to know if you're going to be part of it. I can't go through this again unless I know you're going to be with me one hundred percent. He's been through so much—neglected by his parents…abandoned by a foster family who'd promised him for ever—Simon needs, deserves, people willing to sacrifice everything for him. So do I.' She was braver than he, putting everything on the line and facing facts where he wasn't able to. It sucked that she was giving him a choice because then he had to make it.

'I just…can't.'

'But you already are. Don't you see? You're already part of our lives. All I'm asking is that you'll commit to us. I love you, Matt.'

The words she thought would fix everything only strengthened his case against this. It didn't matter who loved who because in the end they'd come to resent each other for it anyway. Love tied people together when the best thing could be for them to go their separate ways and find their own paths to happiness. Quinn and Simon would be better off without someone who'd learned to be selfish enough to want a life of his own.

'And what? Do you honestly think telling me that will erase my memory? I told you from the very start I didn't want anything serious. Adopting Simon sounds pretty damn serious to me. I told you I don't make promises I can't keep—that's why I was very sure not to make any.' Even as the words came out of his mouth he wanted to take them back, tell her he was sorry for being so harsh and take her in his arms again. He couldn't. Not when he was trying to make her see what a lost cause he was and how she'd be better off without him. He wanted her to hate him as much as he hated himself right now. It would be easier in the long run for her to move on by thinking he was capable of such cruelty when, actually, his own heart was breaking that this was over.

Quinn's blood ran cold enough to freeze her heart, Matt's words splintering it into tiny shards of ice.

It was happening all over again.

Just as she thought things were slotting into place, a man had to ruin everything.

Matt mightn't have verbally promised anything but the rejection hurt the same as any other. More so since she'd seen how he was around children, with Simon. They could've been great together if he'd only chosen them over his bachelorhood.

It didn't feel like it at the moment, but it was best she find out now he wasn't the man she thought he was than when Simon started calling him Dad.

Her son was her priority more than ever and she wasn't going to subject him to a string of fake relatives who'd dump them when they got tired of playing house. She couldn't be as logical in her thinking as Mr McGrory; her emotions would always get the better of her common sense.

'Yes, you were. How silly of me to forget you had a get-out clause.'

'Don't be like that, Quinn. We had a good time together but we both want different things.' He reached out to take her hand but she snatched it away. He didn't have the right to touch her any more and she couldn't bear it now she knew this was over. It hurt too much.

'We want you. You don't want us. Plain and simple. There's probably no point in drawing this out.' She unfurled her legs from beneath her to stand, faking a strength she didn't possess right now.

Matt took his time getting up. Contrary to every other night he'd been here, Quinn wanted him gone as soon as possible. She wanted to do her ugly crying and wailing in private. A break up was still painful whether you saw it coming or not and she needed a period of mourning before she picked herself up and started her new life over. One without Matt.

'I'll look into transferring Simon's care to another consultant.'

'No. I never wanted him to suffer as a result of our relationship. He deserves the very best and that's you. I think we can be grown-up enough to manage that. If not, I'll stay out of your way and let you get on with it.'

Appointments at the Castle were never going to be the same. The fairy tale was well and truly over but she hoped there was still some sort of happy-ever-after in sight even without her Prince Charming. She would miss his supporting role at the hospital as much as out of it. He'd got her through some of those darkest days but she couldn't force him to want to be around.

He nodded, his professional pride probably making the final decision on this one. 'Of course. There's no point in causing him any more disruption than necessary. We should probably make alternative arrangements for the dog too.'

She was the worst mother in the world, before she'd even officially been handed the title. Simon was going to lose his two best friends because she couldn't keep her emotions in check.

'Maybe you could email me your schedule and we'll work something out.'

She knew Matt didn't have the time, not really. The dog had been another pie in the sky idea that they hadn't fully thought through. Maisie was going to end up as another casualty of their doomed affair if they didn't take responsibility for their actions.

'You should take her. We got her for Simon's benefit after all, and it would prevent any…awkwardness.' He clearly wanted a clean break with no ties that weren't strictly professional.

The quick turnaround from an afternoon where he couldn't keep his hands off her was hard to stomach.

'I suppose if Simon's going to be here permanently there's no reason why we can't take her on.' Yet deep down she was still hoping for one just so there'd still be some sort of tenuous link between them.

Matt didn't appear to have any such sentimental leanings.

'I should go.' He turned towards the door, then back again, as if he wanted to say something more but didn't. Only an uneasy silence remained, giving her time to think about the days they'd had together, and those they wouldn't.

'Yes.' She'd always been too much for any man to consider taking on and there was no reason this time should've been any different. Now the last hope she'd had for a *normal* family had been pounded into dust, she had to make the most of the one she had. From here on in it was just her, Simon and Maisie.

She watched him walk away, telling herself she'd started this journey on her own and she was strong enough to continue without him.

The first tears fell before Matt was even out of sight.

He daren't look back. It had taken every ounce of his willpower to walk out of that door in the first place, knowing he was leaving her behind for good. Another glimpse of Quinn in warrior mode, those spiky defences he'd spent weeks breaking down firmly back in place, and he might just run back and beg for forgiveness. That wasn't going to solve anything even if it would ease his conscience for now.

She was a strong woman who'd be stronger without him, without putting her hopes in someone who could never be what she needed—a husband and a father for Simon. If he was out of the picture, at least in a personal capacity, they stood a better chance of a stable life and he, well, he could return to the spontaneity of his.

He pushed the button on the key fob to unlock the car door long before he reached it so he wouldn't start fumbling with it at the last minute and betray his lack of confidence in his decision-making. Once inside the vehicle he let out a slow, shaky breath. This was the hardest thing he'd ever done in his life because he'd *chosen* to walk away; it wasn't a decision forced upon him.

She'd told him she loved him. He loved her. It would have been easy to get carried away in the romance of the situation and believe they could all live happily ever after but real life wasn't as simple as that. Unfortunately, loving someone always meant sacrificing his independence, something he'd fought too hard for to let it slip away again so soon.

He started the car and sneaked a peek back at the house, hoping for one last glimpse of Quinn before he left. The door was already firmly shut, closing him out of her home for ever. He would still see her from time to time at the hospital but he was no longer part of her life. From now on Quinn, Simon and Maisie were no longer his responsibility. Exactly what he'd wanted. So why did he feel as if he'd thrown away the best thing that had ever happened to him?

CHAPTER TWELVE

'HOW ARE YOU, Simon?' It had been a couple of weeks since Matt's world had imploded. He'd taken a back seat, letting the nurses change the boy's dressings to give him time to get used to the idea he wasn't always going to be around.

It had been harder for Matt than he'd expected. Of course, he'd kept up to date on the boy's progress, interrogating the staff who'd treated him and scanning his notes for information. None of that made up for seeing him, or Quinn, in person.

He could operate and perform magic tricks for hundreds of other patients and their families but it wasn't the same. Apparently that connection they'd had was one of a kind and couldn't be replicated.

'Okay.' Simon eyed him warily as he'd done way back during the early stages of treatment as though trying to figure out if he could trust him or not. A punch to Matt's gut after all the time they'd spent together, and it was nobody's fault but his own.

He'd had a sleepless night with the prospect of this one-on-one today. Although Quinn had kept to her word and stayed out of sight whilst he did his rounds it didn't stop his hands sweating or his pulse racing at the thought she was in the building.

'How's Maisie?' he asked as he inspected the skin already healing well on Simon's face.

'Okay.'

He definitely wasn't giving anything away. Perhaps he thought sharing too much information was betraying Quinn in some way. It wasn't fair that he'd been stuck in the middle of all of this. Matt hadn't hung around for the nature of the break-up conversation between mother and son. It must've been difficult to explain his disappearance when they'd tried so hard to keep their relationship secret from him.

Simon's reluctance to talk could also be because he saw him as another father figure who'd abandoned him, in which case he'd every right to be mad at him. It was still important he trusted Matt when it came to his surgery.

'I miss her around the place, even though my shoes are safer without her.' He never would've imagined his place would be so lonely without the chaos, and he wasn't just talking about the dog.

'Is that why you don't want to see us any more? Did we do something wrong? I promise I won't let her eat any more of your stuff.'

The cold chill of guilt blasted through Matt's body and froze him to the spot. He couldn't let Simon think any of this mess was his fault when he'd been nothing but an innocent bystander dragged into his issues. They were his alone.

It was the earnest pools of green looking at him with pure bewilderment which eventually thawed his limbs so he could sit on the end of the hospital bed.

'What happened between me and Quinn…it wasn't because of anything you, or Maisie, did. We've just decided it's better if we don't see each other.' This might've been easier if they'd co-ordinated their story at some point over these past weeks in case he contradicted anything he might've already been told.

At least Quinn mustn't have painted him as the bad guy if Simon thought he should somehow shoulder the blame. It was more than Matt deserved given his behaviour.

'Don't you like each other no more?'

If the situation had been as simple as Simon's point of view they would've still been together. He liked—loved—Quinn and she'd been fond of him enough to want him to be a part of their family. On paper it should've been a match made in heaven but he'd learned a long time ago that reality never matched up to rose-tinted daydreams.

'That's not really the problem.' As much as he'd tried, he couldn't switch off his feelings for Quinn. Not seeing her, talking to her or touching her hadn't kept her from his thoughts, or his heart. In trying to protect himself he'd actually done more damage.

How could he explain to a five-year-old he'd lost the best thing that had ever happened to him because he was afraid of being part of a family again, or worse, enjoy it too much? The one thing he was trying to avoid was the ultimate goal for a foster kid.

'She misses you. Sometimes she's real sad when she thinks I'm not looking but she says she's going to be my new mummy and we'll have lots of fun together.'

It didn't come across as a ploy concocted to get Matt to

break down and beg to be a part of it all again but he was close to breaking when Quinn was only a corridor away.

'I tell you what, after this surgery I'll have a chat with her and see if we can all go out for ice cream again some time.' They'd done the hardest part by making the break; meeting up for Simon's sake surely couldn't hurt any more than it already did. She still had Simon, and the dog, but the knowledge he'd saved himself from playing happy families didn't keep him warm at night.

The bribe did the trick of getting Simon back onside again and prevented any further speculation about what had happened. If Quinn had a problem, well, she'd simply have to come and talk to him about it.

He was just glad he and Simon were back on speaking terms again. He was such a different character from the withdrawn child he'd first encountered and Quinn was to thank for that. A part of him wanted to believe he'd helped in some small way too, aside from the cosmetic aspects. Despite all of his misgivings about becoming too involved, it was good to know it wasn't only his heart which had been touched by their friendship.

He hadn't realised quite how much until they were back in theatre, Simon asleep and completely at his mercy. For the first time in his career, Matt hesitated with the scalpel in his hand.

He would never operate on any of his sisters, or his nieces, because he was too close, too emotionally involved, and that could mess with his head. The consequences of something happening to someone he loved because he wasn't thinking clearly was a burden he could never live with.

Yet, here he was, hovering over a boy who'd come to mean so much to him, with a blade in his hand.

Simon *was* family, as was Quinn, and he'd abandoned them for the sake of his own pride. He'd always wondered how his life would've panned out if he'd shunned the responsibility thrust upon him to concentrate on his own survival. Now he knew. It was lonely, full of regret and unfulfilling without someone he loved to share it with.

His skin was clammy with the layer of cold realisation beneath his scrubs.

'Is everything all right?' One of the theatre assistants was quick to notice his uncharacteristic lapse in concentration.

'Yes.' He was confident in his response. He had to be. When he was in theatre he couldn't let his personal issues contaminate the sterile atmosphere.

He took a deep breath and let his professional demeanour sweep the remnants of his emotions to the side so he could do what was expected of him. It would be the last time he'd operate on Simon and he wasn't looking forward to breaking the news.

Quinn would never get used to the waiting. For some reason today seemed worse than all the other times Simon had been in surgery. The can't-sit-still fidgets were part parental worry and part running-into-an-ex anxiety.

With Matt still treating Simon it made an already stressful situation unbearable. There was no clean break like she'd had with Darryl. She hadn't seen him for dust once she'd insisted on going ahead with the fostering plan. This time she faced the prospect of seeing the man who'd broken her heart at every hospital appointment. She never knew which day might be the one she'd catch a glimpse of him to drive her over the edge.

Sure, things were going well with Simon in his recovery, and the adoption, but that didn't mean she could simply forget what she and Matt had had together. Could've had. She'd loved him and she was pretty sure he'd loved her, though he'd never said it and he hadn't been willing to trade in the single life for her. That was going to come back and haunt her every time she laid eyes on his handsome face. Out of Simon's sight, she'd cried, listened to sad songs and eaten gallons of ice cream straight from the tub but she hadn't reached the stage where she was ready to move on. She wasn't sure she ever really would.

No one got her like Matt; he seemed to know what she needed, and gave it to her, before she did. Except for what she'd wanted the most. Him. That's why it hurt so damn much. He'd known exactly what it would do to her by walking away; he'd told her long before she'd figured it out for herself. She could do the parenting alone, she just didn't want to.

For her, Matt had been the final piece of that family puzzle, slotting into place to complete the picture when there had been a void between her and Simon. Without him, she feared there'd always be a sense of that missing part of them and who knew where, or if, they'd ever be truly complete again. All she could do was her best to give Simon a loving home and pray it could make up for everything else.

Missing boyfriend and father figure aside, Simon had been making great progress in terms of his recovery and schooling. Those days of being a *normal* mother and son no longer seemed so far out of reach. It was only on days such as this which brought home the memories of the fire and the extra worry she'd always shoulder for Simon's welfare.

The thumbs up from the nurses was always the cue

she was awaiting so she could relax until he came around from the anaesthetic. This time her relief was short-lived as Matt came into view to add more stress to her daily quota.

'Did everything go to schedule?' It was the first time she'd spoken directly to him since they'd confronted the painful truth of their non-relationship so there was a flutter which made its way from her pulse to her voice. Worse, he was frowning, lines of worry etched deeply enough on his brow to put her on alert. Matt wasn't one to cause unnecessary drama on the wards and if he was worried about something it was definitely time to panic.

'Yeah. Fine... I need to talk to you.' He dropped his voice so other people couldn't hear and thereby induced a full-on panic attack.

It was never good news when doctors did that. Not when they were grabbing your arm and dragging you into a cubicle for a private word. Her heart was pounding so hard with fear, and being this close to him after such a long absence, she was starting to feel faint.

'What's happened? Is there an infection? I've tried to keep the dressings clean but you know what boys are like—' Her breathing was becoming rapid as she rattled through the possible disasters going on in her head.

Matt steered her towards the bed, forcing her to sit when the backs of her legs hit the mattress.

'He's fine. There were no problems or complication. I just can't treat him any more. I'm sorry but—'

The blood drained from her head to her toes and her limp body sank deeper into the bed. The moment things seemed to be going well for Simon, she'd messed it up. She couldn't let him do this because of her. Simon needed him.

'Is it me? Next time I'll stay out of the way altogether. You don't even have to come onto the ward. I'll talk to the nurses or I can get Mrs Johns to bring him to his appointments. I'll do whatever it takes. I don't want to be the one to mess this up.'

Any further resolutions he had for the problem were silenced as Matt sealed her lips with his. The stealth kiss completely derailed her train of thought, leaving her dazed and wanting more. She touched her fingers to her moist lips, afraid it had been a dream conjured up by falling asleep in the corridor.

'What was that for?' she asked, almost afraid of the answer.

'It was the only way to shut you up so I could finish what I was saying. Well, probably not the only way, but the best one I could think of.' He was grinning at her, that mischievous twinkle in his eye sending tremors of anticipation wracking through her body, but she still didn't know what there was to smile about.

'But why? Why would you feel the need to kiss me after dumping me and then telling me you're dumping Simon too? It doesn't make any sense. Unless this is your idea of a sick joke. In which case I'm really not amused.' Her head was spinning from his bombshell, from the kiss and from the way she still wanted him even after everything he'd done.

'Do I need to do it again to get you to listen?' He was cupping her face in his hands, making direct eye contact so she couldn't lie.

'Yes,' she said without hesitation, and closed her eyes for one last touch of him against her lips.

Whatever the motive, she'd missed this. She hated herself for being so weak as she sagged against him and let him take control of her mouth, her emotions and her dignity when she should be railing against him for putting her through hell.

Although she kissed him back, she remained guarded, wary of getting her hopes up that this was anything more than a spontaneous lapse of his better judgement. Once the pressure eased from the initial flare of rekindled passion, she broke away.

'What's this about, Matt?'

He raked his hand through his hair before crouching down so they were at eye level.

'I've missed you so much.'

Her stomach did a backflip and high-fived her heart but she kept her mouth shut this time. Words and kisses didn't change anything unless they were accompanied by a bit of honesty. She wasn't going to fall into that same trap of hoping she could change a man and make him want to be a permanent fixture in her life. In fact, she might draft that into a contract for future suitors so she could weed out potential heartbreakers. Although a Matt-replacement seemed a long way off when the real one was still capable of upsetting her equilibrium to this extent.

'I can't do Simon's surgery any more because I'm too close, too emotionally involved. It's a conflict of interests and one which means I have to choose between my personal and professional roles.'

'I don't understand. You're *choosing* not to treat him. Why is this supposed to be good news?' As far as she could see he was simply kicking them when they were down.

'I'm choosing you. If you'll still have me? Seeing Simon today in that theatre…it was like watching my own son go under the knife. It made me realise I'm already part of this family. I love you, Quinn. Both of you.'

She was too scared to believe he was saying what she thought he was saying. There'd been weeks of no communication from him and heartache for her and somehow now all of her dreams were coming true? She wasn't so easily fooled by a great smile and hot kisses any more. Maybe.

'What's changed, Matt? The last time we saw each other you were telling me the very opposite. Are you missing the dog or something? I'm sure we can make arrangements for a visit without forcing you into another relationship.' Okay, she was a little spiky but she'd every right to be after he'd ripped her heart out and she'd spent an age trying to patch it back up. If she meant anything to him he'd put up with a few scratches as he brushed against her new and improved defences.

The frown was back; she might have pushed him a tad too far.

'That's what I'm trying to tell you. I miss you all. This time apart has showed me what I'm missing. I don't want to end up a lonely old man with nothing but expensive furniture and fittings to keep me company. I've seen a glimpse of what life is like without you and Simon and it's not for me. I love you. I want to be with you, raising Simon, or a whole house full of Simons if that's what you want.'

'There's nothing I want more but only if that's truly what you want this time. How can I be sure you won't change your mind when the adoption comes through or there's another troubled kid on the doorstep? There can't be any room for doubt, Matt.' She pushed back at the flutter of hope beating hard against her chest trying to escape and send her tumbling back into Matt's arms.

He stood up, paced the room with his hands on his hips, and she knew she'd called his bluff.

'That's what I thought,' she said as she got to her feet, her voice cracking at the joyless victory.

'Wait. Where are you going?'

'To see Simon.' He was the only reason she hadn't completely fallen apart. She had to be the strong one in that relationship and he'd need her when he woke up and heard the latest bad news.

Matt stepped quickly into the path between her and the door to prolong her agony a while longer.

'What if I move in with you? Would that convince you I'm serious? I'll quit my lease, sell everything. I'll take a cleaning job at the hospital if it means I can stay on. I don't care about any of it. I just want to be with you.'

That made her smile.

'I think the hospital would give anything to keep you here given the chance.'

'And you?' He had that same worried look Simon had when he thought she didn't want him and in that moment she knew he meant every word. He was laying himself open here and this level of honesty was simply irresistible.

'Well, you know I'm a sucker for a stray so I guess I'll keep you too.' It was easier to joke when she was secure in his feelings for her.

'Tell me you love me.' He gathered her into his arms, a smile playing across his lips now too.

'You're so needy.'

'Tell me,' he said again, his mouth moving against hers.

'I love you.' She'd tried to convince herself otherwise

since he'd left but it was a relief to finally admit it aloud without fearing the consequences.

'I love you too. And Simon. And Maisie. And this mad, dysfunctional family we've created.'

'I think there's someone else who's going to be very happy to hear the news.'

'Let's go get our boy.' Matt took her hand and led her towards Simon's room to complete the group love-in.

Quinn's heart was so full she didn't think she'd ever stop smiling.

Now her family was finally complete.

* * * * *

HEALING THE
SHEIKH'S HEART

ANNIE O'NEIL

This one is for all the gals who worked on the series. I was a first timer and you made it a wonderful experience. A special shout out to the fabulous Fiona Lowe, who always helps me keep my head screwed on, and Karin Baine, my partner in googly-eyes.

CHAPTER ONE

"Next!"

Sure, it was clichéd, but so was the interview Idris had been forced to bring to an abrupt halt. How superficial did these people think he was?

His name on a hospital wing for having his daughter's surgery at the Chelsea Children's Clinic? *Ridiculous.* The money wasted on ribbon-cutting ceremonies and plaques should be spent on the children. In hospital. Wasn't that the point of a large donation? Not lavish displays of wealth and largesse. He had one concern and one concern only—bringing the gift of sound into his little girl's silent world. He turned at the gentle *ahem* prompt from Kaisha, all too aware this was exactly the sort of thing Amira couldn't experience.

"Are you ready for the next one?"

"Are there many more? I don't know how much more of this misplaced adulation I can take."

His assistant appeared by his side, scanning the print-outs on her leather-clad clipboard. The one with the royal crest that always ramped up the anxious-to-please smiles of his interviewees. Surgeons at the top of their games! He sucked in an embarrassed breath on their behalf, using the three-two-one exhale to try to calm himself.

"No, Your Excellency. We've only got three more."

"Kaisha, please." He only just stopped himself from snapping. "It's *Idris* when we're alone. There's only so much sycophancy a man can take in a day. You, of all people, know how important it is we find the right doctor for Amira."

"Yes, Your... Idris." Kaisha winced, did a variation of a curtsy, then threw her arms up in the air with the futility of getting it right and left the room. They both knew there was no need for a curtsy. They both knew Idris's glowering mood was virtually impossible to lift. He'd worn his "thunder face," as Amira liked to call it, near enough every day for the past seven years.

Despite his headache, an overdose of London's medical glitterati and a growing need to get out and stride off his frustration in one of London's sprawling royal parks, Idris smiled. Kaisha was loyal, intelligent and the last person he should be venting his frustration on. He'd hired her because she specialized in Da'har's rich history. Not for her skills as a PA. Perhaps he should hire her a PA to take up the slack.

He cupped his chin, stretching his neck first one way, then the next, willing the tension of the day to leave him... if not the penthouse suite altogether.

He crossed the impressive expanse of the suite's main sitting room. The "trophy suite" no less. Even he had winced at the pompous moniker but the location and views were incomparable. Nothing was off the shelf at Wyckham Place. Handcrafted tables, bespoke art pieces hung to match the modern, but undeniably select, furnishings and decor. He lived a life of privilege and preferred this type of understated elegance to flashy shows of gold-plated wealth. Apart from which, Amira liked the view of the London Eye and the Houses of Parliament the penthouse suite afforded. Anything to bring a smile to his little girl's face. She was so serious all the time. Little wonder, he supposed, without a mother's tender care and a father more prone to gravitas than gaiety.

His eyes hit a mirror as they left the view—the image confirming his thoughts. Hard angles, glinting eyes and the glower of a man with the weight of the world on his shoulders. There was a time when all he would've seen in return was a broad smile. When life was little short of perfect.

His gaze snagged on his grimace. Losing his wife had all but ripped his easily won grin straight from his face.

He looked away. Self-reflection had been another casualty. All that remained was his daughter's happiness and the well-being of Da'har. If a nation's character could run in a man's genes he knew he embodied all that the small Gulf nation stood for. Pride. Strength. Resilience.

His dark eyes hit the solid door of the suite, beyond which were two of his most trusted employees. Beyond them, at the lift, two more. And in the foyer of the hotel more waited, innocuously, in plain clothes. They were meant to provide a sense of security. Today it felt stifling.

A sudden urge overtook him to tug on a hat and walk out into the streets of London, bodyguards left behind none the wiser, and become…no one in particular. But finding the right surgeon for his daughter was paramount. He'd tolerate near enough anything for her. Even torture by fawning hospital officials. He was mortal, after all. A true god would have foreseen the complications his wife had endured during the birth of their beautiful daughter. A truer one would have saved her.

"How long has Amira been at the zoo?" Idris called over his shoulder.

Kaisha appeared by his side again. "Only an hour or so, Your—Idris. As you requested, they cleared the zoo of other patrons so Amira could have a private tour."

He wondered, fleetingly, how Kaisha did that. Just… appeared. Maybe she'd been in the room the entire time and he simply hadn't noticed. One of his recently "acquired" traits.

Not so recent, he reminded himself. The seven longest years of his life. The only light in that time? His beautiful daughter.

"Excellent. Amira always takes ages with the giraffes and penguins. And remember, I don't want her anywhere near the hotel until we find the right person. If I have to pay to keep the zoo open longer, that's not a problem."

Even Idris didn't miss the pained expression Kaisha tried to hide from him as she lifted her clipboard to hide her features.

"What is it, Kaisha?"

"It's just…"

"Out with it!" Patience might be a virtue but it was most likely because it was in short supply. Particularly in his hotel suite.

"You've seen most of the specialists already and haven't bothered to hear any of them out."

"They all seemed more interested in attaching the Al Khalil name to their hospitals—or the Al Khalil money, rather—than in my daughter. She's the entire point of this exercise. Cutting-edge medicine. The best money can buy. Not getting my name spread across London! If Amira hadn't wanted to see that musical I would've flown everyone to Da'har and not wasted my time."

Kaisha, to her credit, nodded somberly. She had heard it all before. In between each of the interviews today, in fact. And the day before. Any patience in the room was Kaisha's alone. Idris was more than aware he had a tether and was swiftly approaching the very end of it.

"Right! It's the next person on the list or we're off to Boston Pediatrics or New York ENT. Enough of this nonsense. All right?"

"Yes, Your Ex— Idris." Kaisha gave a quick smile, proud

to have remembered the less formal address in the nick of time. "Shall I fetch the next candidate?"

"We might as well get it over with," Idris grumbled, settling back into the only chair that comfortably accommodated his long limbs. "Who is it, please?"

"Uh—yes, sorry—it's Robyn Kelly. Dr. Robyn Kelly. *Salaam Alaikum.*"

Idris looked up sharply. The voice answering him was most definitely not Kaisha's.

Alssamawat aljamila!

The pair of eyes unabashedly meeting his own were the most extraordinary color.

Amber.

Lit from within just as a valued piece of the fossilized resin would be if it were held up to the sun. Mesmerizing.

The sharp realization that he was staring, responding to this woman in a way he had only done once before, made him bite out angrily, though she bore no blame for his transgression.

"How did you get in here?"

"Walked," she answered plainly, her wayward blond curls falling forward as she looked down. "With these." She pointed at her feet, clad in the sort of trainers he would've expected to see on a teenager. His eyes shot back to hers when he heard her giggling as if he had just asked the silliest question in the world.

"Oh!" She popped a finger up as a sign he should take note. "Your...I think they're your bodyguards...kindly let me in to 'powder my nose' a few minutes early. Hope that was all right. And it's Robyn with a *y* not an *i*—i.e., not like the little birdie up in the trees but pretty close! Blame my parents," she finished with a playful shrug.

He narrowed his eyes, assessing the new arrival as coolly as he could considering she looked about as dangerous as a baby lamb. Even so, no one got past his bodyguards. Ever.

And yet this amber-eyed sylph had done just that. What if she'd found Amira and stolen her away? His heart seized at the thought.

Pragmatics forced him to blink away the foolish notion with a stern reminder that this…"Robyn"…was very human and that his daughter was safe and well.

His gaze returned to Robyn. A couple of inches above average height. About his age—midthirties. Slender. At least what he could see of her, as most of her body was hidden beneath an oversize trench coat that would've been stylish if she'd bought the correct size or used the belt as intended rather than as a long rope to swing round and round like an anxious cowgirl as she awaited his response. A wild spray of golden curls. Untamed. A makeup-free face. Evidence the "nose-powdering" was a euphemism. Her cheeks were pink…with the cold, perhaps? By Da'harian standards, the day was wintry. A three-year stint at an English university had taught him the on-again, off-again late-summer rainstorms were normal. In keeping with the storm-tossed treetops quaking along the riverbanks below, Robyn Kelly was looking similarly windswept and ever so slightly unkempt.

Perhaps more faerie or wayward pixie than sylph, then.

The mythical creatures, he suspected, didn't giggle. Nor did they tug their fingers through their hair when it was too late to make a good first impression.

Even so—he shifted in his seat—it was easy enough to picture Robyn in gossamer with a set of diaphanous wings taking flight over the palace gardens of Da'har.

Mercifully, he caught a glimpse of Kaisha appearing, and gave his throat a quick clear as if it would shunt away the images Robyn's presence elicited.

Kaisha shot an apologetic look at Idris. She didn't seem to know how Robyn had entered the suite any more than he did. "Dr. Kelly, could we offer you some coffee or—"

"Bless you, love! I'd kill for a good old-fashioned cup of builder's." Robyn's face lit up with a bright smile at Kaisha's instantly furrowed brow. "Apologies!" She laughed. "I forget English is your...what is it—third or fourth language?"

"Fourth." Kaisha smiled shyly.

"Fourth! I should be so lucky." Robyn's amber eyes flicked to Idris as if to say, *Can you believe this girl?*

"And such different languages, as well. If I remember from our emails, you have the Da'har dialect, Arabic, French and English?"

Kaisha nodded.

"Impressive. The only other language I speak is 'menu.' Builder's *tea*," Robyn explained, hardly pausing for breath. "It means brewed strong and with a healthy dollop of milk."

"Not cream?"

"No, love." Robyn shook her head with a gentle smile. "I'm not so posh as all that. And if you have a couple of biccies tucked away in there somewhere so much the better." She turned on the heel of what the cool kids would call her "trendy kicks" to face Idris. "I'm sorry. This is all a bit whirlwindy of me, isn't it? Shall I begin again? A bit more officially?" She stuck out her hand without waiting for an answer. "Dr. Kelly from Paddington Children's Hospital and you are...?"

"Sheikh Idris Al Khalil," he answered, rising to his full height and accepting her proffered hand, bemused to have to introduce himself at all.

"Great!" Robyn gave his hand a quick, sharp shake and just as quickly extracted her hand with a little wriggle as if he'd squeezed it too hard and not the other way around. "Amira's father." Her eyes darted around the room as she spoke. "Excellent. All right if I just throw my mac here on the sofa or would you rather I grab a hanger from somewhere so you could hang it up on...?" Her eyes continued to scan the room for an appropriate place to hang her soaked raincoat while he found himself completely and utterly at a loss for words.

No one had asked him to lift so much as a finger for them since...ever. Not that he minded lending a hand to a person in need, but...her lack of interest in his position in the Middle East, let alone the world, was refreshing. If not slightly disarming.

He arched an eyebrow as she twisted around, untangling herself from the tan overcoat and about three meters' worth of hand-knitted scarf, muttering all the while about "British summers."

She pulled off the coat, managing to get an arm stuck in one of the sleeves, went through a microscopic and lightning-speed thought process before, rather unceremoniously, yanking her arm out and turning the sleeve inside out in the process. She gave an exasperated sigh, bundled the whole coat up with the scarf and tossed it into the corner of the überchic sofa before flopping onto the other corner in a show of faux despair.

He felt exhausted just watching her. And not a little intrigued.

Idris flicked his eyes away from Robyn's, finding the golden glow of them a bit too captivating. More so than her ensemble: a corduroy skirt that had seen the washing machine more than a few times, a flowered top with a button dangling precariously from a string. The trainers... More student than elite surgeon.

She was a marked contrast to the four preceding candidates who had all looked immaculate. Expensive suits. Silk ties. Freshly polished shoes. All coming across as if their mothers had dressed them for their first day at school. He huffed out a single, mirthless laugh. Little good it had done them.

"What? Is there something wrong?" Robyn asked, her gaze following his to her cream-colored top dappled with pink tulips, a flush of color hitting her cheekbones when her eyes lit on a stain.

"Ah! Apologies!" she chirped, then laughed, pulling her discarded, well-worn leather satchel up from the ground where she'd dropped it when she came in and began digging around for a moment before triumphantly revealing a half-used supersize packet of wipes. "We just had congratulations cupcakes at the hospital for one of the surgeons who's newly engaged and I shared one with a patient while we were reading and—" she threw up her hands in a *What can you do?* gesture "—frosting!"

She took a dab at the streak of pink icing with a finger and he watched, mesmerized, as the tip of her tongue popped out, swirled around her finger, then made another little swipe along her full lower lip. "Buttercream. I just love that stuff! Doesn't stop the children from getting it absolutely everywhere, though, does it?"

She began scrubbing at her top with the wipe, chattering away as she did. "Bless them. Being in hospital is bad enough, but having to worry about manners?" She shrugged an indecipherable response into the room, clearly not expecting him to join in on the one-sided conversation. "Then again, if the hospital weren't on the brink of closing I probably wouldn't be here making a class-A idiot out of myself. I'd be in surgery where I belong."

Her eyes flicked up and met his.

"Uh-oh." Her upper teeth took hold of her full lower lip as her face creased into an apologetic expression. "Out-loud voice?" Again, she didn't wait for an answer, shook her head and returned to her task. "That's what they get for sending the head of surgery and not PR!"

Idris watched near openmouthed, trying to divine if *she* was mad or if *he* was for letting her ramble on, all the while dabbing her blouse a bit too close to the gentle swell of her...

He forced his gaze away, feeling his shoulders cinch and release as Robyn's monologue continued unabated. She hadn't noticed. Just as well. He was in the market for a surgeon, not a lover.

"We, meaning everyone at the Castle—aka Paddington's—*obviously* imagine Amira is a gorgeous little girl, and I, for one, can't wait to meet her. So!" Robyn dropped the used wipe into her satchel and clapped her hands onto her knees. "Where is she?"

"I'm sorry?" Idris crossed his legs, leaned back in his chair, all the while locking eyes with her. He was used to conducting interviews. Not the other way around. Who was this woman? Minihurricane or a much-needed breath of fresh air?

"Amira?" Robyn prompted, panicking for a second that she'd walked into the wrong Sheikh's suite in the wrong fancy hotel. All the fripperies and hoo-ha of these places made her nervous. Or was it just the Sheikh? Idris.

He had breathtaking presence. The photo the hospital had supplied with his bio had been flattering—pitch-black eyes, high cheekbones, dark chestnut hair—a tick in all of the right boxes, so that was little wonder. But in real life?

A knee-wobbler.

She only hoped it didn't show. Much.

She tried a discreet sidelong look in his direction but the full power of his dark-eyed gaze threatened a growing impatience.

He had said he was Idris Al Khalil and not the long-lost son of Omar Sharif, right?

"Amira," she repeated, unsuccessfully reining her voice back to its normal low octave. "Where did you say your daughter was?"

"Out," came the curt reply.

Huh. Not a flicker of emotion.

Still waters running deep or just a protective papa bear?

Not the way she usually liked to do things, but then she wasn't in the habit of "pitching" herself to be the surgeon of choice, either. One of the few things she solidly knew about herself was that when it came to Ear, Nose and Throat surgeries, she was one of the best. If she thought there was someone else better for the job she wouldn't have even showed up. But this was her gig. She'd known it from the moment she saw Amira's case history.

She tipped her chin upward, eyes narrowing as she watched Idris observe her in return. His black eyes met hers with a near tactile force. Unnerving.

She looked away. Maybe this was some powerful sheikh-type rite of passage she had to go through. She crinkled her nose for a moment before chancing another glance at him.

Yup. Still watching her. Expectantly. Still super-gorgeous.

She pursed her lips. He'd better not be waiting for a song and dance.

She glanced at her watch.

That was about half a second used up, then.

Looked up at the ceiling—eyes catching with his on the way up.

Still staring at her.

She remembered a trick one of her colleagues taught her. Pretend he was in his underwear. She gave him her best measured look all the while feeling her blush deepen as she pictured all six-foot-something of Idris naked, which was really…much nicer than she probably should be finding the experience.

This whole staring/not staring thing was a bit unnerving. Part of her wished she'd brought a sock puppet.

Robyn! Do not resort to sock puppets!

She clapped her hands onto her knees again.

"So…what do I call you?"

His dark eyebrows drew together into a consternated furrow.

"Idris."

"Oh!" She blinked her surprise. "Phew! I was a bit nervous there that I was meant to bow or 'your highness' you or something. Idris. Great. Beautiful name. I believe that's after one of the Islamic prophets in the Qur'an. Yes? Did you know it's also a Welsh name meaning 'ardent lord' or 'prince'? Fitting, right?"

"I am neither a prophet nor a prince," he answered tightly.

Okay. So he was a king, or a sheikh, or a sheikh king. Whatever. It made no difference to her, not with how full her plate was with the hospital on the brink of closing and an endless list of patients Paddington's could help if only its doors were kept open. Besides—she chewed on her lower lip as she held another untimed staring contest with him— she was just making chitchat until his daughter showed up.

Blink.

He won. Whether or not he knew it. Who could stare at all that…chiseled perfection without blinking? He had it all. The proud cheekbones. The aquiline nose. Deliciously perfect caramel-colored skin. The ever so slightly cleft chin just visible beneath more than a hint of a five o'clock shadow. She didn't know why, but she was almost surprised at his short, immaculately groomed dark hair. He would've suited a mane of the stuff—blowing in the wind as he rode a horse bareback across the dunes. Or whatever it was sheikhs did in their spare time. The color of his hair was run-your-fingers-through-it gorgeous. Espresso-rich. Just…rich. Everything about him screamed privileged. Polar opposites, then.

Of course she'd blinked first.

"Well, you know there's also a mountain in Wales— Idris's Chair. And just look at you there—sitting in a chair."

She raised her eyebrows expectantly. Most people would, at the very least, feign a smile.

Nothing.

"It rhymes!" She tacked on with a hopeful grin, trying her best to keep her nerves at bay.

Nothing.

His lips, though clamped tight, were…sensual. She'd already noticed he curved them up or down to great effect. Disconcerting in a man who, on all other counts, embodied the definition of an alpha male. The perfect amount of six-foot-something. For her, anyway. She liked to be able to look a man in the eye without too much chin tilting. If she were in heels? Perfect. Match. Not that she was on the market for a boyfriend or anything. She bit down on the inside of her cheek to stifle a guffaw. As if.

He looked fit. Athletically so. She would've laid money on the fact the hotel swimming pool had seen some well-turned-out laps this morning from the spread of his shoulders filling out what had to be a tailor-made suit. She tipped her chin to the side, finger tapping on her lips, wondering if she could drum up the Arabic word for *tailor.*

"Here we are! I even found a mug! The butler told me builder's tea always has to come in a mug. Preferably with a chip, but I'm afraid this one has no chips."

Robyn lifted her gaze, grateful to see Idris's assistant arrive, face wreathed in a triumphant smile, carrying a tray laden with tea fixings and a huge pile of scrummy-looking biscuits. Were they…? Oh, *wow.* Dark chocolate–covered ginger biscuits. In abundance!

"These are my absolute favorite!"

"We've done our research. Let us hope," Idris continued in his lightly accented English, "that you have done yours."

The words were a dare. One she'd needed no prompting to resist.

"It's actually been fascinating going over Amira's notes.

It's kept me up at night." She saw a flash of something indecipherable brighten Idris's dark eyes. "In the best possible way."

Kaisha set the tea tray down between them.

"Heavens! There are enough biscuits here for an army! Is Amira coming with a group of her friends?"

"No. This is just for you," she answered, her beautiful headscarf swishing gently forward as she leaned to pour a cup of mint-scented tea for Idris and herself from a beautiful china teapot.

"Oh, you are a sweetie. Thank you. It's Kaisha, isn't it?" Robyn asked.

"That's right."

Robyn repeated the name. "In Japanese it means enterprising, or enterprise, I think." She found herself looking to Idris for confirmation. He looked like a man who had answers in abundance.

"I thought you said you weren't a linguist, Miss—"

"Doctor," Robyn jumped in with a smile. It was her whole life—her job at Paddington's—and heaven knew she'd far rather be defined by her work than her less edifying home life as a spinster.

"Doctor," Idris corrected, eyebrows lifting as if he were amused by her insistence upon being called by her rightful title. "For someone who professes to only speak 'menu' you seem to know your way around the world's languages."

"Oh, yes, well…" She felt her cheeks grow hot. Again. Not a handy time to have a creamy complexion. She twisted her fingers together, hoping they would help her divine the perfect way to confess just how much of a nerd she was. Nothing sprang to mind so she dove into the pool of true confessions. "I've studied quite a few sign languages from around the world. It comes in handy as an ENT specialist. Many countries share similar signs for the same word, but it's always useful to know the word in the spoken language given we have patients joining us from around the world and a lot of them—as many as I can encourage actually—are lip readers. So—" she signed as she spoke "—that is why I had prepared for meeting Amira and not you."

"I see." Idris's dark-as-night eyes widened and she felt her heart sink. Why, oh, *why* did administration see fit to send her out on these meet-and-greet jobbies? She got too nervous. Talked too much. Way too much. She really would've preferred to meet the child—or patient—as the administrators insisted on calling them, on her own.

Patient. The word gave her shivers. The people who came to them at a time when they were sick, or injured and needing a healing touch—they were all *children*. Children with names and faces, likes and dislikes, and in some cases, the ability to knit the world's longest scarf.

Her fingers crept across the couch and rubbed a bit of the damp wool between her fingers. The gift was as precious to her as if the children she'd never have had made it for her. An ectopic pregnancy had seen to that dream. So her life was filled with countless "adoptees."

Children.

"Patient" sounded so *clinical* and she, along with the rest of the staff at the Castle—as the turreted building had long been nicknamed—wanted the children who came to them to be treated with individual respect and care. With or without the hospital gown, tubes and IVs. Row upon row of medicines, oxygen tanks, tracheal tubes and hearing aids. They were *children* for whom she tried her very best to make the world—or at least Paddington Children's Hospital—a better place to be.

If Amira's records were anything to go by—and Idris was willing to accept the cutting edge treatment she thought her hospital could offer—Robyn knew, with the right team of surgeons, specialists and, annoyingly, *funding*, she could help his little girl hear for the very first time.

So…it was suck it up and woo the Sheikh, help his daughter and save the hospital in the process.

CHAPTER TWO

"LET ME START AGAIN."

Idris's growing impatience won out over the desire to return Robyn's infectious smile. "I wasn't under the impression we had started *anything*, much less the interview I was expecting to conduct."

He knew he was being contrary but this woman unnerved him. Her watchful tigress eyes flicked around the room on a fruitless quest to come up with reasons for his terse response. She wouldn't find what she sought there. In the immaculate soft furnishings and discreet trappings of the überwealthy. The answer to his coldness stood guard at the surrounds of his heart. Unreachable.

And she would have to do a bit more than smile and catch him off guard to be the one he chose to operate on his daughter.

He was the wall people had to break through to get to Amira. He'd lost one love of his life to the medical "profession." He'd be damned if he lost another.

He shifted in his chair, well aware Robyn was already unwittingly chinking away at some of his usually impenetrable defenses. This woman—ray of light, more like—was a near antithesis to everything his life had been these last seven years. Where he was wary and overprotective, she was virtually bursting with life, enthusiasm and *kindness*.

He didn't think any of the other surgeons had so much as spoken to Kaisha other than to say "tea" or "coffee." Perhaps a nod of dismissive thanks, but in his book, consideration was everything. Particularly in his role as leader of Da'har. Every decision he made about the small desert kingdom would, ultimately, affect each citizen. As such, he took no decision lightly, altered no laws of the land to benefit one group of people and not another. Life on this small planet was already unjust enough on its own. He'd learned that the hard way. And regrouped out of necessity.

The last thing the people of Da'har needed was a leader drowning in grief at the loss of his wife. Seven years ago his newborn daughter had needed a father with purpose. Direction. So he'd shut the doors on the past and sharply fine-tuned himself to focus on Amira and the role she would one day take on as Sheikha of Da'har and all her people. People whose voices she now longed to hear.

"Where are all the toys?" Robyn asked pointedly.

"I'm sorry?" Idris swung his attention back toward her, not realizing his thoughts had wandered so far away.

"Toys? You did bring your daughter with you, right? And she's seven so…" He watched her brightly lit eyes scan the immaculate sitting room. "Where does she play?"

"She's at the zoo with Thana."

Kaisha's eyes widened at his words. He knew as well as she, he would normally never tell a virtual stranger his daughter's whereabouts. Or to call him Idris for that matter. He'd offered no such "common" courtesy to the surgeons he'd met before Robyn. Something about her elicited a sense of…comfort. Ease. She exuded warmth. Albeit, a higgledy-piggledy variety of warmth—but she seemed trustworthy, nonetheless. Which was interesting. Trust wasn't something he extended to others when it came to his daughter.

"And Thana is her…?" He bristled at Robyn's open-ended question. He never had to face this sort of questioning in Da'har. Or, generally, anywhere else. His wife's death during childbirth had been international news. Where their wedding had lit up television broadcasts, her funeral had darkened screens around the globe. It was near impossible to explain how leaden his feet had felt as he'd followed her casket, Amira's tiny form tightly swaddled in his arms, the pair of them making their way toward the newly dug grave site. He swallowed the sour sensation that never failed to twist through his gut at the memory.

"Her nanny."

Robyn winced. He could see she remembered now. The myriad expressions her face flashed through and finally landed on was something he recognized too well.

The widowed Sheikh and his deaf daughter...all alone in their grief at the loss of the Sheikha.

So.

He quirked an appraising eyebrow.

She *had* done her research, after all. Just wasn't going to any pains to prove it.

"Right!" Robyn pulled open the flap to her satchel and pulled out a thick sheaf of papers, which she knocked into an exacting rectangle on the glass coffee table. "I generally prefer to do this sort of initial 'meet' with the child. Amira," she corrected. "While I am relatively certain the type of surgery and treatment I am proposing will suit her case, I also like to make sure it suits *her*."

"What do you mean?" None of the other surgeons seemed to care a jot about Amira's thoughts on the matter. They just wanted to showboat their latest clinical trials... for a price, of course. A large one.

"When someone who is profoundly deaf has hearing restored, it can be quite shocking. Not all deaf people, you may be surprised to learn, *want* to hear."

"That is not the case with Amira."

Robyn gave him a gentle but firm smile before continuing. "It would be *preferable* to hear that from Amira. Sometimes what a parent desires for their child is different from what the child themselves wants. Tell me, how does she communicate?"

"She mostly reads lips, although—" he raised a hand as Robyn's own lips parted to interject "—we have our own sign language of sorts. As I'm sure you are aware, there is not yet a regionally recognized sign language between the Arab nations as there is in America or here in the United Kingdom."

Robyn was nodding along, the tiniest flicker of "been there, done that" betraying the fact he wasn't telling her anything she didn't know already.

"And is her lipreading in Arabic, French and English?"

Hackles rising, Idris checked the volume of his response. "Da'har's local dialect is what interests her most as the people of my kingdom are the ones she will one day be Sheikha to. Though she speaks a smattering of the others as we travel together regularly. Do bear in mind, *Doctor*, she is only seven."

"I have met some very savvy seven-year-olds in my day." Her chin jutted forward decisively.

Was she mocking him? Amira was the most precious thing in his life. He was hardly going to overwhelm his already serious little girl with an endless stream of tutors and languages when life was innately challenging for her.

When his eyes met hers, he was heartened to see Robyn's countenance matched her words. She seemed to have...*respect*...for her patients. He notched up a point for her. A small one. But a point, nonetheless.

"Shame." Robyn was shaking her head, fanning out some of the papers she'd brought. "It's much easier to learn multiple languages as a child. The younger, the better, some say. Particularly if it's not in a scholastic setting." Her eyes made a derisive skid across the decidedly "grown-up" hotel suite.

"Actually…" Kaisha interjected shyly. "Amira's English is pretty good and we have been practicing some British Sign Language. She seems to enjoy it."

"You've not told me this!" Idris knew it wasn't something to be angry about—but why would they keep this from him? A small twinge of concern that his own serious demeanor might be the reason teased at his conscience. Then he dismissed it. He was who he was. A father who put his daughter above everything.

"It was a surprise. For Dr. Kelly." Kaisha jumbled the words together, then launched herself into some fastidious note-taking to avoid any reaction Idris might have.

"That's excellent!" Robyn gave a fingertip pitter-patter clap.

"British Sign Language is closer to French—so if she takes that up as well, it sounds as though she's got some solid grounding in the wonderful world of the polyglot!"

Kaisha beamed with pride.

"Hold on!" Idris unsuccessfully tried to rein in the women's enthusiasm. "What has all of this got to do with the operation to restore her hearing?"

"Everything," Robyn replied solidly.

"And why is that?" Idris asked, now feeling sorely tested.

"Because there is always the chance it might not work."

A thick silence settled between them as he took on board what none of the other surgeons dared suggest. Failure. It was a courageous thing to admit.

"I thought you were one of the best."

"I am," Robyn replied without so much as a blink of an eye. "But Amira's case is a tricky one and the treatment I'm proposing has never been done in exactly this way. Not to mention, I've never done it in tandem with gene therapy."

"Gene therapy?" Idris's hackles went straight up. It sounded invasive. Dangerously so.

"Don't worry...don't worry." Robyn waved away his concerns as if they were minor. "This is really exciting stuff. During my time in Boston Pediatrics—"

"I thought you were based at Paddington's."

Was *nothing* as it seemed with this woman?

"I am," she confirmed patiently, then gave a self-effacing laugh. "Unlike most of the human race I like to take my 'holidays' at other hospitals. See what my fellow comrades in the Ear, Nose and Throat world are up to."

"So...you *work* on holiday." It came out as a statement.

"I never feel like I'm at work," she replied, looking shocked he could think otherwise. "I love what I do. So, really, I'm living the dream!"

Idris saw something just then—the tiniest of winces as she spoke of her "perfect life."

That she was passionate about medicine he had no doubt. But there was something missing, something personal. Which was what she seemed to be making this whole affair by the constant reminders that Amira wasn't available for "inspection."

He gave a dissatisfied grunt at the thought, smoothing away an invisible crease on his trousers.

Work and play might be one and the same for Robyn, but he had yet to get a handle on what it was she was actually going to *do* for his daughter apart from test her emotional elasticity. What was she expecting? A picket fence lifestyle for a girl who had lost her mother at birth and would one day rule a nation, all the while coping with profound deafness?

If she could handle that with the grace and charm she exhibited on a daily basis, Amira would certainly be able to handle...

Ah...

Idris put two and two together, suddenly seeing the sense behind everything Robyn—*Dr. Kelly*—was saying. One devastating loss was big enough. Something she would have to live with forever. The second? Her dream of being able to hear the voices of the people she would one day serve as leader?

He glanced at his watch, wondering how long it would take to bring Amira back from the zoo. Then again, he still hadn't heard Robyn's surgical plans. He was hardly going to give her hope before he'd heard Dr. Sunshine's proposal.

"Okay, Idris—Your Highness. This is the part for focusing." Robyn's entire body looked as though it were ready to spring from the sofa as she spoke. "I am particularly excited about the different components of this surgery. I think Amira—when I eventually meet her—will be pretty interested to learn she'll be one of the first children to receive a 3-D printout of not one but two inner ear bones. The stapes or stirrup, and the incus—or anvil as it is commonly known. I'm guessing you're relatively *au fait* with this terminology, right?" She didn't pause for an answer, just a quick glance in his direction as she pushed a couple of maps of an ear in his direction highlighting the work she proposed to do. Then, from her seemingly bottomless pit of a satchel, she pulled out a large model of an ear.

"This was more for Amira's sake, but as she's not here, you'll do."

"How very kind," Idris answered dryly. Whether or not Robyn took any notice of his tone was beyond him as she was utterly engrossed in taking apart the pieces of the gigantic model to reveal a beautiful side view of the intricately constructed organ.

"As she was born prematurely, it looks as though a couple of Amira's middle ear bones had some trouble developing completely, leading to the conductive hearing loss and—for whatever reason, it could be her diet, could be all the other factors a preemie has to go through—her body hasn't quite caught up with the development she should have gone through by this point. It's also apparent that the sensory hairs in her ear were damaged at some point. It could have been in the gestational period, but I think it is more likely it was during the labor. Sometimes the use of medicines that are beneficial to the mother can affect the baby—"

"Stop there. I've heard enough."

Idris clenched his teeth, feeling the telltale twitch in his jaw as he did. No one had so much as dared to suggest Amira's hearing loss had been caused by the medical treatment his wife had received. He'd never hold his wife's fight for survival accountable for his daughter's condition. At first he'd thought it had been punishment for being too happy. A beautiful wife, a nation who adored the pair of them, a child on the way... The lightning strikes of how cruel life could actually be had been blunt and unforgiving.

Robyn leaned forward and reached out a hand, taking one of Idris's in her own. His instinct was to yank his hand away. It had been years since he'd known the comforting touch of a woman. Years since he'd thought such a thing would ever be possible after he'd lost his beloved wife. If Robyn noticed, nothing in her expression betrayed the fact.

"This is a big step," she began, the warmth of her fingers beginning to mesh with his own. "For you *and* your daughter. I would rather call the entire thing off if you feel it's too iffy. There is always the option of cochlear implants or bone conducting hearing aids. They do offer excellent opportunities for many hearing-impaired children, but given the damage to Amira's sensory hairs, I believe they'll offer minimal aid in your daughter's case. If you like I can show you the details for the other surgeries."

"No need." Idris extracted his hand from hers and stood, suddenly impatient to get things under way. His own fears, his need to control the situation, would have to be controlled. For Amira's sake. Putting all of his faith in a surgeon for his daughter's well-being terrified him, but something about Robyn told him she would do everything in her power to do what she could for Amira.

"We will do the surgery, as you prescribed, but on one condition."

"Oh! I…uh…" She threw a look over each shoulder as if expecting the condition to appear from behind the sofa.

Idris bit back a smile. She was clearly a doctor, through and through. A negotiator? Not so much. Children seemed to be the medium through which she communicated with the rest of the world. Adults, less comfortable terrain. Or was it just him that made her squirm? A flash of sexual prowess shot through him. Fleeting—powerful enough to leave aftershocks.

"What exactly is this condition?" Robyn shot him a wary look when a giraffe didn't pop up behind her. "I don't dance, sing or play poker if any of those are your poison."

"You will come to Da'har."

Her eyebrows shot up and her mouth popped into a pretty O as she took on board his proposal. She wanted him out of his comfort zone…and it looked as though his request meant she would have to leave hers.

"Why?"

"To spend time with Amira, of course. As you requested," he couldn't resist adding.

Robyn jumped to her feet, raising her hands in protest.

"There's no need for me to leave the hallowed shores of Blighty to do my best in surgery." Her eyes zigzagged between him and Kaisha as if trying to divine a hidden meaning in the request. Demand? Even he wasn't sure. What he did know was if he was going to acquiesce to her demands she'd better be prepared to meet him half-way. Putting his daughter's future in the hands of virtual stranger? Not an option.

"When we're in Da'har—"

"Oh, my goodness me! Let's not count our camels before they hatch!" Robyn laughed nervously, faltered, regrouped, then put on what he suspected was a self-taught stern expression as she wagged a finger at him. "I don't exactly remember saying I would come along. I am the head of surgery at a very busy hospital that—"

"Is under threat of closure and relocation outside of London? Riverside, I believe the new site is called?" he finished coolly.

He was no game player, but if Paddington Children's Hospital was on the brink of an unwanted closure, he had the means to change that. His pockets were deep. Very deep. But his daughter's welfare came first. The thought of losing Amira under any circumstances chilled him to his very marrow. Something just as deep-seated told him Robyn was the woman to perform Amira's surgery, but only after a few more boxes had been ticked. "You will come to Da'har to allay my concerns—"

"Concerns?"

A piercing shot of anger coursed through Idris that she could even dare to suggest he would feel otherwise.

"Yes. Concerns. Shall I spell it out for you? A *father's* concerns. Surely, Dr. Kelly, you are not unfamiliar with the love a parent has for a child?"

Robyn went deathly still. She blinked, hiding behind her eyelids a look of pure, unadulterated grief. When she opened them again, her eyes bore little of the light they'd shone with earlier and Idris knew he was at fault for unearthing a deep sorrow. A hollow victory if ever there was one.

"I will have to talk to the board," she said. "Ensure appropriate replacements can be made…"

"Good." He gave a curt nod, his tone back to its usual brusque efficiency. It wasn't as if he could comfort her. Pull her into his arms and tell her whatever it was that had thrown a shadow over her sunlit eyes would one day be better. He was proof that time was not a healer of all wounds.

"Right. Very well, then. When shall we book your flight? Or, if you care to join us, we will be taking the jet back. Is it tomorrow afternoon, Kaisha? Amira's booked in to see a premiere of some sort tonight—a musical—otherwise we'd be off today."

"You're going to see *Princesses and Frogs*?" Robyn shoved her dark thoughts away, grateful for the distraction. The highly anticipated musical had been sold out for months and months. She'd been hoping to bring some of her friends from the hospital...well, patients, but they always ended up finding a way into her heart no matter how "doctory" she tried to be.

"Yes. Very nice seats, I'm led to believe. Would you care to join us?"

Robyn barked out an ungainly laugh. "I doubt you'd be able to get extra tickets at this point."

"It won't be a problem. We always book out the Royal Dress Circle."

She cringed as Idris caught her raised eyebrows, even more embarrassed at her reaction to the show of wealth when he finished, "In case Amira would like to bring along a friend or two. As you speak British Sign Language, you could be useful if she needs some additional interpreting along the way. Is there anyone else you'd like to invite along?" She felt his eyes traveling down to her bare ring finger and protectively covered her left hand with her right.

She fidgeted for a minute under his cool gaze, then crossed her arms, in a B-grade show of giving his question a few moments' consideration. Idris didn't need to know she was a dedicated singleton. One whose daily torture and pleasure it was to enter Paddington's and spend day after day surrounded by children knowing she would never have one of her own. Lacerating her heart by getting close to yet another young patient was always a risk. One she'd have to take if it meant saving the hospital that had saved her in her darkest days. Her hands, as they always did, crept down to protect the area where she would have carried a child if things had gone differently. If life had been kind. She blinked. Kind. Idris hadn't known much kindness at the hands of Mother Nature, either.

"It would be great if I could come along...to meet Amira." Her brow crinkled as she continued. "In the light of which, I really don't think it's necessary to take up your time and resources to go to Da'har."

"Nonsense. Expense is the least of my problems." Idris tutted, crossing to the sofa where Robyn was sitting. She watched, wordlessly, as he picked up the crumpled ball that was her raincoat and shook it out. The scarf one of "her" kids had given her fell to the ground. When she bent to pick it up, she conked heads, rather impressively, with Idris.

They rose simultaneously, hands clamped on foreheads. As comedy moments went...this was up there. Except neither of them were laughing.

His eyes...those *beautiful* near black eyes of his held on to hers as if they were speaking to each other. A silent conversation winging its way, effortlessly, to her very core where she was feeling rather heated and a little bit...*giddy*.

Da'har was *meant to be nice this time of year.*

Idris regrouped more quickly than Robyn and all she could do was watch his lips as he spoke.

"If you need a few days to rearrange your schedule..." She watched as his Adam's apple dipped and resurfaced. Was he feeling it, too? "I'm quite sure the hospital administration will be…flexible…about your hospital duties when they understand the complexities surrounding your upcoming surgery."

"It's not the surgery I'm worried about." Her fingers flew to cover her lips. *Gulp.* She was really going to have to curtail her out-loud voice.

"Dr. Kelly, I'm not certain how much your administrative team has told you about me, but in order for this surgery to go ahead I'm afraid there are a few hurdles to leap. My daughter is my utmost priority and as much as you want to understand Amira, I need to understand you."

"Oh, no, no. I don't go under the microscope." *Not a chance.* No one—no matter how sexy, powerful and unnervingly sensual they were—no one opened up her private life for inspection. Case. Closed. She dug her trainers into the thick carpet and gave a shake of the head, wishing she'd commandeered her wild spray of curls into some sort of obedience. "Nonnegotiable."

"My daughter, my rule book."

"Ha! Wow." Despite her best efforts to stem her response, she snorted. "Someone's a little used to getting what he wants."

He quirked an eyebrow in response; a ribbon of heat flickered through her belly as she watched his lips part to respond to her, a full octave lower than usual.

"And someone's going to have to learn to be a bit more flexible to get what she wants."

Robyn could've sworn she saw the hint of a smile on his lips before he continued briskly. "You will, of course, need to meet the team you will work with for the surgery in Da'har before I allow it—"

"*Allow* it?" *Sorry, pal.* Sheikh or no sheikh, she and she alone decided whether or not the surgery was green-lit.

"Yes. Allow it," Idris replied, entirely unaffected by her

interior monologue. "I make decisions about Amira and no one else. It's the job of a parent to protect, is it not?"

Robyn bit down hard enough on the inside of her cheek to draw blood as he continued. She'd never be a parent and, as such, was denied any right of reply. This time her silence drew venom.

"How else do you recommend I look after my daughter's welfare?" Idris snapped. He would move heaven and earth for Amira. Retaining control of her medical treatment was paramount. If he had control, he could ensure nothing would happen to her. Loss—the aching, hollowed-out-heart kind of grief he had felt when his wife had died—was not something he would ever go through again. He pressed his lips tightly together as Robyn began, again, to fight her corner.

"By trusting me and the other physicians at Paddington's to do our very best—as we always do," she replied, only just managing to keep the bite out of her own voice. Kaisha, Idris noticed, was inching her way out of the room.

"Then you will do your very best in Da'har."

"Oh, no, no, no." Robyn's index finger went into overdrive. "Not for the surgery. That will happen here." She pointed in the general direction of Paddington's, wagging her finger as if that were the decision maker. "It's Paddington's *world-class facilities*...or nowhere."

The air crackled between them and for just a moment Idris saw a strength in her he doubted few people were privy to. A confidence in her abilities—under her terms—to which he was going to have to acquiesce.

Interesting.

What was it that made Robyn tick? Gave her the strength to disagree with him when everyone else was busy falling over themselves to appease. What would it be like to share the responsibility of Amira's care with someone he trusted?

The thought instantly brought him back to his senses. He had no one. Amira's care was his and his alone.

"I can get you anything or anyone you like to work with in Da'har. What does it matter where the surgery takes place?"

"Everything!"

They both froze. Idris felt his features recompose themselves into the unreadable mask he'd worn for so long while the tiniest of twitches on Robyn's face betrayed a fight against the unwelcome sting of tears. His chest tightened. Yes, he wanted control—but not on these terms.

"Isn't a surgical theater the same anywhere?"

Robyn shook her head, clearly not yet trusting herself to speak.

"My daughter's welfare is paramount. She is happiest in Da'har."

"My patient's welfare is paramount and, as such, *I* am happiest operating at Paddington's."

"Tell me, what's so special about it?"

His softer tone suggested a change of tack. One Robyn felt herself drawn to. Even so, she didn't share. Not even her colleagues knew about the ectopic pregnancy that had ended her dreams of having a family of her own. All they knew was that Robyn poured her heart and soul into Paddington's and was as much a part of the place as the very bricks and mortar.

"Spend time in Da'har with us." A smile—one he should use more frequently—accompanied Idris's words. "If you meet my terms, I will meet yours."

"You mean the operation will be at Paddington's?"

"So long as you join us in Da'har. The sooner, the better."

A trip to Da'har.

Her lungs strained against the thought. Even so...something told her this was a throw-caution-to-the-winds moment. It was not like she was facing a life or death decision. What harm could seeing a children's musical and a couple of days in Da'har do in the greater scheme of things apart from scare her witless by yanking her straight out of her comfort zone?

So she'd have a handful of days not knowing if she was coming or going. Days that could change the face of things at Paddington's, making every moment of scrutinizing looks from the desert kingdom's leader worth it.

Idris's eyes bore down on her as he waited for an answer, a shift of his jawline betraying his impatience.

Her tummy flipped.

And...breathe.

See? Survived the first step.

Robyn gave a quick nod and stuck out her hand in as businesslike a fashion as she could muster. "I trust there will be chocolate-covered ginger biscuits where we're going?"

Maybe not quite as grown-up as she'd been aiming for.

"More than enough." Idris's voice deepened as he mirrored her nod, engulfing her hand in both of his as he did. Why hadn't she noticed how large his hands were before? And how *strong*. And gentle enough in their strength to make her feel...*delicate*.

Crikey. If only she could take a pile of those ginger biscuits back with her and curl up in a corner until every last crumb of them had disappeared. A sugar high might be the only way she'd have the strength to go through with this harebrained scheme.

"Kaisha," Idris called over his shoulder, hands still encasing hers as if they were precious jewels, "can we get the rest of Dr. Kelly's biscuits put in a basket or something so that she can bring them back to the hospital. To *share*." He arched an eyebrow at her, all but proving he'd read her mind.

* * *

A few moments later, a flame-faced Robyn was jabbing at the lift buttons, a wicker basket swinging from her arm laden with enough ginger biscuits to feed an army.

C'mon, c'mon, c'mon! Where was the elite and exclusive service when you needed it? She could feel the Sheikh's bodyguards train their eyes on her, hoping they read nothing into the jiggling she could feel beginning as a hit of nerves overtook her entire upper body.

He'd seen into her *soul*.

How was that even possible? Less than an hour with Idris—Sheikh Idris Al Khalil. Her polar opposite if ever there was one, and yet...

She shot a glance over her shoulder again and grimaced. If the muscle men evaporated she could start banging her head against the controls hoping to knock some sense into herself at the same time. What on earth was she doing? Agreeing to up stakes and hang out in a desert kingdom with the cool-as-a-cucumber mind reader? Her private life was exactly that and she didn't know how many more X-ray vision looks she could deflect.

A low groan filled the space around her. A droning moan of despair. Oh, wait. *She* was making that sound. Oops.

She turned around and flashed the bodyguards a quick smile, which grew brighter when she heard the lift ping and the doors click-clack open.

The sooner she could get back into the comforting surrounds of Paddington's, the better.

CHAPTER THREE

"He said *WHAT* exactly?"

Robyn scanned the sea of expectant expressions, wishing she weren't the center of attention. Limelight and Robyn were not a good combination. But these people were her friends as well as her colleagues. The surgeons and doctors who were pouring their hearts, minds and endless energies into keeping the doors of Paddington Children's Hospital open.

"Well, Dominic, um…" *Why did they send me?* "Biscuit, anyone?" She pushed the basket of sweets to the middle of the surgical ward's central desk and forced on what she hoped was a winning smile.

"Claire said *you* said *he* said you'd have to go to Da'har."

"Hold on a minute, Alistair. You know how I feel about riding the gossip train." She tsked, then gulped as the sea of expectant faces grew more impatient.

"For heaven's sake, Robyn! I'm not engaging in idle gossip, I'm trying to learn if there is even the smallest sliver of a chance we can save Paddington's from this ridiculous move out to Riverside!"

"You know, you have a lovely voice, Alistair. Is that what drew you to him, Claire? The voice?" The more the group stared at her, the more tongue-tied she became. "Can't I just send out a memo or something?"

Rosie Hobbes—still glowing from her recent engagement to Dr. Marchetti—turned her flame-haired bob and made another stab at extracting information from Robyn. "You don't need to give us a blow-by-blow account of what happened with His Excellency, but the key details would be useful."

"You mean Idris?" Robyn crinkled her nose. Rosie's fiancé was, after all, a duke and no one went around calling *him* His Excellency.

A general *"ooh"* that said, *Look who's on first-name terms with the Sheikh*, circled Robyn like an ever-tightening snare.

"Just because most of you lot got swept away with spring fever and are all loved up doesn't mean I can't carry on with a *professional* relationship!" She could've added in a bit about the pregnancy chair having done far too much work this year, but no need to turn herself into a human voodoo doll. Wide eyes continued to stare expectantly. Provocatively. Annoyingly.

"It's August. Cupid's month off. I have it on good authority."

"Methinks the lady doth protest too much," Alistair teased, giving his fiancée, Claire, a little nuzzle as he did.

It wasn't as if Idris was all gorgeous and irresistibly off-limits or anything.

"If you're on a first-name basis," Rosie chimed in, "he's obviously keen for you to do the surgery."

"He is," she conceded. "But when I told him I would only do the surgery here at the Castle, Idris said he would only agree if I went to Da'har."

His name felt both foreign and familiar when she spoke it. A sweetness upon her tongue. Not a sensation to get used to. "Besides, a first-name basis doesn't mean I have to fly out and see his magical desert kingdom by moonlight, okay?"

Maybe Alistair had a point.

"Robyn!" Rosie persisted. "You don't want to move out to the business park of so-called 'Riverside' any more than the rest of us do. Paddington's must stay open. We just want to know if there's anything we can do to help you."

Apart from dropping the playground teasing about Idris, nothing sprang to mind. This was solidly on her shoulders. Unfortunately.

"No, not really. I should probably speak with Victoria about his proposal."

"Your chic Sheikh has asked you to marry him?" Matthew teased, receiving a jab in the ribs from Claire as Robyn's mouth screwed up into an *"eww"* face.

"Is it possible that he's not a chic sheikh?" Rosie asked with false innocence.

"Or that he's not really a sheikh?" Victoria posited, another biscuit disappearing from the ever-diminishing pile.

"Maybe the chic Sheikh already has five wives and our Robyn really deserves to be wife number one."

There was a collective nod of heads.

"Get your heads out of the registry office! The lot of you!"

Too cranky.

She opened her mouth to fix the mood-change grenade she'd tossed into the midst of the group, gaped like a fish for a moment, then dove in. "He obviously loved his late wife very much and from his…less than warm demeanor, I can happily inform you he will be bending his knee and asking me to marry him in—oh, just about never." She grabbed a biscuit and ran her finger along the edge before looking up at her peers. "And don't look so surprised!"

Marriage had been on the cards once, but after her epic fail in the baby-making department? Never again. She needed to contain the situation. Set them straight.

"Don't make fun of my chic Sheikh."

The eyes trained on her collectively widened.

That probably wasn't the best way to handle it, Robyn.

"Gah!" Robyn cried, zigzagging her index finger around the group with her stern expression on full tilt. "All of you are very, *very* silly."

And she would miss them heart and soul if the hospital were to close. Which only meant one thing.

She'd need to buy a suitcase.

She shushed their teasings and proddings, then put on her I'm-the-head-of-department face.

"Idris wants me to go to Da'har for a few days to get to know his daughter better." She looked around the group to garner support that she shouldn't leave Paddington's.

"So go!" Dominic urged. "I'm pretty certain I speak for Victoria when I say this. If it'll help Paddington's—*go*."

"Dominic," she pleaded, "this is your bag, not mine. I'm bound to make an idiot out of myself or put my foot in it."

"Is not going worth compromising the Castle's future?" Alistair's question hushed the group collectively.

"Not fair! You all know how much this place means to me." Paddington's was her heartbeat. Her lifesaver. The job offer to work here had come the same week she'd had her insides removed and her relationship had imploded. It had literally pulled her out of the dark and into a new world of possibility. Of hope that, even though she would never be a mother, she could dedicate her life to helping other women's children survive. Thirteen years later she was still here—but soon Paddington's might not be.

Her eyes moved from surgeon to doctor to paramedic to nurse. Each of them an unwitting role-player in her fight to survive her darkest days. She brightened as an idea struck. "Why don't *you* go to Da'har, Dominic? I already said I'd go to the theater with him. I'll meet Amira there. I'm sure we'll hit it off just fine and then, once the show's over, I'll let His Excellency know it'll be you and not me who'll be joining him in Da'har."

"What?" Rebecca barked through a mouthful of ginger biscuit. "You're going on a sheikh date?"

"Yeah, right. Just like the genie is going to pop out of the bottle and make all my wishes come true when I—uh—rub it."

"Hold on a minute." Dominic raised his hand before giving Robyn's shoulder a gentle rub. "As fun as all of this is, Robyn, you are the Castle's head of surgery, not to mention the doctor who would be performing Amira's treatment. You should not only be going to the theater on your sheikh date, but you should be preparing yourself to eat dates with the Sheikh from afar in Da'har."

"I thought you said we were done rhyming." Robyn grabbed a biscuit and took a defiant chomp. Hopefully it would help mask the jitters launching a Mach-force invasion on her nervous system.

"We are. And you are done prevaricating. Get out the Factor Fifty, my friend. You're going to Da'har." Dominic grinned.

She widened her eyes to appeal to her fellow surgeons. "Being in the operating theater? Piece of cake. I've already thought of an amazing team, and on the cab ride back I checked with one of the specialists at Boston, and he's already looking into flights. It would take his research global. The whole publicity thing? That's your terrain, Dom. You're the one who can get it all over TV."

"And you're the one who can do the surgery that will get Paddington's the right kind of press. But *only if* you go to Da'har and win over the Sheikh!" He finished with a persuasive smile all the while fixing her with his bright blue eyes, and for just a moment she could see why Victoria had fallen for him. Not that she thought of anyone, ever, in that way anymore. Except that a certain pair of inky black eyes flashed into her mental cinema. She blinked them away, forcing herself to focus on the words coming out of Dominic's mouth.

"We can clear your schedule from tomorrow—" He raised a hand to stop Robyn from interjecting, proving just how right she had been to put him at the helm of the PR campaign to save the hospital from closure. He flopped an arm around her shoulders as she squirmed beneath the imploring gazes of her colleagues.

She was great with children and in surgery. Being the object of everyone's undivided attention was—

"Oops—easy there, Ryan!" She lurched out from underneath Dominic's arm to steady the young boy as he tried out his new crutches along the hospital corridors. "Big step up from the wheelchair, eh?"

Ryan beamed up at her, too focused on staying upright to answer back. The seven-year-old had come such a long way from when he'd first been brought in after the horrible primary school fire. He was one of dozens of children now recovering in leaps and bounds because of the help they received here at Paddington's. Help they might not be able to get if she didn't get over herself and board a plane to a place she'd barely heard of let alone was familiar with.

She turned back to the cluster of colleagues awaiting her response. "Fine." She shook her head with a sigh and a halfhearted smile. "You win. I'll go."

A smattering of applause followed her as she grabbed another biscuit and offered Ryan gentle encouragement as he made his way back along the corridor to his room. If he could fight the odds, so could she.

Idris tapped his foot impatiently. Where *was* she? Kaisha, at his request, had rung the hospital to confirm Robyn was coming and had given her the times.

"You said we'd be in the royal circle, didn't you?"

"Yes. I made it clear she was to tell security she was to be allowed through to our section."

As if she'd need it.

"You said seven-thirty, didn't you?"

"Yes. Three times," Kaisha replied neutrally, fingers skidding along her tablet to check the confirmation email that had accompanied the phone call.

It was at moments like this that Idris was a little surprised Kaisha didn't hand in her notice or tell him to put a sock in it. He was hardly a bundle of laughs at the best of times and this was about the tenth time today he'd been insufferable. Not that he was keeping track or anything; it was just…there'd been a shift today. A shift in the currents of his life, as if things were changing course. He had little doubt what shape the change had come in—blond hair, amber eyes…

Change or no, Kaisha shouldn't be the one to take his discord in the neck.

He signaled for her to put her tablet away.

"Stop. Don't worry. The curtain goes up in a minute or two—just…"

Just what? Go out into the whole of London and find her? Bring the production to a halt while they waited? One meeting and she'd already threaded herself into his psyche—a single gold thread in a tapestry of too much unhappiness.

He cleared his throat and reenergized his tapping. Golden presence or otherwise, the woman was late. He wasn't unaware the fault could be his own. It was very possible he'd been too harsh. Shaping his own fears into too acute a display of anger.

He leaned across to Amira and dropped a kiss on top of her curtain of ebony hair as she diligently worked her way through the program, her index finger distractedly fiddling with a loose tooth. He fought the urge to tell her to leave it be. His parents had allowed him free rein to be a child and he owed it to his daughter to do the same. She would bear full responsibility for ruling Da'har one day. For now? She could worry about her loose tooth.

Amira turned to him and pressed one of her small hands onto his knee, mouthing and signing, "Daddy! You're jiggling the entire balcony!"

"I'm sorry, darling. Just excited for the princesses. Aren't you?"

"Of course," she signed, her brows knitting together as she did. "Do you think there will be dancing frogs?" Her fingers lifted and twirled upon her palm as if it were the stage and her fingers the dancers.

"I can't see why not." He gave what he hoped looked like an enthusiastic nod.

Dancing frogs! Definitely not his *milieu*, but if it lit up his daughter's somber expression, then so much the better.

He looked up sharply as the lights began to dim and the initial glimmerings of the musicians warming up drew to a halt in the orchestra pit. He felt his daughter's eyes on him as he responded to the sound of the trill of a flute, a few seesawed notes upon a violin, the rich scales running along the length of a cello, and his heart ached for her. Ached for the day when she would be able to hear what he did. Music. It had played such a huge part in his life before Amira's mother died. The foundation of so many moments. And when the doctors had told him they had lost her, along with his wife's beautiful smile went his passion for singing.

Some murmuring to his right caught his attention. His security staff were—were they laughing with someone? A flash of bright blond curly hair answered how such a thing was possible.

Robyn Kelly.

Like a bright, energetic force of nature—springtime in human form—she entered the area prepared for Idris and his daughter. He felt himself pluck at his suit's lapels, then run a hand through hair he knew didn't need revamping. *Primping!* His facial features tightened at the thought. She was here to impress them. Not the other way around.

Robyn was walking backward, still laughing at something one of the security guards had said, and when she turned around he was struck, just as dramatically as he had been the first time, by the rich amber luster of her eyes. If she hadn't collided with one of the seats and stumbled, he would have likened her to Persephone. But the Greek goddess had turns of darkness which could turn the world cold and decayed. There didn't seem to be anything that wouldn't flourish underneath the warmth of Robyn's smile.

Curiosity struck as she looked up with an embarrassed smile and inched her way along the row of seats toward him. All too quickly he saw the hidden sadness he'd unearthed earlier when her eyes lit upon Amira and then moved to him. A darkness only she was privy to. And, as their eyes met again when she approached him with a mouthed apology for her lateness, he knew in his heart it was true. There were depths to this woman—hidden sorrows she bore on her own without malice or fury in the way his own grief often manifested itself.

A hint of rain and fresh flowers wafted toward him as she settled into her chair, unlooping the strap of her satchel from around her neck. She scanned the location and again, as an expectant hush filled the theater, mouthed how impressed she was by the seats. She then leaned forward and gave a little wave to Amira.

He watched, mesmerized, as his daughter...*smiled.*

What was it about Robyn that brought about such open joy?

His eyes were locked on Robyn's fingers as she introduced herself to Amira—speaking in Arabic first, then the same again in English.

"Robyn," her slender fingers spelled.

"Like the bird?" his daughter asked, eyes clearly glued on Robyn's lips, her tiny fingers mimicking the Arabic sign for *bird*.

"Very close," Robyn deftly signed back. "Shall we use that as my name?"

Idris's eyes flicked between the two—leaning across his lap as if he weren't there, barely cognizant of the curtain lifting above the stage as Amira and this mystery of a surgeon in Mary Poppins mode decided Robyn's sign language name would be that of little bird.

It suited her.

Robyn's fingers continued signing at lightning speed, mouthing the words as she did that they'd carry on the discussion later and come up with a suitable name for Amira during the interval. In the meantime, she drew their collective attention to the warm wash of light and sequined princesses filling the stage—it was time for fairy tales.

As Idris settled back against the seat, he caught himself smiling. It was fairly clear in this particular scenario who was playing the frog.

"May I sit here?" Amira's dark eyes were huge and hopeful.

Robyn watched Idris's face for a reaction.

Who could say no to *that* face?

Not to mention the wash of relief she felt when the seven-year-old pointed at the seat where Idris had been sitting before the interval.

"It is fine with me." She nodded. Hopefully not too eagerly.

Amira's happy smile was such a reward she had to freeze her own grin for a moment, hoping to mask a jab of concern. A shift in the "seating plan" was a double-edged sword. The second her eyes had lit upon the gorgeous little girl, Robyn's heart had swooped up and cinched tight.

An instant connection. And she knew where that could so easily lead. No matter how often she tried to view children as *work*, they always ended up becoming so much more. The number of times she'd opened up the door to her heart only to suffer the excruciating pain of loss…

It was nothing more than a parent would feel. Of course. And that thought alone threatened to blind her for an instant, sorrow eclipsing pragmatism with the knowledge that she would never be a mother herself. Never have the right to love a child as much as she so often did.

She shook her head clear. She'd promised Victoria she would come see the musical as per Idris's request. All part of the deal to save the hospital. It wasn't personal. It wasn't a reminder she'd never have a child of her own. It was a moment to *savor*.

Little-girl-heaven moments, she called them at Paddington's. This was just an out-of-context meeting made more pronounced by the gilt-edged theater, the front row royal balcony seats, the amazing musical and a certain dark-haired, glowering sheikh begrudgingly shifting over a seat so his daughter could sit next to the British interloper.

She grinned as Amira plopped down with a satisfied nod—the female version of her father. Big brown eyes. A black sheet of polished ebony hair. A heart-shaped face and a near permanent expression of earnest intent on her face.

Amira's beauty was hardly a surprise given the gene pool she'd sprung from. Not that Robyn thought Idris was gorgeous or anything… It was just a question of science and personal preference. Just a little. *Okay, a whole lot.* But she had, on her lightning-fast internet search on the way to the theater, also seen how very much in love he'd been with his late wife—another beauty. It explained the imperiously arched eyebrows and pursed lips when he looked at her—a discombobulated mishmash of science and too much heart on her sleeve.

"So what did you decide upon?"

"Sorry?" Robyn looked up to Idris.

"Amira's sign language name."

"Oh!" Robyn leaned forward so that Amira could see her lips, as well, and began signing. "We forgot, didn't we? What would you like your name to be?"

"I want you to pick it," Amira replied somberly.

"Me?"

When Robyn glanced across at Idris, she saw his eyebrows were raised as high as hers felt.

"Maybe we should wait."

"But what if I don't see you again?"

This time she could practically feel Idris's gaze burning into her—expectant. She hadn't exactly given him an answer, had she?

Victoria's words rang in her head again. "We can delay your surgeries, but we can't put off saving Paddington's. We're down to the wire. He may be our last chance." Then she'd added the line that always spurred Robyn into action. "Just think of all this could do for the children."

Unable to meet Idris's questioning gaze, she shifted in her seat, putting her full focus on Amira.

"What do you say we pick the perfect name another time?"

Amira's shoulders slumped a little, while in the corner of her eye she saw Idris's stiffen.

"When I come to Da'har," Robyn amended, not daring to look toward Idris.

She was certain there would be a look of triumph in those dark eyes of his if she met his gaze now. Unwitting or no, he had found her weak spot. The challenge of a parent to even attempt to love their child as much as they did. Their own flesh and blood. How could she, a barren spinster, ever understand what it meant to love a child?

It was possible. Robyn had felt the deep love again and

again. Experienced the pain of loss as many times. And would have to bury her pain if she were to save Paddington's.

Amira looked up at her father, face alight with happy disbelief. As the lights began to lower she swung her head first to Robyn, then to Idris and back again in taut anticipation of the second act.

How to improve upon dancing frogs and swirling princesses? Robyn could hardly stop a giggle from burbling forth. Amira's excitement was contagious.

She had to fight the urge to reach across and hold hands with the little girl, settling on folding her hands in her lap like a reserved nun.

She tsked herself.

If she'd been by Ryan's bedside, the poor lad back at Paddington's who had well and truly captured her heart, she would definitely have taken hold of his hand without hesitation. Or Penelope Craig, with whom she'd spent countless hours reading and rereading the childhood classics. Princesses in attics. Wannabe ballerinas. Discovering magic gardens. She followed Amira's bright eyes as the little girl pushed forward in her seat and leaned against the red velvet balcony ledge to take in the spectacle unfolding in front of them. So…alive! This little girl deserved, at the very least, a shot at having her hearing restored.

So what was making going to Da'har so *difficult*?

When she saw a large hand protectively rub across his daughter's shoulders, she knew the answer instantly.

Idris.

He'd made an impact and it was unsettling her. The man obviously adored his daughter, but his cool reserve felt… not judgy, but…

Critical.

As though each and every thing she did were under a microscope. It made her all squirmy and un-surgeon-like.

Well, tough. This was *her* surgery. *Her* terms. Except, of course, for the parts that were his terms. Rearrange her plans, her surgeries, fly thousands of miles away from her life here and—

A sudden change in the orchestra's music caught her attention. Lots of minor chords and eerie lighting filled the theater as the evil Frog King took his long-legged, menacing strides across the stage toward the beautiful fairy princess, bravely facing the man—frog!—who could change everything with the flick of a—

Before she knew what was happening, Amira had clambered into her lap, eyes still glued to the stage, her little hands reaching for Robyn's so she could be wrapped in the safety of her arms.

Instinct took over. Her arms slipped around Amira's waist, a delicious wash of little-girl aroma filling her senses and she looked to Idris for—what exactly? Approval?

His expression was unreadable. And fleeting. She caught a slight twitch in his jaw as he turned back to the musical as if his daughter was always crawling onto the laps of virtual strangers for a cuddle.

Too much too soon. The vibe was coming off him loud and clear.

Only one way to solve that problem.

She scooped up Amira and handed her toward Idris. His eyes widened, and ever so slightly his implacable expression softened as he reached out his arms and took his daughter, her bright eyes still entranced by the unfolding action of the proud Frog King and the courageous fairy princess.

No chance of art imitating life up here in the royal balcony! Robyn plucked her work pager off her waistband and made a *What can you do?* shrug of apology, scooped up her raincoat and skulked out of the auditorium like the coward she felt.

When she dared to turn around and peek through the red velvet curtains, it was as if she had never been there at all. Amira's arm had snaked around her father's neck as he held her close. Father and daughter. An unbreakable bond.

Robyn turned and all but ran down the stairs, gulping in lungful after lungful of London's cool night air when she pushed through the double doors out onto the street. She held her arm up to hail a taxi, then abruptly dropped it. She could walk to the hospital from here.

A brisk walk would take thirty, maybe forty minutes from the West End given the amount of energy she had to burn. She'd limit herself to an hour at the hospital. Just a chance to peek in on the little sleeping faces. The ones she wouldn't let herself get attached to except, of course, on a professional basis. Hopefully, little Penelope Craig wouldn't be there. Too much time in the cardiology unit for that wonderful little girl.

With each click of her boot heels she added a mental note to her ever-growing tick list.

Sort out her surgeries.
One or two days max in Da'har.
Arm's length.

That was where she'd keep Amira. No more cuddling during the scary bits of West End musicals.

And, of course, her gloweringly attractive father would have to be sure he knew his place. The man had more than a little Mr. Rochester running through him. An image of herself as Jane Eyre flickered into her head and out again when she remembered Jane had to have all that awful tumbling about in the moors in the cold and wet. August in Da'har would be sunny and enriching—not that desert kingdoms had ever been on her radar.

Would she get to wear a gauzy and enigmatically mysterious ensemble? Curly toed silk shoes? Ride a camel?

Her foot caught on the pavement and she only just stopped herself from taking a nosedive onto the hard concrete.

Serves you right, daydreamer.

Back to the checklist.

Her mind shot into the familiar gear of Only Look Forward, Do Not Look Back as the rain began to fall around her in a mist. At first it added a bit of ambience to the evening until heaven wearied of its indecision and cranked open a full-blown downpour.

List-making became more succinct at this point.

Perform the surgery.
Don't get attached. To anyone.
Job done.

"A *fortnight*?"

Idris held the phone away from his ear and looked at the receiver as if he were going mad. Most people would give their right arm to stay at the palace for a day let alone a couple of weeks. He cleared his throat, drew a swift outline of a bird on the hotel notepad and tried again.

"Yes, Dr. Kelly. A fortnight."

Silence.

He obliterated the bird under a thick layer of lead, snapping the pencil tip off in the process. He didn't know why, but this whole business of getting Robyn on board felt more akin to...wooing than asking and receiving.

"Dr. Kelly—a fortnight or we go elsewhere."

Robyn stared at her phone receiver—almost expecting to see Idris's face through some sort of telephonic portal. When she heard him continuing, the irritation in his tone made her relieved this wasn't a teleconference.

"Kaisha will sort out all the particulars and I will be the contact for everything involving Amira and her medical treatment."

"There's no need for that."

"Yes," he said. "There is."

"Whatsoever you desire, Your Excellency."

Since when had she morphed into a courtier?

Robyn hung up the phone without any of the usual niceties and stared out into the corridor where the hustle and bustle of Paddington's continued as if nothing at all had changed in the world.

It had, though. All of the fear that had been gripping the hospital as it rallied its troops under the threat of closure had just taken on a seismic shift. And the responsibility for which direction that shift took was on her. She could almost imagine a tiny halo-wearing Victoria appearing on her shoulder and asking, "Well, Robyn? Are you going to save us?"

She tried to picture Idris with a little pair of horns and a trident on the other shoulder, but he kept turning into a shirtless Poseidon standing—poised for action—at the prow of a beautiful handmade ship, willing to do anything for his daughter's well-being. Even acquiescing, just a little, to an ENT specialist if it meant his little girl would hear one day.

The sacrifices parents made for their children never failed to humble her. The very same sacrifices she would have given to have a child of her own.

Just thinking of Amira brought back the incredible sensation of holding her in her arms last night at the theater. The little-girl limbs, all curled up, sending out wafts of little-girl scent…

"Knock-knock?" Victoria rapped lightly on Robyn's door frame. Victoria wasn't wearing her usual paramedic uniform. She looked like she was power dressing for a meeting. Another reminder of just how important the decision she'd made to go to Da'har was.

Robyn stared at Victoria for a moment, realizing her arms were still holding the invisible child on her lap. She dropped her hands, limp and empty, to hang by her sides. The ache for a child to love would never be appeased.

"So? Are you packing your bikini and sunblock?"

"Ha! I don't think that's considered traditional garb in Da'har."

Victoria looked at Robyn closely. She was good at reading people and today was no different.

"You don't *have* to go, you know."

That answered that, then.

Victoria's brow crinkled with concern, her hand unconsciously slipping to her very pregnant tummy.

Robyn looked away and then up to Victoria's kind, hazel gaze.

"The problem is, my friend, not whether I can bear to go...but whether I can bear *not* to."

"With the future of the hospital at stake, you mean?" Victoria bravely put words to the elephant in the room.

"Yeah." Robyn nodded. "Which is why I said yes."

Victoria's face lit up, her face a real-life version of the sunbeam smiley face on her notepad. "You did? Oh, that's great, Robyn. It's really great! I'm off to meet the board now so I'll let them know." She stepped away from the door frame, then quickly poked her head back into Robyn's office. "If that's all right."

"Of course it's all right." Robyn nodded, laughing at Victoria's burst of enthusiasm. "Now, leave me be. I've got tons to do before I can even think about sunblock!"

"Ugh..." Victoria sighed, leaning her cheek against the doorframe. "I'm totally jealous. The beautiful ocean, the warmth, the freshly squeezed orange juice and the amazing baguettes... And fruit! Think of the amazing fruit bowls—"

"Don't you have a meeting to go to?" Robyn stemmed the flow of excitement with a faux schoolmarm purse of the lips. One aimed more at herself than Victoria. She needed to see this as work only. Not pleasure. "You're making me hungry."

Victoria left with a flutter of her fingers, humming as she went.

At least she'd made *someone* happy.

With fresh resolve, Robyn pulled her keyboard across the notepad full of doodles, masking the grumpy face and thundercloud.

The next few weeks weren't going to be so much of a trip into the unknown as a magic carpet ride into a world where anything was possible.

Fingers crossed that "anything" included restoring Amira's hearing. If the surgery failed?

She gave a quick thumbs-up to Ryan as he steamed by on his crutches.

The surgery couldn't fail.

The hospital's future depended upon it.

CHAPTER FOUR

IDRIS'S STRIDE WAS a single long-legged one to her two. Maybe even two and a half. Robyn was no shorty, but she was practically having to skip to keep up with him. And it wasn't as if she'd *asked* him to show her to her room, so he could drop the whole "being put upon by her presence" thing. Surely a sheikh would have at least a handful of servants to hand. And yet…there'd been no one other than Sheikh Idris Al Khalil himself opening the door to a very un-palace-like palace when the driver dropped her in the semicircular drive of the stone-and-clay building nestled amongst an acre or two of lush gardens.

She ran a few steps, making an exaggerated clatter on the tiles as she eventually caught up.

"It's really beautiful," she tried.

"I'm so pleased you think so."

His body language was the opposite of a delighted host. Didn't they do charm school in Da'har?

Then again, she had been very reluctant to agree to come in the first place so maybe they were a match made in heaven.

Ha! When cats could fly. Or something like that.

"I trust this will do?" Idris flung open a pair of intri- cately carved wooden doors and stepped to the side so that Robyn could enter the bedroom…or…was it an entire *suite* of rooms?

"Idris, it's—" She gave him a gob-smacked double take. "That was a rhetorical question, right?"

Her question went unanswered. Just a slight tightening of those sensual lips.

"It's beautiful, but I don't need—"

He raised his hand and shook his head. "We'd like you to be happy with your rooms during your stay here."

Robyn bit back a less than civil response that might have included words like *enforced* and *commanded* and instead reminded herself that the entire reason for being here in Da'har was because of Paddington's. And one very darling little girl.

"We can put you up in another suite if this isn't to your liking."

"No!" She waved him off as if "settling" for the grouping of rooms she could have easily fit her entire flat into was something she could just about come to terms with. It was the only cover she could come up with to mask the fact she was all but drooling over everything her eyes had lit upon so far.

Four stories of stone, jewel-colored tiles rose above a massive internal courtyard of the palace, whose centerpiece was a vast shallow pool tiled with what looked like millions of little squares and diamonds. A virtual jungle flourished and tumbled from the plenitude of balconies, dipping their jungle green leaves into the expansive pool.

Who knew such a place existed? Perhaps it was where they washed His Royal Excellency's rose petals.

She sniggered, then quickly covered her mouth, aware she was very likely suffering from a severe case of visual overload.

Idris impatiently cleared his throat, to which Robyn offered a polite smile in return. She took a few steps into the room, shoes immediately sinking into sumptuous carpets her high-heels-weary toes just itched to dig into. What had she been thinking when she'd put the ruddy things on in the first place?

Dressing to impress?

Hardly.

She twiddled her toe around a swirly design on the carpet, reminding herself she was here for work and to spend time with Amira.

"Out here is your courtyard." Idris had disappeared from her side and was opening a pair of French windows leading to a lushly gardened patio.

"If you like you can take your breakfast here—"

"Oh! I thought I'd be dining with Amira," Robyn cut in, flopping back onto the bed and only just escaping suffocation by a generosity of silk-covered throw pillows...and a bouncy mattress, too!

She looked up at Idris from her prone position, aware her eyes were perhaps a little too sparkly after the playful bed-tester moment.

His gaze was penetrating and decidedly cool. Chilly slivers of discomfort shot through her veins. She was just testing the bed, for heaven's sake! Give a jet-lagged woman a break!

She pushed herself up awkwardly amid the sea of luxurious bedding, her eyes leaving his to seek purchase on item after item of discreet comforts and immaculate design.

Truthfully? She was still a bit shell-shocked from handing over her surgical roster. She'd lectured and double lectured the team on the importance of attention to detail before being practically pushed out of the hospital and into a waiting taxi by Victoria.

Then there was the first-class flight to Da'har. A first. She had automatically turned right upon boarding the plane and was instantly turned around and steered left by flight attendants who all seemed to have been briefed that she was a guest of His Excellency's.

"The en-suite bathroom is just through here."

Her eyes followed the length of Idris's fingers, loitered just a moment, wondering what their touch upon her skin would elicit, then zoomed past them on to an arched doorway.

Carved marble. *Natch.* To go with the intricately tiled floors that had stretched out before them as they'd worked their way from one end of the surprisingly comfortable palace to the other.

She looked at Idris, a bit taken aback to find his black eyes continuing their indecipherable inquisition.

"You wouldn't mind grabbing me a couple of extra towels, would you?"

Idris's eyes widened as his eyebrows all but shot past his hairline. His very thick, very rake-your-fingers-through-me hairline.

"Ha, ha!" Robyn made a goofy face. "Kidding!"

So much for acting all mature and aloof when she got here. What she wouldn't give for a pair of scrubs and a surgical theater.

She swung her shoulders side to side, wondering why on earth Idris was just standing there staring at her until she couldn't bear it any longer and braved breaking the awkward silence.

"Any chance of seeing Amira? Maybe she can give me the full Monty tour of your pal—palatial home." Still a little weird to call his house a palace. Still a little weird to be in Da'har.

"By 'full Monty' you mean…?"

One of Idris's eyebrows remained aloft while the other dipped into a studiously displeased crinkle.

"Um…" An image of jolly blokes down at the pub doing

stripteases morphed into strobe-lit flickers of Idris tugging off his loose-fitting linen shirt to reveal—

She dragged her eyes away from the expanse of chest and forced herself to meet his detached gaze. She shifted, stupidly nervous he'd poked his head into her mental cinema and not enjoyed what he saw. He'd seen other things, too. Hurt. Loss. Defensiveness.

An urge to have him see more, know more about her, began to override her nerves, and retreated just as quickly. She didn't trust herself to share the real Robyn with a man who seemed to value his privacy as much as she did.

"I'd love to see the place through Amira's eyes and I'm sure you're very busy with, um, ruling your kingdom?"

"I've largely cleared my schedule for the duration of your visit."

Ah.

Unexpected.

Unwanted.

"Not to tend to me, I hope!"

"More to look out for my daughter's interests," he replied dryly.

"Of course."

How could haughty and arrogant look so…so…*rip my clothes off, please?*

Actually, there probably wouldn't even be a "please" in there. Just commands and expectations of obedience.

Which opened a whole other doorway to sexy she'd never thought of before.

Robyn's cheeks streaked with heat. She was going to have to find something to blame for all of the illicit thoughts crowding out her common sense. She seemed to have left the Robyn whose life was only about Paddington's back in customs.

That Robyn was familiar. That Robyn she could deal

with. *That* Robyn had something to fill her every waking moment with! Patients. Surgeries. Research.

This one? The one thinking all sorts of sassy inappropriate things while waiting to see a little girl who was tucked away somewhere in this cavernous palace? This Robyn was really, really in need of something to do.

Idris turned sidelong to her—offering next to no signs of leaving and absolutely no show of being satisfied with what he saw as his ebony eyes raked the length of her.

There might have been a few meters separating them, but his eyes didn't just look...they *inspected*. His gaze felt tactile.

Being naked in front of a million penguins would've felt less awkward.

Her nicest and most conservative "London suit" was making her feel itchy and trapped. When she'd landed, she'd been surrounded by men wearing weather-appropriate *dishdashas*—the collarless ankle-length gowns that looked more cooling than constraining. As did the women's *abayas*. Long, loose-fitting fabrics fluttering prettily in the breeze seemed far more appealing than her snug wool skirt and jacket combo. Blasted British summer! It had been perfect ten hours ago in London.

Idris was wearing Western clothing—a loose-fitting linen top and dark linen trousers—but unlike her, he seemed entirely unaffected by the late-afternoon heat.

Robyn rocked back on her stupidly uncomfortable "business" heels and gave her new...what was he? Boss? Benefactor? Whoever he was, she gave him a sidelong look that she hoped showed him the last thing she was going to do with her time—her precious time—was stand here like a von Trapp child waiting for the whistle blow that would allow her to be dismissed and *do something*. Idle hands and all that.

"Is there some sort of code word I'm meant to be using? Something that will get the ball rolling here?"

Idris's eyebrows tucked together in the center of his forehead and just as quickly drew apart. "You've never had a holiday, have you, Dr. Kelly?"

Who made you Mr. Insightful of the Year?

"Perhaps there's an element of truth to what you say…" she allowed, wondering why she was speaking like an eighteenth-century duchess.

"Have you not ever done anything just for fun, Dr. Kelly?"

Why did he keep saying her name all the time? He'd charmed her into agreeing to leave the hospital; it was fair to say they could follow through on the first-name basis thing.

"It's Robyn," she said through gritted teeth. "And I think we've got a little case of the pot calling the kettle black here, don't you?"

She suddenly realized, as the words hit their intended target, that the two of them were birds of a feather. Maybe not in the billionaire-ruler-of-a-country department, as she ran a department that could easily *spend* a billion…or two.

But in the all work and no play department, Idris seemed as ill at ease with this unexpected "holiday" as she did.

She stood there, unexpectedly transfixed as Idris processed what she'd said. It was, it slowly dawned upon her, unlikely that people ever spoke to him so…frankly. Saw that his solid stance, indecipherable mood and cool response to her agitated shuffling were all defense shields against the less protected business of being human.

Their gazes meshed and the shock waves of heat detonating throughout her body at the union were unlike anything she'd experienced before.

She didn't dare think how she'd respond if they were actually touching.

A shudder of awareness shifted down her spine as she tried to regain control, knowing if she were to open her heart to the man standing before her, she would be powerless to defend herself.

Idris abruptly turned on his heel and left the room. *Her* room.

The one where Robyn would undress tonight and stretch, catlike no doubt, along the length of the bed that he wished he hadn't seen her enjoying so much.

What had he been thinking inviting Robyn to Da'har? To the palace? His *home*? The one place he could hide away from the world and all of the things he didn't want to feel.

Yes, he wanted Robyn to get to know Amira, his cherished little girl, but had he really wanted things to feel so personal?

His jaw tightened at the thought.

Absolutely not was the answer to that one.

He tried to hold back the surge of attraction he'd felt for Robyn just now in long-legged purposeful strides toward his office.

"Daddy!"

His daughter jumped out from behind a tree in the central courtyard, signing his name and mouthing the word in the Da'har dialect he longed for her to hear.

He scooped her up into his arms and swung her around, tightly embracing Amira in his arms as he wheeled around to find Robyn standing at the far end of the courtyard.

"Yes?" he asked, placing his daughter on the cobalt-and-jade-colored tiled bench surrounding the fountain.

"I—I was looking for Amira." Robyn faltered, eyes still locked on his until in a swish and a whirl, Amira, too, saw Robyn and flew from the fountain's edge up and into Robyn's arms as if she were a long-lost...

Oh, no. He didn't dare say "mother." But the smile that lit

up on Robyn's face as she scooped his child up in her arms? It was loving. Unrestricted by the cruelty of life as his was.

A sting of jealousy went through him as he saw the pair of them, gabbling away in a mix of heaven knew what, fingers flashing, eyebrows jigging around, mouths exaggerating words.

Idris caught himself staring at Robyn's lips—a beautiful dusky shade of rose—and for the second time felt a rush of attraction he hadn't thought possible. Whether it felt like betrayal or destiny he couldn't tell. The first word that came to his head told him all he needed to know.

Malikah.

His wife's birth name had crowned her queen before he had fallen in love and made her a true one. Never had the nation known such collective joy as the day they had married.

Never had the nation borne such grief as the day she had died giving birth to their daughter.

This precious jewel of his who was— His eyes zapped across the courtyard. Was Amira laughing?

His eyes widened as he took in the sight and rarely heard sound of his daughter's laughter. Robyn was tickling Amira's little tummy, eliciting burble after burble of giggly laughter.

Extraordinary.

She was normally such a stern little girl.

Took after her father, everyone said. Took her future responsibilities incredibly seriously for such a young child.

He'd taken the words as praise. Had felt *prideful* his daughter's tendencies were to take seriously the role she would eventually hold as Sheikha, and yet...

The sound of her laughter—more beautiful than that of all the birdsong in the land—swept a slash of doubt across his clean conscience.

Robyn rose from her kneeling position and took Amira's hand in hers, realigning her features into a hopeful expression.

"Amira and I need your help," she said.

"Oh?"

Winning comeback, Your Excellency. And since when did he speak to himself in the third person? Life had made certain he knew that he, too, was only human when his wife had been taken from him. He shook his head. Robyn might be suffering from jet lag but he was suffering from... brain lag.

"Yes, we need your help." Robyn signed something to Amira, who turned her expression, now very grave, toward him. "We've got a bit of a language barrier and hoped you could help."

Amira mouthed and signed their "secret" language. They'd developed it over the years as a sort of father-daughter shorthand. And right now his daughter was very emphatically telling him Robyn's shoes were silly, too hot to be worn in Da'har, and needed to be changed. As was her suit. They should go to the souk.

Idris's eyes widened.

She'd never asked such a thing before.

They rarely left the palace grounds excepting public celebrations where he and his security team could keep their watchful eyes upon her.

"We can get someone to fetch everything Robyn needs," Idris replied.

"It could be fun!" Robyn interjected. "I've never been to the souk," she added, her shy smile prizing apart his decision not to leave the grounds.

"Nor has Amira." Idris addressed this solely to Robyn in a tone few would mistake as approving. There was a reason this was so. Why her outings were predominantly only for state occasions.

The crowds, the frenetic bustle, the chaotic mayhem the market could burst into without a moment's notice. Even with bodyguards he had never thought the journey appropriate. Not for a little girl. Not *his* little girl.

"It would be madness if we were to just appear at the souk." He pressed his heels against the tiled floors, rising to his full height. "Not *fun*."

He felt a tug on his hand.

Amira's fingers wrapped around just one of his as her other hand curled into a soft little fist and rubbed in a circle over her heart.

Please.

Sign language was an evocative thing.

Her expression mirrored the word.

Please.

He thought back to his own childhood. Free of bodyguards. Endless hours wandering the souks and sprawling communities fanning out from the exquisitely designed city center. Speaking to the people whose lives he would one day hold responsibility for. Listening…

Exactly!

Listening.

It would be difficult for Amira. Too difficult. Too many people who would crowd and surround her, keen to tell her their stories with no means of communicating.

Stories she might one day hear if this infuriating blond woman standing in front of him, elbows akimbo, loosely curled hands propped on hips, would see some ruddy sense in the decisions he made.

No souk.

Not today.

He felt a tug on his fingers and looked down at the little, expectant face tipped up toward his.

Two against one.

He rolled his eyes heavenward only to have them land on a smiling Robyn upon their descent.

This, he was beginning to think, was going to be an awfully long fortnight.

"This is such fun, don't you think?" Robyn smiled cheerfully, seemingly immune to Idris's increasingly dark mood as they obeyed his daughter's insistent beckoning to enter another clothing store.

Idris made a noncommittal grunt. *Fun* wasn't exactly the word he would've chosen. The perfect recipe for an ulcer was more like it. Ditching the security guards at his daughter's insistence meant he was the one weighted with the bags and boxes of clothing and scarves Robyn had accrued.

Thus far.

Or should he say, the items Amira had accrued on Robyn's behalf. The poor woman was as powerless as he was in the face of Amira's untapped shopping gene.

Idris ruled, with meticulous detail, an entire *kingdom*, for goodness' sake! And here he was being pulled willynilly down the never-ending twists and turns of the maze that was the capital city's largest souk.

"Just one more?" His daughter struck her most forlorn and wide-eyed expression.

He had to smile as she didn't bother waiting for an answer and tugged him into the store—walls all but hidden by silks, tunics and headscarves.

Robyn's arrival seemed to have transfigured his serious little girl into little less than a high-powered personal shopper as she inspected the beautiful fabrics and clothing items on display, then casting an appraising eye over Robyn, who was, he had to admit, playing along rather wonderfully.

She would turn and sashay and kneel down so Amira could hold the fabrics up to her strawberries-and-cream complexion, every now and again, flicking those amber eyes up to meet his for what exactly he wasn't sure.

Approval?

The stirrings of something he hadn't felt in a long time— seven years to be precise—told him all he needed to know. They'd done enough shopping for today.

"I think your daughter would do well in Paris!" Robyn stood up, laughing, when Amira rejected another ream of richly colored *sarwals*—the formfitting trousers that drew a man's attention directly to a woman's ankle.

He could feel his jaw tighten at the thought of Amira growing up at all. His little girl. His precious little girl.

"My daughter does perfectly well in Da'har."

"I wasn't suggesting—" Robyn protested, then stopped, her eyes glued to his as if trying to divine why he'd gone all prickly. "Of course she does," she said gently. "Just look at her."

His eyes stayed on Robyn just a moment longer as she turned to watch Amira inspecting pairs of traditional leather shoes much to the shopkeeper's delight. She used her own form of communicating, a mix of mouthing the words in the local Da'harian dialect and miming movements or pointing. She was never inhibited by her inability to communicate in the traditional fashion. Never one to behave as though she had a disability. For her, this was normal. A normal Idris couldn't bear for her to endure. She deserved every gift of the senses he had and more! She was his daughter, for heaven's sake! The woman standing next to him was the one who could make it possible. He hadn't realized how frightening it would be to invest so much faith in one person. So much hope.

For her part, Robyn appeared openly charmed with Amira's mad-dash shopping bonanza, her eyes shining with unchecked delight. What she didn't know was that the little girl, beaming, expertly folding and unfolding the headscarves, was *bargaining*, for heaven's sake, negotiating for this *dishdasha* or that pair of harem trousers—she wasn't the little girl he saw very often. And watching her come to life as she did with Robyn was more painful than he could have imagined.

They were moments Amira should be having with her mother. The mother she would never know. He turned again as Robyn joined his daughter, each of them running an appraising finger along the intricately designed sandals, their heads bent together—one black as midnight, the other impossibly golden—and his heart cinched even tighter.

"All right, then." His voice sounded jagged amid the happy buzz and hum that had filled the shop mere seconds earlier. "Time to go."

Drawing any sort of banter out of Idris on the car ride home was proving next to impossible. The pulling-blood-from-a-stone variety.

His jet-black eyes were trained on the roads as they whizzed past the beautiful structures that made up the old town. A vividly modern section of the city lay closer to the airport, looking every bit the hotbed of Middle Eastern business Da'har was purported to be.

She turned to peek at Amira, who had fallen asleep amid the tumble of boxes and shopping bags, her beautiful little face framed in tissue paper and silk ribbons.

Focusing very stoically on the beautiful capital city was the only way Robyn could stem a sudden stingy tickle and tease of tears. She scratched her nails along her legs as they balled into fists.

You can love her from a distance.

She squeezed her eyes tight.

You shouldn't let yourself love her at all.

"Everything all right?"

"Yes, fine." She looked up, surprised Idris had noticed

her change of mood at all. "Just a long day, is all." An end-less future without a child of my own...

"If you look just over to your right—" he slowed the speed of the four-by-four "—you will see the Museum of Swords."

"Of *swords*?"

"Absolutely. There are a few of my father's in there and—" he chuckled more to himself than her as if remembering the rake of a man he may once have been "—one or two of mine."

Clear as day she saw Idris tugging not one but two wide-lipped scimitars from horn-and-ivory cases, crossing the flashing blades in front of him, shielding Robyn and Amira from...camel-riding marauders intent on kidnapping them from their Bedouin tent—carpets and all!

"Goodness."

Idris unleashed a full-throated laugh at her prim, English response. Little did he know she was busy A-Thousand-and-One-Nighting it now that she had a more appropriate wardrobe. Or was it the *someone* playing the dashing knight who'd unbuckled her imagination?

She felt her lips purse at the thought, barely hearing him as he talked her through each of the buildings they passed.

She didn't *fancy* Idris.

He was too...too gorgeously unattainable to plain old crush on.

Unh-unh. Apart from which, there was the very obvious point that men like him didn't desire people like her. He was serious to her scatty. He could do limelight. She'd rather hide in an operating theater than be the object of attention. He was a sun, she was an orbiting moon—happy to enjoy the light and heat and *electricity* of his presence from afar.

Hmm. Maybe she did fancy him. Just a little.

Her gaze lowered and slid toward him as she tilted her

chin to make it look like she was memorizing the facts he was rattling off rather than ogling him.

Idris Al Khalil was beautifully sensuous in the most masculine of ways. Strong-featured. Stoic. Commanding. And she? While they were about the same age, she felt past any sort of prime she might have had. No, she wasn't *old*, but...losing the ability to have children all that time ago seemed to have stolen something from her. Perhaps as losing his wife had stolen that rare, wonderful laugh from Idris. Her fingers pressed into her lips to stem a sigh.

"And this, over here—" she followed his fingers as they lifted off the steering wheel and pointed to her left "—is the Old Castle."

The structure rose from the ground as if it had been there a thousand years. More opulent fortress than French château, there were acres of towers and soaring walls, wooden shuttered windows closed against the late-afternoon sun that made the air smell hot and heavily spiced.

"So, you live in the...New Castle?"

Again, Idris laughed, but as it faded away, so, too, did the light she'd seen in his eyes as he pointed out the architectural jewels in his family's crown.

"No," he replied. Then again, harder. Flintier. "No."

He turned a corner from one street to the next, the light shifting to a rosy golden hue as the sunset caught the harbor city in its full glory.

"This was the New Castle."

A broad avenue stretched out before them. Something akin to the Mall leading up to Buckingham Palace. Something fit for a king. At the top of the avenue was a gloriously modern structure, resplendent in its nod to traditional architecture, unerring in its thrust toward the future.

It was a modern-day Taj Mahal, she knew at once. No longer a palace to be lived in, but a seven-year-old testament to love.

Out of the corner of her eye, she saw Amira stir and wake, her eyes blinking into understanding as to where she was. Her little hands pressing against the window as she blew kisses to her mother's tomb.

Another hit of emotion burned the rims of Robyn's eyes so strongly she was forced to turn away from it all. Idris's stoic profile, the little girl lost in thought over a mother she'd never know and a palace standing in the midst of Da'har's many people—empty and alone.

CHAPTER FIVE

"Let's have a fashion show, shall we?"

Robyn looked as astonished as Idris felt hearing that collection of words coming out of his mouth.

Fashion show?

And yet…

All of their moods had taken a discernible dip after they returned but somehow the somber atmosphere didn't seem fitting with Robyn around.

He'd had seven years of walking around like the god of thunder and retribution, perhaps a new turn as…something else was in order.

"Come along." He nodded toward the large pile of untouched boxes and paper-wrapped packages. "We weren't dragged across Sanhella's largest souk just to sit here watching you grow more and more uncomfortable in that suit of yours."

A hot flash of primal instinct took hold of him as he pictured Robyn revealing for them, veil by veil, the layers of delicate silks and diaphanous wraps concealing her slender figure, currently unartfully hidden in the boxy suit she'd arrived in.

"I really don't think that's necessary." Robyn shook her head, clearly uninterested in displaying her wares, silken or otherwise.

A flush crept up the length of her neck as she busied herself with finishing off a savory pastry parcel they'd brought home from the souk, a parting gift from a vendor who'd spotted them loading up Robyn's purchases.

"I insist," he said, wincing at the unintended harshness in his tone, and tacked on smile, hoping it would soften the moment. He'd have to work on his "order" voice before Amira could hear. He'd have to work on a lot of things.

He glanced over at his daughter innocently finishing the picnic dinner they'd opted to have in the central atrium, her little brows furrowed together in their usual cinch as she worked out the spices and scents each savory morsel afforded.

There were servants and formal dining rooms and even more formal rooms for impressing visitors in the government buildings—not too far away—but this house he'd designed after Amira was born was their sanctuary.

He was surprised to realize having Robyn in his home felt right. As if she were someone who immediately saw it for what it was—a retreat from the world and a reminder of everything that was beautiful as his heart fought the darkness that so often threatened to consume him.

"Would a single showing along the catwalk suffice?" Robyn asked as a put-upon soldier might inquire of a general demanding his boots be polished every fifteen minutes.

He nodded curtly. Too curtly given the internal ticking off he was giving himself for just that sort of brusque behavior. Behavior that had near enough held everyone he had once loved at arm's length. Friends, advisers—aunts and uncles who no longer knew how to deal with the coldness he knew exuded from him the day his heart had all but withered and died. The only thing that had kept him alive was the little girl sitting across from him. The one throwing him a "fix it now, Daddy" look as Robyn's discomfort increased.

"Please," Idris asked, palms turned upward in an open appeal to her generous spirit. "Please show us how you look in your new outfits."

Under Idris's dark-eyed gaze...Robyn felt as if there was no escape. As if he were looking straight through to her very soul. His long-lashed eyes easily swept aside the bluster and Englishness she hid behind, seeing instead the particles making up the invisible essence that was her spirit. The very kernel of who she'd become in the aftermath of her painful loss. And yet he didn't know a thing.

That she was a woman who ached. A woman who felt the loss of her unborn child as if it had happened yesterday.

Idris moved his hands forward in a genuine entreaty for her indulgence, eyes shifting toward Amira, then back to hers.

The request wasn't just for him. It was for his daughter, and no points for guessing how powerless she was in that department.

Little Amira had all but wrapped her around her finger and she'd only been in the country a handful of hours. Ridiculous!

She swept some invisible crumbs off her cheeks, hoping the gesture made excuses for the pink she knew was there, and pushed up from the cluster of pillows she'd been leaning on while they ate.

"There's a powder room off to the left," Idris directed once she'd filled her arms with packages, much to Amira's delight.

Of course there was.

And, if she asked, there would probably be someone to come along and help her figure out how to make the best of the meters and meters of fabric Amira had selected. The fact there wasn't a collection of servants lining the atrium had her feeling grateful, if not a little surprised, that Idris seemed to live so privately.

The palace bore a far more personal touch than she would have suspected. Idris was all cut glass and black marble, but this place—this *home*—looked as if someone had conjured up the mythical Hanging Gardens of Babylon. But, as he'd told her over supper, it had all come from Idris—from his thesis project in university where he'd studied architecture and, of course, politics.

What a project! A love letter to the traditional architecture of his land, with secret, little hidden-away connections to the modern world. Wi-Fi, built in radios, tablets lying out of sight, but always within reach, if ever a person wondered what if…and the answer was only a tip and a tap of a keyboard away.

The more he spoke, the more she saw this place was the dream child of his complicated mind, the heart that had known such sorrow and a mind that bore, surprisingly, an extraordinary imagination. For a man who came across as being utterly rigid about his beliefs and ways, his home was almost whimsical.

She turned just before going into the changing room and saw he was watching her. Two of the boxes tumbled out of her hands and as she lurched to catch them she managed to lose her grip on the bags dangling precariously from her fingertips.

She dropped almost gratefully to the floor to collect everything up, then crawled into the changing room—mercifully out of sight.

Wow, did she hate the limelight.

"Another one!"

Robyn gave a playful eye roll and turned back toward the changing room.

So far they'd seen three outfits and, with each one,

Robyn had softened and relaxed in the "glare" of her audience's eyes.

Idris felt a tug on his sleeve. His daughter was facing him, her face alight with excitement and hands whirling with a rapid-fire list of demands.

Pull the curtains together. Robyn needed a place to have a "proper" entrance. Where was her dress-up box? Could she please wrap his head in a turban and draw on a mustache. Why should Robyn be the only one to dress up?

Laughing, he pulled his daughter into his arms, rose and swirled her around, eliciting squeals of delight as he swung her over the fountain's edge.

A phone call later, boxes appeared and Idris found himself near enough nose-to-nose with his daughter.

Robyn peeked out from the changing rooms only to find curtains had been drawn between the two columns she had been using as a stage. She'd heard Amira's squeals earlier, and now could hear the little girl's laughter. She chanced a glance between the curtains, her own lips twitching into a smile as she saw the scene unfolding before her.

With a face as serious as a general's, Amira had one hand planted on her father's head as she fastidiously went about drawing on the curliest mustache Robyn had ever seen with the other. Idris sat patiently, his caramel skin becoming less visible beneath the swirling magnificence of his daughter's artwork. Amira pulled back and eyed her handiwork. Idris pulled a couple of faces, giving the drawn-on mustache life and eliciting another peal of laughter from his daughter. Next, she pulled a length of opalescent silk out of a wooden crate and gave it swirl after swirl upon his head until he had a beautifully wrapped turban atop his head. He jumped up and struck a pose on the side of the fountain for her, feigned losing his balance so well Robyn almost jumped through the curtains to help—

Help what? Interrupt a beautiful moment between a father and daughter? For every part of her that ached to be with them, enjoying the moment, there was another part reminding her that this was not her world. Not her life. Arriving in Da'har had felt akin to handing over her passport to a different universe. Not just the different sights and sounds, but different feelings, responses. She sucked in a deep breath. English Robyn would run back to her room and hide rather than show off the outfit she felt strangely at home in. She blew the breath out, pulled her shoulders back and smiled. She wasn't English Robyn right now—she was the Little Bird of Da'har and she felt as though she could fly.

"How's this?" Robyn asked, sweeping open the drapes of the changing rooms and spinning along the "catwalk" in a swirl of diaphanous fabrics. The light chiffon lifted and floated as Robyn's hips and shoulders shifted and moved against the silky softness.

Idris looked up and was instantly mesmerized. If Robyn was amused by his mustache and turbaned look, she didn't show it. If anything, she looked emboldened.

As she sauntered one moment, then twirled another, Robyn looked as he imagined she would have as a younger woman—a giggling girl playing dress-up. And at times, when his eyes caught with hers, he saw a woman discovering a sensuality blossom within her. A sensuality she'd never known she possessed.

Until now.

Idris sat upright, utterly transfixed as their eyes locked. His body grew taut with desire for her.

He wanted Robyn. Wanted to pull her to him, shift away the deep emerald chiffon and lace headscarf with a sweep of his fingertips. His hand twitched. One step led to the next as imagination and desire melded into one. He would take hold of the back of her head, his other hand slipping onto the weightless silk that caressed her back and pulled her to him so that he could taste the bright red of her lips, her mouth. Urgently. Hungrily.

The sound of his daughter's clapping jarred him into the present. Into reality.

Their eyes still caught together, Robyn's body frozen mid-twirl, Idris tried to communicate all the things he couldn't say—couldn't put a voice to. As Robyn's eyes widened, then narrowed with understanding, shame and anger obliterated the romantic notions.

Robyn wasn't here to be his lover. Not even a friend. Her presence here was strictly business and he was a fool to think—even for a moment—she could be anything to him but a means to an end. The solution to his daughter's plight.

"Perhaps we've had enough fun for tonight."

"Yes," Robyn said. "I think I'll turn in straightaway if you don't mind." She turned to go, tripping as she did. The first time that night. For the past hour she'd felt beautiful. Graceful.

Amira rushed up to her when she realized Robyn was leaving and wrapped her arms around her waist.

Robyn gave her a quick squeeze and dropped a kiss on top of her head, then hightailed it to her room, desperate to hide the tears she knew would come.

"Excellent!" Robyn accepted the pile of folders from Dr. Hazari. "These are all of her records?"

"His Excellency said to ensure you had everything you need."

Robyn didn't need a mirror to tell her that her eyebrows were knitting together. All she wanted was a little "me time" at a hospital. Amira's actual records were just a bonus.

"Has he—? You haven't spoken with him this morning, have you?"

"Of course," he said. "Her Royal Excellency's medical papers aren't something we just hand over to anyone."

"No," she said. "Of course not." She looked at the papers and then back to Dr. Hazari. "And you just pick up the phone and call him?"

"On matters relating to Amira—yes. Absolutely. He is always available to speak when it is about his daughter."

"How very...*accessible* of him." No staff, no go-betweens. A protective lion of a father.

She gave Dr. Hazari a smile of thanks, turned her attentions to the files and found she could only see one thing.

Idris Al Khalil.

The caramel skin. The proud set of his cheekbones drawing her attention first to the ebony sheen of his eyes, then tugging her along the descent toward the full, deep red of his mouth. Her pulse quickened at the memory of his lips parting when she had last appeared "onstage," an emerald headdress skating along the edges of her blond hairline, an even deeper green *dishdasha* skimming her skin as Idris's inky gaze unleashed prickles of anticipation across her entire body.

The man had haunted her dreams. That alone had been miracle enough because sleep had been a long time coming after she'd left him and those hauntingly evocative eyes of his.

Enough!

She snapped the folders into a precise pile and began meticulously working her way through them, ignoring the little tugs and pulls of guilt teasing away the well-stitched hemline of her conscience. So what if she'd snuck out of the palace and found her way to the hospital on her own. That's what guidebooks were for. Right?

A few hours in the hospital wouldn't hurt anyone. Especially not the impenetrable fortress that was Idris.

She squeezed her eyes shut against the image that had kept her awake well into the night. Idris's usually implacable expression softened.

A smile crept onto her lips. And it wasn't just the memory of his swirly mustache. It was the whole picture. The proud father indulging an excited daughter. The host enjoying his guest's discovery of his country, his home. It was a side to Idris she suspected few people saw. A warm, loving family man at home with face painting and a spontaneous fashion show.

And when their eyes had met?

She couldn't help a little happy hum as she relived the moment. Idris's gaze had held something stronger in them than approval. They had sparked and fought the same thing she was feeling when she looked at him. Desire.

She sucked in a deep breath and held it.

Longing. Passion. Love.

She didn't do those sorts of things. Not now. Definitely not in the future. And all because of the past she'd never laid to rest. A past she'd had to deal with on her own.

How quickly news of an unexpected pregnancy had turned into the darkest of horror films. She'd been so happy. A wonderful boyfriend. Maybe a marriage? The ectopic pregnancy. Too advanced. Low to no survival rate. For herself and the child unless…

She looked up from the sofa where she'd been sitting and wondered if her subconscious had led her here.

The maternity ward.

Just like any hospital she'd ever been to, there was the row of beautiful babies, swaddled in soft blankets of pink or blue. Little eyes clenched tight against the world they'd only just entered, lips puckering, fingers reaching for the mother they were inextricably linked to.

Her baby hadn't come to term before they'd had to end the ectopic pregnancy threatening her life...but, oh, how she had ached to hold him. *Would* ache so long as she drew breath. It still astonished her how impossible it was to forget that tiny little child.

The breath released from her chest in a whoosh of regret.

She picked up her phone and did a quick calculation. Too early to call the hospital. Then again, surely *someone* she knew would be on night shift. She tapped the little green phone receiver icon, needing to hear a familiar voice.

"Is this how you always conduct your research?"

A shiver of recognition slipped along her spine, pooling in her belly.

Maybe not that particular voice.

She looked up from the phone, scanned past the pair of long legs, along the arms crossed over a linen-shirted chest and up, past the...stubble? Interesting. Idris was normally immaculately well-shaven.

"If you mean by going to a hospital to look at all of Amira's records, then yes," she replied with more verve than she felt.

She stood so she felt less like a five-year-old being told off outside the headmistress's office. It didn't stop her cheeks from burning, though. As she rose, Idris didn't take the customary step back one generally hoped for in the personal space department. Proximity only made her response to him deepen. She tilted her chin up and met his gaze with as much defiance as she could muster. Difficult, when her body was a bit busy doing its own thing—heart rate accelerating, the whoosh and roar of her body temperature soaring as her eyes met his. The physical need to reach out and touch him was near enough overwhelming every practical bone in her body.

"I meant sneaking out of the house and causing great distress to my daughter, who thought you'd left. Thought you weren't interested enough in spending time with her to do the surgery." His lips pressed together tightly as if he could've said more but was biting the words back against his better judgment.

All the swirly feelings swooping around Robyn's body like giddy hummingbirds plummeted into a weighted mass in her gut.

"I didn't think—"

"Precisely," Idris cut in. "You didn't think. I'm hardly surprised to learn you don't have children of your own if this is how you treat children under your care."

From the streak of pain searing across Robyn's amber eyes, he knew in an instant he'd been cruel.

She stood, frozen in place, visibly digesting the sour spill of words he'd spat in anger. What could he have said instead? That he'd woken to discover an empty room, no sign of Robyn anywhere in the palace, his little girl's stricken face when she thought Robyn had fled? How could he tell her he'd been frightened, too? That he'd been left on his own again. That fear had manifested itself as rage.

"You'll be happy to hear, Your Excellency, I can't have children. A—a *procedure* I had in my twenties made sure of that."

He tore his gaze away from Robyn's, unable to bear the burden of guilt he bore for the sorrow in her eyes.

"I'm truly sorry," Robyn continued, her voice devoid of the light it usually carried. "I never meant to hurt Amira. Or to pull you away from her to hunt me down." Robyn gave the files a distracted look and swiped at her eyes where she'd lost the battle with a handful of tears. She looked up at him, cheeks flushed, voice hoarse with emotion. "And I never meant to hurt you."

In that moment, Idris was consumed by a need to hold her in his arms until all the hurt and pain he'd caused went away. How could she be so generous with her apologies, so *heartfelt*, when he had been so unkind?

He opened his arms and pulled her toward him, unsurprised to feel her stiffen, then—much to his amazement—feel her relax into his embrace, laying her cheek against his chest as if seeking solace in the beat of his heart.

He did his best to steady his breath, quell the racket thumping around his rib cage, a little too aware of Robyn's wildflower scent, the soft femininity of her hand pressing against his chest.

He laid his cheek alongside her temple, astonished that Robyn, despite having seen his darker side, was bringing the man he'd once been back out into the light. The one who comforted, smiled and laughed. The one who enjoyed being *alive*!

For seven years he'd been shut off to that man. More attuned to one who saw the world through a filter of grief, frustration and fear for his daughter's well-being.

And yet, here he was, holding Robyn in his arms, conscience pricking at the harsh judgments he'd made as if he alone were bearing the weight of the world.

He traced his fingers along Robyn's temple, drawing them to her chin, only realizing as he caressed her cheek with the back of his hand that she was wearing a headscarf. Sky blue. It matched her personality, full of light and optimism.

The Da'harian style had seemed so natural on her when he'd first caught sight of her on the sofa; he hadn't even thought to remark on it. Or perhaps his relief at finding her had made him blind to everything else.

He held her close, neither of them saying anything, their breaths joining in a growing cadence with the other's.

They shared the understanding of loss. He knew that now.

This and a thousand questions filled his mind as he

stroked her cheek with the backs of his fingers, relieved, at last, to feel her steadied breath upon his wrist. He crooked his index finger and tipped her chin up toward him, telling himself it was to ensure there were no more tears in her eyes, but the ease with which he could have leaned down and kissed her all but blindsided him.

Robyn blinked at his wide-eyed response to her, then gave a shy smile as she gently extricated herself from his embrace.

"Was that our first fight?"

"I suspect, my dear, it won't be our last."

My dear?

He checked himself. Best not to get too carried away. Emotions could far too easily take the helm when it came to Amira. They'd had a moment. Nothing more. He shook his head again, taking a step backward, only to barely avoid colliding with a passing nurse.

"Your Excellency!" The woman turned when she saw who he was, blanched and performed a quick bob.

He clucked away the gesture with a smile and a shake of the head. Adulation of any sort had never suited him. Earning the respect of his people was all that mattered.

"So!" He turned back to Robyn, masking his discomposure with what he hoped was a businesslike nod. "I suppose meeting our Ear, Nose and Throat specialists was on your tick list."

"Yes." She nodded, relieved to be back on familiar terrain. "I really would like to meet the entire team if possible. It would be particularly helpful to see where and who will be giving Amira her aftercare."

"Won't you be doing that?"

"Immediately after the surgery, of course I will, but... when you both return home, I'll be at Paddington's. Or wherever we end up if this closure goes ahead."

Her smile seemed unnaturally bright. As if she were

forcing on the same show of bravura he was in the wake of the moment they'd just shared. Pain, loss and the unexpected understanding that neither of them was alone.

The reminder that Robyn would be in and out of their lives so briefly shook the new sense of grounding he'd felt since she had come into their lives. He had borne so much alone that having her here felt like putting back together the pieces of a puzzle he'd never known had come apart.

"Well." He returned the artificially cheery smile. "Isn't it lovely we still have the best part of a fortnight together to sort out all the particulars? Now that I can allay Amira's fears about your mysterious vanishing, I trust I can safely leave you to your own devices here at the hospital for a handful of hours. We will, however, look forward to you joining us for lunch back home. And," he continued, trying his best not to stare as her mouth formed an inquisitive moue, "I hope you don't mind, but I have organized for some of your new things to be packed. We're going on a little trip this afternoon."

"Oh?"

His announcement seemed to have reduced her to monosyllables and widened eyes, but he noted with a satisfied smile that it was the first time she hadn't protested.

"Right, then." He gave a curt nod. "Shall I leave you in Dr. Hazari's capable care?"

Robyn nodded, her dazed expression mirroring everything he was feeling internally. There was something they shared now. A silent understanding of the burdens of grief. One he made no effort to hide from the world, while she… Robyn bore her grief for her own loss with tenacity and a fierce show of happiness. The light to his shade. The two essential components to make an object real.

He ground his teeth together and lengthened his stride. A walk rather than the high-speed drive he'd made to track Robyn down might be in order.

He was letting her under his skin. Too much. Too deep. And far too personal for his liking.

Robyn's presence here was solely for Amira, he reminded himself, putting meter after meter behind him in quick succession. None of this was personal excepting where it affected his daughter and her well-being. It was the only logical explanation for the surge of emotion he had experienced this morning.

He pushed open the doors to the hospital and looked out onto the busy street.

The early-morning bustle of the day sped past him as people went about their daily lives, blissfully unaware their leader was very busily trying to yank Cupid's wayward arrows out of his chest.

CHAPTER SIX

"WELL, THIS IS all a bit mysterious." Robyn tried her best to keep the trepidation out of her voice, but could see she'd been unsuccessful when Idris all but rolled his eyes.

So much for finding her way back into his good books. He'd been aloof ever since he'd left the hospital. Well. If aloof meant not around, then he had been extra aloof.

Not that she could blame him.

This was a business trip, not a touchy-feely sobfest about her bad luck in the procreation department. Her focus was meant to be on Amira and Paddington's future. Two diligent hours of work at the hospital later, she was back at the palace, wearing her best winning smile, trying to make up for the morning's unintended gaffe.

She felt a tug on her hand. Amira. "Do you like horses?" she asked.

"Very much." Robyn nodded emphatically. Riding had actually been one of her favorite escapes a few months after she'd had the hysterectomy. Work had been her first escape. But on the days she found being with the children at the hospital was too much to bear, she'd take herself away for the weekend, hire a horse at a stables and ride and ride and ride until the pain—for a moment at least—had ebbed away.

She looked up at Idris—something she seemed to do automatically now. Whether it was to check for his approval or to see what he was thinking she wasn't sure; all she knew was that in the space of a few days her mind's orbit had changed and Idris... She shook the thought away, reminding herself those who wore wax wings were never wise to fly too close to the sun.

"Are we going riding?"

"Something like that," Idris said with a quick nod.

No smile. No flash of a shared passion. Nothing. Subconscious or not, it told her one thing. She was here to learn and listen, not to get excited or become attached as too often happened when it came to the children who unwittingly pulled her heartstrings. With the way Amira was affecting her, Robyn was beginning to feel like the entire string section of a full-blown orchestra! No matter how hard she tried, remaining scientific and critically indifferent was impossible.

Caring made her a better doctor. But it came with a risk. Caring made the failures, or, more pointedly, the losses... cut too deep. That she was her own worst enemy was one way of looking at things. Hell-bent on destroying what little peace of mind she had would be more accurate.

Robyn squared herself to Idris wishing he'd treat her more like the highly respected surgeon she was than some thorn in his side. Being here, after all, wasn't her bright idea.

"Any chance you're going to tell me what it is we will be doing?"

A flash of irritation lit up his eyes. No attempt to try to hide it, either.

His behavior rankled. She felt as though Idris had thrown her into an emotional boxing ring. Round one, attacking her with his words, laying bare her biggest sorrow. Round two, pulling her into his arms, caressing her, holding her until her tears had dried. Now here she was in round three at arm's length again with little chance at gaining ground.

"We're going on a little trip. Away from the capital."

Amira nodded, her little heart-shaped face so earnest as she read her father's lips all the while weaving her fingers through Robyn's.

When their hands were as one, Robyn's heart skipped a beat—a warning sign that she was getting too close. Wanting too much to have a family of her own.

Idris reached across and took Amira's other hand, compelling the little girl to release her own, take a hop-skip and stand by her father's side.

Knockout.

"I thought you might like to see some other parts of the country," Idris began, mercifully oblivious to her internal monologue. "It will be informative for you both to meet the people Amira will one day rule. See why her future, and the success of her operation, are so important."

Robyn looked down at the little girl, relieved to see a smile of anticipation on her face.

"Are we going to your favorite places?" Robyn signed and spoke.

Amira shook her head no, and gave a little jump of excitement.

"She's not traveled extensively in the country," Idris said, drawing Robyn's attention away from his daughter.

"Why not?"

It was a simple enough question but Idris seemed to need time to formulate the best answer. An overprotective parent? It was hard to blame him. She'd be gun-shy, too, in his shoes.

People began appearing out of doorways, arms full of luggage and packages.

"What's all this?"

"Supplies, mostly. Not all of it will be in the vehicle we take, but there will be a few follow-up trucks with us.

I never like to go into the…less fortunate parts of Da'har without bearing gifts."

"I thought gift giving was normally *to* someone in your position, not the other way around," Robyn quipped lightly.

"No." Idris's lips tightened, his gaze darkening even further. "That's not the case in Da'har."

With a quick move of his eyes, she watched as he reminded himself his daughter was present. The man who ruled the land, the one setting an example for his daughter, took over the impatient, irritable one she seemed so easily to elicit.

"My family, just the two of us now—" he nodded to his daughter "—have benefited enormously from the natural resources of this kingdom. I make no show of hiding either my gratitude or my good fortune in being born into the ruling family of Da'har. It is inevitable that society— no matter the largesse of its leader—will suffer at least some inequalities."

Robin flushed under the intensity of his gaze as he spoke.

"There will always be people richer than others. Just as there will always be those who seem happier, more intelligent or naturally gifted with incomparable beauty."

He paused for a moment, eyes narrowing as they raked the length of her. If he was trying to tell her she was beautiful, he was going to have to work on the delivery. If he was trying to tell her otherwise… Her breath caught in her throat.

Don't go there, Robyn.

"We try to make the imbalance of life's offerings less obvious. Bringing gifts is our way of doing this. I thought we would also stop by the hospital. The storerooms will be made available to you if you'd like to collect some things and hold a small clinic for one or two of the tribal communities we will be visiting."

"Oh, I'd love that!" Robyn clasped her hands together, trying her best to push the "examination" out of her mind.

She bit down on her lower lip and watched as he delivered a few instructions to an approaching staff member. A part of her ached for him, was forgiving of his mood swings. He was a man doing his very best to find his place in the world after only just surviving the initial, suffocating waves of grief he must've experienced when he lost his wife. A man trying as best he could to raise his daughter.

A flurry of commotion took over as Amira's nanny appeared and took her away to change. Robyn's newly purchased clothes had disappeared from her room and were being loaded into a car somewhere inside the vast compound.

"Ten minutes. The car will be at the front of the house. Don't be late," Idris instructed as he turned away to leave.

She nodded her assent, not that he was looking at her to notice, then looked around the extraordinary central courtyard of the house with fresh eyes. The fountains, the beautiful tiles, the comfort of it all…was this who Idris really was? Had inviting her here been his way of showing Robyn his gentler side?

She sat on the edge of the fountain, drawing her fingers across the surface of the pool, flowered lily pads moving in the tiny current she'd created. She wondered, for a moment, if this was what she'd done to Idris's life. Created a disturbance. Or—her lips turned up into a grin as she whirled her finger around in a circle—stirred things up for the better.

She looked up from the aqua pool, eyes moving from balcony to balustrade soaking in the beauty, trying to remind herself what she knew about Da'har.

Unlike similar kingdoms comprised of several tribes, Da'har had never experienced civil unrest. The rule—while held by one family—was far more progressive than in many of its neighboring countries. The city, what little she'd seen of it, sang of a place where tradition and progress met on an even footing. The same things were embodied, here in Idris's home. History and a look toward the future. A place that exemplified all that was good that had come from Da'har's rich, cultural past.

Such a contrast to the starkly modern palace he had been living in when he had been married. Perhaps, when there had been life and love in it, its sharp angles and cool facade had taken on a different hue.

She ran her fingers through the water again.

Idris's heart was in the past. It seemed to be the place where his decision making came from. That painful, hollowed-out place where light was a scourge to the grief he'd so clearly settled into.

How, she wondered, would his daughter be able to duck out from under his protective wing with an eye to the future?

A sigh whooshed out of her chest. The pair of them had so much responsibility. And, weighted with grief as Idris's story forever would be, could make seeing a new future— a *different* future—next to impossible.

"I feel like a chauffeur with the pair of you sitting back there!"

"We're very busy drawing everything we see," Robyn playfully retorted. "And hadn't you better keep your eyes on the road? Precious cargo and all that!" She was feeling strangely protective of the bond she and Amira were sharing—just a simple exchange of words, but the teaching of signs and sometimes sketches on the large notepad they had balanced on their laps was letting Robyn into Amira's world. Showing her just how much the somber little girl understood and could communicate.

"I thought I'd show you things, items of interest, along the way," Idris grumbled. "But I can't get a word in edgewise with the two of you going on about camels and birds and who knows what else."

"If I didn't know better, I'd say you were jealous!" Robyn replied absently, eyes still on the drawing of a…was that a solar panel next to the waves?

"I am *not* jealous."

Robyn sat upright and looked into the rearview mirror, her eyes just missing Idris's irritable glance. When his gaze returned to the mirror and meshed with her own, she saw a bit of *relief.* As if a mutual need for the other was confirmed within that brief moment. A need she hadn't yet acknowledged.

A heat grew in her belly and the atmosphere shifted from playful to taut as Amira, thankfully, remained deeply engrossed in her drawing.

Idris returned his focus to the road, but she could see from the stiffening of his shoulders he had felt it, too. The connection.

"It is tricky," Robyn began tentatively, "with Amira needing to read lips. I don't want her to feel left out." Idris's eyes remained focused on the road. He was leading a relatively impressive group of vehicles through the countryside. When he'd said Robyn could "raid the store cupboard" at the hospital she hadn't expected a warehouse.

"Of course," Idris replied stiffly as if that had been the point he'd been trying to make all along. "She is the reason you're here."

"Although—" a surge of chance-taking overtook her "—most children her age aren't all that interested in what adults yammer on about."

"Most children her age don't have a country to be responsible for."

"True." Robyn leaned forward, resting her arm on the back of the empty passenger seat. "If you're fishing for compliments about your daughter, I can tell you for free, she's exemplary."

"And the rest of your advice?" Idris's lips twitched with something. Pride? Humor? Or another streak of irritability she seemed to have a knack for tapping? "Does that come with a price tag?"

Robyn laughed. Whether he was annoyed or not she lived in a far different world to Idris and his bottomless coin purse. "If it's medical advice you're after, and I didn't need to pay my rent or eat, I would work at Paddington's for free. Especially if it meant keeping the doors open longer."

"Sounds like you mean it."

"I do! Being head of the surgical ward is—well, I don't so much like the public side of things, but helping the children, working with the children… It really is my passion."

"Even though—"

"Yes," she answered quickly. "It's hard sometimes, I admit, but…"

"And how about this move to the outskirts of London—"

"To Riverside Hospital?" It was hard to keep the derisive tone out of her words, but she was grateful for the change of conversation topic. Surprised, in fact, he'd brought it up at all.

"Yes." Idris nodded, eyes occasionally meeting hers in the rearview mirror as the city sights began drifting away and the road curved into an ever-increasing expanse of desert. "What would be so bad about moving there?"

"Everything!"

"Won't it have new facilities, new equipment?"

"It would be a soulless replication of what we have now. A business park of a hospital." *Just like that palace of yours—sitting empty in the middle of such a thriving city.*

"And the reason for the move?"

"The board wants to sell the site. It would," she acquiesced with a sigh, "bring a lot more money to the hospital—but a lot of added expense for all of the patients and their families with the travel, the hotels." She pulled herself up short. "I feel like I'm giving a speech and that's not really my turf."

"No? It was sounding quite convincing to me."

This time she was certain he was smiling.

"I think speech making is more likely your terrain."

"When necessary," he conceded. "But this—" He drew his hand along the view spreading out before them as they crested a steep hill. "This is the terrain that sings to me."

Robyn was speechless. The capital city was on the sea and very beautiful, but the vast peninsula they were overlooking now was absolutely breathtaking. A huge sprawl of orchards and marshland and the most extraordinary coastline was spilling out beneath their hillside vantage point.

"No wonder..."

"No wonder what?" Idris asked.

"You're so passionate about Da'har. It's absolutely beautiful."

"No more so than—" Idris stopped himself short, forcing himself to tear his gaze away from Robyn for fear of betraying what he really wanted to say. That she was beautiful. Fiercely intelligent. Passionate about children when others in her shoes would have walked away.

Being with her brought life back to parts of him he'd long ago consigned to the past.

"No more dedicated than you are to Paddington's," he said instead.

"Birds of a feather, us two."

From Robyn's tight reply, he wished he'd just said what he'd meant to.

No more beautiful than you are.

Pretending he was unaffected by her beauty was increasingly difficult. He was beginning to wish he had selected one of the potbellied, middle-aged *male* surgeons who'd all but kowtowed to him for the honor of doing Amira's surgery. But Robyn?

She didn't kowtow. She didn't beg.

First impressions? A scatterbrained wood nymph. The more he grew to know her, the more he appreciated how right he had been to go with his gut. Much like him, she was a woman who didn't bother with charades. She was the best and didn't need to try to impress. It wasn't arrogance. It was simply the way it was. Her commitment, lauded skill and ability to help his daughter weren't the only factors at play.

He was *moved* by Robyn. She reached places in his heart he had slammed shut for good, and the thought of opening those doors, of letting himself love again? It was easier to imagine Amira being able to hear than envisioning himself happy and in love.

"What are those?" He followed the line Robyn's finger drew, catching glimpses through the side mirror of his little girl's face pressed up against the window, her eyes actively absorbing everything she saw. This was a first for her and he felt a twinge of remorse they hadn't done this earlier. That he'd opted to drive instead of sit alongside her and tell her his childhood tales of exploring the nooks and crannies of the fertile valley below them.

"It's a solar farm. For the orchards and farms," he explained.

"The orchards? I would've thought there was more than enough sun to ripen the crops."

"You're right on one count. We have more than enough sun, but not enough water. What you can't see, beyond the mountain range at the far end of the valley, is a desalination plant. We built it out of sight of the handful of villages that populate this valley as it is less than complementary to the rural setting. The electricity made helps pump the water from underground tunnels here into marshlands and into reservoirs for the orange groves and pomegranate orchards."

"It all sounds incredibly well thought out."

"These are the types of decisions I enjoy making," Idris said, surprised to hear the depth of feeling in his own voice.

"Did you study all of this? The hydro, the salination, solar-powered orchard-crafting?" Robyn laughed as she garbled the multilayered technologies, and he found himself chuckling along with her.

The team of engineers he'd worked with to put together the complementary power and hydration systems would've died of shock. It had been one of the first projects he had put together in the wake of his wife's death when he had been a shell of the man who had ascended to the throne. Where he had once felt there was nothing he couldn't overcome, he now saw what all those who came into contact with him must've spotted a mile off. A man embittered by life. Angry. Hollowed out by the cruel twist life had taken on an otherwise blissfully happy ride.

"You remember, of course, that I studied architecture in university," he explained. "I also took a higher degree in urban and rural planning. So much of the region—the Gulf Peninsula—is turning to desert faster than we can find ways to fight the loss of precious agricultural land. If farmers abandoned their crops and moved to the cities, we as a nation would be forced into an untenable position. My people must have food and water. The rest…?" He paused, eyes scanning the lush agricultural land below he played a key part in maintaining. But the swell of pride wasn't for himself. "I want Amira to have a country able to fend for itself when it is her turn to rule. A country that hasn't been savaged for its resources for my own gain without thought for the ramifications."

"That is very noble," she said, feeling deep in her heart that a man who cared this deeply was both generous and kind—no matter the steely exterior he presented to the world.

As if to prove her point she watched as his jaw clenched while an eyebrow arched in displeasure at her words.

"There is no nobility in it when there isn't a choice. It is the *responsibility* of a father to look after his daughter."

"I know, but I don't think you see Amira that way. As a responsibility." Robin's voice was softer now. A welcome whisper in his subconscious telling him what he already knew. He did it for love. A love he found difficult to show for fear of ever experiencing the pain he had endured seven years ago.

"Just as well," he said, his voice gruff with emotion. "We've a busy few days ahead of us. All of us."

His lips pressed and tightened—a cue to Robyn that the conversation was over. As she relaxed back into the deep seat of the luxury four-by-four, he inhaled the sweet meadow blossom scent her movement left behind.

For every part of him that wanted Robyn near, that enjoyed having her as a confidante, a friend, there was another very active, near brutal part of him that knew having her close was akin to stepping in quicksand. If he were to fall in love with Robyn Kelly, there would be no going back. She deserved nothing less than a man's entire heart and he didn't have that to offer.

His nation and his daughter had endured enough. His future would be a solitary one.

CHAPTER SEVEN

"HOLD OUT YOUR HANDS!"

Amira could hardly contain her giggles, while her father's face was a picture of fastidious concentration.

"This is your grandfather's secret technique. Pay close attention." He tightened his grip on the knife and made a final and sharp incision.

"Oh!" Robyn cried. "Careful."

"And they all come out. Quickly, your hands! Just like this!"

Amira and Robyn held their hands out as gem after gem of ruby-colored fruit cascaded into their open palms. She'd never seen such beautiful pomegranates, let alone picked them from a tree jeweled to the hilt with them.

"So." Idris closed his sharp pocketknife after swiping the blade along a few tree leaves and plucked a couple of seeds from Robyn's cupped hand. "What do you think?"

He popped them into his mouth, and as his eyes connected with hers, the sun-warmed scent of his body swirled around her like an aphrodisiac. Her gaze shifted from his dark eyes along the straight-as-an-arrow line of his nose and landed on his mouth, her own lips parting as she watched the tip of his tongue slip out to retrieve a drop of juice. She stood, mesmerized, as one of his teeth bit down on his lip until slowly, agonizingly, the fullness of it was released, the color intensified by the skid of tooth against his very full, very kissable mouth.

Everything about the moment screamed erotic: the warm orchard and ocean-scented evening air; stars pinging out against the ever-increasing darkness above the sea as the waves hushed and whooshed upon the sand, advanced and retreated. Advanced and retreated. Candles flickered in abundance inside the hurricane lamps dotted liberally about the "campsite" Idris's staff had set up for them three days into their journey.

An entire crescent of perfect beach, just for them! Bedouin-style tents with a luxury of mattresses, pillows… Everything she would have imagined an Arabian warrior would be privy to. The canopy-tented "living room," the solar-powered showers hidden by gently billowing canvases, the bed so large she could sleep on it diagonally without the slightest of concerns—none of these were set out to impress her. It was how the very real Sheikha-in-waiting and her father, the powerful and benign leader of all they had seen on their extraordinary trip to this seaside retreat, lived. Not ostentatiously, but it was undeniably luxurious.

She chanced another glance at Idris and was instantly snared by the intensity of his returned gaze. Unable to move, the only thing she could remember to do was breathe.

Was the pull of attraction mutual? The same type of magnetism that bound the moon, the earth and the sun. Utterly organic. Completely undeniable.

Her body had no resistance to fight the waves of desire being near Idris elicited. Proximity as he took a single step closer toward her only magnified the sensations, the tingles of response. His unblinking gaze, knowingly or not, was turning her very essence into a heated, molten pool of longing.

She lifted her hand, only just stopping herself from reaching out to caress the dark outline of his evening stubble when Idris quickly averted his eyes to remind her they weren't alone.

Amira, thankfully, was oblivious to their otherworldly moment brought on—no doubt—by too much time in the sun and not enough...

Not enough what? Common sense?

Probably.

Robyn sucked in a quick breath of air and plopped down on the rattan sofa awash with pillows, patting the space beside her for Amira to come and finish off the pomegranate seeds her father had prepared for her after another wonderful picnic dinner.

Idris took a seat across from them underneath the large, open tent his staff had arranged for them to enjoy their supper and the sunset.

Just as well, she chided. Amira was why she was here, not...not having *moments* with the last person on the planet she should be getting all swoony over. Not that she was swoony or anything. Not much, anyway.

"So." Idris eventually broke the silence, well aware something had passed between them. Something overtly sensual. "I suppose it's time for Amira to head to bed."

"Already?" Robyn's expression was slightly stricken as though she were planning on using his daughter as a shield to protect herself from being ravaged by him. The thought was far too easy to picture.

Robyn's golden curls splayed out on the rich colors of the throws and blankets that made up his bed. Her slender limbs moving, responding beneath him as he—

"Do you read to her?"

Idris's eyebrows furrowed together in near disbelief. "You do remember my daughter is deaf, Dr. Kelly?"

Robyn stiffened at the use of her formal title and he instantly regretted the patronizing tone he knew came too easily. More so when he saw his daughter was following the words being shaped by his lips.

Amira blinked, almost in confusion at the version of the father neither of them much liked. Cold. Unfeeling. Indifferent. All things he was most definitely not feeling now, but needed to fight.

Robyn saw the interchange and busied herself with scrubbing a wet wipe over Amira's hands, giving a kiss to each of her fingertips after it had been cleaned. She looked across to Idris when she gave Amira a wipe to do the same for her.

"Has anyone taught you how reading to the deaf needs to be a slightly different experience?"

He shook his head no. Communicating and educating his daughter was incredibly complex. He had, much to his shame, relied on the hope that one day the miracles of modern medicine would eradicate the need to explore all the various teaching techniques a deaf child required when his energies should have been spent on working with deaf educators—taking advantage of his daughter's quick and eager mind.

One look from Robyn and he felt disappointed in himself. As Robyn had said, the operation wasn't necessarily going to be successful. But he would empty the family's coffers to the very last coin if it would make it so.

"I have a book in my bag I think she might enjoy. The vocabulary might be a bit advanced for her reading level." Robyn's voice was neutral, but those amber eyes of hers spoke volumes.

This isn't about you, they said. *Your ego. Your hopes. This is about your daughter and her welfare. Right. Now.*

"Would you like to show us?"

The light he so enjoyed seeing returned to Robyn's eyes at his request.

"Very much." She thanked Amira for cleaning her

hands, then explained what she wanted to do—sending the little girl to run and fetch the book.

"We could have sent someone." Idris felt the thunderclouds gather again.

"Children," Robyn said firmly, "enjoy helping. It makes them feel a part of things."

"I give her everything she needs."

"No one is saying otherwise." Robyn folded her hands together on her lap as if they would provide the calm she needed to keep her response in check. "Sometimes what a child needs more than *things* is to be *needed*."

Idris sat back against the pile of scarlet and white pillows, wondering what had made this woman so strong. No one spoke to him like this. Ever. And yet...they were all things he needed to hear. The voice of reason to the black-and-white view of the world he'd adopted after his wife had died.

"Here she is." He beckoned his daughter to come over and join him, wrapping a protective arm around her shoulders as she held the book up for Robyn to see.

"Great!" Robyn signed as she spoke in a steady clear voice. "Idris, if you wouldn't mind reading the story, I will sign along with my own narration. That way you can see the difference."

"Won't you just be repeating what I say?"

"Not exactly. Sign language isn't a word for word translation. It's more..." Her eyes flicked up to the soft billows of fabric hanging above them, the candlelight adding gold to the luster of her richly colored irises. "Signing a story is more often a case of capturing the essence of the tale, details when necessary, but a big mix of using your face and your expressions to tell the story, as well. Often in written language, so much is implied and, in this case, they need to be explained. Sometimes just using the pictures in the book along with a sign is helpful. Here, let me show you."

She crossed to where he and Amira were seated and sat next to him, her scent immediately causing him to lose focus and stiffen.

The entire reason he'd sat across from her was to shake off his body's unbidden response to Robyn, not compound it! And yet, her focus was entirely on Amira, the book he held in his lap and showing him, as he imagined she would show any parent trying to do the best by their child, how to read a story.

"So!" Robyn clapped her hands together and gave him a quick look. "Shall we begin? If you just start with the title."

"Beauty and the Beast," Idris read dryly. "I suppose you find that funny."

Robyn looked up at him, her face a picture of innocence and then began to sign. Her fingers widened as she fanned them across her face with a beatific expression in her eyes, then abruptly crumpled her face into a grumpy mirror image of his own, fingers curling in an angry twist in front of the face before she looked back at him with a grin.

"It's just a fairy tale. Don't be scared."

Idris gave her his best sidelong look. "Shall I continue?"

"Yes, please do. This is excellent fun!"

Much to his surprise, Idris did actually enjoy telling the story "Robyn-style." He read the story aloud, one line at a time, and Robyn would either repeat the line verbatim—particularly if it was about an action—or, if it was more subtle, she would explain it fully until Amira's eyes lit with understanding. Seeing Robyn's slender fingers spell things out alongside the pictures in the beautifully illustrated book and then take flight, usually up toward her face where her expressions alone told the tale of a young woman traded by her father in exchange for a single, exquisite rose by a hideous monster who was really a handsome prince cast under a spell for cruel, selfish behavior.

Idris, despite an inclination to slam the book shut at the constant flow of similarities, found himself engaged. He grew nearly as wide-eyed as his daughter when Beauty left the Beast behind only to discover him half-dead for grief at the loss of her and ultimately transformed into the handsome prince he had once had the chance to be.

"And that," Robyn said with a satisfied smile at the sight of her openmouthed audience, "is how you tell a story in sign language!"

"Very...persuasive." Idris chose his words carefully. It could just be coincidence that art was imitating life a bit too accurately. Who knew? Maybe that magic carpet bag of hers had an entire library of fairy tales and myths in it. Fiction. That was all it was, he reminded himself as his daughter's sleepy form began to press against him. "It's definitely time for this little one to get her beauty sleep." He scooped her up in both arms, Amira's long black hair swishing across his arm as he brought her forehead up to meet his lips for a kiss. As he dropped the kiss on his daughter's brow, he looked up just in time to catch a glimpse of Robyn's tear-filled eyes as she looked out to the sea, her hands wiping at her cheeks as she walked briskly out into the darkness toward the retreating tide.

"Are you happy with your tent?" he called after her. It was a ridiculous question. She'd been sleeping in the same high-caliber Bedouin-style tent for the past three nights they had been touring. It was every bit as luxurious as the palace. Tonight, however, with the glaze of tears in her eyes, he was vividly aware she would be on her own and he wanted, much to his surprise, to be with her. All of them. Just as he had with his extended family when they'd come to this very same beach when he was a child. The whole lot bundled into the extensive bedroom, telling stories, laughing, until one by one, eventually, they had all drifted off to sleep with the sound of the waves as their lullaby.

"Very," came the tight reply, shoulders stiffening at the realization she hadn't quite escaped his notice.

"I'll just put Amira down."

He saw her nod her head, working her way to the shoreline, only the phosphorescence of the foam visible in the inky darkness now enveloping her.

"Here." Idris's voice broke into the still night air. "For the cold."

Robyn started as she felt a soft cashmere wrap being placed on her shoulders. She didn't need to turn to identify the voice or the fingers staying just a moment longer than she would have thought necessary to ensure the wrap would stay.

"Thank you for the story. Amira loved every moment of it."

"My pleasure." She kept her gaze straight ahead, somehow finding it just a bit too painful to look him in the eye. Not with everything she was feeling. The weightless, out of control, topsy-turvy journey that was falling in love. Because that was what was happening. Despite her very best efforts, she was falling in love with Idris. At least, with the man he was when he let his guard down. When he reveled in showing them the best way to open a pomegranate. When he tightened his grip on the steering wheel as he spoke of his country's transformation from tribal outpost to international stalwart on both financial and political fronts. The way his eyes lit when he looked first at his daughter and then, on occasion, at her.

What she couldn't bear was the wall she regularly saw slide into place when whatever it was that was happening between them grew too intense.

But he was right, wise even, to keep the wall between them strong. He belonged here. A modern-day knight for a country that needed a strong leader—someone unafraid to face the future on his people's behalf.

Robyn was half in love with the country, as well, but her place was at Paddington's. Behind the scenes. Doing what she did best beneath the harsh glare of the surgical lamps…

"Come." Idris tipped his chin toward the soft light of the tent. "Sit with me awhile."

"I should probably make a few calls. Check in with the hospital." She winced apologetically, backing away from the hand he'd held out to place on the small of her back.

He noticed the move but said nothing, folding his hands behind his back, as if he'd intended to do so all along.

"Actually…it's probably best we speak before you make that call."

Robyn's sense shot to high alert. "You don't want to cancel the surgery, do you?"

"No, no. Nothing like that." He shook his head and took a seat in an armchair, gesturing that she should sit on the sofa across from him while they spoke. "It's just, seeing you here, with Amira—the both of you discovering what I love about Da'har so much—I'm beginning to think it would be best if we had the surgery here. She's had so much change already—"

Robyn's head was shaking no, no, no, before her mouth caught up with her. "I will only do the surgery at Paddington's. With great respect to you and your team, it's where I am most comfortable. Where I will be able to ensure I will do my best work."

"This is not what I want!" Idris slammed his fist against the wooden table sitting between them, the force behind his gesture so intense it sent the reverberations of his anger straight through to Robin's core.

She sat bolt upright and locked eyes with him. "Not everybody always gets what they want, do they, Your Excellency? As you yourself once said, life isn't fair."

The words furled out from her mouth like a whip—snapping with a ferocity she hadn't realized she'd possessed.

"You won't stop me from protecting Amira." Idris's voice was low, a near growl. "I have the power to stop this thing—whenever I choose."

And that was when she saw it clearly. The fear. The living terror that something would happen to his daughter and he would be powerless to change it. Her heart ached for him, but he had to see that micromanaging wasn't love. Trust and faith and courage—those were the fibers that made love strong.

She took a deep breath and looked him in the eye again.

"I owe Amira my absolute concentration in the operating theater. The one place she will receive that is Paddington's. You can't control everything, Idris. Least of all me. Perhaps it's time to focus on what you do have rather than what you don't."

"I have a daughter who can't hear!" His voice rose again.

"You have a loving, joyful, curious, amazing daughter who would do anything for you if only you'd let her."

He let the words sink in, his body visibly battling a need to vent his frustration.

"Can you promise me absolute success in Paddington's?"

"No," she said plainly. "But what I can promise is my very best."

Robyn's hands curled into fists to hide the tremors that would betray her to Idris.

He considered her silently for a moment, his body still taut with his ferocious need to protect his daughter. She felt naked beneath his gaze and it took all her courage not to look away. She wriggled some more strength into the line of her spine, all the while meeting the depths of his ebony eyes when running away would have been the easiest option.

"What is it?" Idris asked, his voice unexpectedly softening, teasing away the harshness of his steely-eyed expression. "What is it you didn't get that you wanted so badly?"

"A child," she said simply, her eyes bravely linked to his so he could see the truth in them. "A child of my own."

"You would be a wonderful mother." The words came without reservation and she felt them in her heart.

"Alas!" The corners of her lips tipped upward, parting with a bittersweet smile. "It is not to be."

"Do you mind my asking why not?"

She sighed, pressing her hands between her knees, hunching her shoulders up around her ears. "It's not a very nice story."

"Whatever it is, you've lived to tell the tale. Someone very wise once told me I should focus on the positive."

She arced an eyebrow at him. It wasn't strictly what'd she'd said, but it had been the message.

"I'm paraphrasing," he intoned with a gentle smile.

"Of course." She knew the smile she was offering him in return was wan, but she felt a strength growing in her. One that might lend a voice to her story.

She tipped her head and gave him a sidelong look. His expression wasn't as enraged as she might have expected after their fiery exchange. It was, in fact, one that spoke of a new understanding. Perhaps a realization that holding his daughter as tightly to him as he did could be restrictive rather than loving. That holding on to the grief and fear of the unknown that had come with his wife's death might be suffocating his heart and soul—rather than enlightening them.

Robyn tugged the edges of the shawl around her shoulders and tucked her feet up and under her on the cushioned sofa. She was going to have to get comfy if she was going to spill this particular pot of beans.

"You're difficult to say no to, you know."

"You're difficult in your own special way, but let's not

worry about that now." Idris reached across and took one of her hands in his, his thumb giving her palm a few short rubs before releasing it and settling back in his chair. "Please. I want to know."

The candlelight flickered off the dark shine of his hair, but his black eyes were lit entirely from within.

"A little while ago," she began, then laughed softly before correcting herself. "A long time ago actually, since forty is looming out there."

"What? Forty looms for the both of us."

She couldn't help it. She snorted. "You're a whippersnapper at thirty-five."

"You can barely be into your thirties."

"Thirty-seven," she corrected, not a little pleased to see his eyes widen with genuine disbelief. Idris didn't do social niceties so she knew it had to be real. "Guess that makes you my boy toy!"

Oh, wow. Did you really just say that?

"Does it, now?" Bemused didn't even begin to cover the expression she received in return.

"Can we just forget I said anything?"

"Probably for the best," he conceded, a twinkle of humor coming to the fore.

"Anyhow—" she gave him a soft smile and a nod of thanks for wiping the slate clean "—when I was in my very early twenties, still in med school, I was in a relationship and fell pregnant."

"You were married?"

"No." She didn't meet Idris's gaze, her fingers busy toying with the tassels on the ends of the shawl he had placed protectively on her shoulders.

"Was he not an honorable man?"

She looked up, surprised to see the flare of protectiveness surge through him on her behalf.

"He was, but what happened to the two of us…it was tough." It surprised her how easy it was to speak to Idris. The man who seemed so solid, so absolute about his opinions—he wasn't sitting there, body taut with tension to judge her, but to defend her if necessary, and she hadn't felt that sort of security in, well, ever. The rest of the story came out in a whoosh of information. The medical school romance, the unplanned pregnancy. "I hadn't realized how much I had wanted a child until I was pregnant and John was a good guy so we thought, why not? Why not have a child?"

"So what happened?" Idris pressed, concern weaving through his voice.

And this was the hard part. "It was an ectopic pregnancy." She shot him a glance, and instead of feeling strange telling him about the intimate details, she felt relief. He didn't seem squeamish or put off. Just profoundly interested in what had happened to her to change her life so much that she would always feel a longing for something she could never have. She went on to tell him about the cervical pregnancy. The fetus had implanted so near her uterus it had sustained a gestational sac. She had known the chances of the baby surviving were rare, but abortion hadn't been a choice she'd wanted to make. There had been bleeding. Too much bleeding. And ultimately a hysterectomy to save her life, but not the life of her child.

"The ramifications of what had happened to me—to my body—were too much for John and we drifted apart. There was a job offer from Paddington's that lifted my heart out of the abyss and now it's just me and my work!" She put on the bright smile she was so accustomed to pasting on at moments like these. The ones where she wondered if she really had healed and moved on from that devastating day.

There were no visible scars, but she would be in complete denial not to admit that the emotional fallout ran deep.

"I am so sorry, Robyn. You didn't deserve that."

"No one does," she quipped, pulling her hands back as she saw him come forward to offer her a comforting caress. Feeling his touch, the soft shift of his thumb along the back of her hand, along the length of her arm, would tip her over the edge, and this was a work trip. She might be great at giving advice, but taking her own seemed nigh on impossible.

"You know, I really do have to make a few calls to the hospital. Check up on how things are going." She pressed up from her chair and gave her legs an unnecessary brush for sand.

"Surely they would get in touch with you if they needed anything." Idris rose with her, his body language still hovering between his usual reserve and a newfound intimacy sprung from the fears and sorrows they had shared.

It was an intangible line the pair of them could cross— a shared discovery of all the joy just waiting to fan out before them—if only life were so easy. Idris didn't want *her*. He wanted his daughter to hear. And he would do anything in his power to make it happen. So, Robyn did a quick internal round of shutting the doors to everything she'd laid bare before him and gave Idris a bright smile.

"There are a few things I wanted to make sure are under way as regards Amira's surgery. If we're still green-lit, that is?" She crossed her arms protectively, the delicate fabric of the shawl between them a reminder their futures were linked now…at least professionally speaking. And that was the part she needed to secure.

"Very well."

Robin watched as the shutters slammed shut in Idris's eyes. His lips pressed tightly together to form a straight line as the cool, icy distance she'd felt the very first time they met sent shivers along her spine.

Again, she knew sleep would be some time coming and, when it did, there was little mystery as to who would haunt her dreams.

CHAPTER EIGHT

As DAWN BROKE Idris squinted against the sun's glory while it crested the mountain peaks encircling the valley and seaside cove where their camp lay. He stretched and pushed himself up and out of the tangle of bedsheets that hadn't seen much sleep, elbows coming to rest on his knees, fingers templing, thumbs pressing into his brow as he sat in a contemplative silence he hoped would bring some peace.

Restlessness won out. He tugged on a pair of swimming trunks hoping a long swim could achieve what his normally very controlled mind could not. He slipped his feet into his sandals, aligning the tan lines with the bands, suddenly appreciating how much he had been in "holiday" mode for the past few days. Traveling with Robyn and his daughter had been something he hadn't experienced for a while. Years, in fact. It had been…fun.

Very much like the childhood his parents had ensured he'd had. Not at all similar to the one he afforded Amira.

He rounded the corner of his three-sided tent only to find a very anxious-looking Robyn nibbling away on her tidy manicure, twisting her slender body this way and that in the loose confines of a light cotton dress. The spaghetti string straps gave a clear view of her slender shoulders and the soft swoop and curve toward her breasts. No brassiere or bikini straps, just two triangles of cloth forming an eye-catching V in the center of her décolletage.

The traditional clothing she'd been wearing had never afforded him so much… *Robyn*…and there was no denying he liked what he saw. She turned and noticed him watching.

Unable to look away, he shifted his gaze along the soft arc of her breasts, her nipples tightening against the thin cotton as if he had reached out and caressed them between a finger and thumb or given them a swift lick with his tongue. A shot of desire slammed through him as the possibilities developed and grew. There was no one around at this hour. His tent was bathed in the apricot and gold light only a Da'harian sunrise could elicit. His fingers twitched, each hand longing to play its part in separating Robyn from her dress. Not by the gentle slipping of one strap and then the next in a slow, luxurious unveiling, but with a sharp, brusque rent of the flimsy fabric so that he could see all of her at once, then decide slowly, luxuriously, where and how he would begin to touch and caress her naked body.

He surprised himself by taking a step forward. Just as quickly he ground his heels into the sand and his jaw into a tight clench, mind dictating to matter that he needed—he must—keep his primal response to her in check.

"You seem to have been lying in wait. I can only assume it was for me?"

Idris knew he sounded more growly than he would have liked, but he didn't like losing control and the unbidden jags of longing that just looking at Robyn unleashed in him needed to be tamed.

Her eyes widened with a combination of relief and nerves, both quickly evolving into something altogether different as he watched her eyes slip from his face and down to his bare torso.

Electricity crackled through him again as her lips parted and she unconsciously licked her lips before shifting her heavy-lidded gaze upward to meet his. Her hands dropped to her sides and whatever it was that had been disturbing her seemed to have left her completely as she opened and closed those rose-red lips.

"Care to join me for a swim?"

It wasn't a request. He needed to get in the deep, cool seawater. Now.

"Ah, no, it is—rather, that is, I was—" she stammered out a few false starts.

"Come on. Spit it out." He reached into his tent and grabbed a towel, wrapping it around his waist to increase the divide between them.

"The press have got hold of the news."

His focus swung from lust to protective in an instant.

"About Amira?"

"About the surgery, yes."

"What calls did you make last night?"

"I rang the hospital. Paddington's." Her brow crinkled into tight furrows of concern.

"Who did you speak with?"

Robyn held her hands up in protest as he approached. "Please. No, Idris. I'm so sorry. I only spoke to one of my colleagues about where to place the 3-D printer and—"

"Word leaked out," he finished for her, arms crossing over his chest as he tried to put the information into some sort of order before he spoke again.

Robyn nodded somberly, rubbing her thumb again and again across the palm of her other hand as if it would expel the nerves that roller-coastered through her gut. If he decided to withdraw consent for the surgery now, the future of Paddington's could only be closure. Coming to Da'har had been scary enough. Now she was going to have to well and truly fight to save the one thing that meant the most in the world to her.

She could virtually see the thoughts flicking through Idris's eyes as he dismissed option after option. She'd told him to loosen the reins of control and *wow*! What a back-fire.

A sudden clap of his hands jolted her to attention.

"First things first, I'll cancel the visit to Amaleet today."

"To see the children singing and the hawk display?"

She received a curt nod, a distracted glance.

"What on earth for? The press won't be there, surely! Amira was so looking forward to being with the other children."

Was she defending Amira or Paddington's? Had the futures of both become equally important? Robyn's hand moved instinctively to her heart.

"We'll go another time, when the children aren't there," Idris continued, his statement making little to no sense.

Was he wrestling with his need to control everything? This sort of thing—a media leak—was precisely what he wouldn't want for Amira. Robyn, of all people, understood the desire for privacy. The fact news of the surgery would be hitting all of the British newspapers at dawn made her sick. For herself, the promises she'd made to Idris of absolute privacy and, most worryingly, for the future of Paddington's.

Robyn watched as he shifted his jaw from left to right as if tasting the results of his decision. "Perhaps, if we cancel the other children she can see the hawk display."

"Don't you think she wants to do these things with other people? The same way you experienced them as a child."

"It's safer for her this way. Easier."

"Amira's deaf, not agoraphobic!" Robyn protested.

"And Amira's my daughter, not yours."

If he had slashed her with a knife the words could not have cut deeper.

She took a step back, barely able to contain the slug of grief rising in her throat.

Idris was drawing his line in the sand—in concrete more like—and Robyn would have to respect it. She'd promised him privacy and had landed him on the front page.

She swallowed all the things she could have said. All the feelings near enough choking her as she widened her tearless eyes. She may have fallen at this hurdle, but would not give Idris the satisfaction of seeing her cry.

"In which case, it's best I return to England. I've spent enough time with you," she added hastily.

She was going to have to have a talk with her "out-loud" voice.

"I think you'll agree it's probably best if I got back to Paddington's and began organizing things. Particularly under the circumstances."

"No. You will stay in Da'har," Idris replied, his temper barely contained. "As discussed."

Forcing on a braver face than the one she knew it was masking, she, too, pressed her heels into the sand for better grounding and drew a deep breath before jabbing an accusing finger in his direction.

"I know you are Amira's father, but either our talk last night meant absolutely nothing to you, or you are suffering from a rather severe case of floccinaucinihilipilification." She sucked in another breath, feeling her confidence whoosh out of her with the word she'd summoned from only heaven knew where. An attack of Englishness forced her to tack on, "If you don't mind me saying."

"I'm not certain I know *what* it is, let alone if I'm suffering from it." Idris arced an imperious eyebrow. Something, Robyn now knew, he only did when his curiosity was piqued.

Ha!

"The action or habit of estimating something as worthless," she explained with a sniff.

"In other words, dismissing the opinions of others?" The eyebrow lifted again.

"Well…" She etched a heart shape into the sand with her toe. "I'm not *entirely* sure if I would have put it precisely as you did. But yes." She raised her eyes to meet his, surprised to find Idris smiling.

"I'm not so sure you are as shy of asserting yourself as you profess, Dr. Kelly."

"Robyn," she gently corrected, a warm hit of pride tickling at her heart as she spoke.

"Very well, then. I won't cancel the day's events. We carry on as—" Idris paused to give her a conciliatory smile "—as the doctor ordered."

Robyn's smile flattened into a grimace.

"Why the frown? You just got what you wanted, my dear. Usually a victor smiles."

Robyn cinched her lips back into a facsimile of a smile. "This isn't about winning or losing, Idris. It's about what's best for your little girl. If you would just hang up the 'underaged curmudgeon badge' you so proudly wear you might be able to see sense for once!"

"Underaged curmudgeon?"

"Yes." She gave him an indignant little nod. "You're far too young and gorge—" She swallowed the rest of her sentence and started again. "You're far too young and gifted a leader to be this grumpy. It's usually Victorian gentlemen with gout who are this consistently horrid."

"You think I'm horrid?"

"I…might. Just a little," she squeaked, fingers held up in a tiny pinch, as her lungs strained against the huge breath she'd sucked in realizing she was about to tell him what she really thought.

And what she really thought was that underneath the

thick layer of defensiveness there was a kind, loving father. A generous and thoughtful leader. A man whose capacity to love had… She was struck with an unexpected hit of disappointment that he had chosen never again to be open to the pure, enriching love between a man and a woman.

"You're right." Idris gave her a begrudging nod.

"About the gout?"

"Don't be ridiculous. I'm as healthy as an ox." He struck a pose and only released it when he was quite sure Robyn had appreciated quite how healthy he looked. Just as quickly his entire demeanor transformed into a businesslike mode. "We'll hold a press conference. *You* will, that is. We shall organize it at the television station back in the capital when we return. For now we will complete our trip. As scheduled."

Idris's eyes twinkled, his chin tilting to the right, lips pressing forward and that eyebrow of his arching in a self-satisfied sort of way.

Which was great, except… She raised her hand as if she were a girl back in school needing to ask for permission for something to which she already knew the answer was no.

"Is there any chance we could skip the press conference part?"

"Not even a sliver of a chance." He squared himself to her, arms crossing over the broad expanse of caramel-colored chest she'd fastidiously been trying to avoid staring at, as if crossing his arms put an end to the matter. And for the moment, it did, because the gesture near enough short-circuited her brain again. It wasn't so much the soft whorls of dark hair around the burnt-sugar areolas, but the arrow of hair between his taut stomach muscles and his hip-skimming swimming trunks. All a bit much in the visual overload department. Particularly when her mind needed to be one hundred percent focused on sorting out this PR palaver.

"What if you were to release a statement, or even deliver the statement?" she posited. "Surely people are more interested in what *you* have to say..."

"I think you will find, Dr. Kelly," Idris dryly replied, "it is your surgical skills and medical prowess the people are curious about. It would get you the much-needed publicity I am sure Paddington's requires in the face of this financial uncertainty. Come now—what was it you said I was suffering from earlier?"

"Floccinaucinihilipilification?"

"Yes. Let's not hope it's catching now, shall we?"

Her mouth went dry and she felt a funny, tickly, scratchy sensation in her throat. The same one that always threatened to squeeze her larynx into oblivion whenever the thought of speaking publically started worming its way through her nervous system. So she'd been the pot calling the kettle black. So what? This whole thing was about Idris and Amira—not about her!

"Couldn't we just use some of your gazillions and get ourselves a body double to do it for me?" she said, only half joking now that the words were out.

Idris's lips tweaked upward a couple of times before he drew them in and released them after a drag beneath his teeth. "*Gazillions* isn't a word I tend to use in reference to my wealth."

"Apologies." She fluttered her hands between them as if it would erase what she'd said and huffed out a defeated sigh. "I just...oh! This is so embarrassing since you're so good at it, but I absolutely, positively, couldn't find anything in the world more terrifying than giving a press conference."

Idris leaned his weight back on one foot and gave her a sidelong look. "Even when the future of Paddington's is at stake?"

"You're not threatening me, are you?"

"Not in the slightest. I'm just saying this is a news leak we need to harness. Gain control. You know I don't like it when things are out of my control and I know you will do anything to save Paddington's. I think it might be time to take a spoonful of your own medicine, Robyn."

As he spoke, his eyes raked across her and for the second time that morning she felt her body respond to his visual caresses. Her breasts pressed up against the brushed cotton of her overworn dress. Something she'd thrown on for an early-morning walk along the shoreline as she fought for the right way to explain to Idris that she'd lost control of the ship she hadn't been steering all that well in the first place.

"If it's all right, I'd like to think about it."

"Think about what you'll say?"

"Think about whether or not I'll do the press conference," she corrected, knowing the wince crinkling her nose and shooting her eyebrows up to her hairline wasn't really giving her the in-charge-of-the-situation look she'd been going for. Her teeth bit down on her lower lip too hard, too fast, and as she ran her fingers along the lip to feel for blood, she knew if she looked up, her cheeks would once again burn with response at being the object of Idris's heated looks.

"What if I agree to do it with you?"

Her eyes shot up, her fingers stilling along her lip as an injection of hope surged through her. "Really? You'd do that for me?"

"I'd do it for Paddington's."

Idris knew damn well he was offering to do the press conference for Robyn, but telling her so would be akin to opening a vault whose doors were already bulging with unshared revelations.

Unwittingly, Robyn was bringing him back to life. She enabled him to see the blessings he had instead of focusing on all those he didn't. She was of the simple-pleasures school of life and it was serving him well to have her remind him of the importance of them. He turned at the gentle shift in the wind and inhaled the sweet scent of a woman.

Robyn was growing increasingly uncomfortable underneath the weight of Idris's gaze as he absorbed the impact she'd made on, not just him, but his daughter, too. He'd rarely heard Amira laugh before, and now—he cocked his ear upward—he could make out the giggly laugh only a tickling session with her nanny might elicit. A tickling session the nanny would never have attempted before Robyn.

"Good. Well, then, if you'll excuse me, I'm off for a swim." He untucked the towel from his hips and swung it over his shoulder as if the entire matter were settled.

"We'll carry on with our tour of Da'har as scheduled, and in three days' time, we will give a press conference. If you could let the appropriate parties know, I would be grateful."

He strode away, a smile on his lips as he felt her turn her head to watch as he strolled off into the morning surf. He liked having her here and was loath to think of a life without her in it. In some capacity.

Perhaps, he mused, his lips quirking back up into a grin, his "gazillions" could help secure Paddington's future, freeing her up for periodic visits to Da'har. Amira would love to see her again. He was sure of that and he—

Idris stepped into the sea and took a sure-footed dive into the incoming waves.

Yes.

He would like that very much, as well.

It was incredibly difficult to fume when all Robyn was feeling was abject terror.

A press conference? In front of...*press*?

Five hours, a car ride across the mountains toward

Da'har's central desert region and a breathtakingly delicious lunch hadn't done a jot to dissipate the growing panic over what she knew she had to do. A lunch of cardboard cutouts would most likely have done the same trick. And yet, the publicity the innovative surgery could generate was too important for the hospital to refuse. It was the whole reason she'd agreed to this harebrained trip.

Her eyes flicked across toward Idris.

Well.

Mr. Tall, Dark and Sheikhy may have had something to do with it, as well. But it had *definitely* started with a Paddington's Only remit, she assured herself. No romance here. Not in this heart!

She glanced across at Amira—right up front near the falconry experts, the sun glinting off her dark hair, happy as a lark in the center of a whole gaggle of children despite Idris's earlier protests. She felt a smile twitch and form. She'd won that discussion, anyway.

This moment made the soul-digging glares Idris had scorched into her psyche worth it. Amira was giggling away and pointing, the children making up their own sign language on the spot to explain everything. Sign language that involved lots of jumping and soaring arms, hands turning into beaks snapping up unsuspecting prey.

Knowing how much more Amira could enjoy the interaction if she could hear, especially later when the children would sing for her, Robyn just had to perform the surgery.

Which meant…she would have to do the press conference.

She squeezed her eyes shut against the falconry display and willed the images of popping flashbulbs and whirring cameras to disappear. Did photographers even use flashbulbs anymore?

Her lids flew open again, squinting sharply against the glare of the late-afternoon sun.

"Aren't you enjoying the display?" the increasingly familiar voice rumbled into her ear, his scent wafting and twirling around her as he leaned in to demand her full attention. If they hadn't been all alone in the shaded viewing tent she might have— What? Might have fled? Kissed him? Laid herself out on the pile of cushions and cried, *Take me now!*

A twirl of heat took hold below her belly and she squelched the wickedly, sensual thoughts from her mind as best she could.

She gave him a quick smile and nodded. The part of her that was able to focus *was* really enjoying herself. Two men in traditional dress were riding bareback on a pair of ridiculously beautiful chestnut stallions. The falcons rode, perched on the leather tether strapped to each man's forearm, flying upward toward the blinding light of the sun, then spiraling downward when they caught the prey other men sent heavenward in catapults designed for the show. It was a huge blur of color, action and raw strength.

"Perhaps you'd like to see me in action?"

Idris's eyes were still on the display, but had that been a note of hope in his voice? Her jaw dropped. Was he *flirting* with her?

Too easily she could picture him in one of the loose silk tops, the center slit of the cobalt blue fabric bearing down the length of his midriff. She could practically see the cloth fluttering behind him as he galloped, exposing the golden expanse of his bare chest and stomach. A heated bolt of attraction crackled down her spine, pooling luxuriously below the waistline of her silken *sherwal*, despite frowning most sternly against the sensation.

Not good. Her body's response to merely *thinking* about Idris's naked torso told her she'd need to chain herself to a tent pole in order to resist leaning forward for just a teeny-tiny touch. Precisely the reason she should have stayed at

Paddington's in her scrubs and working instead of coming to this wonderland that brought such light and...frisson to Paddington's most generous benefactor.

"A display may put us slightly behind schedule, of course." Idris's voice went slightly gravelly as he continued. "Riding in this heat is sweaty work."

Another burst of warmth showered through her at the thought of Idris standing beneath a cascade of water heated by the desert sun.

The inside of her cheek took a punishing blow as she tried to bite away the vision. She'd already had to scurry away once this morning when he'd strode off into the sea, knowing that watching him emerge from the water with that bronzed body, all dappled with drops of water, glistening in the morning sun...*agh!* Too much stimuli for her to compartmentalize.

Particularly with this blinking awful press conference hanging over her head.

"Don't worry about riding just for me. I'm fine."

Robyn shook her head in a solid "no" against the offer, but when a laser shot of disappointment streaked through Idris's dark eyes, she did an about-face so quickly she almost made herself dizzy.

"Now that I think about it... Yes. Absolutely, yes. I would love to see you in one of those shirts astride one of the stallions—"

She only just managed to stop midflow, a little too aware she had just opened her private thoughts to inspection.

Idris's lips, sensual beasts that they were, twitched forward, almost into a pucker. First a smile, then a frown was formed, and she couldn't help feeling like a starstruck teen as her heart began thumping in sporadic thuds, all but lurching straight up into her throat as she awaited his response.

"You wouldn't want to deny Amira a chance to see her father's prowess with a horse, would you? Maybe you'd inspire her to take up riding," she lamely tacked on, knowing her craving to see Idris at his rugged, shirtless, stallion-riding apex was a request best left unfulfilled.

"Of course," Idris answered, his features, as they most often were, recomposed into something unreadable even in the broad light of day. "My daughter has often told me she'd like to see me bare my chest to the elements, taking a horse under my command, teasing it into submission."

Robyn's eyes widened, then narrowed. "I do believe, Your Excellency, you are playing with my mind."

"Well spotted, Dr. Kelly."

She dipped into a small curtsy, and lowered her gaze. When she tilted up her head and dared to meet those black eyes of his, it was as if the invisible pane of glass between them had disappeared. The pounding of horses' hooves on the dunes accompanied the rhythm of her heart as Idris took her hand in his and raised it to his lips, eyes glued to hers as he pressed his mouth to the back of her hand.

Fireworks didn't even begin to cover her body's response to Idris's touch.

Feeling his lips upon her skin sent undulating waves of yearning through a bloodstream she was sure had been running on idle until Idris's kiss slammed it into high gear.

Idris let go of Robyn's hand as spontaneously as he had brought it to his lips, hoping to consign the action to a moment of madness, knowing full well the moments leading up to it had been laden with intent.

"I'm going to check on Amira."

He could feel Robyn's eyes on his back as he took the swift, long-legged strides he needed to work off whatever alchemy she had unwittingly bestowed on him. He'd thought the relationship he'd had with his wife was a once-in-a-lifetime experience. Now he knew he was wrong.

Robyn had found an entire fistful of keys with which to

open his heart—door after door of revelation. And it simply wouldn't do.

He had a kingdom to run. A daughter's welfare to look after. A future… His breath caught as he thought of the instant and unfillable void that would be left in his life when Robyn went back to London. In their lives.

He shook off the scowl as he approached his daughter and placed his hands upon her slight shoulders. The children all turned to face him, their expressions suddenly somber, eyes wide as saucers as they looked upon their leader.

It was decision time. He felt Amira twist out of his hands and look up to him. She knew as well as he did this wasn't "normal." Playing with children as if she were just any old child. But she wasn't a regular. She would one day be responsible for the future of the very children she was playing with.

And he wouldn't have her embarrassed by the singing display he knew was coming next. These sorts of displays could wait until after the surgery.

He stretched his neck, hearing the tension kink and pop as he did. The surgery that was dependent upon Robyn. He would have to do his utmost to ensure it went ahead—no hitches.

"The musicians have asked us to go to the tent for the singing." Kaisha appeared by his side, her tone ever neutral.

"No." He shook his head firmly, giving Amira's head an apologetic stroke as he did. "It was mostly for Robyn's sake, but—"

"What was for my sake?" Robyn asked, tucking her headscarf protectively around her shoulders. The deep green of the scarf had shimmers of gold woven through it, adding luster to her amber eyes. He resisted the urge to get lost in them, putting on the blinkers that had seen him through the last seven years.

"Singing. If you really want to hear them sing, we can

organize it back at the palace after Amira has gone to bed. I don't want her to be embarrassed."

"Why would she be embarrassed?"

"You, of all people, shouldn't have to ask that question." Idris felt his fingers tighten protectively around his daughter's shoulders.

"There are some wonderful ways to interpret music," Robyn protested, quickly kneeling down in front of Amira. "How would you like to hear your daddy sing to you?"

"You're just being cruel!" Idris protested in a low voice. "Why ask a question like that so close to the surgery? Of course she'd like to hear my voice. All of our voices, but she can't."

"No." Robyn looked up, her blond curls already escaping the confines of her scarf. "It's not cruel. It's realistic." She began signing as she spoke. "Your father is going to sing his favorite folk song to you." Then she fixed him with her eyes, a spark of defiance flaring in them as she did. "Get thinking. We've got to tell the musicians what they're about to play."

Enta eih.

Who was this woman? Powerful goddess or stubborn mule? For a split second Idris was grateful his daughter couldn't hear when he muttered a word not fit for any ears.

A bustle of activity ensued as, with Kaisha's help, Robyn scuttled everyone up to the open-sided tent prepared for the performance. He set off after her, his hand easily encircling her wrist as he pulled her around to face him.

"What is it you think you are doing? Public humiliation? Is that what you want for Amira?"

"How dare you!" she shot back. "How dare you think for a single moment I would do that to Amira."

"Then why do this? She is deaf!"

"Not for long if I have anything to do with it, and as

such, she needs to be used to the same lives you and I are lucky enough to lead."

"What?" He couldn't keep the sneer from his face. "A life dedicated to nothing but work?"

She turned away, for just a moment, as if he had slapped her. After scraping her chin along her shoulder, she faced him again, the tiniest of twitches appearing at the corner of her eye. "I meant living a life where it is far too easy to take the most precious of gifts for granted."

Idris didn't have to ask her what she meant. He saw it all in her eyes. The same longing he felt. The same struggle to break free from the locks and chains they'd imprisoned themselves with after grief struck in cruel, body-numbing blows.

"Sing to your daughter. I'll interpret."

It wasn't a plea. It was an entreaty to do the right thing.

Complex emotions poured into his heart, threatening to drown out his ability to think, let alone remember the words to a simple folk tune.

He'd never sung to Amira. Not once. And the understanding of that simple deprivation struck him hard. He'd been so busy protecting his child from what he thought would harm her, he had denied her the simple connections a parent and child could share. He grimaced and swallowed the strong sting of emotion at the back of his throat. Yet another thing he'd never succumbed to since his wife had died.

A few minutes later, at Robyn's suggestion, Idris was holding his daughter in his lap. Robyn stood across from him alongside the musicians and the children who had climbed onto a small set of risers.

"Whenever you're ready." Robyn nodded, almost too frightened to breathe. She could barely believe Idris had consented to her idea, let alone taken on board the all-too-real fact that she'd *volunteered* to stand in front with the performers. But this was important.

Idris and Amira would have a steep learning curve to climb as the little girl entered the world of the hearing, and the closer the bonds they shared, the easier going forward would be. Her own childhood was woven together by her mother's lullabies and she couldn't imagine Amira not knowing the sensation of being sung to.

Robyn closed her eyes against Idris's unblinking gaze and imagined herself back in the London theater where she and Amira had first met. She'd signed for her then. This would be no different.

The moment the music began Robyn knew she'd vastly underestimated how different this scenario was. Her hips began to organically shift and move in time to the music— the handful of unfamiliar instruments transforming the space around them as if they'd taken a magic carpet ride to a different time and place. The collective sound of the children's voices thickened and swelled into one perfect voice and her eyes locked with Idris's as he, too, began to sing. His attention was wholly undivided. The words sung in Da'harian by the children, English by Idris, were being sung directly to her.

The lyrics of the song, while simple, were heartfelt and pure. They told the story of a poor shepherd boy who'd fallen asleep beneath a pomegranate tree, dreaming of the girl he hoped to marry when he made his riches from the flock who grazed around him.

Robyn signed the words; her body's movements encapsulated the rhythm and pacing of the music. Idris's rich baritone would be vibrating from his chest through to his daughter's back—a sensation every bit as powerful as hearing the song would one day be. It cinched her heart tight to see his daughter pull his arms tight around her as the drama of the story unfolded.

Translating became more intuitive as the song's journey through the young shepherd's imaginings built and unfolded. Robyn's eyes moved between Idris and Amira, her fingers flying to tell the unchecked dreams of the solitary young man. His hope that he'd one day be brave enough to ask the questions lying in wait upon his lips. It became impossible to separate the lyrics from the man singing before her.

Her body felt alive with possibility. Was she being serenaded? Was Idris telling her what she was only just realizing she felt for him? Was he telling her he loved her, too?

A surge of happiness threatened to split her heart in two as Amira, in the midst of a powerful drumming sequence, leaped to her feet, pulling her father up by both hands, and began to dance. Idris willingly complied, singing the chorus at full volume, his head thrown back as he scooped up his daughter and they twirled and spun to the hypnotic beat of the music.

When the cadence of the music slowed and the children's voices lifted softly in sync with the instruments, Idris shifted his daughter to his hip, her small hand on his heaving chest, both of their eyes solidly on Robyn as she interpreted the final chorus Idris had now begun.

The shepherd, Idris sang, was jarred from his sleep when a fruit fell from the tree. The thud of the pomegranate upon the ground woke him from a perfect dreamworld only to discover all of his sheep had gone and he was left with nothing but the sour scent of the broken fruit spoiling in the heat of the burning sun.

The music dwindled away and Robyn was left standing, her body frozen, as if she herself were caught between the conflicting worlds of hope and reality.

Amira's fingers were skating across Idris's lips and he pressed them to his daughter's small fingertips, giving them each a small kiss, his eyes still very much linked to

Robyn's, his chest sucking in breath after life-affirming breath.

She turned abruptly, no longer able to stand in the remains of the words Idris had sung. Was it love he was feeling? Had it been love she'd seen in his eyes?

Or had he been trying to tell her what was inevitable? That theirs was a relationship never to be realized. Or worse. He could be telling her everything she'd thought had passed between them over the past week had all been in her head and there had never been any love at all.

CHAPTER NINE

"Dr. Kelly should be in the center," Idris directed the men setting up the nametags on the table, all the while looking over his shoulder to see where on earth she had got to.

"Are you sure?" Kaisha shot him a worried look and he didn't blame her.

They had spent large chunks of the past two days in the hospital at Robyn's request as she drilled the details of the surgery into her head.

He glanced at his watch. Twenty minutes until they would be live. Members of the press were already lurking outside the hospital doors. Some, he suspected, may have already wheedled their way in.

He and the press already had an...*understanding*. They left Amira out of the limelight, and he didn't shut down their businesses. He was all for democracy, but he valued privacy much, much more.

Where on earth was she?

He rocked back on his heels and worked his way through the past forty-eight hours. His eyebrows lifted in a satisfied arch as the answer came to him.

Sure enough, a few moments later he caught a glimpse of Robyn's tangle of blond curls hidden behind the foliage of an untamed succulent in the far corner of the central courtyard—a tiled maze of fountains, flower gardens and palms where patients and their families could escape the more sterile environment inside the hospital.

"Feeling up to facing your adoring public?" He sat down on the long slab of mahogany she was perching on, a clutch of note cards in her hands.

Robyn barked out a short laugh. "If I could hide back here and use a secret microphone, it would be much better."

He nudged her gently with his elbow. "You know you're up to it. Even Amira could talk you through the surgery at this point you've practiced on her so much."

"Would she like to do it? The press conference?"

He widened his eyes and gave her a very solid, "No."

Robyn turned to him, an embarrassed smile playing on her lips. "I've been horrible, haven't I?"

He lifted up his fingers and left a couple of centimeters between his thumb and index finger. "Just a bit horrible. The rest…" Their eyes clicked and with the connection along came the surge of endorphins he experienced whenever they shared a moment. "The rest of you has been *tolerable.*"

Liar.

She swatted away his hand and laughed, for real this time. "You should be the one who's nervous."

"Why would I be nervous?" he riposted. "I have chosen the best surgeon for the job." He meant it, too. The more Robyn fine-tuned her explanation of the groundbreaking treatment, turning the complicated medical language into layman's speak, the more confidence he had in her abilities to give his daughter the gift of hearing.

He still couldn't shake the incredible feeling of dancing with Amira in his arms, singing at top volume, his daughter's hands pressed on his chest as he sang, her eyes glued to his lips, absorbing the story he told as actively as any hearing child might. It was a moment any father and daughter would have been lucky to share. For that alone, he owed Robyn an unpayable debt of gratitude.

The buzz of her phone broke into the shared silence his comments had brought and she shot him an apologetic smile as she dug, like a sorceress, into the depths of her bag and retrieved her mobile.

"Message," she said, her lips tightening as her eyes scanned the note.

"Everything all right?"

"No," she answered tightly. "One of the patients I was hoping wouldn't need to be readmitted has just been brought in."

"Anything I can do?" Idris offered inanely, but seeing the color drain from Robyn's cheeks showed him just how much she cared and he didn't like the helpless feeling it elicited.

"Not unless you've got a secret stash of millions you don't need," she replied, her thoughts clearly elsewhere.

She'd obviously meant it as a throwaway comment. Robyn had never asked him for a single thing. She was still trying to offer him money for the clothes they had bought at Amira's insistence, some of which she was wearing now.

The ensemble she'd chosen for the press conference was a beautiful sky blue, enhancing the rich coloring of her eyes, the soft pink of her lips and, now, the growing pink flush on her cheekbones as she became aware of the intensity of his gaze.

He shook his head and gave her knee a perfunctory pat.

"The best thing you can do for this patient—"

"Penelope," Robyn filled in.

"The best you can do—we can do—for Penelope is get on with this press conference. Bring the publicity you and your team deserve at Paddington's."

Robyn nodded. "I know. I just really can't bear all the attention. It genuinely terrifies me."

"Don't be scared." Idris, against his better judgment, took her hands in both of his and held them tight. "You were there for Amira and me yesterday in a way no one has been before. Today we are here for you."

The look she gave him in return was so filled with gratitude he had to fight not to pull her to him, holding her close as he had done once before.

With members of the press lurking everywhere it made things more complicated. The last thing he wanted was photos giving the wrong impression of their relationship taking precedence over the press conference. He could see the headlines now: *Royal Scandal! Passion Not Parenting!*

If only they knew how incredible a parent Robyn would be to his little girl. Their instant connection, the smiles, the *laughter*! Amira would be hard-pressed to find someone else to better fill the space her mother had left in her wake.

Idris's chest instantly hollowed as the air swept out of his lungs.

A mother for Amira.

She had a mother!

A mother she'd never known. Never would.

Robyn offered...possibility.

He looked down at Robyn's fingers, nervously tip-tapping against his hands, and swallowed away the conflicting thoughts. With a sharp breath, he placed her hands back in her lap, wishing he'd never taken them up at all. Robyn didn't need any diversions. Nor did he.

"Come." He rose and tipped his head toward the lecture room where everything had been set up for them. "Leave that enormous bag of yours and let's go dazzle the media."

An anxious smile crept onto Robyn's lips. "You'll be in the room, right?"

A simple question, but the look in her eyes was so much more complex. The only thing he could think of in response to the hope alight in those amber eyes of hers was, *As long as you need me, I'll be there.*

The words were still ringing in Robyn's ears as she settled herself into the chair at the center of the table. "As long as you need me, I'll be there."

She was beginning to think forever might be just about long enough, but she would take right now as a starting block. She'd seen something in Idris's eyes just then. Something she knew a glance in the mirror would reveal in her own.

Love.

She loved him. She loved Amira. Heck! She loved Da'har with its varied landscape, the rich culture, the way Idris steered it boldly into the future with a solid understanding of his nation's past. And knowing all of these things, owning them in her heart, gave her strength to lift her head up from her notes and begin to speak.

She found herself boldly looking directly into camera lenses, explaining the finer points of the gene therapy they hoped Amira would benefit from. When a reporter would ask her a question, instead of her insides being reduced to a wobbly jangle of nerves, she felt her spine straighten, and clear, concise answers come out of her mouth. At moments, it was almost as though she was looking at herself through the reporters' lenses, seeing a confident, intelligent, capable woman.

"And what of Her Highness?" one particularly insistent reporter asked. "How aware is the Sheikha of what will be happening to her?"

"Very much," Robyn answered. "I have explained the surgery and gene therapy to her—along with her father's input, of course—until I was confident she fully understood the process."

"Aren't you just setting her up for disappointment?" another jumped in.

"How do you mean?"

"If it doesn't work."

"That's always a possibility," Robyn replied, astonished she wasn't scooping up all of her paperwork and fleeing. Admitting something she was going to do could be a failure was not normally something she conceded to with confidence. But this time around, it felt as if part of her had been in hiding and had finally come out into the light for a grand reveal. All of the trust and confidence her colleagues had invested in her suddenly had merit. She knew where it had come from. The fire. The newfound strength.

It came from the enigmatic and utterly engaging Sheikh of Da'har. The dark-haired man sitting alongside her as she spoke, hands folded loosely on top of his knee, nodding, occasionally offering a supportive smile as he invested the most precious thing of all in her abilities: trust.

He was telling the world loud and clear he was trusting Robyn Kelly with his daughter's well-being and the swell of pride she felt in that knowledge was all she needed to make the press conference a success.

She leaned forward, eyes scanning from reporter to reporter, and spoke with a voice she hardly recognized as her own. "There are only a handful of hospitals in the world capable of such cutting-edge surgery. And of that handful, we at Paddington Children's Hospital are the only ones brave enough to do it."

"You mean *you're* the only one brave enough to do it?" shouted a reporter with a British accent.

Robyn shrugged. Wasn't that apparent? It was hardly her style to jump up and shout, "Yeah! I'm the best in the world!" She turned at the unexpected sound of Idris's voice.

"I think you'll find Dr. Kelly is in a league of her own. There is no one else to whom I would entrust my daughter's care. And just so we are clear—" Idris leaned forward, forearms pressed on the table, chin cocked to one side, the press mimicking the gesture as if magnetically drawn to him "—Her Royal Highness is living a rich and full life. This is not a win or lose situation. This is all gain." He shot Robyn a grateful look before continuing. "Dr. Kelly is the only surgeon I would trust to take on such a monumentally important surgery and Paddington Children's Hospital has the very best of facilities for the intricate surgery. Their long-established record of succeeding where other hospitals have not has earned my complete confidence. If, for whatever reason, her hearing is not restored, my daughter will continue to live a meaningful and well-balanced life— not least of which will include one day taking the reins of leadership in Da'har."

All eyes swung to Robyn. She surprised herself by meeting the gape-jawed looks with a confident smile. "Thank you very much for coming. The next time we see you will be in London after what we expect will be a successful surgery."

She stood and gave a slight bow of the head as she'd seen many Da'harian women do when a conversation had finished. A quick glance over her shoulder as she turned to walk out of the auditorium told her Idris was close enough for her to hear his whispered words. "You dazzled them."

Lil' ol' plain Jane Robyn Kelly! Barren spinster. The woman who knew the nooks and crannies of Paddington's better than she did the cupboards of her own home. And now a media darling! It was one of those moments when all you could do was laugh at the madness of how far she'd come from thinking of herself as the barren spinster of Paddington's.

Getting to this point hadn't been a solo flight, though. It had been a duet.

* * *

"How would you feel about taking a walk with me?" Idris poked his head into Amira's room where she and Robyn had gone to read after supper. He'd looked in earlier and had barely been able to wipe the smile off his face for the last hour. Two heads—one blond, the other dark—pressed together as they worked their way through the intricacies of the elaborate tale. From what he could determine there were swashbucklers, princesses and a rather unfortunately named camel.

"Robyn?"

He took a step into the room, his smile growing softer, more tender, as he took in the sight of the pair of them, fast asleep on Amira's large canopy bed. His daughter was curled in the crook of Robyn's arm, the book having spilled to one side. Robyn's body language was entirely open and loving, even in her sleep. Her cheek was resting atop of Amira's dark hair, one arm protectively wrapped around his little girl's shoulders, the other enclosing Amira in a loose hug. Throughout Robyn's time in Da'har, there had, not even for a moment, been anything awkward or strained about the way the pair were with each other, and in sleep, the relationship they shared seemed, if possible, even more honest. One trusting soul with another.

He watched them for a moment before silently padding over to the bed and gently extracting Amira from Robyn's embrace so that he could tuck her under the covers. She stirred a little as he moved her, sleepily crooking the stuffed elephant she favored under her arm as he pulled up the covers and switched off the bedside lamp.

Walking around to the other side of the bed he wondered for a moment if he shouldn't just leave Robyn. She looked more relaxed and at peace than he had probably ever seen her. A swell of pride took hold of his chest as he remembered how well she had done at the press conference, despite her long-held fear of public speaking. Pride was replaced by passion as the desire to touch her, hold her in his arms, took such strong possession of him; he was lifting her up and out of the bed before common sense could prevail.

Robyn's arms slid naturally across his shoulders and chest, cinching together at the base of his neck as, still half-asleep, she nestled her curly blond head into his shoulder. The touch of her silky hair upon his cheek, intermingling with the wildflower meadow scents that swirled around her, threatened to undo him then and there.

Before he thought better of it, he tipped down his chin and kissed her.

Robyn wasn't sure if she was dreaming or if she was receiving a very real kiss. She clenched her eyes tight, not wanting whatever was happening to come to an end. Hits of understanding came to her.

Idris's scent. Cinnamon and hot sun mixed with pure alpha male.

His touch. Fingertips pressing possessively along her midriff, shifting with intent along the silken top she wore over a pair of body-hugging *sherwal* trousers. A cascade of goosepimples shivered along her spine as more details came to her.

His arms were around her. One around her back and the other under her knees, holding her as if she weighed nothing more than sunshine itself.

His lips, which she could feel hovering just above hers, were every bit as sensuous as she had imagined them to be. The touch of them so soft and evocative… Surely this had to be a dream.

Her eyes fluttered open, lashes brushing against his soft skin, before their gazes locked and an understanding passed between them. The desire was mutual and pressing, unchecked, against doors they both wanted to open.

Her lips parted. She felt the brush of his stubble against her skin as he took possession of her mouth again. Hungry, heated kisses seared her to her very core and all she could think was...more.

Idris's spicy scent intermingled with the sweet taste of his lips. It was impossible to hold in a whimper as he drew his lips away from hers and began to drop kisses along the length of her neck. Softly at first and then, as her senses shot to life at the speed of light, the pressure from his lips grew more urgent. As he reached her throat, and then her mouth, his tongue took advantage of the parting of her lips as a low moan escaped her throat. Lightning jags of response crashed through her, jettisoning her entire body onto another plane of touch alight with electricity.

"I want you."

She could barely believe she'd spoken the words, but they were the truest thing she could say. She did want him. Body and soul she ached for him in a way she hadn't known possible.

Idris accelerated his pace, taking the length of the never-ending corridor in long-legged strides, turning, unexpectedly, into his own suite of rooms, which she hadn't yet seen.

The blur of decor she glimpsed as he carried her toward his emperor-size bed was deeply male. Rich scarlets, the darkest of blues and the raw luster of mahogany melded together to craft the extraordinary sensation of masculine beauty. Something Idris's entire being exuded. Especially now as he laid her out on his bed, chest heaving with ragged breaths, not from exertion but desire.

If he had wanted her to beg she knew she would have.

Never before had anyone looked at her with such longing. She could see the flashes and glints of hunger in his eyes, as if a damn had burst within his psyche. More than anything, she wanted to satiate his every appetite.

Lush, wanton thoughts crowded out the woman Robyn

had thought she once was as a sexual confidence she'd never experienced took hold of her. She pressed herself up to sitting, tipped her chin up so that she could meet Idris's black, sparking gaze and reached out to touch him below his waist where his desire for her was most evident.

He gasped at the contact, instantly pulling her up so that her legs encircled his waist, both hands cupping her buttocks as his lips crashed down on hers with a heated urgency she ached to return. Such was the depth of her need for him, slaking her hunger for Idris's kisses, his touch, would be nigh on impossible.

Idris unhooked Robyn's legs from around his waist, his arms bearing her entire weight just millimeters away from his own as if it would help check his body's primal urges to possess her. Whether she was light as a feather or he was channeling the strength of a Titan—all he knew was he was holding an angel in his arms. Amber eyes. A halo of blond curls. The softest skin he had ever touched.

He laid Robyn onto his bed, standing stock-still for just a moment as he drank in the sight of the wild, desire-fueled woman he'd uncaged. He lowered his knees to the edge of the bed, then fully mounted it, crawling slowly forward as a triumphant lion would approach a prospective mate, to take possession of what he knew he had already won.

The tight line of connection that had drawn them together cinched and became unbreakable.

Idris's lips peeled into a satisfied smile with each whimper and groan of pleasure he drew from her. The simplest of movements—a finger tracing the soft outline of her jaw, his lips skidding across the décolletage of her *dishdasha*, a thumb grazing the sides of her straining breasts as he lowered his mouth to kiss them through the thin fabric—each gesture elicited a complexity of responses.

There was much more than lust in those amber eyes of

hers, and when she whispered into his ear, he could have sworn she told him that she would always be his. Only be his.

An even deeper longing for Robyn shunted straight to his heart, spreading like scintillating pulses through his entire bloodstream. Theirs was a mixture of primal and cerebral, an inevitable union as the stars aligned for them. For tonight, at least, they would be as one.

Robyn's body positively thrummed with need. She began, timidly at first, then insistently, to undo the buttons on Idris's shirt, then his trousers. His impatience matched hers and within milliseconds he had dispensed of his clothes and her own.

When the length of his naked body pressed against hers, a cry of longing so carnal she barely knew where it had come from curled up and out of her throat. Each of his touches was pure erotica. The caress of his hands. The sensation of his bedclothes against her skin as he moved her to where he could please her best. The soft hair on his leg as he wound it around hers, decreasing the ever-diminishing space between them. The wet warmth of his mouth traveling from her breasts to her belly and beyond—all threatened to be her undoing.

Her body became possessed by a need to touch and be touched, to have him inside her, deep and unfettered. After an agony of strokes and teases, Idris slipped a hand between her legs, fingers slowly sliding along the length of her wetness before pulling his hand along her inner thigh until he reached her knee, tugging her leg onto his back as he lowered himself into the hot, eager center of her very womanhood.

It was the first time in Robyn's life she had experienced complete, full-bodied ecstasy at the touch of another man. Her body melded with his as their movements intensified, each of them undulating and pressing together to reach the ultimate release, until finally, when she felt they could fly no higher, everything within her burst into a shimmering cloud of sensation and pleasure. Idris reached the same heated denouement deep within her, his spine arching, belly pressing into hers as Robyn's nails scored the length of his back, eliciting a whimper of the purest satisfaction from her parted lips.

They lay in silence, each of them taking long, full-bodied lungfuls of air as their bodies recovered. Idris shifted to his side, pulling Robyn in tight to him so that her back met his stomach and chest, the beat of his heart pumping straight through to her own. As their heartbeats synchronized and slowed, she knew, at long last, she would sleep without dreams, for everything she could have hoped for was right there next to her.

CHAPTER TEN

DAWN WAS ONLY just creeping into the room when Idris inhaled a deep breath of wildflowers and sunshine—the scent of heaven if ever there was one. It took a moment or two to realize he was still holding Robyn in his arms. If anything, she had nestled in closer in the course of the night; their limbs were softly tangled. Her soft curls tickled and teased the side of his cheek and life seemed near enough perfect until he realized, with a deafening pound of his heart, that Amira might come in at any moment. It happened more often than not. When she'd had a bad dream, or a question about a book she was reading.

Mouth dry, pulse racing, his mind thundered with possibility.

Would it be so bad if she were to find them?

He had ached for the fact his daughter had no mother figure. Someone to speak with about the myriad things only women share with one another. Someone to light up her somber world. Someone who would be there for her when, one day, Amira ascended into womanhood. He knew playing the roles of both mother and father only went so far, and yet... He was already asking her to trust in Robyn regarding the operation. If that were to fail...?

He extracted himself, as gently as possible, from the weave of their limbs, not wanting to wake her before he knew where he stood on...what exactly? It wasn't as if he and Robyn were going to have a life together! She lived in England—in Paddington's by all counts. He had a nation to rule, a daughter to raise—to the very best of his undivided attentions.

The decision to make love to Robyn suddenly seemed careless. Not a decision at all but an impulse. A matter of the heart he should have overruled with his conscience. Falling in love with Robyn—what could that lead to?

A jagged slash of pain rent through him so completely he could have sworn he'd been split in two. Physical proof he had nothing to offer her beyond a heart battered and singed by life's crueler turns.

Robyn. Beautiful, sunlit, optimistic Robyn, who had brought nothing but kindness and light into their lives.

He took another step back from the bed and began yanking on his trousers and then his shirt, as if they would shield him from the desire to crawl back into her arms and give himself over to the unknown.

His lips pressed and thinned against each other.

Robyn deserved more. And he had to slam shut the windows of opportunity that kept blinking at him. Hope. Possibility. Love.

He must lead, if he were to make good on the promises he'd made to the memory of his wife.

Everything for the past seven years had been solely for Amira and Da'har. Blood and country. It was how he'd survived. There hadn't been room in his heart for anything more.

He looked down at Robyn, her face soft with the innocence of sleep.

How reckless he'd been! Selfish even, to have pulled her so close to him when he didn't have a full and open heart to offer her. Robyn deserved every bit of a man's heart.

His heart. But after all he'd been through, it was no longer his to give.

The thoughts whirling in his brain began to compound with viselike strength. How was he going to get out of this without hurting Robyn?

He shook his head knowing damn well how he would deal with it. Precisely the same way he'd made it through the tragedy that had blindsided him all those years ago. By steeling his heart and realigning his focus. Blood and country. Nothing more.

It didn't take Robyn long to figure out something was wrong. Her legs and arms were wriggling about in a luxurious stretch when, still half-asleep, she realized the sheets she was tugging up and over her shoulder were the ones in her own bedroom. She sat bolt upright, her heart stopping dead still, then unleashing in a series of staccato pumps. One for each question flying through her mind. How did she get here? Where was Idris? Had last night been a dream?

She threw back the covers and tugged on some clothes, barely noticing it was perfectly natural for her to reach for the formfitting leggings and loose tunic native to Da'har. All she could think of was whether or not she had done something wrong. Had she upset Idris in some way? Spoken in her sleep about—what? Paddington's?

She tried to push away the hurt she was feeling, certain there was some sort of simple explanation. It wasn't as if she'd been expecting rose petals, a perfect cup of Earl Grey and a plate of freshly baked scones to arrive on her lap, but after the night they'd shared she'd expected...*something.*

No. That wasn't right, either.

She'd expected *someone.*

Idris.

This was a message. It had to be. A cruel one. Depositing her back in her bed after— A shiver of response slipped along her spine at the memory of her night in Idris's arms. Only to be left on her bed as if it had meant nothing?

She sped along the corridor toward his office, little snippets of possibility taking form in her head, then reshaping over and over as she blindly made her way past the tiles, fountains and tumbles of lush vegetation that, until now, had never failed to enchant her.

Was he *ashamed* of what they had done?

Fear stole through her at the thought, chased cruelly by the anguish of loss. The same hollow feeling she hadn't experienced since her hysterectomy.

She'd been right two weeks ago. To want to stay in the UK. She'd told *everyone*! Coming to Da'har was ridiculous. She'd be out of her depth. Destroy any good that might come of doing Amira's operation.

Amira.

Paddington's.

The tight squeeze in her heart made her gasp. She'd let Idris's beautiful little girl slip too far into her heart, as well.

Idris.

A low moan escaped her lips as she thudded her forehead with the ball of her hand. How could she have let this happen when the only thing she should have been thinking of was saving Paddington's?

Idris had it all. Her heart, her body. What she had left of her mind was going to have to be put to exacting use, to regain what little control she had over her future. Over the future of Paddington's. If she had to fall on the sword of sacrifice, she would do it.

Her knuckles stung as she rapped on the carved wooden exterior of Idris's office. Too impatient to wait for a response, she pushed open the thick wooden door only to find a very officious-looking Idris sitting at his desk, pen in hand, a sheaf of papers laid out before him as if it were any old day.

Didn't he know her world had changed when she gave herself to him?

"Is that your luggage?" she asked inanely as a luggage-laden servant walked past from the room where they had spent the night wrapped in the other's arms.

"Yes," Idris replied, looking up from his paperwork as if her presence in his office was a complete mystery. Those dark eyes of his, so expressive the night before, were now impenetrable in their inky darkness. The glacial reserve she'd shivered under upon their first meeting was icily back in place. "It would probably be a good idea to get your things together. I can have someone else do it if you're busy. The plane will leave today at lunchtime."

"Plane?"

"Yes." He nodded as if she'd already been given a run-down of the day's itinerary and hadn't burned it into her psyche as everyone else had. "To England."

"You're sending me back to England?"

His hardened features were a cruel confirmation of what she'd feared but never put words to. Her life would always be a lonely one.

"What about Paddington's?"

The question hung in the air between them until Idris pushed back from his desk with a harsh sigh he knew came across as exasperated when in fact he felt as if the universe was sucking his lungs dry. The look on Robyn's face told him everything he needed to know.

In one swift moment, he had torn each and every fiber of connection they'd shared in their short time together.

But it was the right decision. Whatever it was that had passed between them had to end. No amount of wide-eyed, bewildered amber looks would change his mind.

"We're *all* going to England. I've made the appropriate calls regarding Amira's admission into Paddington's and trust you are well placed to set the wheels in motion on your end. Sooner is better."

Robyn just stood and stared, her eyes swirling with confusion, appalled by his behavior. He fought the urge to cross to her, hold her in his arms and tell her he knew he was being a fool. What would that do other than make things worse? The Idris he'd been over the past fortnight was gone now. The one who had felt happy. Contented. Prepared to face the world, at long last, with a smile. The shadow of a smile disappeared from his face. He couldn't be that man. Not with a daughter to raise. A kingdom to rule.

Robyn's unnatural silence threatened to be his undoing.

"I don't think I need to remind you, Dr. Kelly, that I have responsibilities that override your holiday plans being curtailed. Perhaps it's time to make good on all those promises you made at the press conference yesterday."

Her jaw dropped at his words.

"Dr. Kelly, we've not got much time and I'm quite busy. If you don't mind…" He gave his watch a cursory glance, ignoring the tangle of blond curls whose wisps had tickled along his cheek as they'd lain, limbs tangled together, in silken sheets. The amber eyes that had flickered with desire solely for him. The dusky rose lips that had whispered vows of commitment to him and him alone.

He slammed the door shut on the memories. He couldn't give her his lacerated heart. Not with the loss he'd suffered. Not with an empty palace standing in the center of the capital—a hollow testament to the love he had once had and could never have again. Not with Amira's future at stake.

He gritted his teeth and forced himself to swallow the bitter pill.

This had to end.

"Perhaps you could stop by Amira's room, suggest

some things she might bring along for her stay in the hospital." His dismissive tone did not go unnoticed and, in true Robyn-style, he saw her heels press more soundly to the marble floor.

"Perhaps, as her *father*, you should explain to her what's going on."

"About what exactly, Dr. Kelly? She knew we'd be heading to London shortly."

Robyn staggered back a step, sending him a look of disbelief so powerful it pierced straight through to his soul.

He was handling this about as well as he had handled the loss of his wife—which was precisely the point. He wouldn't—*couldn't*—give Robyn his heart. And his priority was Amira. She was used to the harsher edges of his personality. Sharp contours that had softened with Robyn in their lives.

"Your Excellency," Robyn bit out, her voice now curling with well-deserved disdain, "while I appreciate your time is precious, it is my professional opinion that your priority right now is to be a father."

Idris swallowed the words as if they were poison.

"Are you suggesting my daughter is not my absolute priority?"

"Not at all. But I do know it can be difficult for a parent to put their child through an experimental operation like this. You want what's best for her, but it can be very frightening for both the patient and the parent."

She was giving him an out—an excuse for behaving abominably. One he couldn't take.

"I think you may have misread my intentions when I invited you to Da'har," Idris bit out, the words tasting acrid as they crossed his lips. "My daughter is my one, my only, focus. The flight will be leaving shortly. You'd be well advised to pack your things."

Robyn, to his astonishment, simply stood there, unblinking, her body soaking in the aftermath of his vile words. A jag of anger tore through him that she wasn't finding this as painful as he was. He willed the burning in his heart to turn to ice, barely recognizing his own voice when he finally broke the silence he'd forced upon them.

"Dr. Kelly, let's not add letting down Paddington's to the day's list of things to do."

He'd been certain she would cry. Flee the room. Anything other than stand there and stare at him with her wide, amber eyes.

"You do remember you're human, don't you? That you're allowed to feel pain and fear, just like the rest of us mere mortals."

Robyn's voice was steady as she handed him the olive branch, a move far too generous for someone who'd received such an unkind verbal swipe. Where he had become cold-blooded, she had become brave. A modern-day Boadicea, fearlessly protecting all that she held to be true. If his daughter's welfare weren't at stake, he'd see his own behavior as cowardice. But he had her heart to defend as well as his own and this was the only way he knew how.

Robyn shook her curls away from her eyes and met Idris's gaze with an intensity she hardly knew she possessed. He may not love her, but she would not let him rob her of her dignity in the process.

"If you don't mind me saying, it's not right what you're doing. Living in the past isn't going to help your daughter."

"I most certainly do mind!" His hand slapped against the mahogany sheen of his desk with a resounding clap, making it clear Robyn was stepping into extremely unwelcome territory. "Amira *is* my way of looking forward."

"You're imposing responsibilities on a child that you should be carrying!" she shot back.

"And I suppose your rich and varied experience as a parent enables you to make all these wise decisions?"

Robyn looked away, her throat constricting against a swell of nausea. She knew Idris wasn't biting out at her. He was angry with the world, but whenever the barbs from a frightened parent became personal these were the moments that hurt the most. The judgments people made just because she didn't have children of her own. As if they thought being barren rendered her incapable of empathy, of love.

She closed her eyes for a moment, imagining she was back in one of the family rooms at Paddington's. White coat over sensible attire. Parents looking at her with wide-eyed disbelief that the perfect child they'd created was in hospital. A mixture of hope that whatever she said would fix it all and fear that life as they knew it would never be the same. All of the Pennys and Ryans flickered past her mind's eye and poured the strength she needed back into her heart.

"Idris, Your Excellency, I may not have a child of my own, but I have spent each and every day of my professional life with children and their parents during their darkest hours. I have fallen in love with more of them than I can count. I have grieved with their parents when we have lost them. I have cheered alongside many more when their child, with Paddington's help, overcame some of life's cruelest hurdles. So, yes. I think my experience affords me a certain level of expertise in understanding when a parent's wishes interfere with a child's needs."

"Is that what you think I'm doing? Interfering?" Idris rose from his desk with a surge of unchecked fury that made Robyn grateful for the expanse of desk standing solidly between them.

"No. I think you are loving your daughter to the best of your ability."

"And in your eyes—" his voice grew colder as he spoke "—my 'ability' to love my daughter falls short?"

Oh, you want me to insult you? Kick you while you're down? Tough.

"I think you are capable of much more than you give yourself credit for," Robyn replied, the painful sting of tears teasing at the back of her throat. He may not love her, but she'd be damned if she was going to let him wallow in self-pity. He had life, a daughter, a kingdom! She gave Idris a curt nod. "If you'll excuse me, I'd better get my things together."

When she closed the door behind her, it took everything in her power not to race to her room and release the flood of tears for all that she had gained and lost when she had left the safety of Paddington's behind.

CHAPTER ELEVEN

EVEN THE ROAR of the jet's engines couldn't drown out Idris's thoughts.

Robyn hadn't so much as said a word to him since they'd left the palace. Not that he blamed her. If he could pull back the sand that had swept through the hourglass since this morning he would have. Whatever had passed between them, she didn't deserve the icy blows he delivered with too much ease.

Seven years. Seven years of lashing out at a world that had done nothing but try and make up for the grief he couldn't bear to set aside.

He accepted a glass of sparkling water from the flight attendant, grateful for the fleeting diversion from his thoughts.

Amira, he noticed, was back to her sober little self. The ready smile she'd worn so often over the past week, the laughter, all hidden away.

His lips carved a scowl into the sides of his mouth, knowing they could be smiling and laughing right now if history hadn't ripped his heart out of his chest for daring to love. Trusting that such a perfect happiness would last.

Amira slipped out of the seat beside him, having teased the last of the stories out of him hours earlier. He reached out a hand to touch the long, slick gloss of hair, just missing the connection as she crawled into Robyn's lap. He watched, transfixed, as after a moment's discussion Robyn began to sing to her. His daughter's small fingers traced Robyn's lips as she mouthed along with her, occasionally forming words out loud, and in a bittersweet moment of perfection that nearly brought tears to his eyes, the pair hit a perfect harmony when their voices converged as one.

A flash of insight struck him. How talkative Amira had become since Robyn had been with them. Amira's voice bore the telltale thickness of a deaf child's, instinct unable to conquer the inability to hear, and yet, hearing her join in as Robyn sang about mockingbirds and diamond rings, he wondered how it would sound in a week's time, when Amira could hear her own voice.

Hot, searing pain rammed into his chest as he reminded himself Robyn would play little to no part of Amira's voyage of discovery. He'd made sure of that this morning.

"There, can you see?" Robyn stopped singing and pointed, then signed rapidly as she spoke to Amira. "London."

They each peered out of an oval window, Amira's face alight with interest as Robyn pointed out Buckingham Palace and the London Eye. Even Paddington's signature turrets were easy to spot from the flight path their pilot had taken. It was the place where his daughter's life would be changed forever—where both of their lives had already been changed by this whirlwind of a woman who had burst into his hotel room only a few weeks before.

He shifted in his seat, uncomfortable with the pendulum swing of his thoughts. He'd made his decision.

Even with only ten minutes to go, Robyn would have happily forsaken the luxury of his private jet for a knee-cramping, elbow-jabbing economy seat on an overcrowded commuter plane in lieu of enduring the torture of sitting across from Idris.

His eyes lifted to meet hers, the darkness of his irises, as ever, fathomless and inaccessible.

Her hands curled into fists, gathering up the thick fabric of the skirt she'd worn on the flight out. A pathetic gesture, really. As if her slim fingers could defend her from the churning disappointment and loss she knew she'd finally give in to when this was all over. Already she missed the silken caresses of the clothes she'd worn in Da'har. The exotic, hot scents of the country. Idris's smile.

She sat back in the soft leather seat with a huff. Just thinking of pawing through her bag, finding her key, putting it in the lock of the flat she knew had never been a home, exhausted her. She'd probably slept more nights in the hospital's on-call rooms than at her "nest." It was neither nest, nor home. Just a place she hung her clothes in between surgeries.

Idris's palace in Da'har had been more of a home to her in less than a fortnight than her own had ever been.

Squeezing her eyes shut tight against the thought only let the darkness creep further into her overanxious heart.

She eased one eye open, then the other, blinkering her vision so that she could only see Amira. Her beautiful heart-shaped face. The sheet of ebony hair cascading down her slim, little shoulders. Robyn's chest squeezed tight when she saw the hope and light that lit up Amira's almond-shaped eyes when she realized Robyn was looking at her. Saying goodbye to this little girl was going to be particularly painful.

Swallowing down the tears she refused to let come, she pasted on a smile.

Never mind. She was back in London now. She could jump into a taxi and go straight to Paddington's where everything would right itself back into its natural order once again. What had happened in Da'har was…an aberration. A mirage more like, she silently chided herself. A beautiful, sand and sea and Idris-filled mirage.

She tugged a few folders out of her satchel, blindly training her eyes upon the papers as if the words she could barely focus upon would save her life.

The diagrams and side notes began to pull her back to her comfort zone and at long last she felt a smile begin to creep onto her lips. The surgery wouldn't save a life—but it would most assuredly change Amira's for the better.

As the plane touched down and she turned on her mobile, it sprang to life with some sobering news.

Ryan Walker had had a turn for the worse. The sooner she could get back to Paddington's and help with the fallout, the better. Ryan's brain injury wasn't her area of expertise, but the young boy had had the entire staff rooting for his recovery. Losing him now, when he'd fought so hard against the odds…

What was it Idris was fond of saying in his darker moments?

Life wasn't fair.

She pulled her satchel up onto her lap and unbuckled herself from the luxurious leather seat before giving Idris a quick nod. "I'll see you two tomorrow at Paddington's."

She planted a swift kiss on the top of Amira's head, and the moment the stairs were lowered to the private entrance, she began to run. Lungs burning, feet racing, heart pounding so hard she could hear nothing but the rush of blood in her head. She ran and ran until she was safely in a taxi heading back to Paddington's where she belonged.

The platter of chocolate-covered ginger biscuits stared at Idris accusingly. One side amber, the other inky black. He had half a mind to fling them off the balcony.

"Who on earth requested these?"

"No one. I think they just assumed, given your order from the last time we stayed, you might want them again?" Kaisha answered from under the desk where she had been plugging in the various laptops, mobiles and other electronics they never seemed to be able to travel without these days.

"I don't think we'll stay here next time," he growled. "If there is a next time."

"The hospital has offered you a suite at Paddington's if you prefer. Amira will need to be prepped and ready quite early tomorrow morning, so…" Kaisha crawled out from the desk, managing to intersect him as he stalked from room to room in the hotel suite he wished he'd never taken. It was too awash with memories of his first meeting with Robyn.

Across the suite, Amira's little face was pressed up against the rain-streaked windows as she stared at the iconic buildings they'd seen from the airplane. She was missing Robyn, too—and no amount of sterling British architecture would fill that gap.

Kaisha discreetly cleared her throat as she waited for an answer, only to stumble back a few steps as he wheeled on her, hands splayed out in disbelief.

"They think I'm going to be able to *relax* while my daughter's future is hanging in the balance?" Idris's eyes shot heavenward, realizing as he spoke that this could be the last time he could speak loudly, harshly even, without causing distress to his daughter, whose eyes were still glued to the London cityscape beyond the floor-to-ceiling windows.

He glanced at Kaisha, now slowly backing away from him, a hint of fear all too visible in her eyes. The same look she'd often worn before Robyn had come into their lives.

A streak of remorse twisted his features as he pressed his hands to his face. Had he used Amira's deafness as a means of justifying this way of speaking with people?

"I think it was more so you'd have somewhere private to—"

"To what?" Idris interjected. "Wait and find out if my daughter is still deaf?"

"I believe Robyn—Dr. Kelly, I mean…" Kaisha's voice faded out as the expression on Idris's face grew dark again.

Robyn. The light to his shade. The woman with courage enough to challenge him with what he himself could not bear to confront: his fear. The creeping, terrifying tendrils of laser-sharp fear threatening to drown him in darkness as the moment approached when he would hand over his daughter's welfare to—

The only woman in the world he would trust with her care.

He began to shake his head, eyes searching the growing darkness as night fell over London's skyline.

What had he done? How big a fool had he been?

"Anyone want to run through things one more time?"

Robyn held up her gloved hands and scanned the pairs of eyes peeking out at her from above their surgical masks. Sure they were only practicing on a model, but it was important to mimic the exact conditions in which they would be doing the operation.

Not a single headshake.

Just as it should be.

"May I get the case for the middle ear pieces, please, Rosie?"

"You got it, Robyn."

The flame-haired nurse carried over the special box that would house the miniscule middle ear replacement.

A rap on the door turned all of their heads.

"All right, Leo?" Robyn called out cheerily. "Ready to help out with prep tomorrow?"

The pediatrician stuck his head through the door with

a smile. "Absolutely. Can't wait to be part of history in the making!"

He received a chorus of whoops in response. These were the moments when Paddington's really shone. They were an unbreakable team—particularly in the face of the unknown.

"Rosie, I'm heading down to the Frog and Peach. Meet me there?"

"Mmm?" Rosie stood absolutely still as Robyn loaded the precious pieces into the case, releasing an audible sigh as she did. "Sorry, love. I'll be there in half an hour."

Va bene." Leo gave the door frame a clap and turned to go. "Get your beauty sleep, everyone. And best of luck!"

A chorus of thank-yous went up as the doctors and nurses meticulously returned their equipment to the exact location they would be expecting it in the morning.

"That was nice of Leo to pop in." Robyn pulled down her surgical mask and smiled, hoping the heat in her cheeks didn't betray the slightest—okay, the huge—bit of envy that Rosie had found love.

"I'd love to take all the credit." Rosie laughed. "But I think Leo's more interested in your surgery than me today. The whole hospital is on tenterhooks about tomorrow."

"What a relaxing thought!" Robyn's cheeks flared further. She didn't mind having an audience when she was in surgery, but knowing the future of the hospital was hanging in the balance because of this one, very risky surgery…

It was a lot of pressure she didn't need on top of a deflated heart and ego and the splattered remains of her pride. Maybe she could fling herself on the operating table after Amira's surgery and demand returning cardiologist, Dr. Wolfe, throw a few well-placed stitches into her broken heart.

She smiled at the image her mind's eye conjured and shook her head. See? Losing the man she'd never had wasn't hurting that badly, after all. She was already able to make jokes about it—albeit to herself—but it was precisely the sort of thing she hoped would happen when she'd walked back through the high Victorian arches of Paddington's.

"Why don't we call it a day, then?" Robyn tugged her mask free of her neck, giving the collection of esteemed surgeons and specialists the best smile she could muster. "We'll all need to be here bright and early."

She loitered while they made their way out in twos and threes, some making dinner plans, others announcing their intention to have an early night after grabbing a quick drink at the Frog and Peach. An urge to go with them to the "hospital pub" overtook her. She could have a glass of soda water and lime—her go-to favorite when she wasn't in the mood for an alcoholic drink. Just a chance to relax before heading to her home-not-home. Or not...

The double doors to the surgical theater *phwapped* shut and, at long last, she was alone. She stared at the model they'd been working on, superimposing Amira's little face onto the silicone one in front of her, only just stopping herself from reaching out and stroking the long, ebony hair that wasn't there.

Amira's hair would have to be partially shaved. Just a little bit behind and above her ears. Her bright eyes would be closed, her head tipped to the side so they would have full access to her ear. She'd have a scar—a small one tucked behind her ear—but the surgery would mark her no matter what the result. It would be the first step in a long road, including speech therapy, follow-up gene therapy and some six months' worth of checkups before she should receive maximum hearing. In other words—this was the beginning of a difficult journey for Amira. Maybe she would get her a service dog to see her through the transition. A beautiful hearing dog. The three of them could—

Robyn gasped, unable to stem a sob as reality reared upon her like a wild stallion.

The three of them could nothing. They weren't a threesome. There was no "we" or "us."

The only thing she could do was perform a flawless operation.

No pub. And she wouldn't bother with going home. Twiddling her thumbs on her own would only drive her mad.

Maybe she'd relieve Ryan's parents from the vigil they were holding by his bedside. Poor little chap. He'd been through so much and to fall into a coma at this point? His parents had looked wrecked when she'd stopped in to chat with them. A nap in the family room was probably overdue. She'd offer to read to him.

Her brain scanned through the vast book collection in her office. A fairy tale? Nothing too gruesome, though. She bit down hard on her lip a little too aware she'd need a huge injection of courage, as well.

This was her forte. Her strength. Medicine had always been her right-hand man and she wouldn't be trying the surgery if she didn't have complete and utter confidence in her success.

Then, for once in her life, maybe the planets would align and Paddington's would be saved and she'd never have to think about the man who'd stolen her heart ever again. Perhaps tomorrow she could arrange a nice little case of amnesia…

She laughed and pushed out of the empty lab to go check on the three-dimensional printer, still hard at work making a backup set of the middle ear pieces.

Malleus. Incus. Stapes.

Each tiny, perfectly shaped piece would play a vital role in Amira's ear.

A trill of excitement took spark and held, lighting her smile properly for the first time since she'd returned. Leaving Idris and Amira so brusquely had felt like ripping off one of her own limbs. When the surgery was done and dusted tomorrow, maybe she'd feel whole again.

CHAPTER TWELVE

THE CLOCK HAND dropped a single measly stop. Two hours and forty-three minutes since Amira had been taken into surgery. Each painful second after the last, moments ticking away with the exhaustive slowness of sap running from a tree, drip by even slower drip with no concern for those who lay in wait.

Idris forced himself to sit down in the softly lit "family room." There'd be holes in the practical, overdesigned carpet if he didn't cool his jets.

A low growl formed and flew out of his throat unchecked. He was beginning to wish he'd taken the hospital up on its offer of a suite. Not for the luxury of it, but for the rooftop space. He could pace freely there. Shake his fist skyward. Even the illusion of being able to roar from the rooftops if things didn't go as planned would provide some release to the agony he was feeling.

He thought of Robyn's beautiful face and knew he'd find solace there whatever the outcome.

Solace he didn't deserve.

Those amber eyes of hers, ever generous even though he'd been unnecessarily cruel.

This morning, when she'd entered Amira's room to bring her up to the surgical ward, she'd managed a smile. Some kind words. Her touch, when she'd reached out to put her hand upon his wrist, had been a salve against the strains of the day.

"We'll do our very best."

Those were the final words she'd spoken to him and he believed her. Heart and soul he believed her. Which was a damn lucky thing because the feeling of sheer helplessness encapsulating him now was suffocating.

Every fear that could have come his way was piercing him in psychic knife blows so vivid he was surprised the waiting room wasn't running with blood.

Had he pushed Amira into this?

Was the risk worth it?

An abrupt shift change crowded all his other thoughts away.

It wasn't the risk of surgery he was worried about. How *blind* he'd been. All his anger, the crudely executed rage— it was all cruel bluster to mask the truth that lay within his heart.

He loved Robyn.

Loved her with every fiber of his being. Not to act on that love would be to condemn himself and his daughter to a lifetime of fear and pain that neither of them deserved.

He closed his eyes, fingers spread wide on the sofa cushions as he pictured the woman he'd married nine years earlier. Her beautiful smile, the soft laugh and almond-shaped eyes he saw every time he looked at their daughter.

A warm heat filled his chest as he thanked her for the love they had shared and the daughter she had bravely borne him at the cost of her own life. The heat strengthened and grew within him as he asked for her blessing to leave the days of mourning in his wake and fill them instead with a life of love and laughter only a future with Robyn could bring.

When at long last he opened his eyes, he knew there was only one thing he could do.

* * *

"All right, everyone, are we ready for the stapedotomy stage?"

Robyn took the familiar scan, cataloging the nods and yeses. "Okay, let's get that eardrum elevated and turned."

This was where she was in her element. Where she felt her confidence was best placed. Time became irrelevant. Energy continued unabated. All that mattered was the patient.

Through the operating microscope she watched her instruments as her hands elevated and turned the miniscule eardrum forward.

Robyn's concentration intensified, each movement more critical than the last.

The laser to vaporize select parts of the middle ear. The placement of a platinum piston. Connecting the piston to the second hearing bone—now the 3-D printed incus they had inserted earlier was in place.

Each step required follow-on steps, all of which would take months to be fully realized. But once they had injected the engineered virus designed to encode the ear's crucial microvilli, Amira should, pending the level of swelling, be able to tell them if the operation had been successful.

A cloth was passed across Robyn's brow. She glanced up from the surgical spectacles and saw the clock. Four hours. Only a few more steps to go—none of them rushed—and Idris could see his daughter again. She closed the mental door on what would follow. The only thing she could think about right now was Amira and the chance the little girl might have to hear.

"How long will it take?" His voice was low, but impatience snapped and crackled in Idris's every word. His body was taut with a barely contained frustration. An energy so charged Robyn could easily envision it coiled like a whip ready to lash out in biting snaps and flares at anyone or anything that stood in the way of his daughter's recovery.

She kept her eyes glued on Amira. It was the only way to keep her emotions in check. Of course, she couldn't blame Idris for being anxious, tense even, but he wasn't the only one clock-watching.

"It can take between ten and twenty minutes from now."

"That long?"

The strain had turned his voice hoarse. His tapping fingers drummed out all of the unspoken words on the doorframe.

I've already waited five hours and now you want more of my precious time?

"I'm not sure if you remember," Robyn began cautiously, "but Amira seemed to really enjoy the folk music we heard back in Da'har."

"You think I would've forgotten something like that?" Idris's dark-eyed gaze snapped to her, demanding her attention. She inhaled a deep breath, held it and looked up, almost frightened to see the emptiness in those jet-black eyes she had fallen in love with.

When her eyes met with his, she was physically struck by the story they told. Of course he remembered that day in the tent. They had laughed, sung and danced as a *family* that day. It was one of the pivotal moments, she was certain of it, that had led to their beautiful night back at the palace.

"Well, anyway—" she looked away, unable to bear the memories "—I hope you don't mind but I downloaded some music and thought I might put it on so Amira could wake to it."

"How on earth did you find Da'harian folk music?"

His bewilderment gave him a slightly more human edge, one that softened the sharp lines and angles of the man who held her heart in captivity.

A smile tweaked at the edges of her lips despite the rivulets of anxiety weaving their way through her nervous system. "I had a lot of…extra energy last night. I thought it best if I put it to some use."

"Trawling the internet for arcane folk music?"

"If by arcane you mean beautiful—" she shot back only just stopping herself from launching into a full speech telling him what she well and truly thought of him, how he was behaving, how ridiculous it was to be so miserable when all they had to do was open their hearts to love.

Or something like that.

"I'm trying," Idris ground out, "to *thank* you."

"Well, you might need to work on your delivery," Robyn parried with a huff that collapsed into a sigh. No matter what happened today, her journey with Amira and Idris was over.

Best to retain what few shreds of dignity the situation could afford her. She shifted on the bouncy rubber of her favorite trainers and wished, for the moment, she hadn't worn the smiley-face surgical cap she was only just remembering to take off. Looking goofy while your heart was breaking really was an unneeded lavishing of icing on the misery cake.

"Perhaps, Dr. Kelly, it might be a good idea to play the music."

Both of them stood tall, heels ground solidly into the hard hospital floor, eyes locked and trying to divine if they were fighting or agreeing.

Amira's small body lay between them, her hands resting atop the multicolored coverlet Idris had insisted they use in lieu of the regulation-issue sheets and blanket, her breath coming steady and slow. Robyn ached to touch her, stroke her soft little cheek, cup it with her hand. Kiss her darling sweet brow, tucking a few strands of silky hair back behind her ear, but knowing she couldn't now that Idris was here. Amira wasn't hers to love, but love her she did. With every aching pore in her body. Every bit as much as she loved the girl's stubborn, beautiful, irritating-in-ways-she-hadn't-imagined-possible father. The one whose eyes she could feel burning into her the longer she refused to obey.

Amira shifted ever so slightly. The last thing in the world Robyn wanted was for Amira to wake up and find two scowls hovering above her. Amira, on this day more than most, needed to wake up and see love. Because of her, for her, Robyn dug a hand into her white coat and pulled out her phone, fingers flashing along the touchscreen to find the music that had played throughout the entire surgery, fueling her to do her best.

Idris watched as Robyn, cheeks flushed with emotion, plugged the phone's attachment unit into the speaker and pressed Play.

"It might be a good idea if you sat alongside her, maybe held her hand." Her amber eyes lifted to meet his, then fluttered away just as quickly.

"Should I be facing her, or holding her?"

"Face her," Robyn gently encouraged. "If the surgery went as well as we believe, she should be able to hear you, but her brain will take some time to catch up with everything she is experiencing so you may want to sign, as well. She's used to reading your lips, so just behave as you always have with her."

Idris nodded, his chest constricting with emotion. This would be the first time his little girl would hear him speak. Robyn's calming instructions were the only things keeping him afloat as his mind raced with things to say.

Why hadn't he thought of this before? Would the simplest but truest of sentiments be the best? *I love you.* Or should it be a prayer of thanks? The name of their country. How much would compute with the words she read upon his lips with the sounds she would be hearing for the very first time?

Hello? Or perhaps, *Can you hear me?* So basic, but straight to the point. He cut himself short when he realized he was about to swear with frustration. He certainly wasn't going to have that be the first thing his cherished daughter heard!

The importance of language had never stood out so vividly before. His daughter would be *hearing* him. He clenched his eyes tight and tilted his chin up to the invisible heavens offering prayer upon prayer that the operation had been a success.

Idris tucked his fingers beneath Amira's hand when she stirred again. As her fingers clenched and released upon his own, Idris's blood began to rush and flow with the urgency of a river in a spring thaw. He forced himself to take slow, steadying breaths, not wanting to miss a single moment of his daughter's experience. This was for her. Everything was for her. Having Robyn here with them—the very reason this miracle might occur—was the most natural thing in the world. Without her…

He forced himself to align his scattered thoughts with the music, humming distractedly at first, then with a greater depth of feeling as he realized the reason the tune was striking such an emotional chord deep within him was because it was the very same song he had sung to Amira on that glorious day in the desert. The words came back to him, fitfully at first, and before he knew it, he was singing to his daughter. It was an ever hopeful serenade that would mark the success or failure of the incredible risk they had just taken.

Midway through the now familiar chorus, her small fingers squeezed his. Amira's eyes were still shut tight, but her forehead was crinkling in a show of confusion at first, then suddenly her eyes shot wide open, so quickly Idris forgot to keep singing.

"Keep singing, keep singing," Robyn encouraged, tears forming in her eyes as she took Amira's other hand.

Amira turned to her as she spoke and it was at that moment Idris understood that the surgery had been a success. Tears he'd never spilled flooded his eyes, blurring the beautiful expression on his daughter's face as she took in the same information he was processing.

She could hear.

Robyn had done exactly what she had promised. She'd made his daughter's near impossible dream a reality.

"Would you like to try talking?" Robyn asked Amira.

The little girl nodded, her features crumpling into sobs of understanding at the enormity of the moment. Idris, unable to bear even the tiniest sliver of fear his daughter might experience, forced himself to sing again, his voice so gruff with emotion, but it didn't matter. Not if it would help Amira take the first of many scary steps as she adjusted to the panoply of changes she would experience over the coming months. When his voice cracked, or faltered, Robyn joined in, her soft alto ribboning around his, giving him the strength and confidence to be the man he needed to be in this moment.

Amira's lips parted, her dark almond-sloped eyes shifting in wonderment between the pair of them, now singing like a couple of giggling teens.

"I can hear you," she finally said, tears pouring down her cheeks. "I can hear the song I felt you sing!" She pressed her hands to each of their chests in utter amazement that one beautiful thing had transformed into the other—into sound!

Her head whirled around, eyes narrowing as she sought the source of the other noises in the room. She played the air drums for a minute and signed to Robyn she didn't understand.

"It's music. You're hearing music coming from the speaker."

Amira's lips shaped into an astonished O as she looked at the small phone in disbelief.

"It's just how I imagined it! Beautiful!" she signed, then again and again made the beautiful swooping sign that meant *music*, shifting her fingers into the little bird that symbolized Robyn's name.

"Thank you," she said, turning her full attention to Robyn. "Thank you."

"I am so happy for you," Robyn signed back, her voice catching with emotion. "You deserve all the joy you receive in your new life."

"I'm so happy for all of us!" Amira shouted, then winced at the volume of her voice. "Have I always been this loud?" she whispered sheepishly.

Their collective laughter swirled up and around them, and before Idris could get his head around the fact his daughter had heard his voice for the very first time, she was clambering out from under the covers and tugging him and Robyn into a tight hug as she sobbed and sobbed with disbelief and joy.

As soon as she could bear to break herself away, Robyn excused herself.

She stood at the doorway, watching father and daughter grasp and explore the new world Amira was beginning to inhabit, then turned and fled knowing the happy tears she had shed would now be weighted with sorrow.

"He wants to what?" Robyn had only just managed to splash water on her face, mortified her blotchy, tear-streaked face was going to have to appear on television! "No. Absolutely not. He can do it on his own. Amira is his daughter. This is their moment."

"That's not what he thinks, Robyn." Victoria fixed her with a friendly glare if ever such a thing were possible.

"Who? Dominic?" Robyn's face screwed up in a show of confusion. "Is he putting you up to this?"

"No, silly. Idris Al Khalil—you know, the multi*billionaire* Sheikh of Da'har—thinks so. He chose you out of dozens of possible surgeons to operate on his daughter. You've done what no one else in the world has managed and now you don't want him to sing your praises to the world?"

"Not on television, I don't." *Not anywhere.* It would be too much to bear. She didn't want to hear kind words when the paths their lives were taking would now split and veer off in very different directions.

"Stop being ridiculous. They've already set up a press podium outside the hospital. Half the staff are out there already."

"What?" Robyn recoiled from the friendly hand her friend was rubbing along her arm. "In front of all the Castle's supporters *and* the press? Have you gone absolutely stark-raving *mad*? No, no, no, no, no." Her jaw clamped shut as she rigorously shook her head. Absolutely not. Humiliation one-on-one with Idris was one thing. But in front of all those people?

"Do I need to repeat the *billionaire* part or the *groundbreaking surgery* part?" Rosie intoned.

"I never agreed to do this for the money," Robyn grumbled. She'd never known she would lose her heart, either, but that hadn't stopped her from performing the surgery. Or from a whirlwind of heartbreak picking her up and swirling her around and around in the wake of Idris's rejection. She'd done too much acquiescing to His Excellency as it was. His Glowering Grumpency was more like it.

"Are you going to let a few jitters keep Paddington's from getting the well-deserved publicity your surgery could garner?" Victoria could scarcely keep the disbelief from her voice and Robyn didn't blame her. It was why she'd chosen her to front the campaign. She embodied everything Robyn didn't—confidence, the ability to have a baby, fall in love...

Ugh! Anger, anger, anger.

She didn't do anger, but it seemed to work for Idris—so it was going to have to work for her.

"Robyn." Victoria plopped her hands on each of her friend's shoulders. "You can do this. It'll be five minutes in and out and then you can hide away in the operating theater for the rest of your life if you please. Five. Minutes."

Robyn nodded, a sheepish smile creeping onto her face despite herself. "All right, you win!" She rocked back on her heels, tugged a tissue out of a nearby box and gave Victoria an impressed smile. "Dominic didn't stand a chance with you, did he?"

Victoria, to her credit, flushed with pride, her hands gliding across the ever-increasing swell in her belly. A baby, a fiancé—the paramedic's life seemed fairy-tale perfect after the storms she'd weathered. Robyn was seized by an impulse and pulled her into a hug. "Thanks for everything. You and Dom have done an amazing job handling the Save Paddington's campaign."

"Are you—" Victoria began, her voice muffled in Robyn's shoulder, then pulled back, her lips pressing into a frown as she inspected her tearstained face. "You didn't have a disagreement with the Sheikh or anything, did you?"

"Idris? No!" Robyn protested, throwing in a hand-wave, as if the gesture would punctuate the message she was trying and failing to get across. She was cool. Everything was *fine*.

She muffled a little sobby hiccup behind a fistful of tissues.

Victoria shot her a look, making it clear Robyn was

going to have to work on her fake happy face. But it was the only face she had and all it could do was tell the truth. Her heart was no longer safely tucked away. She'd taken it out to play and had lost the game.

She gave her shoulders a little shruggy shake. "C'mon. Hanging out here isn't doing Paddington's any good. Let's give Idris his press conference and then I could do with a nice glass of wine over at the Frog and Peach if you're willing!"

"It's soda water for me," Victoria gently reminded her, an apologetic wince scrunching her features together when Robyn's eyes flooded with tears. "Maybe we could go somewhere else. Somewhere less...doctory?"

Robyn nodded, knowing if she spoke it would all come out. Her battered and bruised heart that had opened and fallen in love, not just with Idris but with Amira. The gut-wrenching pain at having to say goodbye after feeling, for the very first time in her life, like she was part of a family of her own.

"C'mon. Hand over your makeup bag. Let's get you all freshened up so you can dazzle the masses!"

She let Victoria riffle through her small makeup bag. Powder, a bit of blusher and a fresh swipe of mascara improved things a little bit. They both turned and stared at her reflection. Back to cheery-faced Robyn!

At least on the outside.

"Ready for a bit of stiff upper lip and a smile for the cameras?" Victoria asked.

"As I'll ever be!"

The speed with which the press had gathered made Idris wonder if they'd been here all along. Awaiting the outcome of his daughter's surgery as anxiously as he had.

Good.

All the better. Paddington's deserved all the publicity in the world for their achievements today. For Robyn's achievements.

He turned to face the crowd with renewed vigor.

"The diligent care Dr. Robyn Kelly gave my little girl was above and beyond the treatment any parent would expect for their child."

Idris caught Robyn's eye for just a moment and took heart from her soft, beautiful smile. He hoped she knew he was speaking from the heart and not just trotting out niceties for the sake of a few moments on television. "I think Dr. Kelly knows me well enough by now," he continued, his voice suddenly constricting with a depth of emotion he never displayed in public, "to understand how very much giving the gift of hearing to my daughter meant not only to me but to her. As the future leader of Da'har—" He stopped, forced himself to blow out a steadying breath. "As the future leader of Da'har, my daughter's keenest wish was to be able to hear the voices of the people she would one day lead. In speech…" He turned to Robyn, knowing the only approval he needed was from the woman right next to him. "And in song. Today, not through a miracle of modern medicine but through the sheer determination, intelligence and unparalleled skills of Dr. Kelly and her team, Amira heard her father's voice join with her own in song." He choked back a sob and sucked in a deep breath before plunging forward. "Which is why I would like to announce my intention to make a donation to Paddington Children's Hospital, which should enable them to stay right here in the heart of London where they belong."

Robyn's eyes widened, only just containing a surge of tears.

The instinct to pull her into his arms told Idris everything he needed to know. History was just that. Now was the moment he needed to turn his full attention on the future.

"What surprised me the most along this journey we have taken with Dr. Kelly… Robyn…" He turned to her, stepping away from the podium, and reached out a hand. Reluctantly, her eyes darting to the crowd and the cameras, Robyn extended her hand to meet his. Electric shock waves crackled through him, assuring him he'd chosen to do the right thing.

"Robyn, you have not only restored my daughter's hearing, but you have restored my belief in love."

Conflicting emotions slammed into one another as Robyn tried to process what Idris was saying.

The rush of blood roaring between her ears all but drowned out her ability to hear him and she nearly laughed at the irony of it all—wishing he was signing as he spoke. She forced herself to focus on his lips—that beautiful mouth she had once kissed so passionately. She blinked as she saw his lips shape and form four words, then press together, an expectant, hopeful look lighting up those dark eyes of his. The hundred or so people watching the press conference gave a collective gasp as cameras whirred and clicked like mad.

"I'm sorry." Her fingers flew to her lips, not entirely sure she'd heard him correctly. "Would you mind repeating that?"

She flushed as a wave of laughter rippled across the crowd, swirling and circling around her, proving, once again, that she absolutely did not belong in the limelight.

Idris smiled warmly, lovingly, stroking a hand across the back of Robyn's shaky palm.

"I asked you, my love, if you would do me the honor of marrying me." Idris smiled up at her, looking every bit the ardent lover he had been on that one precious night they had shared. Everything fuzzed and blurred around him. Was he…did he love her?

Scrunching her eyes together tightly, she popped them open again to make sure this wasn't a dream.

"But I thought…" She clamped her lips tight, not wanting the world's press to know they'd shared such an amazing night together that had ended in a humiliating rejection. He didn't want her. He'd made that clear. Hadn't he?

"I've learned so much in our time together," Idris said, his voice so quiet she had to strain to hear him. "Today I saw a future you were not a part of and I couldn't bear what I saw."

He rose, her amber eyes traveling along with his until her chin was tipped up, gazing into his face, seeking answers to myriad questions jockeying for pole position.

"You, Robyn Kelly, more than anyone I have ever met, have taught me the power of love. My country, my daughter and I all need you. We need your light, your laughter, the joy you bring to any situation. Your song is my song. Amira's song. Please say you will be my wife. A mother to Amira." He pressed a tender kiss upon the back of her hand and looked into her eyes, which had more light in them than ever before. "Let's become a family."

"A family?" Robyn repeated the words in a daze. "With you?"

Idris threw his head back and laughed. "Yes, with me! I'll gladly duel anyone who tries to step in and steal my woman." His voice softened again. "If you'll have me."

Robyn's head began to nod in infinitesimal little yeses. They gathered speed until she was nodding and shaking her head, tears springing to her eyes and scattering upon her cheeks.

"Yes!" she finally managed through the joy coursing through her every fiber. *A family.* "Yes."

Six months later

"I think you should be the one to cut the ribbon, Idris." Robyn decisively handed the ceremonial scissors back to her new husband. "You designed all of the changes."

"And you made all of the important suggestions!" he persisted, refusing to accept the silver-plated shears.

"I have a better idea," Robyn said, her smile growing as the possibilities it unleashed took flight. "Let's have Amira do it."

"Open the center?"

"Absolutely!" The idea grew and shone even brighter the more she thought about it. "Come." She grabbed ahold of his hand and took him back a few steps before turning to look at the former palace—once so cold and empty— now virtually abuzz with activity. "Look at what you've created. The Persian Gulf Language Center for the Deaf and Hard of Hearing. It will be amazing."

"You're the one who's amazing," Idris play-growled, nestling into the crook of his wife's neck, enjoying the tickly tease of her blond curls on his face as he did.

"*We're* amazing," she agreed with a big grin, wrapping her arms around his waist and giving him a kiss on his caramel-smooth cheek. "I never knew how much strength came from being a family. Thank you."

Idris laughed again. "We could go on like this all day, but we've got a center to open! A universal Arabic sign language to invent! Come." He safely secured her hand in one of his own and set off toward the front doors of the center. "Let's go find our daughter, see who she's torturing with her newfound listening skills now."

"Da'har beware!" Robyn laughed, taking a skip to catch up with her husband's long-legged strides. "Our girl is going to make the country—and her parents—very, very proud."

She relished the squeeze she received from Idris's hand

at her words and, unable to wipe the smile off her face, turned to face the press who were already beginning to gather for the ceremony and gave them a happy wave.

* * * * *

A LIFE-SAVING REUNION

ALISON ROBERTS

CHAPTER ONE

HE'D KNOWN THIS wasn't going to be easy.

He'd known that some cases were going to be a lot harder than others.

But Dr Thomas Wolfe had also known that, after the very necessary break, he had been ready to go back to the specialty that had always been his first love.

Paediatric cardiology.

Mending broken little hearts...

And some not so little, of course. Paddington Children's Hospital cared for an age range from neonates to eighteen-year-olds. After dealing only with adults for some years now, Thomas was probably more comfortable interacting with the adolescents under his care here but he'd more than rediscovered his fascination with babies in the last few months. And the joy of the children who were old enough to understand how sick they were, brave kids who could teach a lot of people things about dealing with life.

Or kids that touched your heart and made doing the best job you possibly could even more of a priority. It had to be carefully controlled, mind you. If you let yourself get too close, it could not only affect your judgement, but it could also end up threatening to destroy you.

And Thomas Wolfe wasn't about to let that happen again.

He had to pause for a moment, standing in the central corridor of Paddington's cardiology ward, right beside the huge, colourful cut-outs of Pooh Bear and friends that decorated this stretch of wall between the windows of the patients' rooms. Tigger seemed to be grinning down at him—mid-bounce—as Thomas pretended to read a new message on his pager.

This had become the hardest case since he'd returned to Paddington's. A little girl who made it almost impossible to keep a safe distance. Six-year-old Penelope Craig didn't just touch the hearts of people who came to know her. She grabbed it with both hands and squeezed so hard it was painful.

It wasn't that he needed a moment to remind himself how important it was to keep that distance, because he had been honing those skills from the moment he'd stepped back through the doors of this astonishing, old hospital and they were already ingrained enough to be automatic. He just needed to make sure the guardrails were completely intact because if there was a weak area, Penny would be the one to find it and push through.

And that couldn't be allowed to happen.

With a nod, as if he'd read an important message on his pager, Thomas lifted his head and began moving towards the nearest door. There was no hesitation as he tapped to announce his arrival and then entered the room with a smile.

His smile faltered for a split second as Julia Craig, Penny's mother, caught his gaze with the unspoken question that was always there now.

Is today the day?

His response was as silent as the query.

No. Today's not the day.

The communication was already well practised enough to be no slower than the blink of an eye. Penny certainly hadn't noticed.

'Look, Dr Wolfe! I can dance.'

The fact that Penny was out of her bed meant that today was one of her better ones. She still had her nasal cannula stuck in place with a piece of sticky tape on each cheek, the long plastic tube snaking behind her to where it connected with the main oxygen supply, but she was on her feet.

No, she was actually standing on her tippy-toes, her arms drooping gracefully over the frill of her bright pink tutu skirt. And then she tried to turn in a circle but the tubing got in the way and she lost her balance and sat down with a suddenness that might have upset many children.

Penny just laughed.

'Oops.' Julia scooped her daughter into her arms as the laughter turned to gasping.

'I can...' Penny took another gulp of air. 'I *can*...do it. Watch!'

'Next time.' Julia lifted Penny onto her bed. 'Dr Wolfe is here to see you and he's very busy. He's got lots of children to look after today.'

'But only one who can dance.' Thomas smiled. 'Just like a Ballerina Bear.'

Penny's smile could light up a room. Big grey eyes turned their attention to the television on the wall, where her favourite DVD was playing and a troupe of fluffy bears wearing tutus were performing what seemed to be a cartoon version of *Swan Lake*.

'I just want to listen to your heart, if that's okay.' Thomas unhooked his stethoscope from around his neck.

Penny nodded but didn't turn away from the screen. She lifted her arms above her head and curled her finger as she tried to mimic the movements of the dancing bears.

Thomas noted the bluish tinge to his small patient's lips. Putting the disc of his stethoscope against a chest scarred by more than one major surgery, he listened to a heart that was trying its best to pump enough blood around a small body but failing a little more each day.

The new medication regime was helping but it wasn't enough. Penny had been put on the waiting list for a heart transplant weeks ago and the job of Thomas and his team was to keep her healthy for long enough that the gift of a long life might be possible. It was a balancing act of drugs to help her heart pump more effectively and control the things that made it harder, like the build-up of fluid in her tissues and lungs. Limiting physical activity was unfortunately a necessity now, as well, and to move further than this room required that Penny was confined to a wheelchair.

The odds of a heart that was a good match becoming available in time weren't great but, as heartbreaking as that was, it wasn't why this particular case was proving so much more difficult than other patients he had on the waiting list for transplants.

Penny was a direct link to his past.

The past he'd had to walk away from in order to survive.

He'd met Penny more than six years ago. Before she was even born, in fact—when ultrasound tests had revealed that the baby's heart had one of the most serious congenital defects it could have, with the main pumping chamber too small to be effective. She'd had her first surgery when she was only a couple of weeks old and he'd been the doctor looking after her both before and after that surgery.

He'd spent a lot of time with Penny's parents, Julia and Peter Craig, and he'd felt their anguish as acutely as if it had been his own.

That was what becoming a parent yourself could do to you...

Gwen had only been a couple of years older than Penny so she would have been eight now. Would she have fallen in love with the Ballerina Bears, too? Be going to ballet lessons, perhaps, and wearing a pink tutu on top of any other clothing, including her pyjamas?

The thought was no more than a faint, mental jab. Thomas had known that working with children again might stir up the contents of that locked vault in his head and his heart but he knew how to deal with it.

He knew to step away from the danger zone.

He stepped away from the bed, too. 'It's a lovely day, today,' he said, looping the stethoscope around his neck again. 'Maybe Mummy can take you outside into the sunshine for a bit.'

A nurse came into the room as he spoke and he glanced at the kidney dish in one hand and a glass of juice in the other. 'After you've had all your pills.'

'Are you in a rush?' Julia was on her feet, as well. 'Have you got a minute?' She glanced at her daughter, who was still entranced by the dancing bears on the screen. 'I'll be back in a minute, Penny. Be a good girl and swallow all those pills for Rosie, okay?'

''kay.' Penny nodded absently.

'Of course she will,' Rosie said. 'And then I want to know all the names of those bears, again. Who's the one with the sparkly blue fur?'

'Sapphire,' Thomas could hear Penny saying as he held the door open for Julia. If she had concerns about her daughter's condition, they needed to go somewhere else to discuss it. 'She's my favourite. And the green one's Emerald and…the red one's Ruby…'

The relatives' room a little further down the corridor was empty. Thomas closed the door behind them and gestured for Julia to take one of the comfortable chairs available.

'Are you sure you've got time?'

'Of course.'

'I just… I just wanted to ask you more about what you said yesterday. I tried to explain to Peter last night but I think I made it sound a lot worse than…than you did…' Julia was fighting tears now.

Thomas nudged the box of tissues on the coffee table closer and Julia gratefully pulled several out.

'You mean the ventricular assist device?'

Julia nodded, the wad of tissues pressed to her face.

'You said…you said it would be the next step, when… *if*…things got worse.'

Thomas kept his tone gentle. 'They sound scary, I know, but it's something that's often used as a bridge to transplant. For when heart failure is resistant to medical therapy, the way Penny's is becoming.'

'And you said it might make her a lot better in the meantime?'

'It can improve circulation and can reverse some of the other organ damage that heart failure can cause.'

'But it's risky, isn't it? It's major surgery...'

'I wouldn't suggest it if the risks of going on as we are were less than the risks of the surgery. I know Penny's having a better day today but you already know how quickly that can change and it gets a little more difficult to control every time.'

Julia blew her nose. 'I know. That last time she had to go to intensive care, we thought...we thought we were going to lose her...'

'I know.' Thomas needed to take in a slow breath. To step away mentally and get back onto safe ground. Professional ground.

'A VAD could make Penny more mobile again and improve her overall condition so that when a transplant becomes available, the chances of it being successful are that much higher. It's a longer term solution to control heart failure and they can last for years, but yes, it is a major procedure. The device is attached to the heart and basically takes over the work of the left ventricle by bypassing it. Let's make a time for me to sit down with both you and Peter and I can talk you through it properly.'

Julia had stopped crying. Her eyes were wide.

'What do you mean by "more mobile"? Would we be able to take her home again while we wait?'

'I would hope so.' Thomas nodded. 'She would be able to go back to doing all the things she would normally do at home. Maybe more, even.'

Julia had her fingers pressed against her lips. Her voice was no more than a whisper. 'Like...like dancing lessons, maybe?'

Oh...he had to look away from that hope shining through the new tears in Julia's eyes. The wall of the relatives' room was a much safer place.

'I'll tell Peter when he comes in after work. How soon can we make an appointment to talk about it?'

'Talk to Maria on the ward reception desk. She seems to know my diary as well as I do.' He got to his feet, still not risking a direct glance at Julia's face.

From the corner of his eye, he could see Julia turn her head. Was she wondering what had caught his attention?

He was being rude. He turned back to his patient's mother but now Julia was staring at the wall.

'My life seems to be full of teddy bears,' she said.

Thomas blinked at the random comment. 'Oh? You mean the dancing kind?'

'And here, look. This is about the Teddy Bears' Picnic in Regent's Park. Well, Primrose Hill, actually. For transplant families.'

The poster had only been a blur of colour on the wall but now Thomas let his gaze focus.

And then he wished he hadn't.

Right in the middle of a bright collage of photos was one of a surgeon, wearing green theatre scrubs, with a small child in her arms. The toddler was wearing only a nappy so the scar down the centre of her chest advertised her major cardiac surgery. The angelic little girl, with her big, blue eyes and mop of golden curls, was beaming up at her doctor and the answering smile spoke of both the satisfaction of saving a small life and a deep affection for her young patient.

'That's Dr Scott,' Julia said. 'Rebecca. But you know that, of course.'

Of course he did.

'She did the surgery on Penny when she was a baby—but you know that too. How silly of me. You were her doctor back then, too.' Julia made an apologetic face.

'So much has happened since then, it becomes a bit of a blur, sometimes.'

'Yes.' Thomas was still staring at Rebecca's face. Those amazing dark, chocolate-coloured eyes which had been what had caught his attention first, all those years ago, when he'd spotted her in one of his classes at medical school. The gleaming, straight black hair that was wound up into a knot on the back of her head, the way it always was when she was at work.

That smile…

He hadn't seen her look that happy since…well, since before their daughter had died.

She certainly hadn't shown him even a hint of a smile like that in the months since he'd returned to Paddington's.

Had Julia not realised they had been husband and wife at the time they'd shared Penny's care in the weeks after her birth?

Well, why would she? They had kept their own names to avoid any confusion at work and they'd always been completely professional during work hours. Friendly professional, though—nothing like the strained relationship between them now. And Julia and Peter had had far more on their minds than how close a couple of people were amongst the team of medics trying to save their tiny daughter.

'She was just a surgeon, back then.'

Thomas had to bite back a contradiction. Rebecca had never been 'just' a surgeon. She'd been talented and brilliant and well on the way to a stellar career from the moment she'd graduated from medical school.

'Isn't it amazing that she's gone on to specialise in transplants?'

'Mmm.' Sometimes the traumatic events that happened in life could push you in a new direction but Thomas couldn't say that out loud, either. If Julia didn't know about the personal history that might have prompted the years of extra study to add a new field of expertise to Rebecca's qualifications, he was the last person who would enlighten her.

Sharing something like that was an absolute no-no when you were keeping a professional distance from patients and their families. And from your ex-wife.

'It's amazing for us, anyway,' Julia continued. 'Because it means that she'll be able to do Penny's transplant if we're lucky enough to find a new heart for her...' Her voice wobbled. 'It might be us going to one of these picnics next year. I've heard of them. Did you see the programme on telly a while back, when they had all those people talking about how terrible it would be if Paddington's got closed?'

'I don't think I did.' The media coverage over the threatened closure had become so intense it had been hard to keep up with it all, especially since Sheikh Al Khalil had announced last month that he would be donating a substantial sum of money following his daughter's surgery.

'Well, they had a clip from last year's picnic. They were talking to a mother who had lost her child through some awful accident and she had made his organs available for transplant. She said she'd never been brave enough to try and make contact with the families of the children who had received them, but she came to the picnic and imagined that someone there might be one of them. She watched them running their races and playing games and saw how happy they were. And how happy their families were...'

Julia had to stop because she was crying again, even though she was smiling. Thomas was more than relieved. He couldn't have listened any longer. He was being dragged into a place he never went these days if he could help it.

'I really must get on with my rounds,' he said.

'Of course. I'm so sorry...' Julia had another handful of tissues pressed to her nose as he opened the door of the relatives' room so she could step out before him.

'It's not a problem,' Thomas assured her. 'I'm always here to talk to you. And Peter, of course. Let's set up that appointment to talk about the ventricular assist device very soon.'

Julia nodded, but her face crumpled again as her thoughts clearly returned to something a lot less happy than the thought of attending a picnic to celebrate the lives that had been so dramatically improved by the gift of organ donation. The urge to put a hand on her shoulder to comfort her and offer reassurance was so strong, he had to curl his fingers into a fist to stop his hand moving.

'Um...' Thomas cleared his throat. 'Would you like me to find someone to sit with you for a bit?'

Julia shook her head. 'I'll be fine. You go. I'll just get myself together a bit more before I go back to Penny. I don't want her to see that I've been crying.'

Even a view of only the woman's back was enough to advertise her distress, but it was the body language of the man standing so rigidly beside her that caught Dr Rebecca Scott's attention instantly as she stepped out of the elevator to head towards the cardiology ward at the far end of the corridor.

A sigh escaped her lips and her steps slowed a little as she fought the impulse to spin around and push the button to open the lift doors again. To go somewhere else. It wasn't really an option. She had a patient in the cardiology ward who was on the theatre list for tomorrow morning and she knew that the parents were in need of a lot of reassurance. This small window of time in her busy day was the only slot available so she would just have to lift her chin and deal with having her path cross with that of her ex-husband.

How sad was it that she'd known it was Thomas simply because of the sense of disconnection with the person he was talking to?

He might have returned to work at Paddington's but the Thomas Wolfe that Rebecca had known and loved hadn't come back.

Oh, he still looked the same. Still lean and fit and so tall that the top of her head would only reach his shoulder. He still had those eyes that had fascinated her right from the start because they could change colour depending on his mood. Blue when he was happy and grey when he was angry or worried or sad.

They had been the colour of a slate roof on a rainy day that first time they had seen each other again after so long and she hadn't noticed any difference since. He was as aloof with her as he was with his patients and their families.

She'd known it wasn't going to be easy. She'd known that some cases were going to be a lot harder than others but, when she'd heard that he'd agreed to come back and work at Paddington's, Rebecca had believed that she could cope. She'd wondered if they could, in fact, put some of the past behind them and salvage some kind of friendship, even.

That hope had been extinguished the first time their paths had crossed when nothing had been said. When there had been no more warmth in his gaze than if she'd been any other colleague he'd previously worked with.

Less warmth, probably.

The old Thomas had never been like that. He'd had an easy grin that was an invitation for colleagues to stop and chat for a moment or two. He would joke and play with the children in his care and he'd always had a knack for connecting with parents—especially after he'd become a father himself. They loved him because he could make them feel as if they had the best person possible fighting in their corner. Someone who understood exactly how hard it was and would care for their child as if it were his own.

This version of Thomas might have the same—or likely an improved—ability to deliver the best medical care but he was a shell of the man he had once been.

Part of Rebecca's heart was breaking for a man who'd taught himself to disconnect so effectively from the people around him but, right now, an even bigger part was angry. Maybe it had been building with every encounter they'd had over the last few months when they had discussed the care of their patients with a professional respect that bordered on coldness.

Calling each other 'Thomas' and 'Rebecca' with never a single slip into the 'Tom' and 'Becca' they had always been to each other. Discussing test results and medications and surgery as if nobody involved had a personal life or people that loved them enough to be terrified.

It was bad enough that he'd destroyed their marriage by withdrawing into this cold, hard shell but she could deal with that. She'd had years of practice, after all. To see the effect it was having on others made it far less acceptable. This was Penny's mother he'd been talking to, for heaven's sake. They'd both known Julia since she'd been pregnant with her first—and only—child. They'd both been there for her a thousand per cent over the first weeks and months of her daughter's life. He'd been the old Thomas, then.

And then he'd walked out. He hadn't been there for the next lot of surgery Penny had had. He hadn't shared the joy of appointments over the next few years that had demonstrated how well the little girl had been and how happy and hopeful her family was. He hadn't been there to witness the fear returning as her condition had deteriorated again but now he was back on centre stage and he was acting as if Penelope Craig was just another patient. As if he had no personal connection at all...

How could he be walking away from Julia like that, when she was so upset she had buried her face in a handful of tissues, ducking back into the relatives' room for some privacy?

Rebecca's forward movement came to a halt as Thomas came closer. She knew she was glaring at him but, for once, she wasn't going to hide anything personal behind a calm, professional mask.

'What's going on?' she asked, her tone rather more crisp than she had expected. 'Why is Julia so upset?'

Thomas shifted his gaze, obviously checking that nobody was within earshot. A group of both staff and visitors were waiting for an elevator. Kitchen staff went past, pushing a huge stainless steel trolley. An orderly pushing a bed came towards them, heading for the service lift, presumably taking the small patient for an X-ray or scan. The bed had balloons tied to the end, one of them a bright yellow smiley face. A nurse walked beside the bed, chatting to the patient's mother. She saw Rebecca and smiled. Then her gaze shifted to Thomas and the smile faded a little.

He didn't seem to notice. He tilted his head towards the group of comfortable chairs near the windows that were, remarkably, free of anyone needing a break or waiting to meet someone. Far enough away from the elevator doors to allow for a private conversation.

Fair enough. It would be unprofessional to discuss details of a case where it could be overheard. Rebecca followed his lead but didn't sit down on one of the chairs. Neither did Thomas.

'I was going to send you a memo,' he said. 'I'm meeting both Julia and Peter in the next day or two to discuss the option of Penelope receiving a ventricular assist device. It's only a matter of time before her heart failure becomes unmanageable.'

'Okay…' Rebecca caught her bottom lip between her teeth. No wonder Julia had been upset. A VAD was a major intervention. But she trusted Thomas's judgement and it would definitely buy them some time.

His gaze touched hers for just a heartbeat as he finished speaking but Rebecca found herself staring at his face, waiting for him to look at her again. Surely he could understand the effect of what he'd told Julia? How could he have walked away from her like that and left her alone?

But Thomas seemed to be scanning the view of central London that these big, multi-paned old windows provided. He could probably see the busy main roads with their red, double-decker buses and crowds of people waiting at intersections or trying to hail a black cab. Or maybe his eye had been drawn to the glimpse of greenery in the near distance from the treetops of Regent's Park.

'You've had experience with VADs? Are you happy to do the surgery?'

'Yes, of course. It's not a procedure that happens very often but I've been involved with a couple. Do you want me to come to the meeting with Penny's family and discuss it with them?'

'Let's wait until it's absolutely necessary. I can tell them what's involved and why it's a good option.'

Rebecca let her gaze shift to the windows, as well. She stepped closer, in fact, and looked down. The protesters were still in place, with their placards, outside the gates. They'd been there for months now, ever since the threat of closure had been made public. It hadn't just been the staff who had been so horrified that the land value of this prime central London spot was so high that the board of governors was actually considering selling up and merging Paddington Children's Hospital with another hospital, Riverside, that was outside the city limits.

Thanks to the incredible donation a month or so ago from Sheikh Idris Al Khalil, who'd brought his daughter to Paddington's for treatment, the threat of closure was rapidly retreating. The astonishing amount of money in appreciation of such a successful result for one child had sparked off an influx of new donations and the press were onside with every member of staff, every patient and every family who were so determined that they would stay here. Even so, the protesters were not going to let the momentum of their campaign slow down until success was confirmed. The slogans on their placards were as familiar as the street names around here now.

Save Our Hospital
Kids' Health Not Wealth

The knowledge that that announcement couldn't be far off gave Rebecca a jolt of pleasure. Things were looking up. For Paddington's and maybe for Penny, too.

'It is a good option.' She nodded. 'I'd love to see her out of that wheelchair for a while.'

'It would put her at the top of the waiting list for a new heart, too. Hopefully a donor heart will become available well before we run into any complications.'

The wave of feeling positive ebbed, leaving Rebecca feeling a kind of chill run down her spine. Her muscles tensed in response. Her head told her that she should murmur agreement and then excuse herself to go and see her patient, maybe adding a polite request to be kept informed of any developments.

Her heart was sending a very different message. An almost desperate cry asking where the hell had the man gone that Thomas used to be? Was there even a fragment of him left inside that shell?

'Yes,' she heard herself saying, her voice weirdly low and fierce. 'Let's keep our fingers crossed that some kid somewhere, who's about the same age as Penny, has a terrible accident and their parents actually agree to have him—or *her*—used for spare parts.'

She could feel the shock wave coming from Thomas. She was shocked herself.

It was a pretty unprofessional thing for a transplant surgeon to say but this had come from a very personal place. A place that only a parent who had had to make that heartbreaking decision themselves could understand.

She was also breaking the unspoken rule that nothing personal existed between herself and Thomas any more. And she wasn't doing it by a casually friendly comment like 'How are you?' or 'Did you have a good weekend?' No. She was lobbing a verbal grenade into the bunker that contained their most private and painful history.

In public. During working hours.

What *was* she thinking? Being angry at the distance Thomas was keeping himself from his patients and their parents was no excuse. Especially when she knew perfectly well why he had become like that. Or was that the real issue here? That she had known and tried so hard to help and had failed so completely?

'Sorry,' she muttered. 'But, for me, it's never an anonymous donor organ that becomes available. I have to go and collect them so I get involved in both sides of the story.'

Thomas's voice was like ice. He really didn't want to be talking about this.

'You *choose* to do it,' he said.

He didn't even look at her as he fired the accusation. He was staring out of the damned window again. Rebecca found that her anger hadn't been erased by feeling ashamed of her outburst.

'And you choose to shut your eyes.' The words came

out in a whisper that was almost a hiss. 'To run away. Like you always did.'

There was no point in saying anything else. Maybe there was nothing more to say, anyway.

So Rebecca turned and walked away.

CHAPTER TWO

'THE LINE HAS been crossed.'

'Oh?' Thomas had opened the file he needed on his laptop. He clicked on options to bring his PowerPoint presentation up and sync it to the wall screen he had lowered over the whiteboard in this small meeting room. 'What line is that, Rosie?'

He certainly knew what line had been crossed as far as he was concerned. It had been a week since Rebecca's astonishing outburst and he still hadn't recovered from the shock of how incredibly unprofessional she had been.

What if someone had overheard? Members of the press were still all over any story coming out of Paddington's. Imagine a headline that revealed that the leading transplant surgeon of Paddington Children's Hospital described her donor organs as 'spare parts'?

Anyone else could well have taken the matter elsewhere. Filed a formal complaint, even. And was Rosie now referring to it? Had it somehow made its way onto the hospital grapevine?

No. Her expression was far too happy to suggest a staff scandal. He tuned back in to what she was saying.

'...and now that the bottom line's been crossed, thanks to the flood of donations, the government's stepping in to make up any shortfall. It only needs the signature of the Minister of Health and Paddington's will be officially safe. There won't be any merger.'

'That's good news.' Thomas reached for the laser pointer in its holder on the frame of the whiteboard. '*Very* good news,' he added, catching sight of Rosie's disappointment in his lack of enthusiasm.

'Mmm.' Rosie looked unconvinced. 'Apparently there's going to be a huge party organised in the near future as soon as everything's finally signed and sealed but some of the staff are planning to get together at the Frog and Peach over the road on Friday to celebrate early. Guess we'll see you there?'

She was smiling but didn't wait for a response. Other people were arriving for the meeting now and there were bound to be far more acceptable reactions from anyone who hadn't heard the big news of the day. One of the physiotherapists, perhaps. Or Louise, who was the head dietician for Paddington's. One of the staff psychologists had just come in, too, and Thomas nodded a greeting to the head of the cardiac intensive care unit, who came through the door immediately after her.

Everybody in the team who had—or would be—directly involved in Penelope Craig's case had been invited to this meeting, including Rosie as one of the nurses that had provided so much of her care over the many admissions the little girl had had. One of the only people missing as the clock clicked onto the start time of eleven a.m. was her surgeon.

Rebecca Scott.

He hadn't seen her all week, come to think of it. Not that he'd wanted their paths to cross. The shock of their last interaction hadn't been only due to her lack of professionalism. Or that she had so unexpectedly crossed the boundaries of what their new relationship allowed.

No. Thomas had not been able to shake the echo of that vehement parting shot. That he chose to shut his eyes. To run away. And that he had always made that choice.

Did she really think he was such a coward?

He *wasn't* a coward. Had Rebecca had no understanding of how much strength it had taken to deal with what they had gone through? How hard it had been to keep putting one foot in front of the other and keep going?

Obviously not.

No wonder their marriage had fallen apart so easily.

No wonder he had been left feeling such a failure. As a husband *and* as a father.

But to drag it out again and hurl it in his face like that…

It had been uncalled for. Unhelpful. Insulting, even.

And so, yes, he was angry.

'Sorry we're late…' The door opened as Rebecca rushed in to take a seat at the oval table, followed by her senior registrar.

Thomas could feel himself glaring at the late arrivals.

Rebecca was glaring right back at him. 'We got held up in Recovery after our last case. I couldn't leave until I was sure my patient was stable.'

'Of course you couldn't,' someone said. 'We wouldn't expect you to.'

Thomas looked away first. Just in time to notice the raised eyebrows and shared glances that went round the table like a Mexican wave.

'No problem,' he said evenly. 'But let's get started, shall we? We're *all* busy people.'

The tension in the room behind him felt like an additional solid presence as he faced the screen and clicked the pointer to bring up his first slide.

'As you know, we're here to discuss a case we're all involved with—that of Penelope Craig, who's currently an inpatient in our cardiology ward. For those of you who haven't been so directly involved in the last few years, though, here's a quick case history.'

The slide was a list of bullet points. A summary of a clinical case reduced to succinct groups of words that made one crisis after another no more than markers on a timeline.

'The diagnosis of hypoplastic left heart syndrome was made prenatally so Penelope was delivered by C-section and admitted directly to the cardiac intensive care unit. She underwent her first surgery—a Norwood procedure—at thirteen days old.'

He had been in the gallery to watch that surgery. Rebecca had been a cardiothoracic surgical registrar at the time and it had been the most challenging case she'd assisted with. She'd sat up half the previous night as she'd gone over and over the steps of the surgery and Thomas had stayed up with her, trying to make up for any lack of confidence she was feeling. Even as he paused only long enough to take a breath, the flash of another memory came up like a crystal-clear video clip.

He had been in the front row of the gallery, leaning forward as he looked down at the tiny figure on the operating table and the group of gowned and masked people towering over it. Over the loudspeaker, he had heard the consultant surgeon hand over the responsibility of closing the tiny chest to Rebecca. As they changed positions, she had glanced up for a split second and caught Thomas's gaze through the glass window—as if to reassure herself that he was still there. That he was still with her with every step she took. And he had smiled and nodded, giving her the silent message that he believed in her. That she could do this and do it well.

That he was proud of her...

His voice sounded oddly tight as he continued. 'A hemi-Fontan procedure was done at six months to create a direct connection between the pulmonary artery and the superior vena cava.'

Rebecca had been allowed to do most of that procedure and she'd been so quietly proud of herself. They'd found a babysitter for Gwen and they'd gone out to celebrate the achievement with dinner and champagne and a long, delicious twirl around the dance floor of their favourite restaurant.

Those 'date' nights had always had a particular kind of magic. It didn't matter how frantic the hours and days before them had been or how tired they were when they set out. Somehow they could always tap back into the connection that had been there from their very first date—that feeling that their love for each other was invincible. That there could never be anyone else that they would want to be with.

The idea that the night after that surgery would be the last 'date' night they would ever have would have been unthinkable at the time. As impossible as losing their precious child.

Thomas didn't actually know if it had been Rebecca who had done the final major surgery to try and improve the function of Penelope's heart. He'd walked out by then, taking a new job in adult cardiology at a major hospital up north in the wake of that personal tragedy that had torn their lives apart.

He'd run away...like he always did...

Thomas cleared his throat as he rapidly ran through the list of the more recent admissions.

'April of this year saw a marked deterioration in Penelope's condition following a series of viral infections. She's been an inpatient for the last ten weeks and was placed on the waiting list for a heart transplant about two months ago. This last week has seen a further deterioration in her condition and there's an urgent need for intervention.'

The next slide was a set of statistics about the availability of transplant organs and how many young patients were unlikely to make it as far as receiving a new heart.

The slide after that sombre reminder was a picture of a device that looked like a tiny rubber plunger with a single tube attached to the top and two coming out from the base.

'For those of you not familiar with these, this is a ventricular assist device—an implantable form of mechanical circulatory support. Parental consent has been given and it's our plan for Penelope to receive a VAD as soon as theatre time can be arranged.' Thomas sucked in a longer breath. 'Dr Scott? Perhaps you'd like to speak about what the surgery involves?'

Using her formal title caused another round of those raised eyebrows and significant glances. Was it his imagination or did this meeting feel really awkward for everybody here?

'Of course.' Rebecca's gaze quickly scanned everybody at the table. It just didn't shift to include himself.

'To put it simply, it's a straightforward bit of plumbing, really. The device is a pump that uses the apex of the left ventricle as the inflow and provides an outflow to the aorta, bypassing the ventricle that's not functioning well enough.'

Thomas could feel himself frowning. It was fine to describe something in layman's terms for the members of the team with no medical background, like the dietician and the psychologist, but to his own ears it was simple enough to be almost dismissive. Like describing a donor organ as a spare part?

His anger had settled into his stomach like a heavy stone. No wonder he hadn't been that interested in eating in the last few days. Was it going to get even worse when he had to work so closely with Rebecca on Penelope's case? Perhaps the unwanted memories that had ambushed him during his brief presentation had been a warning that it was going to become increasingly difficult to work with his ex-wife. The prospect was more than daunting, especially given that everybody else here seemed to be aware of the tension between them.

David, the cardiac intensive care consultant, was giving him a speculative glance as if he was also having concerns about how this particular combination of the lead carers in this team was going to work. With an effort, Thomas erased the unimpressed lines from his face.

'Of course it's not quite that simple in reality,' Rebecca continued. 'It's a big and potentially difficult surgery and there are complications that we have to hope we'll avoid.'

'Like what?' The query came from one of the physiotherapists.

'Bleeding. Stroke. Infections. Arrhythmias.' Rebecca

was counting off the possible disasters on her fingers. 'Some might not become apparent immediately, like renal failure and liver dysfunction. And some intraoperative ones, like an air embolism, are things we will certainly do our best to control. I guess what I'm trying to say is that there *are* risks but everybody agrees that the potential benefits outweigh these risks in Penny's case.'

Rebecca's smile was poignant. 'As most of you know, Penny Craig is one of those patients you just can't help falling in love with and we've known her all her life.

'I'm sure we're all going to give this case everything we've got.' Her smile wobbled a fraction. 'I know *I* am…'

The murmur of agreement around the table held a note of involvement that was very unusual for a clinical team meeting like this. Heads were nodding solemnly. Rosie was blinking as if she was trying to fight back tears.

For heaven's sake… Did nobody else understand how destructive it could be to get too involved? Was the staff psychologist taking this atmosphere on board and making a mental note that a lot of people might need some counselling in the not-too-distant future if things *didn't* work out the way they all had their hearts set on?

Thomas raised his voice. 'It's certainly all about teamwork and it's to be hoped that we will see a dramatic improvement in this patient's condition within a very short period of time.' He glanced down at the laser pointer in his hand, looking for the 'off' button. 'Thank you all for coming. I look forward to working with everybody.'

A buzz of conversation broke out and more than one pager sounded. David came around to his end of the table. 'I'm being paged to get back upstairs but come and see me when you have a moment? I'd like to go over the postoperative care for Penny in some more detail so I can brief my staff.'

'Sure. I'll be heading up there shortly. There's a four-year-old who was admitted to ICU with severe asthma last night but now they're querying cardiomyopathy. We might need to transfer her to your patch.'

'I heard about that. Page me if you need me in on that consult.'

'Will do.'

The rest of the room was emptying during the brief conversation with David. Everybody had urgent tasks waiting for them elsewhere, including himself. Thomas shut down the programme on his laptop and picked it up, his thoughts already on the case he was about to go and assess. Severe breathlessness and wheezing in children could often be misdiagnosed as asthma or pneumonia until more specific tests such as echocardiography were used to reveal underlying heart disease.

It was a complete surprise to turn and find he was not alone in the room.

Rebecca was standing at the other end of the table.

'We need to talk,' she said.

Thomas said nothing. Given how disturbing their last private conversation had been, he wasn't at all sure he wanted an opportunity that could, in fact, make things worse.

'I'm sure you agree that we can't work together with this kind of tension between us. Especially not on a case like this. Everybody's aware of it and it's destructive to the whole team.'

He couldn't argue with that. And, to his shame, he knew he had to take part of the blame. He had no reason to feel angry with Rebecca for anything to do with her involvement in Penelope's case. He was letting personal baggage affect his relationship with a colleague to such an extent, it was actually difficult to make eye contact with her right now.

He looked down at the laptop in his hands.

'So what do you suggest? That we call in a different cardiologist? In case you hadn't noticed, they've been short-staffed around here ever since the threat of the merger got real. That's why I agreed to take on a permanent position again.'

A brief upwards glance showed that Rebecca's gaze was on him. Steady and unrelenting. He held her gaze for a heartbeat. And then another as those dark eyes across the length of the table merged with that flash of memory he'd had during his presentation—when they'd been looking up at him for reassurance that she had his support when she'd been facing one of her biggest challenges.

A different lifetime.

One in which giving and receiving that kind of reassurance and support had been as automatic as breathing. When success for either of them had created a shared pride so huge it could make it hard to catch a breath and when failure was turned into a learning experience that could only make you a better person. A lifetime that had been iced with so much laughter.

So much love…

It had been a long time since that loss had kicked him quite this hard. A wave of sadness blurred the edges of any anger he still had.

'That's not what I'm suggesting,' Rebecca said quietly. 'Penny deserves the best care available and, on either side of the actual surgery, you are the person who can provide that.'

'And you are the person who can provide the best surgical care,' he responded. 'She deserves that, too.' He closed his eyes in a slow blink and then met her gaze again. 'So what is it that you *are* suggesting?'

'That we talk. Not here,' she added quickly. 'Somewhere more...' She cleared her throat. 'Somewhere else.'

Had she been going to suggest somewhere more private? Like the house they'd lived in with Gwen that Rebecca had refused to sell?

He couldn't do that. What if she still had all those pictures on the walls? That old basket with the toys in it, even?

'I'm going for a walk after work,' Rebecca said quietly. 'Through Regent's Park and over to Primrose Hill. It's a gorgeous day. Why don't you come with me?'

A walk. In a public place. Enough space that nobody would be able to overhear anything that might be said and the ability to walk away if it proved impossible to find common ground without this horrible tension.

Except they had to find that common ground, didn't they, if they were going to work together?

If they couldn't, Thomas would have to add a failure to remain professional to the list of his other shortcomings and this one wouldn't be private—it would be fodder for gossip and damaging for both their careers.

And his career was all he had left now.

'Fine.' He nodded. 'Page me when you're done for the day. I'll be here.'

Out of one meeting and straight into another.

Rebecca only had time to duck into her office and

grab a folder from her desk before heading down to the coffee shop on the ground floor where the committee members in charge of organising the Teddy Bears' Picnic would be waiting for her.

The countdown was on for the annual event that Rebecca had been instrumental in setting up four years ago and this one promised to be the biggest and best yet.

The committee president, a mother of a child with cystic fibrosis who had received a double lung transplant six years ago, waved excitedly at Rebecca and she weaved her way through the busy café opposite the pharmacy on the ground floor.

'We had to start without you, I'm afraid.'

'No problem, Janice. I'm so sorry I'm late.' It seemed to be becoming the theme of her day today, but at least she didn't have anyone glaring at her. Janice was beaming, in fact.

'I've got *such* good news. Your suggestion to contact the president of the World Transplant Games Federation really paid off. We're going to have trouble choosing which inspirational speakers we want the most.'

'Oh? That's fantastic.' Rebecca smiled up at the young waitress taking orders. 'I'll have a flat white, please. And one of your gorgeous savoury muffins.' The way her day was shaping up, it was highly likely to be the only lunch she would get.

'We've got an offer from a man called Jeremy Gibson. He got a liver transplant when he was in his early thirties and had three young children. He's competed in the games for four years now and, last year, he led a sponsored hike in the Himalayas to raise awareness for organ donation and advertise how successful it can be.'

Rebecca nodded but she wasn't quite focused on this

new meeting yet. The way Thomas had looked at her—
after he'd asked if she wanted to call in a new cardiologist for Penny's case…

The tension had still been there. That undercurrent
of anger that she knew had been caused by her telling
him that he always ran away was still there. But there'd
been something else, as well. A sadness that had made
her want to walk around the edge of that table and simply put her arms around him.

To tell him how sorry she was.

For everything.

That was a bit of a shock, all by itself. She was over
the breakup of her marriage.

She was over Thomas.

Who, in their right mind, would choose to be with
someone who simply wasn't there when the going got
too rough?

'And then there's Helena Adams,' Janice continued.
'A double lung recipient who's a champion skier and…'
She consulted a notepad on the table in front of her. 'And
Connor O'Brien—a young heart transplant recipient who
ran in the London Marathon last year.'

'They all sound amazing,' Rebecca said.

'Maybe they could all come,' their treasurer suggested. 'They don't all have to speak. They could just
mingle and join in some of the fun and chat to parents
and kids. And the press, of course. We're going to get
way more coverage this year, what with the threat to
Paddington's already getting so much publicity.'

'We've got three television crews coming,' the secre-
tary added. 'We're going international, apparently.' She
fanned her face. 'This is all getting so much bigger than
we ever thought it would.'

'Okay.' Janice's deep breath was audible. 'Let's get on with everything on the agenda. We've got a lot to get through. Has the bouncy castle been booked?'

'Yes. It's huge. And it's got turrets and everything. I've got a picture here...'

'Oh, it's perfect,' someone said. 'And how appropriate, given that Paddington's nickname is "the Castle"?'

An old redbrick Victorian building, Paddington Children's Hospital did indeed have its own turrets—the largest of which was a distinctive slate-roofed dome that loomed above the reception area of the main entrance.

'What's more important is to decide where it's going to go. I'm not sure the layout worked as well as it could last year and we've got so many extra things this time. The zoo has offered to organise and run pony rides.' Janice looked around the table. 'I know the London Zoo is one of our biggest sponsors and that's why we go over the road to Primrose Hill but is it going to be big enough? Do we need to consider a shift to part of Regent's Park?'

'I'm going to go there this evening,' Rebecca told them. 'I'll take the draft plan for the layout with me and walk it out but I think it'll be fine. We had tons of extra space last year and it was lovely to be on top of the hill and see everything that was going on. Some of the photos were fabulous, weren't they?'

She caught her lip between her teeth, her thoughts wandering again as the other committee members reminisced about last year's success. Should she have told Thomas the reason she was planning that walk in the park after work today?

No. If he'd known it had anything to do with the children and families of both donors and recipients of transplanted organs, he would have run a mile.

They really needed to talk if they were going to be able to work together and he didn't need to know the real reason she was there, did he? It was summer and the evenings were long. She could always stay later than him and sit on the top of the hill with the plan in her hands and make any notes she needed for changes.

It was important that they spent this time together. Before things got any more difficult between them.

And she was looking forward to it. Kind of. In a purely professional sense, of course. She'd feel better when she'd had the chance to apologise for that verbal attack. Thomas hadn't deserved that. She knew he was doing his best in the only way he knew how. That he had probably been doing that all along. It was just so sad that he couldn't see that he'd chosen such a wrong path.

That he, above everybody else, was suffering more because of it.

In retrospect, however, there was another reason why inviting Thomas to share this walk might have been a bad idea. It hadn't occurred to her at the time that a walk up Primrose Hill was an echo of their very first date.

Maybe he wouldn't remember. It wouldn't matter if he did. Just breathing the same air as Thomas was an echo of so very many things and, somehow, they had to find a way to deal with that.

CHAPTER THREE

THE WARMTH OF the summer's evening did not seem to be doing much to thaw the chill that surrounded Thomas and Rebecca like an air-conditioned bubble.

The virtual silence for the brisk walk to Regent's Park had been largely disguised by the sounds of the busy city streets but it became increasingly obvious as they followed a path into the vast stretch of green space.

'Thanks for agreeing to come,' Rebecca offered, finally.

'As you said, we need to find a way we can work together. Without letting our personal baggage interfere in any way with patient care.'

It sounded as though Thomas had rehearsed that little speech. Maybe it had been something he'd said to himself more than once today. Because he'd been arguing with himself about whether or not he could bear to spend any time with her?

Rebecca took a deep breath and did her best not to let it out as a sigh. He was here, walking beside her, so that was a good start. Maybe it was too soon to open the can of worms that was their 'personal baggage.' If Thomas could actually relax a fraction, it could make this a whole lot easier. And who wouldn't relax on a walk like this?

The boat lake beside them was a popular place to be on such a warm, sunny evening. It was crowded with boats—classic wooden rowing boats and the bright blue and yellow paddle boats. The grassy banks were dotted with the rugs and folding chairs of groups of families and friends who were preparing for a picnic meal. There were dogs chasing balls and children playing games on the shore of the lake.

And there were ducks.

Of course there were ducks. How many times had she and Thomas come here with Gwen on those precious days when she wasn't with her caregiver or at nursery school? They'd started bringing her here to feed the ducks way before she was old enough to walk or throw a crust of bread.

Not that she was about to remind Thomas of those times. Or admit that she still automatically put crusts of bread into a bag in the freezer until it was so full it would remind her that she never had the time or motivation to feed ducks any more. No one seeing them would ever guess at the kind of shared history they had. They would see the tall man with his briefcase in his hand and his companion with the strap of her laptop case over her shoulder and assume that they were work colleagues who happened to be sharing a walk home at the end of their day.

Exactly the space they were in, thanks to the boundaries that had been put firmly in place from the moment Thomas had set foot in Paddington's again.

Except that Thomas was smiling. Almost. He had his hand up to shield his eyes as he took in the scene of the boating activity on the lake and his lips were definitely not in a straight line.

His breath came out in an audible huff that could have been suppressed laughter.

'Nobody's swimming today,' he murmured.

It wasn't a lake that anybody swam in. Unless they were unfortunate enough to fall out of a boat, of course.

Like she had that day...

Good grief. She had deliberately avoided opening that can of worms labelled 'shared memories' but Thomas hadn't even hesitated.

Okay, it was funny in retrospect but it hadn't been at the time. Thomas had been inspired by the romantic image of a date that involved rowing his girlfriend around a pretty lake and Rebecca had been dressed for the occasion in a floaty summer dress and a wide-brimmed straw sunhat.

It had been a gloriously sunny day but there'd been a decent breeze. Enough to catch her hat and send it sailing away to float on the water. Thomas had done his best to row close enough for her to lean out of the boat and retrieve the hat but he hadn't been quite close enough. And she'd leaned just a little too far.

The water had been shallow enough to stand up in but she'd been completely soaked and the filmy dress had been clinging to her body and transparent enough to make her underwear obvious. The shock of the dunking had given way to helpless laughter and then to something very different when she'd seen the look in Thomas's eyes. Getting out of those wet clothes and into a hot bath hadn't been the real reason they couldn't get home fast enough.

And now, with Thomas pulling that memory out to share, Rebecca had the sensation that shutters had been lifted. There was a glint in his eyes that made her feel as if she'd stepped back in time.

As if everything they'd had together was still there—just waiting to have life breathed into it again.

It was the last thing Rebecca had expected to feel. It was too much. It wasn't what she wanted. She didn't want to go anywhere near that kind of space in her head or her heart and that made it…what…terrifying?

She had to break that eye contact. To push that memory back where it belonged—firmly in the past.

'Nobody sensible would,' she heard herself saying. 'But we all make mistakes, don't we?'

She hadn't looked away fast enough to miss the way that glint in his eyes got extinguished and her words hung in the air as they walked on, taking on a whole new meaning. That the mistake that had been made encompassed their whole relationship?

The soft evening air began to feel increasingly thick with the growing tension. This was her fault, Rebecca realised. She'd had the opportunity to break the ice and make things far more comfortable between them and she'd ruined it because she'd backed off so decisively. Maybe it was up to her to find another way to defuse the tension. At least she was no stranger to tackling difficult subjects with her patients and their families.

She had learned it was best to start in a safe place and not to jump in the deep end as Thomas had—perhaps—inadvertently done.

'I did that consult you requested on your new patient this afternoon. Tegan Mitchell? The thirteen-year-old with aortic stenosis?'

'Ah…good.' There was a note of relief in his voice as

he responded to stepping onto safe, professional ground. 'What did you think?'

'Classic presentation. Even my junior house surgeon could hear the ejection click after the first heart sound and the ejection murmur. It was the first time she'd come across an example of how the murmur increases with squatting and decreases with standing. She's got some impressive oedema in her legs and feet, too.' Rebecca's lips curled into a small smile as she glanced up at Thomas. 'Tegan, that is, not my house surgeon—*her* legs are fine.'

Thomas didn't smile at her tongue-in-cheek clarification. 'I've got Tegan booked for an echo tomorrow morning. We've started medication to get her heart failure under control but I think she's a good candidate for valve replacement surgery, yes?'

That tension hadn't been defused enough to allow for a joke, obviously. Rebecca nodded. 'Absolutely.'

He didn't see her nod because he had turned his head as the path forked.

'Do you want to go through Queen Mary's Garden?'

'Why not? It'll be gorgeous with the roses in full bloom.'

Thomas took the lead through the ornate gates and chose a path between gardens with immaculately trimmed hedges surrounding waves of colour. Rebecca inhaled the heady scent of old-fashioned roses but Thomas didn't seem at all distracted by the beauty around them.

'How's your theatre list looking for later this week?'

'Not too bad but it can always go pear-shaped at a moment's notice if a transplant organ becomes available— especially if I have to fly somewhere for the retrieval.

I've got two cystic fibrosis kids on the ward now who are desperate for new lungs and I can get called in for other cases, too. I started my transplant training with kidneys and livers, way back. I still love helping with those surgeries when I'm needed.'

'Way back? Five years isn't so long ago.'

'Mmm.' The sound was neutral. Five years could seem like for ever, couldn't it?

As if to push her thoughts where they probably shouldn't really go, a young couple passed them on the wide path. The woman was pushing an empty stroller. The man had a safe grip on the legs of the small child on his shoulders who was happily keeping his balance with fistfuls of his father's hair.

Five years ago she and Thomas would have looked more like this couple than a pair of colleagues. They had been happily married with an adorable three-year-old daughter. They were both juggling careers and parenthood and thriving on their lifestyle even though it frequently bordered on chaotic.

They hadn't intended to have a child so soon, of course, but the surprise of her pregnancy when Rebecca was studying for her finals in medical school had quickly morphed into joy. It had been meant to happen—just like they'd been meant to meet and fall in love so completely. They'd announced the pregnancy to the gathering of friends and family who'd come together to celebrate their low-key wedding and brushed off any concerns about how they would manage those busy early years of hospital training with a baby in their lives.

'We'll cope,' they had both repeated with absolute confidence. *'We've got each other.'*

And they *had* coped. They had known exactly what

specialties they had set their hearts on and Rebecca was chasing her dream of being a cardiothoracic surgeon with as much passion as Thomas put into his postgraduate studies in paediatric cardiology. The firsthand experience of being parents only confirmed what they also already knew—that they were destined to always work with children.

So yes, right now, five years was a lifetime ago. And it had been a long time since Thomas had turned his back on the specialty he'd worked so hard to get into.

'How are you finding being back at Paddington's?' she heard herself asking.

The look she received was almost bewildered.

'I mean, working with children again,' she added hurriedly. 'It must be very different to what you were doing up north…' Oh, help! This wasn't exactly staying on safe ground to get a conversation going, was it?

'It was…a big change…' It sounded as though Thomas was treading carefully—unsure of how much he wanted to say. 'I knew it wasn't going to be easy…'

Wow.

The step he'd voluntarily taken onto personal ground was as unexpected as him referring, however obliquely, to that date when she'd fallen out of the boat. Rebecca had no idea what to say in response. Should she offer sympathy which might immediately lead the conversation into the reasons why it hadn't been easy? To tell him how hard it had been for her, too—to be around children in those grief-stricken months after losing Gwen?

Even now, it could stir the threat of tears that had always been barely below the surface of her existence back then. How often did she have to fight for control? Whenever she heard the cry of a child and the soothing sound of a mother offering comfort. Or she saw the smile of a toddler or heard the delicious sound of a baby giggling. And the hardest thing of all was when she was holding one of her tiny patients herself. Or when a small child held their arms up, expecting the cuddle she would never refuse.

No. She wasn't ready to talk about that. And it would be the last thing Thomas would want to hear about. He had only agreed to this time together in order to clear the air enough for them to be able to work together. Perhaps what was really needed was a way to put more effective boundaries around the past so that they could both move on with their lives.

'No,' she finally said quietly. 'But everybody's delighted that you've come back.'

There was a moment's silence. Was he wondering if she was including herself in that 'everybody'?

'And you're here at such an important time for Paddington's,' Rebecca added quickly. 'You arrived right at the point where we all thought it was the end and then, thanks to the huge drama of that fire at Westbourne Grove Primary School, the media got on board and things started to turn around.'

'Yeah… I did think I might be accepting a permanent job at a hospital that wasn't going to be around much longer. Seemed a bit crazy at the time.'

'But now it looks like it's going to be all right. I know it's not really official yet but it sounds like it's going to be signed and sealed any day now. Are you going to the party at the Frog and Peach on Friday?'

Thomas shrugged. 'I'll have to see how the day goes.'

'Me, too. I often seem to be pretty late getting away once I've caught up on paperwork and things.'

'Same.'

Did they both work such long hours because there was nothing to make them rush home? Rebecca hadn't heard the slightest whisper of gossip that there might be someone else in Thomas's life now. She didn't even know where he was living, in fact.

'I hope this isn't taking you too far out of your way,' she said politely. 'Or keeping you from something you'd rather be doing on a nice summer's evening.'

'It's not a problem,' Thomas said. 'And it's not far to get home. I've got an apartment in South Hampstead.' He cleared his throat. 'And you? You still in Primrose Hill?'

'Mmm.' It was another tricky subject. Buying the basement flat in such a good area had been a huge step in their lives together and they couldn't have done it without the windfall of the legacy from Rebecca's grandfather. Thomas had refused to accept any of that money in the divorce settlement so he'd walked away with almost nothing.

'Keep it,' he'd said. *'Keep everything. I don't want any reminders.'*

Which reminders had been on the top of that list?

The night they'd taken possession and had a picnic on the bare floor of the living area with fish and chips and a bottle of champagne? Had either of them even noticed the discomfort of the wooden boards when they'd made love as the final celebration of getting the keys to their first home?

They'd decided later that that had been the night Gwen had been conceived and that had been as perfect as everything else in their charmed existence.

A sideways glance gave her a moment of eye contact with Thomas and she saw the flash of surprise in

his face. Oh, help! Had he seen what she'd been thinking about just then? The way she'd known he'd been remembering how she'd looked with that dress plastered
so revealingly to her body after her dunking in the lake?

It was too easy to read too much into those glances.
There were too many memories. And yes, some of them
were the best moments of her life but they had been buried under far more overwhelming ones.

Maybe the biggest reminders of sharing that house
were the ones that included Gwen after her birth? Walking round and round that small space, trying to persuade
their tiny human to go to sleep. A floor that was an
obstacle course because it was covered with toys. The
sound of a little girl's laughter that echoed between the
polished floorboards and the high ceilings...

She'd had to live with those reminders and, for the
longest time, tears had done little to wash away the pain
they caused. But gradually—so slowly Rebecca had
barely noticed it happening—something had changed
and sometimes there was comfort to be found in them.

Gwen's room might have become an office but occasionally, when Rebecca was working there late at night,
she would remember going in just to watch Gwen sleep
for a moment. She would take that warm, fuzzy miracle
of loving and being loved so much and wrap it around
herself like the softest blanket imaginable. Sometimes,
Thomas would come with her and they'd stand there
hand in hand and the blanket would be wrapped around
them both. And it would still be around them when they
went to sit on the big, old couch that dominated the small
living room. Or it would be an extra layer on the antique
brass bed that was big enough to almost touch both sides
of their bedroom.

The couch was still there.

And the bed.

Were the memories that lingered even after all this time something else that Thomas had been so desperate to get away from?

Rebecca had chosen to stay. To live with those memories.

To cope with the loneliness of losing all that love…

CHAPTER FOUR

THEY'D BEEN WALKING in silence for a long time, now.

Thomas stole a sideways glance at Rebecca. What was she thinking about?

What had they been talking about?

Oh, yeah, where they were living.

She was still in that house they'd chosen together. Had he imagined it or did she still remember the way they'd celebrated when they'd picked up the keys and had finally been alone together in their first, real home? The idea that he'd caught a glimpse of that memory in her eyes when their gazes had touched might have been purely projection but even if she had forgotten that particular night, there was no way she could escape all the other memories.

He couldn't begin to imagine being able to have done that himself. How could you escape from memories that made you feel as if your heart was being ripped out of your chest when they were all around you? When even the walls had soaked up the sounds of a newborn baby's cry and an infant's laughter and the first words of a toddler?

It was just as incomprehensible as choosing to take your career into an area that held memories that were still too raw to go near. To actually take a child into an operating theatre to harvest organs when you knew the kind of grief the parents were experiencing had to mean you could shut yourself away completely.

To stop caring to the extent that it was possible to think of those organs as 'spare parts'?

Thomas could feel the muscles in his jaw tensing so much they made his teeth ache.

No wonder their marriage had failed.

Maybe they'd never really understood each other.

Their route had taken them right through Regent's Park now and they were walking past the perimeter of London Zoo. A screech of some excited animal could be heard—an orangutan, perhaps? Thomas hadn't been near a zoo for five years and he wasn't comfortable being this close. There were memories everywhere, here. A lazy Sunday afternoon, pushing Gwen's stroller down the paths and stopping to try and capture her expressions when she saw the animals and birds. The penguins had been her absolute favourite and she'd shrieked with laughter every time they waddled close to the fence.

They'd bought a stuffed toy penguin in the zoo shop that had been almost as big as she was but it had to be tucked into bed with her that night. And she'd fallen asleep, still smiling...

Thomas waited for the jolt of pain that always came with memories like that. He could feel his muscles tense and his face scrunch into a scowl, as if that would somehow protect him.

Rebecca seemed oblivious. She was heading for the other side of Prince Albert Road, clearly intent on getting to Primrose Hill and that was good. The further away from the zoo they got, the better. He wouldn't have to mentally swat away more memories.

Like the way Rebecca's face would light up with pleasure when they watched the otters which were *her* absolute favourite.

Or that photograph that someone had offered to take of them as a family, beside the huge, bronze statue of the gorilla just inside the entrance to the zoo. He'd been holding Gwen with one arm and had his other arm around Rebecca. Their heads had both been level with his shoulders and he must have said something funny, because they'd both looked up at him as the photo was taken and they were all grinning from ear to ear.

Looking so happy…

His scowl deepened as they reached the entrance to Primrose Hill Park because now they were going past the children's playground.

For a split second, his gaze caught Rebecca's as they glanced at each other at precisely the same moment. He knew they were both thinking the same thing—that the last time they'd been to this playground, they'd been with their daughter.

They'd probably both looked away from each other in the same moment, as well.

There were more memories, here. More jolts of pain to be expected.

Except…that first one hadn't arrived yet.

That was weird. How could he actually have such a clear picture in his head of something like Gwen being tucked up with her toy penguin and not feel the same crippling blast of loss that he'd had the last time his brain had summoned something like that from that private databank of images?

As if he needed to prod the wound to check whether it was possible that it had miraculously started healing, Thomas let himself think about it again. He could see Gwen's dark curls against the pale pillowcase, her cheek pressed against the fluff of the penguin. He could see the sweep of her dark lashes become still as sleep claimed her and he could see the dimples that came with even the smallest smile.

And yes, he could feel the pang of loss and a wash of sadness but it wasn't really pain. He could—almost—feel his own lips trying to curl up at the corners.

Instead of relief, this awareness that something had changed brought something far less pleasant with it.

Guilt?

Was he somehow failing Gwen by being less traumatised at being reminded of her loss?

Maybe grappling with a sense of failure was familiar enough to be preferable to something strange and new.

He'd been over this ground often enough in the past few years. How he'd failed Gwen as a father because he hadn't been able to keep her safe.

How he'd failed Rebecca as a husband because he hadn't been able to keep their marriage alive.

But how could it have worked when they were such different people? People who had never really understood each other?

'Do you mind if we stop for a moment?'

'Not getting puffed, are you? We're not even at the top of the hill.' Unbidden, another memory ambushed him. 'I seem to remember you ran up here the last time we did this. Faster than I managed.'

Rebecca's face went very still.

She hadn't forgotten that moment in time, had she?

Their very first date. A walk in the park and the decision to get to the top of the hill to admire the view.

'Race you!'

'Last one there is a rotten egg!'

She'd won that race but she'd had to throw herself onto the grass to try and catch her breath. And Thomas had lain down beside her and neither of them had bothered to look at anything more than each other between those lingering kisses. The walk down the hill had been much, much slower. Holding hands and exchanging glances so frequently, as if they needed to confirm that they were both feeling the same way—that they'd found a hand to hold that would get them through the rest of their lives…

Oh, man, this walk together really hadn't been a very good idea, had it? It was doing his head in. This was all so hard and exactly what he'd been determined to avoid when he'd chosen to come back to Paddington's.

But Rebecca was staring down the hill, her face still expressionless, seemingly focused on something that had nothing to do with any memories of their first date.

'I just need to check something.'

'What?'

'Um…' Rebecca's eyes were narrowed against the glare of the sun as she looked down the slope. 'We need a flat area for both the pony rides and the bouncy castle…'

Thomas blinked. 'You've lost me.'

'I'm on the organising committee for a big picnic that's happening soon. It's our fourth year and it's going to get a lot more publicity this year because of Paddington's being in the spotlight with the threatened closure. We need to make sure there are no glitches, so I'm checking out the plan.'

Something like a chill ran down Thomas's spine.

'I saw the poster in the relatives' room. It's for transplant patients, yes?' He could hear the chill in his tone. He didn't want to start talking about any of this. Except that this was the reason they couldn't work well together, wasn't it? And that was why they were here now.

They *had* to talk about it.

'Not just the patients. It's to celebrate everything that's good about organ donation in the hope of getting people more aware and making it easier to talk about.' Rebecca's tone was cautious enough to reveal that she, too, recognised they were approaching the real point of this time together. 'It's for the patients and their families, of course, but also for all the people who devote their working lives to making the success stories happen. And…and it's for the people on the other side, too. Some people have contact with the recipients of their child's organs and…and even if they don't, it's a day where they can celebrate the gift of life they were able to provide.'

Julia had said something about a parent like that but it was in the 'unthinkable' basket for Thomas. To see another child that was having fun at some amazing picnic with pony rides and a bouncy castle because they had a part of *his* daughter?

The chill in his spine held an edge of horror now.

Did *Rebecca* know a child like that?

He wasn't going to ask. *He* didn't want to know.

Refreshing that smouldering pile that was the anger that had been ignited last week was a preferable route to feeling either so disturbed by unexpected memories or guilty about things he had or hadn't done in the past.

'Yes,' he heard himself saying aloud. 'I guess you need to drum up a good supply of those *spare* parts.'

The silence that fell between them was like a solid wall. Impenetrable.

It stretched out for long enough to take a slow breath. And then another.

They weren't even looking at each other. They could have been on separate planets.

And then Rebecca spoke.

'I should never have said that. I'm sorry. It was completely unprofessional. And…and it was cruel.'

'I couldn't agree more.'

'It's not what I believe,' she said softly. '*You* know that, Tom.'

It was the first time she'd called him Tom since he'd come back and it touched a place that had been very safely walled off.

Or maybe it was that assumption that he knew her well enough to know that she would never think like that.

And, deep down, he had known that, hadn't he? It had just been so much easier to think otherwise. To be angry.

'So, why did you say it, then?'

'You've been so distant ever since you came back. So cut off. I don't even recognise you any more.' There was a hitch in Rebecca's voice that went straight to that place that calling him 'Tom' had accessed. 'I guess I wanted to know if the man I married still exists.'

His words were a little less of a snap this time.

'I haven't changed.'

'Yes, you have.' He could feel Rebecca looking at him but he didn't turn his head. 'Something like what we went through changes everyone. But you…you disappeared. You just…ran away.'

There was that accusation again. That he was a coward. The reminder of how little she understood came with a wave of weariness. Thomas wanted this over with. He wanted to put this all behind them effectively enough to be able to work together.

He wanted…peace.

So he took another deep breath and he turned his head to meet Rebecca's gaze.

'Everyone processes grief differently. You should know as well as anybody that it's not a good idea to make assumptions.'

'But that's the problem,' Rebecca whispered. 'It always was.'

'What?'

'That you *didn't* process it. You shut yourself away. Emotionally and then physically. You left me. You left Paddington's.'

That was unfair.

'I didn't *leave* you. It was *you* who asked for the divorce.'

'You did leave me.' Rebecca's eyes were bright enough to suggest gathering tears. 'You started walking away the day Gwen died and I felt more and more alone until the idea of staying in our marriage was worse than escaping.'

Thomas was silent. He had a horrible feeling that those words were going to haunt him from now on and that they would be harder to deal with than an accusation of cowardice.

'You don't even want to talk to me any more. You've been here for months now and you've avoided anything that doesn't have something to do with a patient. You can't even ask whether I've had a good day, let alone talk about something like the Teddy Bears' Picnic. And…' Rebecca was clearly struggling to hold back her tears now. She sniffed inelegantly. 'And you never smile. And you call me Rebecca. Or Dr Scott. Like I'm…a complete stranger.'

Thomas closed his eyes for a moment. It was true. He'd created as much distance as he could to try and make their first meeting easier and he'd kept it up. For months…

'I… I'm sorry.'

Rebecca nodded. She sniffed again and then scrubbed at her nose with the back of her hand.

'Excuse me. I don't have a hanky,' she said.

'Neither do I.' Thomas wished he did. Offering one could have been an olive branch. And they needed an olive branch.

'You're right,' he said slowly. 'I have been distant. I knew it was going to be hard working with children again. I thought I'd be making it a whole lot harder if I spent time with you, as well.'

'You don't have to spend time with me to be friendly. Just a smile would do. Or saying something friendly that made me feel like a person and not just a surgical consult.'

Thomas nodded. 'I could do that. Something like "Have you had a good day?"'

It was Rebecca's turn to nod. But then her breath escaped in a huff of sound that was more like a sob. 'Actually, I've had a horrible day. Ever since you glared at me for being late for the meeting this morning and everybody was reminded of how much you hate working with me.'

'I don't hate working with you. You're the best surgeon I have available. I think…your skills are amazing.'

'But you'd rather it was someone else with my skills.'

'You probably found it easier to work with the cardiologist I replaced.'

She shook her head this time. 'Not professionally. You're the best, too.'

'But personally,' Thomas persisted, 'you don't find it any easier than I do.'

'Only because you hate me.'

Thomas sighed. 'Oh, Becca... I could never *hate* you.'

The short version of her name had slipped out, as Thomas turned to look at her directly, so he could see the effect it had. Her face became very still but something in her eyes changed. Became softer. Like a smile that didn't reach her lips.

And something softened inside Thomas, too.

'Come here,' he said gruffly. 'Friends can have a hug, can't they?'

CHAPTER FIVE

THOMAS WOLFE WASN'T the only person in the gallery to watch this particular surgery.

Rosie Hobbes was sitting beside him, alternatively watching the screen that gave a close-up view of what was largely obscured by the gowned and masked figures below and leaning forward to watch the whole team at work.

'I've never seen the insertion of a VAD before.'

'No. It's not common. Especially in children.'

'Do you think it'll work?'

'It will certainly buy us some time. The only thing that could guarantee more time is a transplant. This is a bridge which should give her a much better quality of life while we're waiting.'

Rosie was looking down into the theatre again. At the small chest now open and so vulnerable.

'Life's so unfair sometimes, isn't it?' she murmured.

'Mmm.' Thomas couldn't argue with that. He had firsthand experience of exactly how unfair life could be. So did the surgeon he was watching so intently.

The last time he had watched Rebecca operate had, ironically, been on this same patient, when Penny had been only about six months old.

Life wasn't only unfair, it had patterns to it. Circles. Or were they spirals? A kind of pathway, anyway, that could take you back to places you'd been before. Places where memories could be looked at through a lens that changed with increased distance or wisdom.

Did you choose to follow those pathways with the familiar signposts, Thomas wondered. Or were they somehow set in place by fate and always there, waiting for you to step back onto them? Spirals could go either way, couldn't they? They could go downwards into tight loops that sucked you into a place you didn't want to be. Or they could lift you higher into loops so wide that the possibilities were no more than promises.

He was, very unexpectedly, back on one of his life pathways. Ever since that walk with Rebecca the other day when they'd reached some kind of truce and sealed it with that hug.

Or maybe he'd stepped back onto that path the moment he'd agreed to come back to Paddington's.

It still felt weird.

The way the memories had begun to rush at him from every direction but without the pain he would have expected.

He could think of Gwen and find himself ready to smile.

He could remember Rebecca falling out of that boat and how unbelievably sexy she'd looked in that wet dress...

He had even found himself reliving that hug on the top of Primrose Hill and how it had reminded him—again—of their very first date.

'We're ready to go on bypass.' Rebecca's voice was calm and clear through the speaker system. 'And the pocket for the pump is all set. How's the pump preparation looking?'

The surgeon working on the back table to prepare the device looked up and nodded. 'Ready when you are.'

'Stand by.' Rebecca and her registrar started the task of getting Penny onto bypass. Despite her obvious focus, she kept her audience involved. 'Because we know that this surgery is a bridge to transplant, I'm being careful to leave space for re-cannulation at the aortic cannulation site.'

It took long minutes to get Penny onto bypass and to the point where the heart was stopped. Her life now depended on the oxygen being circulated by the cardiopulmonary bypass machine. It was a procedure that was common and relatively safe these days but it still gave Thomas a sense of wonder at what medicine was able to achieve, along with a dollop of pride that he was able to be a part of this astonishing world.

He was proud of Rebecca, too. He had been perfectly sincere when he'd told her that she was the best surgeon he had available and that her skills were amazing, but he hadn't realised how much better she had become in the last few years. So confident but, at the same time, so exquisitely careful of every tiny detail. His gaze was fixed on the screen again as she inserted a suture.

'This marks the site of the core,' she said, for the benefit of the observers. 'I've used the left anterior descending artery to identify the intraventricular groove. We're going to core anteriorly due to the small size of the left ventricle.'

We. It was Rebecca who was doing the actual task but she'd never shown any sign of developing the ego that some surgeons were famous for. She'd always seen herself as part of a team.

And now Thomas felt like he was part of that team, too. As difficult as it had been to step onto personal ground during that walk, they had found a space just within the perimeter that was apparently going to make it possible to work together without the awful tension of the last months.

Maybe it would even allow them to become friends one day.

It had also given him rather a lot to think about. The quiet conversations between the surgeons, nursing staff and technicians below were only catching the surface layer of his attention as his thoughts drifted back to what was becoming a familiar route.

He'd known that her heartfelt words would haunt him.

I felt more and more alone…

He'd felt alone, too. They might have been walking the same path back then, in those dark days, but they had been nowhere near each other and the distance had only increased.

Looking back, he could see that it had been Rebecca who'd made the effort to reach out time and time again.

'I've kept some dinner for you. It's in the oven.'

'I'm not hungry.'

The bed, where they would lie side by side, should have made them feel less alone but those sleepless hours had been the worst. The slightest contact with her skin would make him flinch and move away.

'It's been a long day. I'm tired.'

But he'd *been* there. He hadn't been running away. He'd been desperately sad. He'd needed more time to try and put the shattered pieces of his life back together and it was something that Rebecca couldn't help with. Not just because she was fighting her own battle but because she was so much a piece of what had been shattered.

His family.

The family that he had failed to protect.

She'd been right to accuse him of being distant ever since he'd returned to Paddington's. Was she also right that he'd coped with his grief by initiating that distance all those years ago? Had he been the one to push them so far apart that there had been no hope of connecting enough to help each other?

How could he have let that happen to the person who'd been his whole world until Gwen had arrived? The only woman he would ever love like that...

'Look at that,' Rosie whispered beside him. 'That's the inflow cannula going in and getting secured to the sewing ring. Dr Scott's incredibly neat, isn't she?'

Rebecca's size had often led people to make incorrect assumptions about her abilities but having such small hands with those long, delicate fingers was a bonus for a surgeon who often had to work on tiny patients. Being so much shorter than he was had always seemed another bonus because it made it easier for children to be drawn to her. At six foot one, Thomas towered over his small patients. And when was the last time he had crouched down to talk to one of them? Had he forgotten the difference that could make in his years of working only with adults?

Maybe he'd forgotten how tall he was, along with ignoring so many other personal things that only intruded on his focus on his work.

Hugging Rebecca on Primrose Hill had made him acutely aware of his height because of the way her head only reached his shoulder. Not that that had ever been a bad thing. As if it was a step from a well-remembered dance, she had turned her head so that it fitted perfectly into the natural hollow beneath his collarbone. It probably wasn't such a good thing that holding her that close had also reminded him of how soft her curves were...

With an effort, Thomas refocused on what he'd come here to watch. Brooding about how much he had failed Rebecca to leave her feeling so unbearably alone that she'd had to escape her marriage was not only inappropriate, it wasn't going to help anyone. The past was simply that—the past. They could only move forward and now they seemed to have found a way to do that.

At least he'd been the one to reach out this time.

To offer that hug that was a physical connection on top of an emotional one.

And it had felt good.

More than good.

As if there was a promise in the air he was breathing now.

The promise of finding peace?

She knew he was watching her.

Not that she'd looked directly up at the gallery at any point but she'd caught movement from the corner of her eye as she'd entered the theatre—her arms crossed in front of her, keeping her scrubbed and gloved hands safe from contact with anything—and she'd known it was Thomas, simply from the impression of height and that measured kind of movement he had these days.

Rebecca wasn't about to let anything disturb her focus. She did allow herself a heartbeat of pleasure that he was there but the only other irrelevant thought that escaped that part of her brain before she closed it down was that the last time Thomas had been observing her work had been during the second cardiac surgery that Penelope Craig had had, when she was still so tiny— only a few months old.

Or maybe the thought wasn't completely irrelevant. The surgery had been a success that time. She was going to do her utmost to make sure it was this time, too.

Finally, it was time to find out. The ventricular assist device had been meticulously stitched into position and Penny had been weaned off the cardiopulmonary bypass.

'We'll start the device at the lowest setting and keep the aortic clamp on to get rid of the last of the air.' Rebecca turned to one of the Theatre technicians. 'I'll need the transoesophageal echo soon, so I can check the final position in the chest without the retractors.'

She took plenty of time to gradually increase the flow of the device while the heart's function and pressures were closely monitored.

'We may not decide on final settings for a few days,' she said, for the benefit of everyone watching. 'Some people leave the chest open for a day to allow for stabilisation but I would only do that if I was concerned about something like ongoing bleeding. This is looking great, so I'll be happy to close. Let's get these cannulas removed and some chest drains in.'

There was movement again in the gallery and Rebecca glanced up to see that some people were leaving now that the procedure was all but over and it had clearly been successful. Thomas was still there, however. He acknowledged her glance with a nod and the hint of a smile.

A smile…

Things had certainly changed in the last few days.

That hug on Primrose Hill had been a turning point. A starting point, perhaps, of a new relationship. One of colleagues who could work together without causing discomfort to themselves and those around them.

Maybe it could even be the start of a friendship?

Rebecca turned back to coach her registrar through the placement of the chest drains. She had to admit that the idea of being friends with Thomas might be pushing things and getting closer than colleagues might not be a good idea, anyway. It had messed with her head more than a little, that hug. Especially coming in the wake of so many memories that had been undisturbed for so long. Not that she'd ever forgotten how it had felt to be held in his arms with her head nestled in that hollow beneath his shoulder but she'd never expected to actually feel it again.

But, like the memories that they'd shared, that hug had stirred up feelings that might be far better left alone.

Like how much she had missed Thomas in her life.

How much she *still* missed him…

No. She missed having a partner but Thomas would never be that man, again. You couldn't rewrite history and too much damage had been done.

Minutes ticked past to add another hour to the long stint in Theatre but Rebecca wasn't about to leave her small patient under the complete care of others. Even when the surgery was completely finished and she had stripped off her gloves and mask and hat to dispose of them in the rubbish, she stayed in the room, keeping a close watch on all the monitors as the team tidied up around Penny and prepared her for the transfer to Recovery. And then she went with them, still watching for any change in pressures or heart rhythm.

It was no surprise that Thomas arrived by her side almost immediately.

'She's stable,' Rebecca told him. 'It's looking good.'

He was scanning the bank of monitors himself. 'You did a fantastic job,' he said quietly. 'Julia and Peter are waiting in the relatives' room. Do you want to come with me to tell them the good news?'

'Of course.' She stayed a moment longer, however, moving to the head of the bed. She put her forefinger against her lips and then reached down to touch Penny's cheek gently. 'Be back soon, pet. Sleep tight.'

Sleep tight, don't let the bedbugs bite...

Had Thomas remembered the final goodnight she had always given Gwen? That soft touch that transferred a kiss and the whisper of an old rhyme that was irrelevant except that it was remembered from her own childhood.

When had it become something she had started to do with her youngest patients?

She couldn't remember. Somewhere in the last few years, it had just become one of those automatic, preferably private things. Like a good luck charm? No. She was too much of a scientist for something like that. It was because she worked with children and you couldn't help connecting with them at a level that was never appropriate or possible with adults.

And maybe it was because she knew, better than most, how precious these little lives were.

If Thomas remembered, he didn't show any sign of it. He was still looking at the monitors, in fact, rather than the small person attached to them. Rebecca's heart sank a little as she followed him from the Recovery area.

They might have made a breakthrough in their own relationship but was Thomas ever going to step any closer to his patients? Allow himself enough of an emotional connection to share the joy that came with success?

He certainly had a smile for Penny's parents.

'I'll let Rebecca tell you how well the surgery went but it was all I could have hoped for. You'll be able to go in and see her very soon.'

Julia burst into tears. Peter put his arms around her and ignored the tears rolling down his own cheeks.

'She'll have to go to intensive care after this, won't she?'

'Yes. But probably not for long. It's amazing how quickly children can bounce back from even open heart surgery.'

'And she's going to be better?' Julia lifted her head from her husband's chest. 'She won't need the wheelchair or to be on oxygen all the time?'

'That's what I expect.' Thomas nodded. He smiled again but the glance at his watch told Rebecca that he was already preparing to move on to his next patient. Stepping back from this emotional encounter with his patient's parents?

Perhaps he wasn't ready for the kind of connection that would allow him to share their intense relief with its glimmers of joy that would become hope. And she could understand that. If you were distant enough not to buy in to the joy, it meant that you were protected from the pain when things didn't go well. With many of the cases doctors like she and Thomas had in their care, the long term outlook wasn't good, so that pain was inevitable. Rebecca had learned to deal with it. To remind herself that it was worth it because of the heavier balance of the joy.

Thomas had chosen to step back.

To run away…

But he had come back. Surely being willing to work with children again was a sign that something big had changed. And there'd been moments during that walk when she could believe that the man she'd married really did still exist somewhere behind those barriers.

Baby steps…

Like the fact that he could smile at her again.

It wasn't as if the distance he kept made the care he provided any less thorough. He went above and beyond what most doctors did which was why it was, again, no surprise to find him in the intensive care unit late that evening, when Rebecca went back for a final check on Penny.

'I met Julia by the elevator. She's finally gone to get something to eat in the cafeteria and then she's coming back to stay the night with Penny.'

Thomas nodded. 'Are you still happy to lighten the sedation level as early as tomorrow morning?'

'Yes. She's been stable ever since the surgery. The VAD is working perfectly. We'll keep the pain control up, of course, but I wouldn't be surprised if she wakes up and wants to get out of bed and put her tutu on. Like Sapphire, there.'

Thomas glanced at the end of the bed where the sparkly blue, soft toy bear that Julia had bought as Penny's post-surgery gift was waiting for her to see as soon as she woke up. But he wasn't smiling. Did he know how desperately Penny wanted to be a ballerina? Did it matter?

'It's very late,' she added. 'What are you still doing at work?'

Had his career become his whole life, the way hers had?

Did he not have someone to go home to?

The thought had occurred to her before, but she'd never heard any hint of what Thomas's life outside the hospital contained these days. It had been five years. It shouldn't be surprising if he did have someone else in his life by now but Rebecca knew how much of a shock it would be.

She wasn't ready to find out.

'It is late,' he agreed. 'I was catching up on some work. Trying to decide whether or not to go to that thing at the pub over the road.'

'Oh, the Frog and Peach. I'd completely forgotten about the celebration drinks.' Rebecca looked at her watch. 'It's only ten p.m. The party should be only just getting going.'

How good would it be if she and Thomas could go to a work function together? To have a drink with their colleagues and make it obvious that they'd found a way to work together again?

'Saving Paddington's is definitely something to celebrate,' she said, looking up to catch his gaze. 'Shall we pop in? Just for a quick drink?'

He hesitated and she could almost see him following the same train of thought she'd just had.

'Sure,' he said. 'Why not? Give me a few minutes to sort what I've left on my desk and I'll meet you in Reception.'

CHAPTER SIX

WEIRDLY, THERE WAS almost nobody from Paddington's still at the Frog and Peach by the time Rebecca and Thomas arrived.

There were plenty of people, and an enthusiastic game of darts going on in one corner, but the only two remaining staff members were Matt McGrory, the burns specialist at Paddington's, and Alistair North, a paediatric neurosurgeon. They were standing at the bar, their glasses almost empty.

'Where is everybody?' Rebecca asked. 'What kind of party is this?'

'We started early,' Matt said. 'On the dot of six p.m. Some people are working tomorrow and others had families to get home to.'

'I was sure Quinn would be here. She's been so involved in the campaign to save the hospital.'

'Oh, she was.' Matt's smile reflected the kind of glow that only newfound love could bring. 'Simon's babysitter could only stay till ten, so she had to go home.'

'How *is* Simon?' Like many of the staff members at Paddington's, Rebecca's heart had been caught by the case of five-year-old Simon, who was Quinn's first foster child, when he'd been badly burned in the fire at West-bourne Grove Primary School.

But Matt was still smiling. 'He's doing great. The scars on his face are looking brilliant thanks to the wonders of spray-on skin. His arm will take a bit more work but the best thing is that his self-confidence seems to be growing by the day.'

'Maybe it's because you and Quinn are together?' Alistair suggested. 'Giving him a real family?'

'I'd like to take the credit but I reckon Maisie has to take most of it.'

'Who's Maisie?' Thomas asked.

'She's a rescue dog we rehomed. Gorgeous collie-cross. Simon adores her, and it's helping in ways we never expected. Like when we went to the park the other day. These kids about Simon's age came over and wanted to pat his dog and help throw the ball for her and I swear they didn't even notice his scars.'

'Oh, that's brilliant,' Rebecca said.

'Claire was here to start with, too,' Alistair said. 'It was the perfect opportunity to share the news that we've decided to stay in London.'

'That's great news,' Thomas said.

'She was looking forward to catching up with you,' Alistair said to Rebecca, 'but she's getting tired pretty easily these days so she went at the same time as Quinn.'

'I'm not surprised she's tired.' Rebecca smiled. 'Didn't I hear a rumour that you've got twins on the way?'

'Yes.' Alistair had the same kind of glow that Matt did. 'Not sure how that news got leaked so fast. It's very early days so we're being careful.'

Rebecca felt a pang of something poignant. She remembered what it was like to be so in love. To be so sure that you'd found the person you wanted to spend the rest of your life with. To be expecting a first baby...

Hopefully, these new couples within the ranks of their colleagues would have the happy-ever-after that she and Thomas had missed out on.

'I'll have to catch up with them both some other time,' she said. 'I wanted to tell Quinn what a great job she did. She put a lot of effort into that committee.'

'I'll tell her you noticed,' Matt said. 'She's over the moon about the result, that's for sure.' His smile broadened. 'I believe she's now on a new committee that's going to be organising the official celebration bash.'

Rebecca laughed. 'That sounds like Quinn. Any word on what sort of party it's going to be?'

'Black tie, from what I've heard. A big dinner with lots of speeches.'

'I'll look forward to it.'

'Me, too,' Alistair said. 'In the meantime, can I buy you guys a drink? It's good to see you out and about for once, Thomas.'

'Ah...' Thomas's gaze slid sideways. Towards the door? Was he thinking that the fact that this wasn't really a work function any more was a good reason to bail?

'I'll have a white wine,' Rebecca said quickly. 'Is it still red for you, Tom?'

Her heart skipped a beat. Unexpectedly, she wanted him to stay. She wanted time with him away from the hospital again, like they'd had on that walk through the park.

Maybe it wasn't the best idea but she wanted...what? To see a glimpse of the real Thomas again? The one that had called her 'Becca' and given her a hug?

'Sounds good,' he said. 'But I'll buy them. Can I get you something else, Matt? Alistair?'

'No, thanks,' Alistair said. 'I'll finish this but then I'd better head off, too. Got an early ward round tomorrow.'

They clinked glasses when the drinks had been poured.

'Here's to Paddington's staying exactly where it should be. For ever.'

'Paddington's,' Rebecca echoed. 'It's been quite a fight, hasn't it? Let's hope there's no final glitch that stops it becoming official.'

'How could there be?' Matt said. 'It feels like we've got the whole of London on our side now.'

'How amazing was it for Sheikh Idris to have made that donation?' Alistair said. 'We wouldn't be celebrating now if it wasn't for him. Can you imagine being *that* rich?'

'No.' Rebecca sipped her wine. 'But I can imagine loving my daughter enough to want to thank the people who helped her. And save the place where the miracle had happened.'

Oh, help! That was a heavy thing to say, given the company. No wonder Thomas was draining his glass of wine. The bartender noticed instantly and raised a bottle as well as his eyebrows. Thomas nodded and his glass was refilled. He glanced at Rebecca's glass and then caught her gaze and she nodded acceptance of the unspoken offer.

Why not? It had been a long day and they both had things to celebrate other than a successful campaign to save the hospital they both worked in. They shared a patient who'd come through some pretty amazing surgery today.

And they were making a fresh start on their new relationship.

It was already feeling easier and Alistair had obviously noticed a difference. She hadn't missed that glance he'd shared with Matt when they'd seen them come in together and he'd made a point of telling Thomas that it was good to see him being social.

It was Rebecca that he seemed to want to talk to now, however.

'I was looking for you earlier today. Sounded like you were tied up in Theatre for a long session. Interesting case?'

'It was. You don't often get to insert a ventricular assist device.'

'Ah, that's little Penelope Craig, isn't it? I heard about that. Did it go well?'

'It's working perfectly,' Thomas put in. 'We'll just have to hope that it buys enough time for her to get a transplant.' He turned away to respond to something Matt said and, within moments, the two of them were engrossed in conversation.

Alistair was looking thoughtful as he took a step closer to Rebecca. 'That's what I was wanting to give you a heads-up about.' He lowered his voice, even though nobody would have been able to overhear their conversation in this noisy bar. 'I've got a case in ICU at the moment. Six-year-old boy. We're going to repeat tests in the next day or two but I don't think we're going to find any signs of brain activity. He could become a possible donor in the near future.'

Rebecca's nod was solemn. 'I know the case,' she said quietly.

Who didn't? This little boy—Ryan Walker—had been

the most seriously injured child in the dreadful school fire at Westbourne Grove that had been the catalyst to turn the attention of the media onto the plight of Paddington Children's Hospital's impending closure. Any real recovery from his severe head injury had always been unlikely and, only a few weeks ago, he'd had a major setback with a new bleed in his brain. He'd been on life support in the intensive care unit ever since.

If he was declared brain-dead, and his parents were willing to consider the idea of organ donation, then he would become one of Rebecca's patients. It was not often that she became involved at this stage. Retrieval of organs was usually somewhere else, from a patient whose family had already accepted that there was no hope for their own child and who had the generosity of heart to realise that their tragedy could provide hope for others.

'Have the parents been spoken to?'

'Not yet. They're still coming to terms with how bad things are. I think they're still hoping for some kind of miracle. I suspect that discussion is going to come after the next electroencephalogram. I was hoping to maybe include you in that family conference. To introduce the subject of possible organ donation?' Alistair sighed and then finished his drink. 'And now I really must get home and make sure that Claire's been putting her feet up.'

Matt followed Alistair's lead and Thomas and Rebecca found themselves alone at the bar when they'd really only started on their refilled glasses.

A waiter walked past, carrying plates from the kitchen and the smell of the hot food made Rebecca turn her head.

'Have you eaten?' Thomas asked.

'No. I didn't find the time. I'll grab a sandwich when I get home.'

'I've just realised I missed dinner, too. Not a good idea, drinking on an empty stomach.'

'No…' She'd wanted him to stay here and give them some time together, but dinner seemed like an intimate thing to do.

But friends could have dinner together, couldn't they?

Of course they could. It was what friends did.

'I think I saw some Yorkshire puddings with that roast beef that went past.'

'Oh.' Rebecca pushed any lingering doubts aside. 'I'll bet they have fish and chips with mushy peas on the menu, too.'

'Let's find out.'

Within a matter of minutes, they found themselves at a quiet corner table, menus in hand and, a commendably short time after that, they had delicious, hot meals in front of them.

And it was much easier than Rebecca had expected. They'd done this a million times together in the past and they could eat and chat without it being a big deal. They talked about Penny and the surgery.

'I'm glad you came to watch,' she admitted.

'So am I,' Thomas said quietly. 'You've come a long way, Becca. Did it occur to you that the last time I watched you operate was also on Penny? When she was about six months old?'

'Mmm…'

He hadn't been around for the last surgery on Penny, though, had he? He'd gone by then and had taken any hope of salvaging anything from the wreck their marriage had become.

A silence fell between them, which made the background conversation of other customers and the music from the juke box increasingly noticeable. Rebecca took a sip of her wine. And then another.

When the Ricky Martin song with its strong Latino beat started playing, the silence between them suddenly became charged.

Some memories only needed something like a few bars of a song to make it feel like they'd happened yesterday.

Salsa dance classes had been a form of exercise Thomas had been dragged along to when they were at medical school.

'It'll keep you fit,' Rebecca had assured him. *'And it's the best stress relief. Just what we'll need when it comes to exam time.'*

Who knew what an excellent dancer Thomas would turn out to be? Or how much they both found they loved it?

Rebecca hadn't danced in more than five years.

From the look on Thomas's face, neither had he.

The wine had to be blamed for the lack of thought on Rebecca's part. For the crazy urge that she couldn't suppress. Maybe it was the memory of the kind of stress relief it could provide. A cure for the slightly awkward silence? A distraction from both memories she didn't want to sink into and the prospect of the kind of conversation she might have to have with Ryan Walker's family in the near future?

'I love this song,' she heard herself say as her smile grew. 'Are you up for it?'

Friends could dance together, couldn't they? Without it being a big deal? It wasn't that much of a step up from having dinner together and that had been fine until a few moments ago. Maybe she wanted to recapture that feeling of being comfortable in each other's company.

Thomas was looking stunned. It was clearly the last thing he had expected and just as obviously he had no idea how to react.

Rebecca helped him out. She put her glass of wine down and stood up, holding out her hand, already turning towards the tiny square of a dance floor that the pub offered.

It didn't matter if he was only being polite, so that she wouldn't be embarrassed by being the only person on the dance floor, but something inside Rebecca's chest melted as he hesitated for only a moment before following her. He touched her fingers, caught her hand in his and then pulled her close.

They could have been back in one of those Tuesday night dance classes. Or even at the one competition they'd entered, just for fun. The muscle memory came back within moments and they moved together as well as they always had. Thomas's lead was so smooth and so easy to follow that Rebecca could simply let the music flow over them and enjoy every step and twirl and dip.

It was over too soon. The next song was a slow one and the kind of dancing that would require was definitely not appropriate between friends. Rebecca didn't even risk a direct glance at Thomas as she headed back to their table.

'Thanks,' she said. 'Can't remember when I last had a dance.'

'Me, neither.'

* * *

Another silence fell. Were they both thinking back to when that might have been?

Thomas certainly was.

And it wasn't that difficult because he hadn't been anywhere near a dance floor in the last five years. Rebecca had been the last person he'd danced with.

The realisation released a flood of memories. Just snatches. How reluctant he'd been when Rebecca had come into class that day at med school, waving a flyer advertising the start of a new term for salsa classes.

The laughter and fun of those Tuesday nights when they'd both been complete beginners, fumbling their way through the steps and trying not to trip each other up.

The satisfaction of moves becoming automatic enough to be able to enjoy the music and hold Rebecca in his arms at the same time. To see the joy on her face and feel it in the response of her body.

Their wedding dance...

How much harder it had been to dance with her as her belly expanded in pregnancy but it hadn't stopped them.

There had always been music on when they were at home together. How often had they paused for a moment as they passed each other? When a brief touch or hug could morph into a dance move or two?

Gwen had loved it. As a baby she'd beam at them from her bouncy chair. As a toddler, she'd demanded to join in.

Maybe that was actually the last occasion that Thomas had danced. When he'd held the small hand of his daughter in the air so she could twirl around. When he'd scooped her into his arms and then bent down to dip her head close enough to the floor to make her shriek with laughter.

Oh, God!

That memory hurt.

Was the pain the reason his gaze sought Rebecca's? Did he need the comfort of a connection with the only other person on earth who would understand how much it hurt?

He saw the moment that connection fused. The way her eyes filled with tears.

'Oh, *Tom*…'

Her lips were trembling. He saw the first tear escape and roll down the side of her nose.

How embarrassing would it be for her to break down in front of all these people in the pub? It would be worse than finding herself alone on the dance floor. Pulling out his wallet he put down more than enough cash to cover their dinner.

'Come with me,' he said, taking her hand. 'Time we got some fresh air, I think.'

She held it together until they were out on the street. Until they'd walked far enough to be away from the sound of the regulars at the Frog and Peach enjoying their Friday night out. And then she stopped and pulled her hand from his, so that she could cover her eyes.

'I… I'm sorry,' she choked. 'It's just that I… I remembered the last time I saw you dancing…'

Thomas clenched his jaw. 'Me, too. With…with Gwen…'

The sob sounded like it was being torn from Rebecca's heart.

'Sometimes,' she whispered, 'I miss her *so* much…'

There was nothing Thomas could do other than take

her in his arms. He needed to hold her. He needed someone to hold him back because those tears were contagious.

'Same,' he muttered.

They stood there for what seemed like the longest
time. Against a wrought-iron fence, out of the way of
people who passed with barely a glance at the embracing couple. Cars and buses and taxis thundered by on the
busy road. The world continued to spin but, for Thomas,
it had paused. There was nothing but this holding. And
being held.

And then Rebecca shifted in his arms and looked up
at him and her wet cheeks gleamed under the light of a
nearby lamppost. Her eyes were huge and dark and…
and so very, very sad.

There was nothing Thomas could do other than to
dip his head and kiss her.

Gently.

Slowly.

With enough tenderness to let her know that he understood.

That he felt exactly the same way.

CHAPTER SEVEN

THIS WAS WHAT had been missing from her life for so long.

Being held when she felt so sad.

Knowing that someone else understood how she felt.

Rebecca closed her eyes and fell into that kiss. There was no way she was going to question the wisdom of what was happening or what the consequences might be.

She'd been waiting for this moment for ever. She just hadn't realised it.

That touch of lips on hers was so heartbreakingly tender it should have made her want to cry but, instead, it covered the source of the tears that had already been falling and smothered them like sand on the embers of a fire.

It was the feeling that someone genuinely cared about her.

Loved her, even…

No. Not *someone*. There was only one person who had ever made her feel quite like this. Only one person who could really understand exactly how she felt, because he had been there and he felt the same way.

Tom…

The name escaped her lips on a sigh but Rebecca didn't realise it was audible until she felt the change in the way she was being held. The tension in the muscles of his arms was instant—preparation for being taken away?

Yes. Thomas was letting her go as she opened her eyes. He was turning his head, too, but not before she'd seen the glint of tears in his eyes and something that looked a lot like…regret?

And then he ran his fingers through his hair, raising his face to the streetlamp above them. His eyes were tightly shut.

'Sorry,' he muttered. 'I shouldn't have done that.'

Why not?

Because it meant that he was throwing away the rule book about keeping so much distance between them?

Because he had another partner that he'd just cheated on? The lines of pain on his face suggested that that was the more likely explanation.

The chill that ran down Rebecca's spine actually made her shiver. But she was still aware of the warmth that kiss had delivered. The comfort of feeling that he still cared.

Did *she* still care? Judging by the urge to erase those lines of pain around his eyes and mouth, apparently she did.

'It's okay, Tom.' Rebecca touched his arm. 'We were both upset. It's my fault. I… I shouldn't have asked you to dance. Dragged us both back into the past like that.'

He opened his eyes and looked down at her and she could see nothing but sadness in his eyes.

'It never goes away, does it?'

'No.' But Rebecca pulled in a deeper breath. 'It does change, though. It gets less painful. There are good things to remember, too.'

His nod was slow. One corner of his mouth lifted a little.

'Yeah...like how much she loved to dance. She was such a happy little thing, wasn't she?'

Rebecca nodded. Gwen had been the happiest of children. She would wake up with a smile on her face and her arms outstretched to greet the people she loved and the new day that would always bring excitement. And she spread that happiness around her with such abundance that anybody nearby would catch it and then give it back and it would get bigger every time.

The world without Gwen had lost so much light. It was still dark in places and Rebecca knew it wouldn't help to step any closer to those corners. It wouldn't help her and it might well drive Thomas back to where he'd been—unable to find any way out.

'It's okay,' she said again. 'It didn't mean anything more than sharing a memory. It...it wasn't cheating or anything.'

'*Cheating?*' Had Thomas taken a step back or did it just feel like he had? 'What's that supposed to mean?'

Rebecca bit her lip. This was really overstepping boundaries. A shared past was something they couldn't avoid but Thomas had been very clear that his current personal life was out of bounds. They were just beginning to feel their way into what could become a friendship. Making a reference to his sex life was more than awkward.

It was excruciating.

He was still waiting for a response. Frowning, now, as if he was fitting pieces of a difficult puzzle together.

'Did you feel like *you* were cheating?' he asked quietly. 'Are you...*with* someone, Becca?'

'No!' The word came out more vehemently than she had intended. As if the idea of being with someone was shocking. She followed it with a huff that sounded incredulous. 'Not me, I thought *you* might be…'

There was a long moment of silence. Rebecca shivered again and wrapped her arms around her body. She didn't dare meet his gaze. Instead, she turned her head to look along the footpath. In the direction she needed to take to go home.

To escape?

Thomas cleared his throat. 'I'm not,' he said. 'Are you?'

Rebecca raised her gaze. 'No.'

Their gazes held. The question they both wanted to ask hung like a cartoon bubble over their heads. Until they both spoke at the same time.

'Has there been…?'

'Have you…?'

Another pause. And then it happened again.

'No,' they said in unison.

The silence had a stunned echo to it this time.

It was Rebecca who broke it.

'Why not?' she whispered.

'Why?' he countered.

'Because…because it's been five years. And I know… I know how lonely it can get.'

Thomas looked away. 'Guess I haven't been ready,' he said. 'I focused on work enough for that to be all that mattered.'

'Me, too,' Rebecca admitted. 'And the time just kept going past. I'd forgotten how long it was until…until you came back to Paddington's. I guess I've just taken things day by day for so long, it's become engrained. I never look too far into the future.'

'And I discovered that it's better never to look too far into the past.'

Rebecca felt herself become very still. This was a huge admission, wasn't it?

She hadn't felt this close to Thomas since…well, maybe since the very early days of their relationship. When it had been so easy to say anything and trust that it would be accepted and understood. When anything seemed possible and glowed with the prospect of real happiness.

It had been a very different kind of closeness at the end—during those awful days when they'd sat in the intensive care unit beside Gwen's bed. Holding each other's hands so tightly that it could become painful—but never as painful as what was happening around them. That connection had been more powerful, perhaps, but far less happy.

With the embrace of that dance still lingering on her skin, Rebecca chose to tap into that first memory of the connection they'd discovered with each other. It made it feel so natural to say more.

'We're both stuck, aren't we?' she suggested softly. 'Living in the present.'

'It's not a bad place to be.'

'But we're still young. There's a lot more to life than work…'

Thomas moved his head in another one of those slow, thoughtful nods. He even offered her the ghost of another smile.

'Like dancing?'

Rebecca smiled back and mirrored his nod.

'I'll keep that in mind.' His faint smile vanished. 'It's getting late. I'll walk you home.'

'No need. It's out of your way. I can get a cab.'

'At this time on a Friday night? You'll be lucky.'

Rebecca wanted to agree. She wanted to walk with Thomas and keep talking. If they did, maybe she could find that connection that seemed to have vanished again.

Or had she imagined it?

Fate intervened in any case. A black cab was heading towards them, with its yellow light glowing to advertise its availability. Thomas raised his arm and it pulled into the curb.

'There you go. I was wrong...' His smile was tight. Relieved? He wanted to get away, didn't he? So that he didn't have to revisit any more painful memories? Or to admit he might have been wrong about anything else—like the way he'd abandoned her when she'd needed him more than ever?

Rebecca opened the back door of the cab. 'Want to share?'

She could feel his hesitation. She saw him open his mouth as if he was about to accept the invitation. And then his expression changed—as though he'd just walked into a mental brick wall.

One of those well-built barriers?

'I'll walk.' His voice had a gruff edge. 'I need the exercise after those Yorkshire puddings.'

She turned her head as the cab pulled away. She could see Thomas through the back window, already heading in the opposite direction.

Alone.

Going back to his apartment where he would still be alone.

As she would when she got back to hers.

It felt wrong.

A lot more wrong than it would have felt last week. Or even yesterday.

She hadn't been wrong about finding that connection again, had she? It was bigger than simply the fact that they'd kissed each other. Or admitted that there'd been no one else in their lives since their marriage ended.

Something had shifted in the layers that had been used to bury what had been their marriage. Had Thomas seen the same glint of what had been uncovered?

Did he realise that the connection they'd had was still there?

That it was possible that it might actually be even stronger?

That wasn't the real question, though, was it?

Rebecca felt suddenly weary enough to rest her head on the back of the seat and close her eyes.

The real question was whether he would want to uncover any more of what had been buried for so long. Whether she wanted that herself.

'And I discovered that it's better never to look too far into the past.'

You wouldn't find anything if you chose not to look. And you could make it easy not to see by kicking the layers back into place.

She hadn't intended to force either of them to look tonight. Asking him to dance had been impulsive and the shared memories that it had provoked had been inevitable.

Had it made things harder?

Judging by the ache in her own heart, Rebecca suspected that it had.

That ache suggested that she'd never really stopped loving Thomas. Getting closer to him again could mean that she was setting herself up for a whole new heart-break—one that could mean she would be stuck for even longer.

Alone. With no partner in her current life or dreams of a family in her future.

Something like a groan escaped along with her sigh.

'You all right, love?'

Rebecca opened her eyes to see the cab driver watching her in his rear-view mirror.

'Almost there,' he added cheerfully. 'You'll be home before you know it.'

She summoned a smile and turned her head in time to see the signpost of her street flash past.

This was where she lived.

But it wasn't a home any more. Not really.

Work was failing to provide the complete distraction that Thomas Wolfe had come to depend on.

He'd spent most of his weekend at the hospital and most of that in his office, writing an article for a paediatric cardiology journal on the relationship between the diagnosis of asthma and dilated cardiomyopathy. He took his time over ward rounds on both Saturday and Sunday mornings but his visits to the intensive care unit were very brief.

Penny was the patient in most need of frequent monitoring but, theoretically, she was under the care of her surgical team at the moment and wouldn't be transferred back to the cardiology ward until Rebecca was happy with her condition. He was on call, of course, if any consultation was needed but, so far, everything was going very smoothly. They'd kept her asleep a little longer than planned but her sedation was now being gradually lifted and it was hoped that she would be awake and ready to move to the ward first thing on Monday morning.

His visits to the unit hadn't coincided with any that Rebecca might be making and that was probably a good thing because Thomas wasn't sure he was ready to see her again just yet.

What had happened on Friday night was still doing his head in. Thoughts kept intruding, even when he should have been completely engrossed in his writing.

A diagnosis of moderate persistent bronchial asthma was made in the four-year-old girl. A year later she was admitted with features of an acute exacerbation, including breathlessness, cough, sleep disturbances and poor response to nebulised salbutamol...

His gaze drifted to the series of chest X-rays he was planning to include in the next section, but he wasn't looking at the evidence of fluid build-up in the lungs.

It was that kiss that was the problem.

Or maybe it had been the dancing.

Then again, he kept remembering—with a slight sense of shock—that Rebecca had told him she was single. That she hadn't been with anyone else in the last five years.

Why not?

It couldn't have been because of any lack of interest on the part of the men she must have encountered. She was gorgeous. Clever. Funny. Such a positive person, too. That was where Gwen's sunny nature had come from. Rebecca had a smile that could light up a room and she automatically looked for the bright side of any-thing, no matter how bad it was.

Even when it was the worst thing imaginable. She'd been the one to bring up the awful subject of organ dona-tion, when they'd been sitting so helplessly, day after day, beside the bedside of their critically injured daughter.

'If there's even the shadow of something good that could come out of this,' she'd said, *'maybe it's the fact that the lives of other people's precious children could be saved.'*

She'd been the one who had arranged Gwen's funeral. The tiny pink casket with bright flowers painted all over it. The pink and white balloons that were released that contained little packets of wildflower seeds. The songs that had come from beloved television shows and Dis-ney movies.

'It's the last party I can ever give her,' she'd said. *'I want it to be what would have made her happy.'*

Oh, God…

So many memories were coming out of the wood-work. He tried to shake them off before that lump in his throat made it too hard to breathe. Before he had to fight back tears, the way he had when he'd made the mistake of kissing Rebecca and could feel the grief of losing her—and Gwen—doing its best to wrap his heart in those vicious tentacles all over again.

But why was she still alone?

She hadn't blamed herself for the accident. She cer-tainly hadn't blamed him. She hadn't even blamed the nursery school who had been responsible for Gwen's safety that day.

She'd moved on. She'd been able to keep working with children. More than that, she'd become involved with the whole transplant side of medicine and even changed the direction of her own career to become as involved as it was possible to get.

If she could handle the emotional side of that, why hadn't she moved on enough to find a new partner? To start a new family, even, which had always been her dream of the perfect future.

There was only one answer that Thomas could come up with.

He'd hurt her so badly, she simply didn't want to risk it again.

And yet, here she was trying to establish a friendship with him. She seemed to want to spend time with him and it had definitely been her idea to have that dance.

It didn't make sense.

She'd accused him of running away. Of leaving their marriage even while they'd still been together.

Did this mean that she was prepared to forgive him?

That it was possible there was more than friendship to be salvaged from the wreck of their lives together?

It had felt like that, when he'd been holding her in his arms while she cried.

When he'd kissed her and felt her kissing him back.

But it was doing his head in.

Part of him wanted nothing more than a second chance.

Part of him wanted to keep well clear of all those memories to protect himself.

But another part still cared enough to be determined not to hurt Rebecca again. He'd failed her once before and it certainly hadn't been intentional. How could he be sure that it wouldn't happen again?

It would be better for everybody if he dismissed the possibility.

He carried on writing.

Respiratory distress worsened to the point that mechanical ventilation was required. The most likely diagnosis considered at this stage included complicated severe asthma, infection, fluid over-load and underlying cardiac disease...

His hands stilled again as he lost the thread of his next sentence. Shutting his eyes for a moment, Thomas tried to force himself to focus. This article was taking a lot longer than usual to pull together but he would get it done; he just needed more time.

And that was the answer to a lot of things, wasn't it? More time.

He could step back from the confusion that a friend-ship with his ex-wife was causing. Given time, he would be able to think more clearly and decide what the best course of action might be. It seemed that trying to set her free by ending their marriage hadn't worked but some-thing needed to happen so that they could both move on in their personal lives.

By finding new partners?

Thomas could feel himself scowling at a computer screen covered with words that were no more than a blur.

He didn't want a new partner.

Worse than that, the thought of Rebecca with some-one else was...unacceptable?

Oh, man, his head really was a mess. And it was start-ing to interfere with his work.

How had he managed to keep his personal head space

successfully separated from anything professional for the last five years?

Because he had been a long way away from Rebecca, that was why. He hadn't had to see her every day. To talk to her and watch her work. He hadn't spent any time with her alone.

And he hadn't even *thought* about dancing with her, let alone kissing her.

Okay, so that wasn't completely true.

With a sigh, Thomas saved his file and closed the programme. He needed some fresh air. A brisk walk or maybe a run that would not only distract him, it might tire him out enough to sleep properly tonight.

A long run. All the way around Regent's Park and Primrose Hill, perhaps.

No. Too many memories, including some very recent ones.

Hyde Park, then. It was closer, bigger and far less familiar.

Safer. For both himself and the woman he had loved so totally.

It was exactly what he had always vowed to do. To put Rebecca's needs above his own.

To keep her safe.

Any working week in a field of medicine that included critically unwell patients was a roller-coaster of good moments, worrying moments and—at the bottom of one of those loops—the really heartbreaking moments that made you wonder if you were up to the kind of stress this job could entail.

Rebecca was about to face one of those low swoops and she had to gather every ounce of her courage to do it.

Walking away from one of the good moments was making it harder. She had just come from the paediatric cardiology ward where her visit to Penelope Craig had coincided with Thomas doing his ward round.

The smile with which he had greeted her had been a relief. She'd barely seen him all week and had convinced herself that she'd wrecked any chance of friendship between them after that night at the Frog and Peach.

Dancing with him, for heaven's sake.

Crying on his shoulder. Was it really so surprising that he'd tried to comfort her by kissing her? It hadn't meant anything but it could well have been enough to have him raise those barriers between them again.

But he'd smiled at her as she entered Penny's room and it hadn't just been a polite greeting. There was a warmth in his eyes that said he was happy to see her. Had he noticed that their paths hadn't crossed in so many days?

Perhaps he thought she'd been deliberately avoiding him and he was relieved, as well. The truth was that Rebecca had been flat out. The Teddy Bears' Picnic was happening this coming weekend and the last minute organisation had taken up every spare second she'd had, and then some, including several very late nights.

So she was weary, and that always accentuated any emotional components of her job.

Everybody was smiling in Penny's room this morning.

'So she can come home next week?' Julia asked. 'And she doesn't need to be on oxygen all the time?'

'Not unless she's getting breathless or becomes unwell,' Thomas told her. 'And that's looking less likely every day.'

'And we can let her do whatever she wants? Go back to school?'

'Not just yet. We'll keep her in until after the weekend and see how she's doing and then we'll talk about school. Let her walk around as much as she wants to and you could take her to the playground.'

'I can dance,' Penny told Rebecca. 'Just like Sapphire Ballerina Bear. Want to see?' She scrambled off her mother's lap, put her arms in the air and turned herself in a slightly wobbly circle. She didn't seem to be in any significant pain as she bounced back from her major surgery. The grin on her face made everybody smile all over again.

'That's fantastic,' Rebecca said. She held out the object in her hand to Julia. 'This is for you. Keep it with you at all times from now on.'

'Oh...' Julia's gaze sought that of her husband and her glance was fearful.

'It's the pager,' Peter said.

'Yes. Penny's on the top of the transplant list now and a new heart could become available at any time. If it does, even if it's somewhere else in the country, you'll get paged and you'll need to come back to the hospital immediately. That doesn't mean that the transplant will definitely go ahead because sometimes unexpected things happen but you'll need to be here and be prepared. We repeat a lot of tests to make sure nothing's changed.'

Julia and Peter both nodded solemnly.

'In the meantime...' Rebecca smiled at Penny who was twirling again. 'Enjoy everything that you haven't been able to do for so long. I'll come back again before you go home in case you have any questions but you've got my phone number, too. Don't hesitate to call.'

'Thank you so much, Dr Scott,' Peter said. 'You have no idea how much this means to us all.'

'Oh, I think I do.' The glance in Thomas's direction happened without thinking and the look in his eyes was better than any smile. They both knew how precious for Julia and Peter this time with their daughter would be. They both knew they were providing a gift they'd never been able to receive themselves.

The connection was most definitely still there.

And, regardless of whether either of them would choose for it to happen or not, it seemed to be getting stronger.

So it was no wonder that her next appointment was a prospect that weighed down both her feet and her heart. She could feel both getting heavier as she slid away from the joy of Penny's visit to the sadness that she knew she would find in the quiet space of the most private room of the paediatric intensive care unit, where six-year-old Ryan Walker had been declared brain-dead late yesterday afternoon.

Alistair North was waiting for her outside the unit.

'Ryan's parents are with him at the moment. They were present for the second round of tests last night and they've been here ever since. I paged you when they were ready to ask about what's going to happen next.'

Rebecca nodded. As a doctor who worked in the field of organ transplants, she was not allowed to have anything to do with the range of tests conducted to confirm brain death. These were normally done twice, by two different doctors, spaced apart by at least twelve hours.

'No inconclusive results, then?'

Alistair shook his head, his face sombre. 'I think it was the angiography that hit them the hardest. The image is so clear when all you've got is a dark space inside the skull with absolutely no blood flow.'

Rebecca nodded. She knew exactly how devastating that kind of image could be.

'His grandparents are in one of the relatives' rooms, looking after his little sister, Gemma.'

Alistair introduced her to Louise and Colin Walker, Ryan's parents, who were sitting, their hands linked and their faces pale with shock, beside his bed.

Wisps of red hair showed under the bandages on Ryan's head and his freckles stood out on a pale little face. Only six years old, this was a tragedy that touched everybody's hearts.

'I'm so very, very sorry,' she said quietly. 'I haven't been involved with Ryan's care since his accident but I know that everything possible was done.'

They both nodded but Colin was frowning. He didn't understand why she was here.

'You asked about what happens next,' Alistair said. 'So there are decisions that need to be made. Difficult decisions.' He cleared his throat. 'I asked Dr Scott— Rebecca—to come because she's had a lot of experience with supporting people to make these kinds of decisions.'

'You mean about…about when we turn off the life support?' Louise's voice broke and she covered her eyes with her hands. 'And what…what happens then?'

'There's no hurry,' Rebecca said gently. 'We can give you all the time you need. And all the support you—and the rest of your family—might find helpful.'

'Rebecca is a surgeon,' Alistair continued quietly. 'There's never a good time to introduce a subject like this, but she's the head of our transplant team. She's come to talk to you about the possibility of Ryan being an organ donor.'

Colin Walker's face became even paler as he joined the dots. 'No,' he whispered. 'How could you even ask?'

'I understand,' Rebecca said into the horrified silence. 'I'm not here to do anything more than introduce myself at the moment. To leave you with some information and my phone number. You can call me anytime at all—day or night—if you have any questions or need to talk.'

Colin couldn't look at her and Louise still had her hands over her face.

'All I ask is that you think about it,' she added softly. 'And I can tell you that the gift of life *can* help—for both sides.'

She glanced at Alistair and he nodded. It was time for her to leave and not seem to be putting any pressure at all on these grieving parents. The subject had been raised and Alistair and the team in the intensive care unit would continue to care for Ryan until they were ready to make their decision.

Walking through the double doors to leave the unit, Rebecca could see a woman coming out of one of the relatives' rooms, holding the hand of a small girl who had bright red curly hair and a freckled button nose. About two years old, she had to be Gemma—Ryan Walker's little sister. Rebecca smiled at the grandmother but kept going. This wasn't the time to introduce herself to the wider family.

It was good that Ryan wasn't an only child. Not that that could change how devastating this whole situation was but Rebecca had thought more than once over the years she'd been involved in this specialty that it could make a real difference in the future. She'd seen it happen on the rare occasions when she'd become involved at this earlier stage of the process of organ donation. These parents were forced to carry on. To stay engaged with all aspects of life—including each other?

Every time, it made her wonder whether that would have made a difference to herself and Thomas and she would feel a beat of her own loss. Not just for Gwen, or for their marriage, but for the larger family that could have been.

She paused in front of the elevators, closing her eyes against the pain of it all.

Maybe Thomas hadn't been so wrong, after all, to distance himself from having to experience it again and again.

She wanted to tell him that. To tell him that she understood. More than she had at the time.

That she could forgive him…

No. Right now she didn't want to talk to him.

She just wanted him to hold her in his arms and comfort her. To remind her that they'd done the right thing when they hadn't hesitated to agree to donate Gwen's organs. When they'd known that they wouldn't be able to hold their precious daughter when she took her last breath.

They would only be able to hold each other.

CHAPTER EIGHT

'I UNDERSTAND.' REBECCA gave Louise Walker's hand a squeeze. 'It's okay.'

Louise looked up at the clock on the wall of this private room. 'Colin will be back soon. He's collecting his parents from the airport. They were on a cruise ship so we've had to wait until they got to a port.'

'He doesn't know that you asked to meet me?'

The distressed young mother shook her head. 'He doesn't want to talk about any of it. Turning off the life support is bad enough but the idea of organ donation is too much for him.'

'I do understand.'

'But I want to do it,' Louise whispered, tears streaming down her face. 'I keep thinking, what if Ryan was the one who was really sick and needed a new heart or lungs or something? If I was one of those parents who was hoping, every day, that a miracle would happen and that an organ would become available…'

'There are two sides to every story,' Rebecca agreed quietly. 'But everybody feels differently and it would be very wrong to try and force Colin to agree to something he can't handle.'

'Dr North says we can take a few days but…it's so

hard. Part of me just wants it to be over, you know? So that we can start trying to put our lives back together.'

'I understand,' Rebecca said again. 'And I don't want you to feel guilty about not making a decision. Or making the decision for Ryan not to be a donor. It's something the whole family needs to be sure about.'

'I know my parents think it's a good thing—that something good could still come out of this whole horrible accident. All these weeks we've had hoping for the impossible.'

Rebecca had to blink away the sudden moisture in her own eyes. Along with the echo of her own broken voice from so long ago.

If there's even the shadow of something good that could come out of this, maybe it's the fact that the lives of other people's precious children could be saved.'

'I think Colin's parents might, too,' Louise added. 'We're all going to come in and spend time with Ryan over the weekend. That will be the time to talk about it again.'

'You've got my number. If I can support you in any way—with whatever decision you make—please call me.'

'I will. And thank you.' She looked up at the clock again. 'I'd better get back. Mum wants to get home so they can take Gemma to the zoo this afternoon. Weird, isn't it? But life doesn't stop, even when it feels like the world should have stopped turning for a while.'

Rebecca let go of her hand, noting how pale and exhausted Louise was looking. 'Have you been away from here at all yourself?'

Louise shook her head. 'Every minute counts, doesn't it?'

The two women parted at the door. Impulsively, Louise hugged Rebecca.

'I think you do really understand,' she whispered. 'It means a lot.'

Rebecca hugged her back. This part of her job often entailed an emotional connection to patients and their families that went above and beyond normal boundaries. Not that she'd ever tell people that she'd been through the same thing herself because that could be a form of pressure to follow her example. That her understanding was genuine seemed to come through unspoken, however, and it was reassuring both to the families she worked with and to herself.

She brought something to this job that nobody else could. It was what she was meant to be doing and she was proud of the difference she could make in the lives of others.

That pride was normally a very private thing that came in moments like this. A public acknowledgement like the one that was to be celebrated at the Teddy Bears' Picnic was very different. Accolades were unnecessary—embarrassing, even—but any discomfort was outweighed by the joy of being with so many people who'd had their lives transformed by organ donation. There was a real need for public education, too, and this year was even more important given the spotlight that Paddington's was still under.

As the head of the transplant team, Rebecca knew that she would be under her own spotlight and she knew the responsibility that she carried. Transplant surgery entailed the kind of drama that people loved to hear about. Showcasing Paddington as an important centre with a track record of great success could confirm how necessary it was for this hospital to remain for generations to come. It could be the final push that would mean its safety was officially guaranteed.

It was a perfect day for the big event.

Not that Thomas had intended to go, but everybody had been talking about it when he'd been in at work doing his usual ward round.

'They want as many Paddington's staff members there as possible, to show how united we all are,' Rosie had told him as she accompanied him to Penny's room. Julia was apparently worried that her daughter was coming down with a cold or something that might delay the possibility of her going home.

'I'm going to meet Leo there, as soon as my shift finishes,' Rosie continued. 'The twins have got their teddies ready for the "best dressed" bear competition at the end of the day and they're so excited by the prospect of a pony ride. It'll be such fun!'

'The Teddy Bears' picnic?' Julia Craig overheard the end of the conversation at they entered her room. 'I wish we could go. Next year.' She smiled at Penny. 'You could take Sapphire.'

'I want to go now,' Penny said. 'I want a pony ride, too.'

'Let's see how you are,' Thomas said. 'Mummy says you've got a sniffle.'

It wasn't anything to worry about but the Craig family wouldn't be attending the picnic this time. Maybe it was knowing that Rebecca would be there that tipped the balance as Thomas left Paddington's early in the afternoon.

It had been so good to see her yesterday when she'd given Penny's parents that significant pager. To see her return his smile and feel like it was still possible that they could be friends without his head getting so messed up.

That they could rewind a little? To forget that dance. And the kiss.

To start again with some better boundaries in place?

Besides, the day was too perfect to spend either in his office finishing that article or stuck in that shoebox of an apartment that had no view of anything green. Thomas pulled off his tie and opened the top button of his shirt. He rolled his sleeves up and kept walking, taking the same route that he and Rebecca had taken that first time they'd spent some real time together since his return.

The sun shone from a cloudless sky but the slopes of Primrose Hill caught a breeze that kept the temperature pleasant enough for the children to enjoy even the more strenuous activities available, like the egg and spoon races and the obstacle course. Thomas walked past the team of volunteers cooking sausages on barbecues and the gazebo that had a queue of children waiting their turn for face painting. He could see a trio of fat, little ponies that had another queue of excited children waiting and he could hear gleeful shrieks coming from inside the bouncy castle.

There were cameras and reporters everywhere, from television stations, both local and national newspapers and magazines.

And there was Rebecca, looking absolutely gorgeous in blue jeans and a white, short-sleeved shirt that had a teddy bear print on it. She had her long, dark hair tied back but it wasn't wrapped up into a knot like it would be at work. It hung down her back in a wavy ponytail that was being teased in the breeze.

She hadn't seen him, because she was focused on the woman she was talking to, and he was partly screened by the man with a huge camera balanced on his shoulder and a young lad who was holding a fluffy microphone on a stick close to the two women. Thomas was simply one of the group of interested onlookers who were watching this interview. He edged a little closer so that he could hear what Rebecca was saying.

'So three people in the UK die every day because of this shortage. At the moment there are over six thousand people on the transplant waiting list and about two hundred of them are children. And many of those children come to Paddington Children's Hospital because we're one of only a few major centres for paediatric transplantation.'

'But there are organs that could be available, aren't there?' the interviewer asked. 'Is it that people don't know it's possible to donate them? Or do they not *want* to?'

'It's complicated,' Rebecca said, 'and it's a difficult subject to even think about for people who are facing the heartbreak of losing a loved one.'

'What is it that you—and all the other doctors and medical staff here from Paddington's—want to happen? We've got a lot of people watching what's happening here. What would you tell them was the purpose of a day like today?'

'Today is about celebrating life.' Rebecca's smile lit up her face. 'Of letting the families that take that amazingly generous step of making organ donation possible realise just how much of a difference they can make to so many lives.' Her gaze shifted as she waved her arm towards the huge crowd of people around them and then it caught as she spotted Thomas.

She didn't break her speech. 'We want people to talk about it. We all think that the sort of terrible situations that lead to organ donation won't happen to us—that they only happen to other people.'

Her gaze was holding Thomas's.

'But, sadly, they do happen to some of us. And if we talk about it before they happen, it might help us make a decision that can change the world for others.'

'I'm Angela Marton and we've been talking to Dr Rebecca Scott.' The interviewer turned to face the camera. 'That's an important message for all of us. And now let's go and meet some of the children and their families here today whose worlds *have* been changed.'

She led her crew away and the onlookers drifted in other directions but Thomas stayed where he was. He was still holding Rebecca's gaze and neither of them were smiling. The moment was, in fact, very close to being tear-jerking.

He began stepping closer at precisely the same moment Rebecca did.

His voice, when he managed to find some words, was raw.

'We did do the right thing, didn't we?'

She knew that he was talking about Gwen. About the decision they'd made to donate *her* organs.

'Absolutely,' she whispered. 'I'm proud of it...aren't you?'

Thomas had to swallow the huge lump in his throat. 'I think I am,' he said softly. 'I've never thought of it like that before.'

Rebecca's smile was as soft as her gaze. In that moment, that look felt as tender and loving as he remembered it being when they were first in love.

'I'm so glad you came today,' she said.

Thomas cleared his throat. 'Me, too.'

He wanted to sink into that soft gaze. To pull it around him for comfort like the softest blanket on the coldest night.

'Want an ice cream? Or a sausage? They're really good.'

Her smile widened until it was as bright as the one she'd given the television crew when she'd said that today was about celebrating life. Their poignant moment of connection was still there, but—as always—Rebecca was finding something positive to move towards.

And he was happy to follow her lead.

'Actually, I'm starving. A sausage sounds perfect.'

How amazing was it that Thomas had come this afternoon?

This was huge.

A lot bigger than Thomas himself probably realised, despite his admission that he had gained a new perspective, but Rebecca wasn't going to allow the beat of fear to diminish the joy that this gathering always bestowed. Having Thomas by her side only made it all the more important to focus on the positive.

It wasn't difficult. Everywhere they went, people came to greet them, eager to share news.

'Dr Scott, remember Tyler?'

The sturdy boy wearing the colours of his favourite football team ducked his head, hiding beneath the brim of his baseball cap. An older brother slung a protective arm over his shoulders.

'Tyler! Of course I remember you. Didn't you move to Manchester?' Rebecca laughed. 'Silly me. I should have recognised the jersey.' She looked up at the boy's parents. 'It's been, what…three years since Tyler's transplant? How's he doing?'

'He made it onto the junior football team last season,' his dad said proudly. 'Got player of the week twice.'

'Wow.' Rebecca looked suitably impressed. 'And you've come all the way to London just for today?'

'We had a minibus,' Tyler's mother told her. 'We belong to a support group for transplant families and we all decided to come for a day out. Tyler and his brother here have been practising to enter the three-legged race. We didn't realise how big it would be, though. Isn't it amazing how many kids there are that probably wouldn't even be alive if they hadn't had transplants?'

'It certainly is.' Thomas joined the conversation. 'But I bet there aren't too many who are player of the week in a football team.'

She introduced Thomas to Tyler's family. A few minutes later, she introduced him to Madeline's family and they learned how her life had changed since her lung transplant two years ago. Stephen was another cystic fibrosis patient who'd received his heart and lung transplant only last year. Piper had been given a kidney as a live donation from her father.

And then there was Ava.

'Rebecca.' Ava's mother, Jude, enveloped her in a hug. 'It's been way too long.'

'I know, I'm sorry. I've been meaning to call you but life's been a bit crazy what with all the organisation for today on top of everything else.' Rebecca's heart skipped a beat as she turned to include Thomas. Would Jude guess? More alarmingly, would Thomas guess that this was anything more than a doctor/patient relationship?

'This is Thomas Wolfe,' she said, the light tone of her voice sounding a bit forced to her own ears. 'He's a cardiothoracic surgeon at Paddington's. He left London before you moved here so he doesn't know Ava yet.'

He doesn't know anything about Ava, she added silently. And he doesn't need to. Not now.

Possibly not ever...

'I think we've got an outpatient appointment coming up with you, soon.' Jude held out her hand. 'Pleased to meet you, Thomas.'

'Likewise. And you, Ava.' Thomas was smiling at the tall twelve-year-old who had long blonde braids and astonishingly blue eyes. 'That's a very well-dressed bear you've got there.'

'It was my grandma's,' Ava told him shyly. 'It was Grandee's idea to give him the waistcoat and monocle. She said he needed to be old-fashioned because he's an antique. Like Grandee.'

'He's going into the competition for Best-Dressed Bear,' Ava's father added. 'Hadn't we better go and get him entered?'

'We won't hold you up.' Rebecca hoped she didn't sound as relieved as she suddenly felt. 'The speeches are going to start soon, too, and I think I need to introduce some of the speakers.'

'You *are* going to come to my birthday party, aren't you?' Ava said as the family began to move on. 'It's a special one.'

'I know, sweetheart. Thirteen. How does it feel to be almost a teenager?'

Ava shrugged. 'Okay, I guess. At least I'll be allowed

to get my ears pierced. *Finally…*' She rolled her eyes at her mother.

Rebecca and Jude shared a smile. Teenage angst starting already?

'It's not far away. What can I bring?' Rebecca asked.

'Nothing but yourself. It's just family.' Jude hugged her again. 'We'll have a proper catch-up, then.'

She got a hug from Ava, as well, and then Rebecca watched them walk away for a little too long. Because she could feel Thomas staring at her? Of course he was. How many patients' families made it clear that they considered their doctor to be a member of their family?

He walked with her towards the main stage where preparations were going on for the guest speakers.

'Ava looks well,' he said, finally. 'How long ago did she get her transplant?'

Rebecca's mouth went a little dry. She tried to keep her tone casual. 'Oh, quite a few years ago now.'

'Did you do her surgery?'

'No…um…they were living in Newcastle then so the transplant was done there. Ava's dad got offered a new—and much better—job last year and it was partly because she could continue her care at Paddington's that they took it.'

'How come you know them so well?' he asked then. 'How did you meet them?'

She couldn't tell him. Did Thomas even know that it was possible for members of a donor's family to initiate contact with organ recipients through the intermediary of the transplant association? That the families could meet if both sides wanted to? Would she ever be able to tell him what an emotional journey it had been to meet the little girl who had received Gwen's heart and how they had welcomed her into their family with such love?

How healing it had been for her?

Janice, the president of the picnic committee, was rushing towards them, a clipboard in her hand that she was waving over her head.

'Yoo-hoo! Rebecca!'

But Rebecca had stopped walking. Because Thomas had stopped and one glance at his face told her that he had put two and two together. He looked as if he'd just been punched in the gut and had frozen completely to try not to collapse from the pain.

'Oh, my God...' he said. 'You know who Ava's donor was, don't you?'

Rebecca said nothing. The noises around her faded to a faint hum. She couldn't say anything.

She didn't need to.

Thomas had gone as white as a sheet.

For a long moment they simply stared at each other. She could feel his shock. The unbearable pain of knowing that a part of his daughter was in another little girl who got to dress up her teddy bear and have a family day out in the summer sunshine.

When, if life was remotely fair, it should have been Gwen.

And then he simply turned and walked away, disappearing into the crowd before Rebecca even had time to blink.

'Oh, thank goodness,' Janice said behind her. 'I've been looking for you everywhere. Are you ready to introduce the speakers? There's a radio station that wants to interview you, as well.'

Desperately, Rebecca tried to catch a glimpse of

Thomas. If ever there was a time they needed to talk, this was it. A time to talk. To hold each other and cry...

And it was impossible.

She had duties she had to attend to. Being the face of transplants at Paddington's wasn't an ego trip. She was representing a hospital in desperate need of the final green light for its survival and she had the chance to say something about that before she introduced those speakers. To thank so many people who had contributed to the campaign and made this an issue that was so much bigger than a local community.

She had to do her bit to save the hospital she loved and believed in.

But what about the man that she had also loved and believed in once? The realisation that this wasn't simply that she cared about him the way she might care for any close friend made her catch her breath.

She *still* loved him...

Still believed in him...

Even a glance might be enough to convey how important that connection still was.

But Thomas was nowhere to be seen.

He had to keep moving.

If he stopped, he'd have to think and Thomas didn't want to think. He didn't want to feel the horror of that realisation all over again.

He'd known there was something odd about Rebecca's connection to that family from the moment they'd spotted each other. She was a part of that family, wasn't she?

Literally. Some of her genes were part of that pretty little girl with the long braids and big, blue eyes.

Some of *his* genes were, too.

It was too much.

She should have warned him. If he'd known, he would never have gone near that picnic today. Oh, he'd known that somewhere out there were several children who'd received the gift of Gwen's organs and he genuinely hoped they were all doing well. But to know who any of them were? To be a part of their lives and watch them growing up, when you couldn't help but think about what your own child might be doing at the age she would be now?

The pain was unbearable and all he could do was try and walk it off.

An hour passed and then another. Thomas wasn't even noticing where he walked. Around the circumference of Regent's Park. Through city streets. Right around Hyde Park. Twice.

He was thirsty. His feet and his legs ached but his heart ached more. So he kept walking until the sun was low in the sky and this day was finally drawing to a close. A day he never wanted to remember.

Exhaustion was helping because he was too tired to think coherently. Too tired to have taken any notice of where he'd been walking for the last hour but it was another shock to realise the automatic route his subconscious had dictated.

He was in his old street. Only a lamppost away from the railings and steps that led down to that basement apartment where he'd lived with Rebecca.

With Gwen...

The pain felt more like anger now.

This was Rebecca's fault. She could have warned him. Could have saved him the agony of these last few hours.

'Tom?'

His name sounded hesitant but laced with a concern

that also triggered an automatic response in his exhausted state. His steps slowed and stopped. He turned.

'How could you?' His voice felt rusty. Broken, almost. 'How could you do that to me?'

He could see his pain reflected in the dark pool of her eyes. A man walked past with his dog and gave them both a curious stare.

'Not here.' Rebecca's touch on his arm was a plea. 'Come inside, Tom. Please.'

He was too tired to resist the touch. Nothing could be worse than what had already happened today but, if it was, he might as well get it over with.

And he wanted an answer to his question. So he wouldn't spend the rest of his life with it echoing in his head. And his heart.

How could you?

CHAPTER NINE

IT WAS WORSE than she feared.

Having forced herself to give her attention to representing a hospital that needed to stay exactly where it was to keep providing the superlative care that young transplant patients deserved, Rebecca had spent the rest of the picnic event and the long tidy-up afterwards worried about Thomas.

Where he was and what he was thinking. How much he might hate her for what had—unintentionally—happened when he'd been introduced to a recipient of one of Gwen's organs.

To find him virtually on her doorstep when she'd finally been able to make her way home had been astonishing. To see the sheer exhaustion in his body language and the anger in his eyes had been frightening. He'd been pushed well past any safety barriers he'd built up over the last few years. And he was blaming her?

At least he'd agreed to come inside. He would be facing ghosts that he'd done his best to avoid but maybe today had shown him that you couldn't avoid them. They would always be there so you had to accept them and, when you did, you didn't have to fear them so much. He was facing some of the grief he'd never processed.

Perhaps this was the first step he needed to take to finally do that?

She'd never imagined him ever being here again. If she'd thought about it, she would have decided that it was the last thing *she* would ever want.

But here they were. And, who knew? Talking now might turn out to be the most honest conversation they would ever have.

Thomas said nothing as he followed Rebecca through the front door and down the tiny hallway. She saw him turn his head as they passed the two rooms on either side, one of which had been Gwen's bedroom and was now her office. The hallway led into the living room where the old couch was still in exactly the same place but she didn't stop there. She took him through to the kitchen and busied herself putting on the kettle and lifting the teapot down from its shelf. Thomas sank down onto one of the two chairs at the small table by the window that looked out onto the shared garden.

The garden where Gwen had taken her first steps...

He said nothing until Rebecca placed a steaming mug of tea in front of him.

'I don't understand. I can't begin to understand why you did any of this.'

Rebecca sat on the other chair. They were close enough to touch but it felt like they were a million miles apart. 'Any of what?'

'The job you do. Having to spend so much time with families who've been destroyed. How you keep it in your life every single day.'

'It *is* in our lives every single day,' she said softly. 'Isn't it?'

'I don't obsess over it,' Thomas said. 'I don't go looking for ways to make it harder. How could you have gone looking to find out who…who was out there…who was still alive because we lost our daughter?'

'I didn't go looking,' Rebecca told him. 'What I did do was to make myself known to the transplant association. I said I'd like to know if they were ever contacted by any of the recipients in the future because I thought it would help me to know that we hadn't made that decision for nothing. That there were lives that had been changed for the better. And…and they gave me a letter that Ava's mother had written more than a year before. It was waiting in the files, in case I ever asked for information. I've still got it, if you'd like to read it. It was addressed to both parents of their donor.'

She could see how painful it was for Thomas to swallow by the jerky movement of the muscles of his neck. He didn't say anything.

'Some of the words are blurry,' she added. 'Jude must have been crying when she wrote it. She wanted us to know that we'd given them a miracle. That they thought of us as part of their family and always would. That they would feel blessed if they could ever get a chance to thank us in person.' Rebecca swiped away the tears that were trickling from her eyes. 'I thought about it for a long, long time but I decided I wanted to meet her. Just Jude. Another mother who'd gone through the agony of facing the loss of her child.'

'But you didn't stop at that, did you?'

'No. The decision to meet Ava took a long time, too, and I was terrified about how I would feel. I cried all the way home. Most of that night, as well. But then I found that it had helped. That there was peace in knowing that we'd done the right thing. That a gorgeous kid like Ava has another chance at life. It really helped.'

'It's not helping me,' Thomas muttered.

'Not yet. But I think it will.'

'What makes you think you know how I feel?' Anger tipped each word, making them as sharp as arrows.

'I don't,' Rebecca admitted. 'But I want to help.'

'By throwing something like that at me? Without even warning me that it was a possibility?'

'That's not fair. I didn't know you were going to be there. We're only just getting to know each other again. Why would I have told you something that I knew you weren't ready to hear? Something that would push you away? I'm sorry it happened like that but...but I'm not sorry I'm part of Ava's life.'

'I don't want to be.'

'You don't have to be.' But, perhaps, even considering that possibility would help him process some more of that grief that he'd just shut away and tried to ignore. The grief that was keeping his life even more stuck than her own?

Their mugs of tea were cold. With a sigh, Rebecca got up and opened the fridge. She took out a bottle of wine and Thomas didn't protest when she put a glass in front of him. The only sound to break the silence for a long while was glass against wood as they picked up and put down their drinks.

It was Rebecca that broke the silence.

'It happened to both of us, Tom,' she said quietly. 'And it was the worst thing that could have ever happened. Nothing's going to change that but it doesn't wipe out the good stuff.'

'What *good* stuff?'

'How much we loved each other. How much we loved our daughter. We were good parents, Tom. We're good people.'

'*Were* we?' Thomas drained his glass. 'Why didn't we keep her safe, then?'

'We weren't even there.'

'Exactly.' Thomas reached for the bottle and refilled his glass. 'We were so wrapped up in our precious careers. Paying other people to look after our kid. If one of us had stayed at home, it wouldn't have happened.'

Rebecca caught her breath. 'One of us? You mean *me*? Are you saying *I* was a *bad* mother?'

His head shake was sharp. 'No. I could have been at home. Or we could have taken turns.'

'What happened was *not* our fault. It could have happened anywhere. We *could* have been there. On a Sunday afternoon when we were going to the zoo, maybe. It was a freak accident, Tom. The footpath is supposed to be a safe place to walk. For anyone, including a class outing from nursery school. Nobody expects a car to go out of control and hit people who are on a footpath.'

'Oh… God…' Thomas covered his eyes with his hand. 'It feels like it happened yesterday.'

Rebecca's chair scraped on the floorboards as she moved it closer. Close enough for her to be able to wrap her arms around Thomas and hold him until the shaking and the tears subsided.

She was crying, too. And at some point Thomas began holding her as much as she was holding him. The daylight was rapidly fading from the room but neither of them thought to move and turn on a light. When they finally unwrapped their arms enough to pull back and see each other's face, it felt like the middle of the night. The way it used to sometimes, when they were in bed together. Naked and vulnerable but…but safe, as well, because they were with each other.

How could she have been so convinced that Thomas could never be a part of her life again? Doubts were being washed away by a flood of remembered feelings. Of that safety. That love…

They were overwhelming. She couldn't stop the whispered words leaving her lips.

'I still love you, Tom. I've missed you *so* much…'

It was so easy to lean closer again and touch her lips against his. Maybe he'd moved at the same time because the pressure was much greater than she'd expected it to be. Nothing like that gentle kiss of comfort they had shared that night after that dance.

This kiss had an almost desperate edge that was like trying to catch hold of something precious that had been lost and was fleetingly in sight again. Or maybe it was the aftermath of a deep, shared grief that was begging for an affirmation of life.

Of love…

Whatever was behind it only got more powerful as lips and then tongues traced such well-remembered patterns. As hands moved to touch skin beneath clothes.

It was Thomas who stood up first, drawing Rebecca to her feet.

It was Rebecca who kept hold of his hand and led him through the darkness to the bedroom.

Had Thomas really believed that today would be one he never wanted to remember?

How wrong could he have been?

But the last thing he could have imagined happening was to be here, like this. In his old bed.

Cradling the woman he had always loved in his arms as she slept in the aftermath of such a passionate physical reconnection.

And how could something like sex have seemed so right when it had come from such a gruelling emotional roller-coaster that had been fuelled by grief and anger and…and bone-deep loneliness?

He adjusted the weight of Rebecca's head on his arm and she sighed in her sleep. Her breath was a warm puff against the skin of his chest.

This felt right.

Walking for all those hours yesterday hadn't dealt with any of those heart-wrenching emotions but it seemed that making love to Rebecca had done more than he could have believed was possible.

Because it had been making love and not simply sex. And for the first time since that terrible accident, Thomas felt at peace.

Exhausted, too, of course. And unsure enough of what his future looked like now to be unable to allow sleep to claim him just yet but he was happy just to be here. To feel as if a small piece of his shattered world had just been put back together.

No. Not a small piece.

The biggest part of it, maybe.

Was that being disloyal to Gwen's memory? From the moment of her birth, she had been the sun that their lives revolved around. The bonus that made them a family instead of a couple. The living promise of the future they'd both dreamed of.

Thomas found himself listening to the silence of the

apartment around them. Could he hear the echo of childish laughter? The patter of small feet running across the floorboards?

They hadn't even thought of pulling the blinds down on the windows when they'd come into this room so there were shards of light from the streetlamp on the road above. If he turned his head just a little, Thomas could see the framed photographs on Rebecca's bedside table and he stared at them for the longest time.

There were three photographs.

One of them was the first photograph of Gwen ever taken. She was lying in Rebecca's arms, only minutes after her birth and mother and baby were gazing at each other as if nothing so incredible had ever happened in the world.

Another was the photograph of them beside the bronze gorilla at the zoo when both the girls in his life had been laughing up at him and he had the grin of the happiest man in the world.

And the last photograph had been taken years before they became a family. Before Gwen had even been a possibility. Newly in love, on a weekend away, he and Rebecca had gone into one of those automatic photo booths. He could remember the strip of black-and-white images, most of which had been them making silly faces. But then they'd kissed.

The tiny photo Rebecca had chosen to put into a heart-shaped frame had been the moment they'd broken that kiss. When their lips were only just apart and they were looking at each other as if there could never be anyone else on the planet who could make them feel like this.

Something tightened in his chest and squeezed so hard that Thomas couldn't take a breath.

Rebecca had been right.

There *was* good stuff that could never be wiped out.

Like how much they had loved each other and how happy they had been together.

He turned away from the photographs to press a gentle kiss to Rebecca's head.

'I love you, too,' he whispered. 'I'm sorry I forgot how much.'

And then he listened again. Yes. He could hear those echoes. And it did make him feel sad but sadness wasn't the only thing he was aware of. He could remember the love and the laughter. The *good* stuff.

The kind of stuff that another little girl's parents were being blessed with when they'd faced the prospect of losing it for ever. A little girl with long blonde braids and blue eyes.

That unexpected flush of pride returned.

Not that he was going to let the worst of those memories surface. It was enough to register this new perspective for just a heartbeat. They *had* done the right thing in making that agonising decision that day. He was proud of it.

Proud of them both.

Thomas let his eyes drift shut, his cheek resting against the softness of Rebecca's hair. In the final moment before he fell deeply asleep, he turned his head a fraction to press another soft kiss to her forehead.

It felt like far more than the start of a new week the next morning.

It felt like the start of a new life.

But new born was also fragile and Rebecca wasn't going to take anything for granted. Not even when their lovemaking at dawn had been so heartbreakingly tender. Something they had both chosen to do that hadn't been prompted by any need for release in the wake of being put through an emotional wringer.

Thomas didn't stay for breakfast.

'I need to get home and changed,' he said. 'What would people think if I turned up to work with you, looking like I'd slept under a hedge for a week?'

'They might think that it was the best news ever.' Rebecca followed him to the door and smiled up at him, her heart too full of joy to hold the words back. 'That Dr Wolfe and Dr Scott had found each other again.'

Thomas was smiling, too. 'Have we, Becca? Have we found each other again?'

The full glow of this reborn connection might be fragile but fragile things needed nurturing, didn't they?

'I hope so.' She reached up to touch his face. 'I don't think I ever stopped loving you, Tom.'

He bent to kiss her. A soft touch that clung for a heartbeat and then another.

'Same,' he whispered. 'But I still need to change my clothes.'

Rebecca watched him climb the steps and let herself dream for a moment. Maybe, soon, his clothes would be back where they belonged—in their wardrobe. And Thomas would be back where he belonged, too.

With her.

The sound of her mobile phone ringing brought her back to the present.

'Dr Scott? Rebecca?'

'Speaking.'

'It's Louise Walker. I'm sorry to ring you so early but… I've been awake all night.'

'That's fine, Louise. How can I help?'

'We decided. Last night. We talked about it with the whole family and we all feel the same way…'

Rebecca's heart squeezed at the pain in the young mother's voice. It didn't matter what the decision was, it had been hard won and she was happy that the whole family was in agreement. Louise couldn't see her nodding, or that she had closed her eyes as she waited out the silence as Louise fought for control of her voice.

'We're ready,' she whispered. 'We want Ryan to be a donor.'

CHAPTER TEN

THE NEEDLES OF hot water in his shower landed on skin that felt oddly raw.

As a young boy, Thomas Wolfe had been fascinated by arthropods—invertebrate creatures who had to shed their exoskeleton because it restricted growth—like grasshoppers and stick insects.

He felt like a human version.

The emotional shock of confronting the very real evidence that parts of his own daughter still existed had cracked the shell he'd been inside for years. Talking to Rebecca had painfully peeled more of that shell away. Being touched and touching with so much love had been the rebirth of the man who'd been hidden. The man he used to be.

Hermit crabs. They were another creature that could emerge from their old shell and start again and he'd definitely been a hermit in an emotional sense.

Was that part of his life over?

Could he start again, with Rebecca by his side?

How miraculous would that be?

The way the water stung was a warning to be careful, however, not to rush anything. Arthropods were at their most vulnerable when newly emerged. He was sure he remembered a statistic that moulting was responsible for something like eighty to ninety per cent of arthropod deaths. They needed time for their new shells to harden.

He needed time, too.

Arriving at Paddington's for the start of the new working week made things feel more normal and boosted his confidence.

There was no need to rush anything. Safety—for both himself and Rebecca—was paramount.

There was a television crew in the area near the main reception desk. Annette, one of the senior members of the team that staffed the desk, waved at Thomas.

'Dr Wolfe? I was just telling these visitors that you're just the person who might be able to answer this query.'

'What's that?' Thomas frowned, trying to remember where he'd seen the perfectly groomed blonde woman who was smiling as he approached. Oh, yes…she'd been the person interviewing Rebecca at the Teddy Bears' Picnic yesterday.

Good grief! With all that had happened since, it felt like a very long time ago.

'I'm Angela Marton,' she introduced herself. 'We're hoping to film a feature on a child that's waiting for a transplant. There was such an overwhelmingly positive response to our coverage from the picnic yesterday. We thought a more in-depth story would help raise awareness of the need for donors. And Paddington's needs all the good publicity it can get at the moment, doesn't it?'

'I can't give permission for something like that,' Thomas said. 'You'll have to speak to our CEO—Dr Bradley—about that.'

'Where is it that you work?'

'I'm in Cardiology.'

'Oh…' Angela's eyes lit up. 'You don't happen to have someone waiting for a heart transplant, do you? A family who might be prepared to share their story?'

'I'm afraid our patient information is completely confidential.'

'Mmm… Of course it is. I totally respect that.'

The look in her eyes suggested otherwise. People were always keen to talk if it gave them a moment of fame, weren't they? Penelope Craig was well-known around Paddington's. Who knew whether an orderly or clerk or even a kitchen hand had overheard things that they could share?

The need to protect Penny and her family from a possibly unwelcome intrusion in their lives made Thomas excuse himself. Hopefully, they could send Penny home today and he wouldn't feel so responsible if their privacy was invaded. His pager sounded at the same time, which added weight to his comment that he was needed elsewhere.

The pager message was to find a phone to accept an external phone call from Dr Rebecca Scott. Thomas felt a beat of excitement as Annette handed him a phone he could use. He couldn't wait to hear Rebecca's voice. He wanted to *see* her again, in fact—the sooner, the better.

It was more than hope that this new beginning was going to take them back to where they'd once been.

In love.

Married.

With a shared dream of a future together…

It was the strength of the *wanting* that made him so aware of how soft this new shell of his still was.

To want something this much and not achieve it had the potential to destroy him all over again. And there would be no coming back from going through that a second time.

He distracted himself from that fear by focusing on a much more mundane detail. It was high time they had each other's mobile numbers, wasn't it? Using a formal contact process like this was not appropriate for anything personal.

Except it wasn't anything personal that Rebecca wanted to talk to him about.

'I'm just on my way into work,' she said. 'I've had a call from the parents of a little boy that was declared brain-dead a few days ago and they've agreed to let him become a donor. I'll get onto the matching processes as soon as I get in. It's just possible that he could be a match for Penny so I thought I'd better give you a heads-up. It would be a shame to discharge her and then bring her straight back in.'

Thomas eyed Angela and her crew, who were now standing near an elevator looking for directions towards Dr Bradley's office. He lowered his voice, anyway.

'How far away is the donor? Will you have to travel for the retrieval?'

'No.' Rebecca's voice was quiet. 'He's in our own intensive care unit.'

'Oh…' Thomas blinked, taken aback. He remembered a snatch of conversation he'd overheard that night at the Frog and Peach, when Rebecca had been talking to Alistair North. He didn't want to know any more, though—like the name or age of this boy. In fact, hadn't he heard something not so long ago? About one of the children who'd been injured so badly in the school fire?

He didn't allow any additional information of who it might be to surface because it felt too close to home.

Too personal. Keeping things as anonymous as possible was the sensible way to handle this.

'Fine,' he said then. 'Thanks for the heads-up. I'll keep things on hold until we know more and then I can either discharge her or initiate the final work-up.'

'Cool, thanks. I'll let you know as soon as possible.'

'Great. And, Becca…?'

Her tone changed, becoming suddenly softer and warmer. He could imagine her lips curving into a private smile. 'Yes?'

'Thanks for last night. For…everything.'

There was a moment's silence. 'I'll see you soon,' Rebecca said, and it sounded like a promise. 'And, Tom?'

'Yes?'

'Maybe you can give me your mobile number?'

His mouth curled into a smile of his own. 'I've got your number from this call. I'll text you mine.'

Penelope was wearing her pink tutu skirt. She also had a diamante, princess tiara on the top of her head. She was sitting, cross-legged, on the covers of her bed, her eyes glued to the latest adventures of the Ballerina Bears. Her toys and games and art supplies were all packed into suitcases in a corner of the room but her parents didn't look happy about any of it.

They looked totally stunned.

'But…' Julia's bottom lip trembled. 'But we were going to take her home today. That's why she's wearing her crown. She's going to be a princess for the day and we've got her carriage waiting. And she's looking so *well*…'

Peter took hold of her hand. 'But this is what we've been waiting for, hon. This could mean years and years of her being well.' His voice cracked and he cleared his throat, shifting his gaze from his wife to the two doctors in front of them.

'Are you sure? This is an exact match?'

'As close as we could hope for.' Rebecca smiled. 'We need to do another blood test on Penny. It's the final comparison of the donor's blood cells and Penny's blood serum to make sure that she hasn't created any new antibodies that might attack the donated organ. It's very unlikely, but we need to check.'

'And if it's okay?' Julia's eyes were wide and terrified. 'When…?'

'The sooner, the better,' Thomas said. 'We've got a hold on a theatre for about two this afternoon.'

Julia's head swivelled to look at her daughter. Penny didn't notice because she was staring at her hands, trying to follow the direction her beloved bears were giving each other.

'You use your thumb and your middle finger,' Sapphire was telling her friends. 'Like you're holding a tiny magic stone…'

Julia tried to hold back her tears. It was her loud sniff that attracted Penny's attention.

'What's the matter, Mummy?'

'Nothing, darling. I'm…happy, that's all.'

'Because we're going home?'

Thomas smiled. 'What is it that you want most of all, Penny?'

'To be a ballerina.' The little girl's smile stretched from ear to ear.

'And what is it that you need so that you *can* be a ballerina?'

'A new heart.' Her tone was matter-of-fact. As if it was a solution as simple as getting a new pair of shoes.

It was Peter who went close enough to the bed to stroke Penny's head. 'What would you say if we told you that you might be able to get that new heart today?'

Penny shook her head. 'But we're going home, today, Daddy. Can we do it tomorrow?'

Then she looked slowly around the room and the television programme was forgotten as the magnitude of what was going on around her sank in. The smile everybody associated with this brave little girl wobbled and her voice was very small.

'Do I have to have another operation?'

'Just one.' Rebecca sat on the chair beside Penny's bed and took a small hand in hers. 'And then we hope there won't be any more. Maybe ever...'

'And the new heart will make me better?'

Rebecca nodded and smiled. 'That's the plan, sweetheart.'

'And I can go back to school?'

'Yes.'

'And I can have ballet lessons?'

'Yes.' It was Julia who answered this time. 'Of course you can.'

Thomas watched the look that passed between Penny's parents as they gripped each other's hands. He could see the mix of fear and hope and he could feel it himself. The protective shield he'd kept between himself and his patients and their families just didn't seem to be there any more.

He looked back at Penny, who was smiling at Rebecca now.

'Okay, I guess it's okay if I don't go home today.'

And then Thomas let his gaze rest on Rebecca's face. That smile that he loved so much. That look she was giving Penny that told the little girl she was the most important person in the world right now. He could feel her determination that she was going to give Penny and her family what they wanted so desperately.

And he could feel his own love for Rebecca that was a big part of the emotional mix in this room. He wanted a successful outcome as much as anybody else here.

He could feel everything with such clarity, it was painful.

Because of his new, soft shell?

He'd forgotten what this felt like. Hope. The anticipation of something so joyful, it made the world look like a different place.

A much better place than he'd been living in for such a long time.

There was nothing more for him to do here. Penelope Craig was Rebecca's patient now, and would be until she was discharged with her new heart to return to the care of her cardiologist. He wanted to be there, though. He wanted to be in the gallery to watch the surgery. To let Rebecca know that she had his complete support and to meet her gaze if she chose to look up and seek encouragement. The way he had when the first surgery had been done on this very child.

How appropriate would it be for him to be there again, now, in what could be the definitive surgery that could give her many years of life? That he could celebrate their new connection by repeating history and letting her know that he believed in her.

That he—once again—believed in *them*?

He also wanted to be by her side when she went to tell Julia and Peter how well it had all gone.

It would be a long surgery. He needed to clear everything else on his agenda today to put the time aside.

The urgent call to the intensive care unit came shortly after the message from Rebecca that said the green light had been given to the suitability of the donor heart and its intended recipient. Penelope Craig was now in the final stages of her pre-theatre preparation.

The patient Thomas had been called to see was a six-month-old baby who'd been admitted and rushed to intensive care in a life-threatening condition. He arrived to see an alarmingly fast trace on the ECG monitor and a baby with a bulging fontanelle who was struggling to breathe and going blue. The baby's terrified mother was standing to one side with a nurse.

'Oxygen saturation is improving with the nasal cannula,' he was told. 'Up from eighty-four per cent on room air.'

Thomas looked at the ECG printout he was handed. 'Looks like a supraventricular tachycardia. Other vitals?'

'Respiratory rate of sixty-five, blood pressure is eighty on fifty and she's febrile at thirty-nine point four degrees.'

'Deep tendon reflexes?'

'Brisk.'

'We could be looking at meningoencephalitis, then. Or meningitis.'

'A spinal tap is next on our list. But we need to get this tachycardia under control.'

'I agree.' The heart rate was far too rapid to be allowing enough oxygen to circulate and it was a very unstable situation. Thomas had his fingers on the baby's arm. 'I've got a palpable peripheral pulse. Let's try some IV adenosine with a two-syringe rapid push. If that doesn't help, we'll go for a synchronised cardioversion.'

The drug therapy was enough to slow the heart rate to an acceptable level. Thomas stayed with the baby a little longer, as treatment to bring down her fever and improve oxygen levels was started. He wrote up lab forms to check electrolyte levels that could well need correction to prevent further disruptions to the heart rhythm.

And then he left, after a glance at his watch told him that Penny would be heading for the operating theatre within an hour or so. So would the donor of her heart. They would be in side-by-side theatres. Other theatres may also have been cleared and there could very well be a retrieval team from another transplant centre waiting to rush precious organs to other children in desperate need.

It was no real surprise, then, to see Rebecca up here.

What shocked him was that she had her arm around another woman who was sobbing quietly, her head on Rebecca's shoulder.

A chill ran down his spine at the realisation that this had to be the mother of the donor child.

He had to walk past them. Despite every ounce of willpower he could summon, Thomas couldn't prevent his head turning. The door to the room was open. His glance only grazed the scene within but it was instantly seared into his memory bank.

A small boy, so still on the bed, his head bandaged and a hand lying, palm upwards as though it had just been released from being held.

His father sitting beside him, his head in his hands and his shoulders shaking.

Rebecca didn't even see him going past, she was so focused on the woman beside her.

'There's still time,' he heard her murmur. 'Go and be with Ryan. And with Peter. He needs you. You need each other...'

The chill didn't stop when it reached the end of Thomas's spine. It seemed to be spreading to every cell in his body.

He was that father.

He could feel the utter desolation of knowing that, very soon, the final goodbye would have to happen. That they would walk beside the bed that their child was lying on until they got as close as they were allowed to Theatre. That they were about to lose even the appearance of life that the intensive care technology could provide.

He could feel his world crumbling around him all over again.

And Rebecca's words unleashed another cascade of terrible memories.

You need each other...

He hadn't been there for her when she'd needed him. Not in any meaningful way. He'd started to pull himself into his shell from the moment they'd taken Gwen further along that corridor that led to the operating theatre and he'd just made himself more and more unavailable.

Not because he'd *wanted* to. Hurting the woman he loved so much was the last thing he would have ever chosen to do. He just hadn't been able to survive any other way.

And who was to say he wouldn't do it again?

Even now, as he walked away from the paediatric intensive care unit, Thomas could feel himself frantically looking for some mental building materials, desperate to try and resurrect at least enough of a barrier to protect himself from this wash of unbearable emotion that seeing the donor's family had induced.

No, it wasn't just an anonymous donor any more.

His name was Ryan, and Thomas clearly remembered having heard the story. He was the little boy who'd gone to school, just like he would have on any other ordinary day. But the unthinkable had happened and he'd been badly injured in that fire at his school.

And he had parents who loved him as much as he and Rebecca had loved their little Gwen.

Thomas took the stairs. He couldn't stand next to anyone waiting for an elevator right now, let alone have the doors slide shut to confine him.

He needed space. A private place to somehow deal with this onslaught of memories that had been buried so deeply he'd thought he was safe from feeling like this again. So he headed up the stairs, instead of down. All the way to the top of the building and through the door that led to the helipad. Empty at the moment, with nothing more than the most amazing view of central London on display. He walked to the furthest corner he could find and stood there, staring at familiar landmarks.

Like the green spaces of the parks and the bump of Primrose Hill where he'd held Rebecca in his arms for the first time since they'd parted and this whole cascade of reconnection had begun. He could see the rooftop and signage of the Frog and Peach over the road where he'd danced with her that night. He could even make out the wrought-iron fences further along the road that marked the spot where he'd kissed her.

He couldn't do it, he realised.

He couldn't allow even a possibility of hurting Rebecca all over again.

Going to the Teddy Bears' Picnic yesterday had been a mistake but it paled in comparison to what had happened between them last night.

It couldn't happen again.

He wasn't going to allow Rebecca to risk her future happiness by being with him. He was the one who couldn't handle these memories.

He was the one who was really stuck. So he was the one who had to set her free to find a new future.

With someone else.

But how—and when—could he tell her that?

Maybe very soon, he thought as his mobile phone began to ring and he saw the name 'Becca' on the screen.

He swiped to answer the call but he didn't get time for any kind of greeting.

'Tom? Where are you?' Rebecca sounded alarmed.

'What's wrong?'

'It's Penny… She's gone missing…'

CHAPTER ELEVEN

'WHAT DO YOU MEAN—gone missing?'

'We can't find her. I came up to see her and check that everything was ready for her to go to Theatre and she's not in her room. She's nowhere in the ward.'

Thomas had already turned away from the view and from any thoughts remotely personal. His stride, as he headed back to the door leading to the stairwell, was verging on a run.

'I don't understand. How could she have gone anywhere? Who was with her?'

'That's just it. No one.'

'What?' Thomas hit the button to release the automatic door with the flat of his hand.

'It was only for a minute or two, apparently. Peter had gone to Reception to meet Penny's grandparents. Julia had dashed to the loo and Rosie responded to an alarm that signalled an emergency in the treatment room. She wasn't needed, in the end, and went straight back but Penny had disappeared. Rosie thought she'd gone to find her mum in the loo but Julia hadn't seen her.'

'She can't be far away. She's probably visiting one of her friends.' Thomas was taking the stairs, two at a time.

'She's not in the ward. We've checked. Everybody's

looking for her. Rosie's beside herself. She thinks it's her fault but it was a cardiac arrest alarm and she said Penny promised to stay in bed.'

'Have you called Security?'

'Yes. They've been all over it for the last ten minutes. Nobody's seen her.'

Maybe Thomas hadn't completely banished personal thoughts. Penelope Craig was still his patient, even though her care was to be in Rebecca's hands for the next little while.

He could understand why Rosie was feeling so bad but Penny's safety was ultimately *his* responsibility.

Like keeping her family safe from the intrusion of that television crew had been, especially today of all days.

To see Angela and her camera and sound people milling around the space near the stairs as he exited on the floor of the cardiology ward was like a slap in the face. The lens of the camera was like a giant eye, swivelling to point straight at him as his presence was noted.

'Dr Wolfe? Is it true that a little girl's gone missing? One that was about to have a heart transplant?'

'No comment.' Thomas pushed past the reporter. How on earth had the news been leaked so quickly?

How hard should it have been to have stopped these strangers finding out anything about Penny? It felt like a personal failure.

And there was a list of other personal failures that it could be added to.

Like not having this special patient in the place that she was supposed to be in order to receive her life-saving surgery.

Like not having been in the right place at the right time to keep his own daughter safe.

And, above all, like not having been able to keep his marriage safe.

He hadn't even heard the last question Angela was calling after him but he raised his hand in a silent 'no comment' gesture. He could see Rebecca in the ward corridor through the double doors. She was amongst a cluster of people that included Penny's parents and grandparents and a man he recognised as Jim, the head of Paddington's security team. Rosie was also there, her face pale and desperately worried.

And, no matter what the odds had been for Penny surviving the surgeries and setbacks she'd already had in her short life, he'd never seen Julia Craig looking this terrified.

'She's probably just found a place to hide,' Jim was saying as Thomas joined the group. 'I expect she was frightened about having to go to Theatre again. We'll find her, Mrs Craig. Please try not to worry too much.'

Julia shook her head. 'She wouldn't just run away— it's not like her at all. And she said she'd stay in bed, didn't she?'

Rosie nodded. 'I was gone such a short time, Julia. I'm so sorry...'

'It's not your fault. I would have left her to go to the loo if you hadn't been there. I've done that a million times.'

'She hasn't been *able* to run anywhere before this,' Peter put in. 'Because she's been too sick. But now... Who knows how far she could have gone?'

'Somebody will have seen her,' Jim said. 'How many little girls do we see wearing a pink tutu and a princess crown? I've got my men everywhere. We're combing the entire hospital.'

'But what if she isn't in the hospital any more?' Julia whispered. 'What if someone's…?' Her breath hitched. 'What if someone's *taken* her?'

'I've got someone reviewing CCTV footage right now. And we've started with the main doors. We've also called in the police.' He turned towards Rebecca. 'How long have we got? When does her surgery have to happen by?'

'We've got a bit of time,' Rebecca answered. 'But that's not the point. What matters is *finding* Penny—as soon as we possibly can.' She ran her hand over her head. 'I can't just wait here. I'm going to start looking myself.'

Her gaze snagged Thomas's as she turned away and his own concern ramped up into real alarm as he saw the fear in her eyes.

Was it at all possible that someone *had* taken Penny? Had she wandered far enough away from the ward for some random predator to spot an opportunity?

It was so unlikely that he would have dismissed the notion as ridiculous up until now.

But, a long time ago, he would have said the same thing about a random car going out of control and mounting a footpath, wouldn't he?

Nothing was impossible, however horrible it might be.

And the fear in Rebecca's eyes was impossible to ignore. As much as he knew he couldn't allow her to depend on him for what she needed, he had to help.

'I'll come with you,' he said.

'We'll try the playground again,' Peter said. 'In case she's come back.'

'And I'll check under every bed,' Rosie added. 'And in every cupboard. She's *got* to be somewhere.'

Jim looked up, ending a call he'd been taking on his phone.

'CCTV from every exit has been checked. There's no sign of her having been taken anywhere and we've got every door covered by security now. She's here. *Somewhere…*'

They started in the wards closest to Cardiology and talked to everybody they encountered.

'Have you seen a little girl? Wearing a pink tutu?'

'No…sorry… We'll keep an eye out.'

'Do you mind if we have a look in the storeroom? She could be trying to hide.'

She was such a little thing, Rebecca thought, moving a laundry bag in its wheeled frame to one side in that storeroom. She'd be able to squeeze into the smallest place.

'I don't understand why she wanted to run away,' she said to Thomas. 'It's not as if this is her first operation. I'm sure I didn't make it sound scary.'

'I'm sure you didn't,' he agreed. 'But who knows what might make a six-year-old kid feel nervous?'

A six-year-old kid?

Just another child?

Thomas didn't seem to be feeling anything like the level of anxiety gripping Rebecca.

'This is *Penny* we're talking about, Tom.'

'Mmm… Maybe the wards are the wrong place to be looking. I wonder if anybody's checked an outpatient area like Physiotherapy. Or the X-ray department?'

He was already walking away from her and Rebecca

stared at his back. It felt like she was being accompanied in this search by a member of the security team. Someone who hadn't known Penny for her entire life and had no personal involvement in her case.

The chill hit her like a bucket of icy water.

Thomas was running away again. Hiding behind those self-protective barriers. Pretending he wasn't involved so he could distance himself from the discomfort of anxiety—or worse. Because he felt guilty? Okay, Penny was his patient but it was ridiculous to assume responsibility for something that had happened when he was nowhere near her. When other people had accepted that mantle of responsibility.

That hadn't stopped him from blaming himself over Gwen's death, though, had it?

It hadn't stopped him believing he had failed as a father.

But how could he do this, when they'd been so close again only last night? When they'd talked about exactly how it *hadn't* been his fault?

Fear stepped in then. How could she have allowed herself to resurrect and sink into those feelings for Thomas? To dream about a shared life again?

This was a tough moment in their professional lives but she needed his support and he was creating a distance that hurt. If they got together again, how long would it be before something important went wrong and she really needed him again?

She couldn't do this.

Because—maybe—she couldn't trust Thomas enough.

But now wasn't the time to think about any of that. Not only was Rebecca desperately worried about the state of mind of a patient she loved dearly, there was a clock ticking. Penny wasn't going to be the only recipient of one of Ryan's organs and there were retrieval teams already arriving at Paddington's. Ryan's surgery would be going ahead whatever happened. If Penny couldn't be found, his heart might have to go to the next person on the waiting list.

Minutes flashed past as they raced along corridors and into every space that might be accessible to a newly mobile little girl. Thirty minutes and then sixty.

Rebecca answered a phone call that informed her that there had still been no sighting of Penny. And then another that confirmed that Ryan would be on his way to Theatre very soon.

'We're running out of time,' she told Thomas as they waited for an elevator to get down to Reception. It had been someone in X-ray who'd thought they'd seen a girl in a pink dress in the toy shop.

Rebecca had to close her eyes tightly to hold back tears of despair.

Surely Thomas could see how upset she was? Just a touch on her arm or an encouraging word would be enough. Maybe even enough to dispel the horrible feeling that he was as distant now as he'd been when he'd first come back to Paddington's.

But he hadn't moved any closer when she opened her eyes as the lift doors slid open.

And he hadn't said a word.

A very pregnant woman, with long, glossy dark hair, stepped out of the lift. She stared at Thomas for a moment and then smiled as she obviously remembered who he was.

'It's Thomas, isn't it? We met in A&E the day of the school fire.'

'And don't I know you?' Rebecca said. 'You're a para-medic, aren't you? And you and Dominic were a big part of the early publicity in the campaign to save Paddington's?'

The woman nodded. 'Victoria,' she said. 'Victoria Christie—but soon to be MacBride. Dom's persuaded me to marry him.'

She was smiling, but the smile suddenly faded. 'I've just come in for an antenatal check,' she said. 'But what on earth's going on around here? There are police officers and reporters all over the place. Reception is crazy...'

Rebecca glanced at Thomas. 'Maybe the toyshop isn't the best place to check, then. If there are already so many people down there, someone would have spotted a little girl in a pink tutu.'

'A pink tutu?' Victoria's eyes widened. 'Are you talking about Penny?'

Thomas had been holding the lift doors open by keeping his hand on them. A malfunction alarm began to sound.

'You know her?'

'I've transported her so often she's like a part of the family. And she's the only kid I know who would sleep in her tutu if she was allowed to.'

'She's gone missing,' Thomas said.

'And she's due in Theatre,' Rebecca added. 'We've got a heart available for her. A perfect match.'

'Oh, my God...' Victoria was looking horrified.

'We've got to go, but can you keep an eye out for her? I'm not sure if anyone's checked Ultrasound or Maternity, yet.'

'Of course I will. I'd spot that tutu a mile off.'

'She's got a crown on today, as well.' Rebecca had to swallow past the lump in her throat. 'She's being a princess for the day.'

Victoria nodded, moved out of their way so they could get into the lift, but then swung back towards them.

'That reminds me of something. Have you checked the turret?'

'What?' Thomas put his hand back into the gap as the doors were closing and they opened again with a jerk.

'We were talking about the turret one day in the ambulance. The big one over Reception? I told her about how, when I was a kid, I'd always thought that a princess lived there but that, actually, it's only a dusty old storeroom full of ancient books and bits of paper.'

'I didn't even know you could get into it,' Rebecca said.

'You're not supposed to,' Victoria said. 'But there's a door. It looks like it's just a cupboard but then you find the staircase. I told Penny about that door. About the staircase...'

It was Thomas who caught Rebecca's gaze as the doors slid shut and the lift began to descend. She could see the hope in his eyes that maybe *this* was the breakthrough they'd been waiting for. A place that nobody would have thought to look because nobody even knew it was accessible?

The glance was unguarded only for the time it took for Thomas to blink. And then he was staring straight ahead at the blank metal of the doors.

'Don't get your hopes up too much,' he murmured. 'It would be a miracle if she'd found that door and hadn't been spotted by someone in Reception.'

As Victoria had warned, the area around the main reception desk was crowded. They showed their official IDs to a police officer who was directing the general public towards a temporary information kiosk that had been set up outside the pharmacy.

The television reporter, Angela Marton, was speaking directly into a camera.

'From what we understand, a child—a small girl who is desperately in need of a new heart—has gone missing, only minutes before her surgery was due to take place.'

At least they hadn't revealed her name, Thomas thought. He put his hand up to shade the side of his face. Angela knew he was a cardiologist and she certainly knew that Rebecca was a transplant surgeon after interviewing her at the Teddy Bears' Picnic. If she spotted either of them, they would have to fight their way through a media scrum to get where they needed to go.

But Angela seemed oblivious to any movement around her.

'This is what it's about, folks. This emergency situation—even more than the tragic fire at Westbourne Grove Primary School—is showing us what this hospital is all about. There isn't a single member of staff here who isn't searching for this little girl right now. Hoping that—any minute now—there will be an end to the dreadful worry her family is experiencing. Everybody cares...*so* much...'

The tiny break in her voice suggested that Angela cared as much as everybody else but Thomas knew that she would lead the pack that would snap at their heels if she sensed a new lead in the unexpected drama she was in the middle of. He tried to shield Rebecca with his body as he led them through the press of people and around the far end of the reception desk.

And there was the door. Inconspicuous enough to be simply part of the wall and tucked far enough behind a rack of filing cabinets that it couldn't be seen from the other side of the reception desk. It wasn't impossible that nobody would have noticed a small girl going through this door. A glance behind him showed Thomas that nobody was watching them as he waited for Rebecca to slip through the gap and then followed her.

The attention of the film crew—and everybody else—had shifted to a group of uniformed people, one of whom was carrying an insulated box. It had to be a retrieval team from another hospital but Angela made a very different interpretation.

'Oh, my… Could that be the heart *arriving*?'

How long would Ryan's family be able to remain anonymous? It was a blessing that the assumption was being made that the heart was arriving from an anonymous donor somewhere else in the country but Thomas could still feel the tension ramping up sharply as he shut the door behind him. Ramping up as steeply as this narrow, spiral, wooden staircase. Round and round they went, leaving the chaos behind them. By the time they got to the top, it was so quiet, they could have been miles away from Paddington's. In a forgotten library, perhaps, with a circular room stuffed full of archived paperwork. The tension was still there but it felt different. As if the whole world was holding its breath.

Dust motes floated in the shafts of light coming through small, latticed windows. The floor was thick with dust, as well, but it had been disturbed. There were tracks in it.

'They look like adult-sized footprints.' Rebecca was whispering as if she, too, felt like she was in a library.

'Who could have been in here? I didn't even know it was possible.'

'Victoria did.'

'Mmm…' Rebecca was staring at the floor. 'Oh, my God, Tom! *Look*…'

And there it was.

A tiny footprint. Of a bare foot. He could even see the outline of where small toes had left their mark in the dust.

He took a step further into the round space. And then another. Far enough to see past a tall stack of boxes. And there, curled up in the corner and fast asleep, was Penny. She had her head cushioned on one arm and her tiara was so lopsided it was almost covering one eye.

His overwhelming relief was echoed in Rebecca's gasp as she came past the tier of boxes but then it evaporated as fast as it had appeared.

Was Penny unconscious rather than asleep? Or *worse*… What if the device helping her heart to pump enough blood to the rest of her body had malfunctioned in some way because of an unexpected, additional stress—like climbing those steep stairs?

Thomas could feel the moment his own heart stopped because he felt the painful jolt as it started again with a jerk. He was crouching by then, his hand smoothing back one of Penny's braids to feel for a pulse in her neck.

A strong pulse…

Penny's eyes flickered open as she felt the touch. She looked up to see both Thomas and Rebecca bent over her and she smiled at them.

'Did you come up to see where the princess used to live, too?'

'We sure did.' It was hard to speak through the tightness in his throat. 'But it's time to go back now, sweetheart.'

'Okay.' Still smiling, Penny held up her arms. 'But I'm tired. Will you carry me?'

'Sure will,' Thomas managed.

'And I'm really, really *hungry*.'

'So you haven't had anything to eat? Or drink?'

His gaze caught Rebecca's as Penny's head was shaking a very definite and rather sad 'no.' At least that was another obstacle to getting her to Theatre that they wouldn't have to worry about.

By the time he'd scooped the little girl into his arms, she was sound asleep again. He stood up and turned and then stopped because he knew that Rebecca needed to touch this child herself—so that she could really believe that this crisis was over.

She had a tear rolling down the side of her nose and Thomas had to blink hard to hold back the prickle in his own eyes. And then Rebecca raised her gaze to his.

'You *do* care,' she whispered. 'As much as you ever did. You try and shut yourself away but it's not who you really are, is it?'

He could see more than relief in her dark eyes. He could see hope.

Hope that he couldn't allow to grow. But how could he destroy it?

'Of course I care,' he said quietly. 'Penny's my patient.'

'And she's fine. We'll get her to Theatre now. Everything's going to be all right.'

Thomas started moving towards the staircase. He would have to go very slowly and carefully. The stairs were narrow and steep.

It might not have been all right, he thought as they neared the bottom. *And it would have been my responsibility. My failure…*

'What?' Rebecca was ahead of him, her hand on the door handle, but her head turned sharply. She stopped moving.

Good grief! Had he spoken those thoughts aloud?

But Rebecca shook her head, as if she didn't believe what she might have heard. She turned the handle and, a moment later, he was stepping back into the real world of Paddington's. Penny stirred in his arms as she heard the exclamations of people around her that rapidly morphed from surprise to become a cheer. Undaunted by all the attention, she was beaming when she caught sight of her mother coming towards them and seemed oblivious to the flash of cameras around them.

'Make way, please.' Thomas held out his arm to clear a path towards the elevators. 'We don't have time for this…'

A hugely relieved Rosie was waiting in the ward to help give Penny a thorough check and get her ready for her trip to Theatre. Thomas and Rebecca worked together until they were both satisfied there was nothing to stop the surgery going ahead. Until the pre-surgery sedation had taken effect.

And, like she had after the VAD had been inserted, Rebecca touched her forefinger against her lips and then touched Penny's cheek to transfer the kiss.

'See you soon, pet,' she said softly. 'Sleep tight.'

It broke his heart how much he loved her for that tiny gesture that spoke of how much she cared, a promise that Penny wasn't going to be alone in what was to come.

It broke his heart to realise just how much he loved *her*...

And how much he was prepared to sacrifice to keep her safe.

Today's crisis could have had a very different ending and, even if it was irrational, he would still feel that at least part of it was a failure on his part.

He couldn't risk failing Rebecca again. Somehow, he had to tell her that but not yet. Not just before she was heading into Theatre for a surgery that was so crucial.

But he caught the glance she threw over her shoulder as she headed for the door and he knew she was picking up this new tension between them. He couldn't let her scrub up with that hanging over her, could he?

'Walk with me?'

'Sure.' Thomas walked by Rebecca's side towards the operating theatre locker rooms. He felt her glance at him more than once but it wasn't until they reached the storeroom that she finally said something.

'I can't leave it like this,' she said. 'I heard what you were muttering under your breath and I can't go into this surgery without saying something.'

Thomas had to lick his suddenly dry lips. 'About what?'

He got a loaded glance as a response to his being deliberately obtuse. Rebecca pulled supplies from the labelled shelves. A small-sized scrub tunic and pants, a cap and shoe covers.

'It wasn't your fault that Penny went missing,' she said. 'You've got to stop blaming yourself for things that you have no control over.'

This was it. A chance to say what he needed to say. Maybe Rebecca would understand.

'What about the things I should have had control over? Like being there for you when you needed me so much?'

Rebecca paused, the bundle of clean clothing in her arms. 'It takes two people to make a marriage work,' she said quietly. 'And maybe it takes two to make it fail. I didn't understand how bad it really was for you. Maybe I was too wrapped up in my own journey. I think I do now, though. When I had to go and speak to Ryan's parents that first time…' She took a slow inward breath. 'It was…really hard.'

Thomas was staring at the bundle of linen in Rebecca's arms but he was thinking of what he'd been holding such a short time ago. He could still feel the shape of Penny in his arms. How small and fragile she was. He could still feel the aftermath of that shock wave of thinking that she might not just be asleep. That they might have been too late. And that morphed into a different shock wave that he would never be able to erase from his memory.

Of arriving in the emergency department to see Gwen when she'd been brought in after that terrible accident. Barely alive.

He'd certainly been too late, that time.

Rebecca could see that her words had triggered memories that Thomas was struggling with.

She needed to go. To get showered and changed and then start scrubbing in for the transplant surgery. Two lots of surgery, because she had to be the one to remove Ryan's heart to ensure the best possible outcome in reattaching the vital blood vessels.

And while she knew she could block out anything

personal when she chose to focus completely on the tasks ahead of her, she couldn't leave Thomas looking so haunted. Not when it felt like she was losing him. She could feel everything they had found between them again—and everything they could find in the future— slipping away. Thomas was running again. Trying to find a safe place behind his barriers. She'd known it was happening during their search for Penny and it had re-kindled all her doubts but then she'd seen the truth in his eyes when he'd been holding the little girl in his arms.

She'd seen the man she had always loved, who was capable of giving just as much love back, if only he could find a way past the burden of guilt he'd been carrying for so long. But the hope of that happening was also slipping away and what she said now might be her last chance of preventing that happening.

His next words confirmed her fears.

'I still feel like I failed Gwen,' he murmured. 'I was her daddy. I was supposed to keep her safe.'

'You were the *best* daddy.' Rebecca's voice was low but fierce. 'It wasn't your fault. There are no guarantees in life, Tom. We can only do our best. We can celebrate our successes and support each other if things don't go the way we hoped.'

'But I *didn't* support you. I can't risk that happening again.'

'So you're just going to give up? Run and hide?' The pain was sharpening her voice now.

'Maybe that's the only way I can keep *you* safe. To make sure I never hurt you again.'

Rebecca's breath came out in an incredulous huff. 'By staying away from me? Do you really think *that's* not going to hurt me?'

She couldn't deal with this now. Later, she would have to process the idea of losing Thomas all over again but, for now, it had to be pushed aside. Through the open door of the storeroom, she could see a bed being pushed along the corridor.

Ryan's bed.

The next few hours were going to test her to her limits. She not only had to use every skill she had to the best of her ability but she would have to ride that emotional roller-coaster from one end of the spectrum to the other.

She had to lose a tiny patient for ever.

And she had to give another one the gift of a new life.

She couldn't do it alone. She needed support and she needed it from someone who was trying to find a way to run away from her—and he believed that, by doing that, he was protecting her?

He couldn't be more wrong.

'Do one thing for me, Tom. Please?'

'What's that?'

'Be in the gallery. Not for this bit…' She would never ask him to do that—not when it would be like asking him to relive the final moments of his own child. 'Just for Penny's surgery?'

He'd been there for Penny's last operation. She could still remember how much confidence it had given her, knowing he was there simply to encourage her. To believe in her.

She needed him there for what would hopefully be Penny's final major surgery.

The bed and its entourage of medics were much closer now. Thomas turned his head and saw it.

Then he turned back to Rebecca. She could see so

much pain in his eyes. But she could see something else, as well.

She could see how much he loved her...

'Yes.' His voice was no more than a whisper. 'I can do that. I'll be there.'

CHAPTER TWELVE

HE WASN'T RUNNING AWAY. But Thomas Wolfe *was* walking away. Temporarily.

He had no intention of not honouring his promise to be in the gallery for Penelope Craig's surgery but he couldn't hang around and wait knowing what was happening in Theatre Two right about now.

There were too many people here, as well. Theatre One was being prepared for Penny's surgery and Theatre Three had just been cleared for a child needing a new kidney. There were retrieval teams here for organs that would be rushed to other parts of the country adding to the congestion.

Thomas needed a space to centre himself. Maybe he needed to convince himself that he was doing the right thing.

That look in Rebecca's eyes when she'd asked him if he thought that removing himself from her personal life wouldn't hurt her...

He'd been so sure that it was the right thing to do.

So why did it feel so very wrong?

The rooftop could be a good place to go, although there might be helicopters waiting to transport those precious organs to their destinations as fast as possible.

He needed to be careful which route he took to go any-where, mind you. The media presence inside Paddington's right now was probably as big as it had been at any time during the whole campaign to save the hospital.

Bigger, even. They had a case that could highlight the importance of this beloved institution with the kind of drama people could lose themselves in. They already had the gripping opening of their story with Penny's disappearance and the frantic search. They had the tear-jerking reunion of the little girl with her parents and now the nail-biting tension of waiting to hear how the surgery had gone. They also knew who the two doctors were who were most involved in Penny's case and the last thing Thomas needed right now was to have a microphone or camera shoved in his face by Angela Marton and her colleagues.

His steps slowed as he neared the main doors that closed this floor of operating theatres and recovery areas from the foyer that contained the elevators and stairwells. Would there be cameras as close as right on the other side of those doors? He turned his head, even though he knew there was no other route to take. The only doors on either side of him led to a couple of small rooms that were used for things like meetings. Or for relatives that had been allowed to accompany a patient on the journey to Theatre but might not be able to cope with anything too clinical.

And that was when he saw them.

Ryan's parents.

They were sitting alone in one of the rooms.

Just sitting.

They were side by side but they weren't holding

hands. They weren't talking to each other. At this precise moment, they weren't even looking at each other.

It was the sense of distance between them that hit Thomas so hard.

He knew they were both feeling utterly lost and that they each had to find their own way to start this most difficult of journeys but…

But if he could go back in time he would change the path *he* had taken.

He knew that this couple had probably asked for privacy after their final farewell of their son but something pushed Thomas to enter their space, uninvited.

To see if there was anything he could do to offer even the smallest amount of support.

They didn't seem to find his presence an intrusion. Maybe they needed something—anything—to give them a reference point in this bewildering new map of their lives. He pulled a chair out and perched on the edge of it, leaning forward as he spoke to them.

'This is the hardest part,' he told them. 'Taking the first steps into a life that's changed for ever.'

'No.' Peter Walker's voice was so raw it was painful to hear. 'The hardest part is knowing that I failed my son.'

It was tempting to break an unwritten rule and reveal something intensely personal but Thomas bit back the words. This wasn't about him.

Except, in a way, it was. Because he could hear himself saying the same thing. He could hear the echoes of it that had bounced around in his head for the last five years and he could see it inscribed in every brick of the walls he had built around his heart.

Where were those walls right now?

He could feel the pain of these young parents as acutely as if it was his own.

Because it still *was* his own?

But it was hearing someone who was the image of where he'd been five years ago saying his own destructive mantra aloud that made him realise how wrong it was.

'You *didn't* fail,' he told Peter. 'Neither of you did.'

Maybe it was the conviction in his tone that made Julia lift her head from her hands and stare at him with the same expression as her husband. Waiting for him to say something else. Something that might give them a glimmer of comfort?

'You loved Ryan,' he said quietly. 'I know exactly how much you loved him because you're going through this right now and you'd only be doing this to give the gift of life to other children because you understand how much *their* parents love *them*.'

Both Julia and Peter had tears on their cheeks. They had turned to look at each other as Thomas was speaking and now they reached out and took each other's hands.

'You understand because that's how much you loved your little boy,' Thomas added. 'And, in the end, that's what really matters. He was loved. And he will always be loved because that kind of love never dies.'

It could be damaged, though, couldn't it?

Poisoned by self-blame. By running away and hiding. It could be lost even though it still existed.

'Help each other.' Thomas could hear the crack in his own voice and he had to pause for a heartbeat to keep control. 'You've got tough times ahead but you'll get through them and—if you can help each other—you can be strong enough.'

It was time to leave them alone now. Thomas stood up but there was one more thing he needed to say.

'Believe that you were the best parents and that Ryan knew how much he was loved. And...' He had to swallow another lump in his throat. 'And be proud of what you're doing right now. Believe me, one day, you'll know it was exactly the right thing to do.'

Stepping out of the room, Thomas didn't even look at the doors that would have taken him away from this area.

He knew now, without the slightest shadow of doubt, that there was something else that was exactly the right thing to do.

And he was going to do it.

It was the last thing Rebecca Scott expected to see.

She surprised herself by even glancing up at the gallery, in fact, because nobody came to watch this kind of surgery. It was hard on everybody and the atmosphere was sombre. Respectful and sad and there were several people in the extensive team in Theatre Two that were openly tearful.

But glance up at the gallery she did.

And there was Thomas.

Standing right behind the glass wall.

His posture told her that he was as sombre as any of them. Probably tearful himself as he grappled with memories that no parent should ever have to experience.

But he was here.

For her?

For himself?

No. As Rebecca stepped in to do her part of Ryan's last surgery, she knew that it was something bigger that had brought Thomas so close.

He was here for them both.

She couldn't tell if he was still in the gallery when she walked out of Theatre Two because she was blinded by tears that didn't stop falling until she'd finished scrubbing in again—this time for Penny's surgery.

Looking up at the gallery in Theatre One was the first thing she did as she entered a space that had a very different atmosphere.

This one was full of hope…

And that was what filled Rebecca as she looked up for a much longer moment this time, her lips curving with just a hint of a smile.

Thomas didn't seem to be smiling but it was hard to tell because he was touching his forefinger to his lips.

Then he touched the glass between them with that fingertip.

And Rebecca could feel that fairy kiss just as surely as if it had been his lips touching her skin. Telling her how much he cared and that she wasn't alone…

From the instant she looked away, her focus was completely on her work. This was the ultimate in the specialty she had chosen to devote her professional life to. A long, painstaking procedure that had moments when it seemed like the most extraordinary thing any doctor could do.

To remove such a vital organ and have a tiny chest open in front of you that had an empty space where the heart should be.

To take another heart and fill that space.

And, best of all, to join it up to every vessel and allow blood to fill it and, with the encouragement of a small, electric shock, to see it begin to beat and pump that blood around its new body.

It had taken a little over five hours from the time Penny's chest had been opened until the final stitches were in place and Rebecca stood back, as yet unaware of her aching back and feet, simply watching the monitor screen for a minute. The green light of the trace was a normal, steady rhythm. Blood pressure and oxygen saturation and every other parameter being measured were all within normal limits.

There were some tears again now, from more than one person in Theatre One, but they were happy tears. This little girl had the chance of a new future. As Rebecca allowed the intrusion of personal thoughts to mix with this overwhelming professional satisfaction, the joy of the potential new future became her own, as well. Looking up, the surprise this time was that Thomas had vanished from the gallery but Rebecca was smiling as she stripped off her mask and gown and gloves and left the theatre.

She knew she would find him waiting for her just outside the doors.

Waiting to fold her into his arms?

He came with her to find the space where Julia and Peter Craig were waiting.

'It's good news,' were the first words they heard. 'Everything went as well as we could have hoped for. Penny has a new heart.'

There were still more tears then. Both Penny's parents needed time to cope with the onslaught of relief and then allow themselves real hope. There were lots of questions to be answered again.

'Where is she now?'

'In Recovery. You'll be able to see her very soon.'

'Where will she go then?'

'Into Cardiac Intensive Care—like last time. We'll

keep her asleep for a few days while we make sure the new heart is working perfectly. She'll probably be in there for seven to ten days.'

'And then…?'

'And then we'll move her back to the ward and Dr Wolfe will take over to keep a very close eye on things, but in two or three more weeks, we fully expect you to be taking Penny home.'

It was a long time later that Thomas and Rebecca finally left their young patient in the care of the very capable team in the cardiac intensive care unit. Neither of them could remember the last time they had eaten anything but it was too soon to do anything as mundane as finding a table in the staff cafeteria.

'Let's get a bit of fresh air,' Thomas suggested.

Rebecca shook her head. 'I can't leave the hospital. I need to be close to the unit for the rest of tonight. Besides, you know how many journalists and television crews are camped out in Reception. One interview was more than enough for me.'

'I'm amazed Penny's parents agreed to it.'

'I think they needed to say thank you. To everyone who helped to search for Penny. To the whole surgical team. And mostly, they wanted to let their donor's family know how much this gift means to them. They did that so well, didn't they? Even that woman who was interviewing us was crying.'

Rebecca's eyes were shining too brightly now, as well. She needed a bit of time away from everything.

'I know just the place,' Thomas told her. 'Come with me…'

He took her by the hand and led her up the stairs. Up

and up, until they found themselves on the rooftop of Paddington Children's Hospital—just in time to see the last of a glorious summer sunset gilding the windows and chimneys of buildings and leaving the tops of the trees in their nearby parks a dark silhouette against a soft glow of pink.

'What a day...'

'I know.' Rebecca closed her eyes for a moment. 'I've never lost a patient when they were supposed to be on their way to Theatre before. I was so afraid Penny wasn't going to get her new heart.'

'But she did. Thanks to you. I can't tell you how proud I am of what you do, Becca. It's extraordinary. And brave, especially for you, but...but I think I understand *why* you do it, now.'

'*You* were brave,' Rebecca said softly. 'Being there for Ryan's surgery. I know how hard that must have been.'

'I'd just been with Ryan's parents. Talking to them.'

Rebecca's eyes widened. 'What did you say?'

'That they needed to believe they had been the best parents. That it was only because they loved their little boy so much that they were able to go through with giving the gift of life to others. That they should be there for each other and...and that they hadn't failed their son.'

'Oh, Tom...' Rebecca put her arms around him and pressed her forehead against his chest.

'That was when I *knew*,' he said. 'That we were the best parents, too. That what we did really is something to be proud of.' He kissed the top of Rebecca's head. 'I don't need to run any more. Or hide. I would never have chosen to get sucked back into the past the way Penny's case has taken me but it's the best thing that could have happened. I don't feel stuck any more.'

Rebecca lifted her head to meet his gaze. She opened her mouth but no words came out.

'We loved Gwen,' Thomas said softly. 'And we loved each other. And love that strong never dies, does it?'

'No, it never does.' Her voice wobbled. 'We'll always love Gwen. And remember her. And miss her.'

Thomas held her gaze. 'We will always miss her and we can't change that but I've missed you, too. I had no idea how much and I can't bear the thought of always missing you when that's something we *could* change. I love you, Becca. I need you—as much I need my next breath.'

'I love you, too, Tom. More than I ever have. You're still the person I fell in love with but there's so much more of you to love now. So many new layers. We've been through so much, haven't we?'

'We're older.' Thomas smiled. 'And wiser.' He dipped his head to place a gentle kiss on Rebecca's lips. 'But you're still the person I fell in love with, too. Just…more beautiful, inside and out.'

He kissed her again and, this time, there was passion to be kindled from within the tenderness. A promise of what was to come.

'I think I learned something important today,' he whispered, when they finally drew apart.

'I know you did.' Rebecca smiled. 'You learned not to hide.'

'And something else.'

'What?'

'That just because you didn't do something perfectly the first time doesn't mean that you failed. It means you can learn something so you can do it better the next time.'

A tiny frown appeared between Rebecca's dark eyes. 'But you know you didn't fail with Gwen. *We* didn't fail...'

'I failed our marriage.'

'We both did.' The frown disappeared and there was a new glow in her eyes. 'But do you mean that you think we could do it better if there was a next time?'

'Not *if*...' Thomas paused to kiss Rebecca again. '*When*. If you'll say yes? Will you, Becca? Will you marry me again?'

'Yes,' she whispered. 'Yes and yes and yes!'

Maybe there would have been more 'yes's' but Thomas didn't need to hear any more.

Besides, he was too busy kissing her.

EPILOGUE

THIS WAS GOING to be an evening that nobody would ever forget.

'Oh, my goodness!' Rebecca had to pause for a moment to take in the scene through the doors ahead of them and Thomas smiled down at her.

'It's a bit of a step up from the Frog and Peach, isn't it?'

'Are you kidding? This is the *Ritz*…'

The magnificent dining room of the famous hotel looked like it belonged in a palace. A halo of chandeliers hung beneath the ceiling frescoes and the soft light glinted on the crystal and silver on the tables. Nobody had expected such a gala party to celebrate the official success of the campaign to save Paddington Children's Hospital but, once again, the generosity of people whose lives had been significantly touched over the many decades that the central London hospital had existed had resulted in an extraordinary donation.

So, here they were—a large group of the people who had been most involved in the campaign had been invited to gather and enjoy an evening to celebrate. They were all dressed in the kind of evening wear that befitted the programme of cocktails, dinner and dancing, along with speeches that would publicly acknowledge the contributions they had all made. The men's black tie outfits were a perfect foil to the splashes of colour in the gorgeous dresses some of the women had chosen to show off.

Rebecca had gone for a classic black dress, however. Maybe because it wasn't the dress that she wanted to show off. Glancing down, she straightened the fingers of her left hand. A tiny movement, but Thomas's smile broadened.

'How long will it be before anyone notices, do you think?'

Rebecca smiled back. 'Let's find out, shall we?'

It didn't matter if nobody else noticed, she thought as she took his hand and turned to follow him to where everyone was gathering for a cocktail before dinner. They both knew she was wearing it for the first time and that it had a special significance. It wasn't the same ring Thomas had given her the first time she had agreed to marry him but it was the same solitaire diamond that had been reset—because they both wanted to keep the best of the old but make a new start.

'Can I offer you the cocktail menu?' a waiter queried. 'Or do you know what you'd like already?'

'A champagne cocktail, please,' Thomas said. 'There's a lot to celebrate tonight.'

'Just mineral water for me,' Rebecca said. 'I'm the sober driver.'

'Och, I've got one of those, too.' The voice behind her with its distinctive Scottish burr sounded amused.

She turned, with a grin, to greet Paddington's paediatric trauma surgeon, Dominic MacBride.

'Not for much longer, Dominic.' Her smile included

the woman standing beside him. 'I wasn't sure you'd even make it tonight, Victoria.'

'It's crazy, isn't it? This baby seems to be determined to stay put for as long as possible.' Victoria's eyes widened as she watched Rebecca take the tall glass of water from the silver tray. 'Is *that* what I think it is on your finger?'

Rebecca's smile felt misty now. 'Yes. Tom and I are engaged. Again...'

'I knew it.' Alistair North turned his head towards them from where he and Claire were standing with Leo and his fiancée, Rosie, and Matt McGrory and his fiancée, Quinn Grady. 'I had a feeling something was going on that night when you were so late at the Frog and Peach you both missed the first party. You thought so, too, didn't you, Matt?'

'It was obvious,' Matt agreed. 'Just a matter of time.'

'Oh, congratulations—this is awesome news.' Claire stepped closer to admire Rebecca's ring. 'Are you going to have a big wedding or just duck into a registry office like Alistair and I will?'

'We haven't got round to planning anything,' Rebecca said. 'But it's second time around so I imagine we'll keep it pretty low-key.'

'Low-key...' Rosie sounded wistful. 'You wouldn't believe the amount of organisation that goes along with getting married to an Italian duke. Not that I'm complaining or anything...' The smile she gave Leo suggested that it was all very well worth it.

'We haven't got round to planning anything, either.' Dominic sighed. 'And it's not going to happen until this little princess decides to make her appearance.'

Victoria looked down at her impressive belly. 'Hear

that?' she said. 'Daddy's getting impatient and I need to be able to wear a dress that doesn't look like a circus tent. It's time to make a move.'

'The sooner, the better,' Dominic added.

Thomas laughed. 'Be careful what you wish for,' he warned. 'Unless you want to avoid all the speeches tonight?'

'I reckon the dancing will do something,' Victoria said. 'And that won't be until all the speeches are finished.'

'Good luck with that.' Rebecca smiled. 'It didn't work for me and we tried a pretty fast salsa when Gwen was due.'

A sudden silence fell amongst the group of colleagues as some cautious glances were exchanged.

Rebecca and Thomas shared a glance of their own.

'It's okay,' Rebecca said. 'You all know our story and we know that you've all been so careful not to say anything but things have changed...' She felt the touch of Thomas's hand as his fingers curled around hers. 'Our first child will always be a very special part of our lives and we want to be able to remember her. And talk about her...'

'*First* child?' Claire was standing close enough to Rebecca to lower her voice and still be heard. 'And is that water you're drinking—like me?'

'Oh, look...' Rosie didn't seem to have heard the quiet comment. 'There's a film crew setting up over there. I didn't think this was going to be televised.'

'Maybe Sheikh Idris and Robyn are making a grand arrival. He's one of the biggest stars here tonight, after all. Without his donation, the campaign might not have been anything more than a protest.'

'No... I don't think so.' Rosie was peering through gaps as people started moving towards the dining tables. 'It's... Good heavens! Is that Julia and Peter Craig—Penny's parents?'

Rebecca nodded. 'There's an ongoing documentary being made about Penny's journey as a transplant patient. It all began the day of her surgery when she went missing and the crew happened to be there to catch the action. Everybody wanted to know what was happening and how things turned out.'

'I was one of them,' Victoria said. 'I was glued to my phone in the ultrasound waiting room, trying to get the latest news.'

'She became the poster girl for saving Paddington's in those last days, didn't she?' Claire added. 'So many headlines. I read somewhere that that was the final pressure needed to get everything signed and sealed.'

'But why are they still following her? Surely the family's got enough to cope with—it's not that long since her surgery.'

'I think Julia and Peter look at it as a way to give back,' Thomas said. 'They want to do all they can to raise awareness of the shortage of organ donors.'

'The committee invited them as special guests tonight,' Quinn put in. 'They *did* become so important as the finale to our campaign. And they're representing all the parents who owe so much to what Paddington's has been able to do.'

'And Penny's doing so well,' Rebecca added. 'I think they're delighted to share that. She's started back at school part time already. And she's started having ballet lessons.'

'Oh…' Rosie looked as if she was blinking back tears. 'That's the best news ever. I'd love to see her dancing.'

'I expect you will—on the documentary. Oh, there's Idris and Robyn arriving and it looks like the official party's going in. That's our CEO, Dennis Bradley, with them. Hadn't we better go and find our table?'

There was a long table at one end of the room where the dignitaries like the CEO, people from Paddington's Board of Trustees and government officials were seated. Idris and Robyn were also at this top table, along with Julia and Peter Craig, but other guests were seated at round tables for six.

Thomas and Rebecca sat with Leo and Rosie and Matt and Quinn. The other tables quickly filled and a silence eventually fell as the Member of Parliament most closely associated with Paddington's stood up to say something. It was a short speech to start the evening where he welcomed everybody, thanked the owner of the Ritz hotel and Sheikh Idris Al Khalil for making this evening possible and finally offered a succinct toast.

'To Paddington Children's Hospital.'

The toast echoed throughout the room as glasses were raised and then a new buzz of conversation broke out. It wasn't often that these colleagues got together socially and none of them were short of things to talk about.

'I can see Robyn's engagement ring from here,' Rebecca said to Rosie. 'It's no wonder she can't wear it at work.'

'I love that she's wearing a dress that's the same green as the emeralds in that ring. And doesn't she look happy?'

'Over the moon happy. I think I'd be exhausted by all that commuting she's doing. I'll bet she can't wait for the wedding and her final move to Da'har. And what about you guys? Didn't I hear that you're moving to Rome?'

'We've decided Florence is better,' Rosie told her. 'Leo's *palazzo* is in Tuscany, and we want to be near his mum.' Her voice trailed off as her attention was caught by Leo, who had been talking to Matt and Thomas but was now frowning at the screen of his phone. 'What's up, Leo?'

'I might just pop out for a moment.'

'Why?'

'I thought I'd ring the babysitter and check on the twins.'

'They're fine. She'd ring us if there were any problems. They'll both be sound asleep by now.'

'I'll just text her, then.'

Rosie shook her head. 'You know what, Leo?'

'What?'

'You're turning into a helicopter parent.'

They both seemed to find this amusing. Quinn was smiling, too.

'Maybe it's something to do with jumping in the deep end as a new parent. Matt and Simon are pretty much inseparable these days. They came up with a joint proposal for me, would you believe? We'd gone out for a picnic and they were both kneeling on the rug while they got things ready and then Matt proposed and Simon told me that I had to say "yes" because he wanted two parents for when he got properly adopted. And then they made me call Maisie and it turned out they'd tied my engagement ring to her collar.'

'Oh, that's so romantic. A real family proposal.'

'Mmm... What about yours, Rebecca?' Rosie had

turned back as Leo put his phone away. 'Was it a romantic proposal?'

'Of course it was.' Thomas had overheard the question. 'A perfect sunset and a view of half of London.'

Rebecca laughed. 'We were on the rooftop of Paddington's—near the helipad.' Then her laughter faded into a smile that was purely for Thomas. 'But yes, it was as romantic as I could have wished for.'

'I know what you mean about jumping in the deep end as a parent,' Rosie said to Quinn. 'You should see Leo. I don't even get a look in as the reader of bedtime stories any more. Apparently I'm nowhere near as good at doing dinosaur voices.'

Laughter and stories continued as the dinner service began. The food served that evening was as amazing as everybody expected, with dishes that featured treats like Norfolk crab, roasted scallops, venison and veal. Dessert delights included a praline custard and a banana soufflé. The three courses of the dinner were separated by speeches and many people were asked to stand and be acknowledged—like Quinn, at their table, for her contribution to the campaign committee. Rebecca missed the last bit of the pre-dessert course speech, however. It was the smell of the banana soufflé that was suddenly too much.

'Are you okay?' Rosie asked. 'You've gone very pale.'

'Bit warm, maybe.' Rebecca fanned herself with her menu, fighting off what appeared to be her first wave of morning sickness. 'Excuse me for a moment…'

With her hand pressed to her mouth, she tried to maintain a dignified walk to the restroom and not break into a run. She was aware that Thomas was following her but there was no time to wait for him.

She only just made it. And when she emerged from the cubicle to splash some cold water on her face, there was someone else doing the same thing at the neighbouring basin.

'I was right, wasn't I?' Claire's smile was rueful. 'How far along are you?'

'We only just found out,' Rebecca said. 'It's too early to tell anybody yet.'

'Your secret's safe with me.' Claire reached for one of the soft handtowels. 'I should be over this after three months, but maybe it's worse when it's twins...'

The door opened and Victoria came in. She was looking as pale as both the other women.

Claire and Rebecca looked at each other.

'I don't think you've got a problem with morning sickness, have you?'

Victoria sank onto the edge of one of the upholstered armchairs in this luxurious restroom.

'I just needed to move. Those straight dining chairs were giving me the most awful backache.' She closed her eyes and blew a long breath out through pursed lips. 'That's better. It's wearing off, I think.' Opening her eyes she smiled at the others.

'Don't mind me. I'll be fine. Go back and enjoy your dessert.'

Except that almost immediately her face tightened into lines of pain again and she bent her head, her arms clasped around her belly.

'I'll stay with her,' Rebecca murmured to Quinn. 'Can you go and get Dominic?'

The door swung shut behind Claire, only to open again almost instantly.

Thomas looked concerned. 'Claire told me that it

looks like Victoria's in labour. Shall I call an ambulance?'

'Yes,' said Rebecca.

'No,' Victoria said at the same time. 'It's a first baby—nothing's going to happen in that much of a hurry. I just need to go to the loo…'

'Not a good idea,' Rebecca said.

'Ohhh…' Victoria gripped the upholstered arms of the chair. 'That hurts!'

The door opened again and Dominic came in. One look at Victoria and his jaw dropped. He reached for his phone. 'I'll call an ambulance.'

'I'm not sure there's time.' Victoria's voice was strained. 'This is crazy but… I think I have to push!'

'Hang on a tick. Let's just check what's happening first. Tom? Can you take her other arm? Let's get her onto the floor.'

Claire poked her head around the door and saw what was happening.

'Oh, heck… I'll stay out here and make sure nobody else comes in, shall I?'

'Please,' Thomas said. 'And call an ambulance. We're going to need some transport very soon.'

It was Dominic who lifted the folds of Victoria's dress out of the way. Thomas knelt behind her so that she could lean on him and Rebecca was holding her hand— or rather, letting her own hand get squeezed in a painfully hard grip.

'What's going on?' Victoria gasped. 'Can I push?'

'There's no cord in the way.' Dominic's voice was shaky. 'And she's crowning. Go for it, hon…'

It only took two pushes and a beautiful baby girl was delivered straight into her father's hands. The first, loud cry of the healthy newborn made Victoria burst into tears. Dominic had tears running down his own face as he put their daughter into her mother's arms and against her skin. Rebecca gathered every soft towel she could find on the shelves to cover them both for warmth and Thomas moved to let Dominic take his position and support his new family. Dominic's hands were shaking as he took his phone out of his pocket.

'Not that we're ever going to forget this,' he said. 'But could you do the honours?'

So Thomas took the very first family photo. Victoria lay against Dominic's chest and he was leaning over her shoulder as they both gazed down at a tiny face with wide open eyes that were staring back at her parents.

Thomas had to clear his throat as he handed back the phone. 'The ambulance should be here in no time.' He caught Rebecca's gaze and she nodded. This brand new family needed a little bit of time all to themselves.

'We'll be just outside the door if you need any help before then.'

Claire was guarding the door on the other side and had Alistair beside her but a small crowd had gathered behind them.

Robyn and Idris were there. And Rosie and Leo, Matt and Quinn.

'We heard her cry,' Rosie said. 'Is everything all right?'

Thomas put his arm around Rebecca's waist and drew her close to his side. 'Everything's perfect,' he said.

It seemed like every couple there needed to draw each other close as they shared the joy of this unexpected event. To smile. To touch. To steal a kiss…

Rebecca leaned closer to Thomas and looked up to bask in the intimacy of eye contact.

'That will be us in the not-too-distant future,' she whispered.

'I can't wait,' Thomas murmured back. 'You?'

Rebecca smiled. 'Like you said…everything's perfect…'

And it was.

* * * * *

JOIN THE
MILLS & BOON
BOOKCLUB

* **FREE** delivery direct to your door

* **EXCLUSIVE** offers every month

* **EXCITING** rewards programme

Join today at
Millsandboon.co.uk/Bookclub